continued . . .

Berkley Sensation Titles by Joyce Lamb

COLD MIDNIGHT
TRUE VISION

TRUE VISION

Joyce Lamb

BERKLEY SENSATION, NEW YORK

THE BERKLEY PUBLISHING GROUP
Published by the Penguin Group
Penguin Group (USA) Inc.
375 Hudson Street, New York, New York 10014, USA
Penguin Group (Canada), 90 Eglinton Avenue East, Suite 700, Toronto, Ontario M4P 2Y3, Canada
(a division of Pearson Penguin Canada Inc.)
Penguin Books Ltd., 80 Strand, London WC2R 0RL, England
Penguin Group Ireland, 25 St. Stephen's Green, Dublin 2, Ireland (a division of Penguin Books Ltd.)
Penguin Group (Australia), 250 Camberwell Road, Camberwell, Victoria 3124, Australia
(a division of Pearson Australia Group Pty. Ltd.)
Penguin Books India Pvt. Ltd., 11 Community Centre, Panchsheel Park, New Delhi—110 017, India
Penguin Group (NZ), 67 Apollo Drive, Rosedale, North Shore 0632, New Zealand
(a division of Pearson New Zealand Ltd.)
Penguin Books (South Africa) (Pty.) Ltd., 24 Sturdee Avenue, Rosebank, Johannesburg 2196,
South Africa

Penguin Books Ltd., Registered Offices: 80 Strand, London WC2R 0RL, England

This is a work of fiction. Names, characters, places, and incidents either are the product of the author's imagination or are used fictitiously, and any resemblance to actual persons, living or dead, business establishments, events, or locales is entirely coincidental. The publisher does not have any control over and does not assume any responsibility for author or third-party websites or their content.

TRUE VISION

A Berkley Sensation Book / published by arrangement with the author

PRINTING HISTORY
Berkley Sensation mass-market edition / June 2010

Copyright © 2010 by Joyce Lamb.
Excerpt from *True Colors* by Joyce Lamb copyright © by Joyce Lamb.
Cover art by Adam Weiss/Getty Images.
Cover design by Annette Fiore DeFex.
Interior text design by Tiffany Estreicher.

ISBN: 978-0-425-23585-0

BERKLEY® SENSATION
Berkley Sensation Books are published by The Berkley Publishing Group,
a division of Penguin Group (USA) Inc.,
375 Hudson Street, New York, New York 10014.
BERKLEY® SENSATION and the "B" design are trademarks of Penguin Group (USA) Inc.

PRINTED IN THE UNITED STATES OF AMERICA

10 9 8 7 6 5 4 3 2 1

For Danielle, Michael, Nikole and Zach

ACKNOWLEDGMENTS

Thanks to:

- Julie Snider, for your always enthusiastic and creative help on PR.

- Glenn and Diane Lamb, best party hosts ever.

- Lisa Kiplinger, Lisa Hitt, Charlene Gunnells, Chantelle Mansfield, Ruth Chamberlain and Karen Feldman McCracken, for being so excited to read the latest manuscript.

- Joan Goodman, Diane Amos, Linda Cutillo, Maggie Hoye, Susan Vaughan and Lina Gardiner, all extraordinary critique partners.

- Grace Morgan, for your absolute wonderfulness as a literary agent.

- Wendy McCurdy, for making me a better writer.

- And Mom, for everything.

CHAPTER **ONE**

Reporter Charlie Trudeau stood on the curb and stared at the stoplight that glowed red in the March sunshine. This was her life at the moment. Ready to make a difference but waiting for someone else to give the green light. Except the light wasn't changing.

The latest story she burned to get into the newspaper, about elderly residents getting ripped off, had been shot down before she'd even gotten the words "local car dealer" out of her mouth. The managing editor had squinted at her over his rimless glasses and growled, "Don't even go there."

So much for journalists being public watchdogs. The drive for advertising revenue had changed much of the newspaper industry from a Rottweiler cornering the bad guy into a fluffy toy poodle begging for a treat. Which meant that using her job to help the innocent, helpless and screwed wasn't going to happen, at least not in Southwest Florida at the *Lake Avalon Gazette*.

"Charlotte?"

Charlie looked up, surprised as much by the sound of the voice as the name. No one but her mother called her that. She glanced behind herself, checking to make sure the woman had indeed waved at *her*. Which was silly, really, to think that another woman with the same given name would be standing right behind her.

"Charlotte!"

The woman hurried across the street toward her. The rev of an engine startled Charlie out of her confusion, and in the next instant, a sporty white car sped full-bore into the intersection, and into the smiling pedestrian. Charlie lurched forward a step, watching in stunned horror as the woman's body pitched across the car's hood, struck the windshield with a horrible thud and flew over the tan ragtop. The car screeched off while the woman's body tumbled wildly across the pavement before coming to a motionless rest, faceup, in the middle of the street.

Charlie tore across the asphalt, fumbling for her cell phone to call 911. She dropped to her knees beside the sprawled pedestrian, the phone pressed to her ear. Come on, come on, *answer.*

Blood trickled from the corner of the woman's mouth, and the side of her face was scraped raw. Who knew what other injuries she'd sustained? But, thank God, she was breathing.

"Hang on," Charlie told her, grasping her limp right hand and gently squeezing. "I'm calling for help."

"911 emergency," a man with a deep voice said in her ear.

She struggled for calm. Don't die. Please, don't die. "I'm at the, uh, the, uh . . . the intersection of Palm and Main. Behind the newspaper. A woman's been hit by a car."

"I'm dispatching emergency vehicles. I'll be back with you in less than a minute."

"Please hurry."

The line went silent. Charlie stared down at the injured woman, not knowing what to do. Should she run to the paper for more immediate help? No, she couldn't leave her unprotected. She could get hit by another car. And Charlie knew that moving an injured person could cause more damage. So she stayed where she was, the heat from the asphalt leaching through the knees of her khakis, the sun on the back of her neck.

"It's okay," she murmured, not knowing whether the woman could hear her but hoping. "Help is coming. Just hold on."

She looked up, expecting to see other witnesses or perhaps the car's driver fretting about whether he or she had just killed someone. But the area was deserted.

Hearing a small gasp, Charlie glanced down. Her racing heart jammed into her throat when she saw the pedestrian's light brown eyes keenly focused on her face, as though she were counting on Charlie to save her.

"Help is on the way," Charlie said. "Just keep breathing for me, okay? Nice and easy."

Her lips moved. She was trying to say something.

Charlie stroked her forehead, trying to soothe her. "Please try to save your strength."

A wet, gurgling sound issued from the woman's throat before she could force the words out. "It's up to . . . you . . . now." She moistened her lips. "Bring them . . . together . . . Charlotte."

Charlie wanted to shush her, to implore her to concentrate on breathing, on hanging on, but she couldn't stop herself from asking, "Bring who together? I don't know what you mean. Do we know each other?"

Instead of answering, the pedestrian tightened her hand around Charlie's with surprising strength and stared intently into her eyes.

"Charlotte," she whispered just before her fingers fell slack, and it took Charlie a few seconds to realize she was staring into the face of a dead woman. Oh, God, no.

The world abruptly shifted, and Charlie was no longer holding a dead woman's hand. She was across the street, sprinting toward the intersection, hope and excitement rising in her chest as she spotted the woman she was looking for.

An engine revs, and I jerk my head up to see a white car bearing down on me. Before I can do anything but flinch, I feel crushing impact, feel myself flying through the air, then the bone-breaking shock of striking the road and rolling uncontrollably.

In the next instant, Charlie was back, kneeling on the pavement, unhurt, her fingers clamped around the dead woman's hand.

Sirens began to scream in the distance.

CHAPTER **TWO**

Charlie stood on the corner with a blanket wrapped around her shoulders, watching the unreal scene play out. Three police cars, a fire truck and an ambulance, all topped with flashing emergency lights, crowded the intersection. Emergency workers milled around the perimeter, waiting for the police to do their jobs before they could do theirs.

A blanket like the one clasped between Charlie's fingers—gray and scratchy—had been draped over the woman's body in the road. Wisps of reddish brown hair escaped from beneath the blanket's edge, lifting lazily on the breeze.

Alive one instant, and dead the next. So fast, so brutal. Shocking.

Charlie shivered, clutched the blanket tighter around her as though it would protect her from the harshness of reality.

"Charlie? Charlie!"

She turned at the frantic voice behind her. It was Mac Hunter running toward her, his thick, dark hair ruffled by the wind. He wasn't looking at her, though, his attention on the body in the road.

Charlie sidestepped into his path, expecting him to focus on her and stop, but he barreled into her, sending them both stumbling. She grabbed at the front of his royal blue dress shirt to keep her balance, and he grunted and brought his hands up to steady her.

The instant his fingers closed on her forearms, the tableau inside her head shifted so that she was seeing the body in the road but from another angle farther away.

Reddish brown hair floats on the wind, and I hear the

horror-filled voice of an older woman gasp, "Oh, Lord, is that Charlie?" Terror seems to shoot to the top of my head on a chilling wave, and suddenly I'm running.

In the next instant, she was back in front of Mac, disoriented and off-balance, her wrists grasped in his hands as he stared down at her as if he didn't recognize her. Then his hazel eyes cleared and a sound that might have been a laugh burst out of him. He pulled her into his arms for a tight hug, burying his face against her neck, his warm breath against her skin. What the—?

"You scared me, Chuck," he murmured, pulling back and gazing down at her.

For once she didn't object to the hated nickname, too startled by the emotion in his eyes. From *Mac*? "I'm sorry I scared you," she said.

He noticed the blanket around her shoulders, and his relieved smile slipped into a frown. "What happened? Are you okay?"

She nodded but couldn't stop herself from glancing at the woman being loaded by paramedics onto a gurney. Not a woman—a corpse. She couldn't suppress a shudder. "I saw her get hit."

"Oh, Christ." He pulled her to him again, hugged her close while resting his chin on the top of her head. She remembered the first time he'd held her like this, three months ago. She'd called him after discovering her beloved grandmother had passed away in her sleep. He'd been there in record time, her best friend, and then they'd gone and screwed their friendship, literally.

He tried to draw her back toward the newspaper. "Come inside. I'll get you something to drink."

"I need to talk to the police, tell them what I saw."

"It can wait a few minutes."

"It was a white . . . Sebring, I think. Convertible, but the top was up. It didn't even try to stop. In fact . . . it sped up."

"Charlie—"

"She called me Charlotte."

"What?"

She raised stunned eyes to his. "Mac, she knew me."

He whistled the *Mission: Impossible* theme as he parked the Sebring and sat for a second to wallow in satisfaction. He'd done it. He'd done what had to be done to protect their secret.

After getting out, he pulled a gray car cover over the convertible. This would hide the damage nicely.

He thought he'd feel some guilt: He'd just killed a woman. But it was a woman who deserved to die. Just like the other one. They'd both known, and he couldn't have them, *anyone*, knowing. Couldn't let the secret out. It would destroy them, and they'd worked too hard for too long to sit back and let the destruction begin.

No, the secret to success was destroying the enemy before they could destroy you.

Mission: accomplished.

CHAPTER **THREE**

Charlie settled at her desk and logged onto her PC, her head spinning a little from co-workers mobbing her the instant she walked into the newsroom. Once they discovered she didn't have answers to their questions about the hit-and-run, they had returned to their usual late-afternoon business. The copy editors on the far end of the room discussed last night's reality TV, loudly debating who *should* have been voted off the island. Two reporters huddled less than three feet from her desk, arguing about who was in charge of doughnut duty in the morning. It was an ordinary day at the *Lake Avalon Gazette*.

Except, for Charlie, it wasn't.

A sharp clap of two hands drew her attention to the center of the newsroom, where managing editor Robert Lewis called out, "Gather around, folks. I have an announcement. Hunter, get your ass over here."

Mac, grinning like a fool, strode to their boss's side. This was *the* announcement, Charlie realized. Mac's promotion. The thing that had ended their . . . what to call it? Fling? Affair? Comfort sex? Whatever it was, it started when Charlie fell apart after Nana's death, and lasted two months, until her father tapped Mac to replace Lew. Which meant Mac had had to choose between their relationship and his dream job. As managing editor, he'd be Charlie's boss, and a long-ago sexual harassment lawsuit had made relationships between bosses and subordinates a major no-no.

To his credit, Mac hadn't taken the decision lightly. But he had greater responsibilities than the average thirty-year-old.

Number one: The sister he'd raised after the deaths of their parents was about to graduate from high school, Mac had vowed to help Jennifer pay for college, and the promotion would nearly double his pay.

"Make it snappy, people," Lew growled, impatient as always. "We don't have all goddamn day."

Charlie joined the rest of her co-workers as they gathered around the large square pillar that served as the newsroom's meeting place. Lew hiked his black pants up to just under his bulging gut and cleared his throat. "As you all know, I've been planning to retire. Instead of taking off next month, though, I've decided to bug out a little earlier. My last day is Friday."

He paused, as though expecting some kind of response, but when no protest appeared imminent, his face colored slightly. As much as they clashed, Charlie felt sorry for him. He hadn't had it easy, being caught between the newsroom staff and her prickly father.

He cleared his throat several times again before going on. "So, effective the day I walk out the door, Mac Hunter will be your new managing editor."

A cheer went up, and Mac's face split into an even broader grin. Charlie joined in the cheering. She might have been disappointed that her father hadn't chosen her as ME—they had never seen eye to eye on how the newspaper should be run—but she didn't blame Mac. He was good at his job. Really good.

Lew slapped him on the shoulder and nodded for him to go on and revel in the kudos of his co-workers, then went back to his desk, his head drooping like that of an abused dog. Charlie felt another wave of empathy for him.

Bypassing the group crowded around Mac, she approached Lew's desk, where he appeared to already be nose-deep in editing.

"Hey, Lew."

He looked up at her and rolled eyes that looked redder than before. "You're not going to harass me some more about that damn Dick's story, are you?"

She almost winced at the reminder that he'd shot down the story before she could even finish pitching it. She'd gotten a tip a couple of days ago that Dick's Auto Sales was cheating elderly customers. At the last minute, the dealer would switch its sales contract for a lease contract. In three years, customers were notified it was time to give back the car they thought they'd bought. Unfortunately, the story seemed destined to languish on Charlie's hard drive: Dick's was the *LAG*'s biggest advertiser.

"I actually came over to tell you how much we're going to miss you around here."

He glanced away, a muscle flexing in his jaw. "Sure you are."

She knelt beside his chair so they were at eye level. "Really, Lew. You've been a good editor. I've learned a ton from you. All of us have."

"Shut the hell up, Trudeau. You're at the top of the list of reporters who can't wait for me to slink off and die."

Her heart squeezed. He was the kind of guy who'd escape into self-deprecation long before showing any kind of emotion. Not knowing what else to say, she patted his forearm.

Suddenly, I'm sitting in an office, facing a bespectacled, somber-faced man in a white coat. "I'm sorry," the doctor says in a steady but grave voice. "I wish there was more I could do." Despair swamps me, followed by a wave of anger, then despair again. Tears spill down my cheeks, hands gripping the arms of the chair. And somewhere in my gut, a gnawing, nauseating ache. The gray-haired doctor says, "We'll do everything we can to make you comfortable in your final days."

And then she was back in the newsroom, on her knees next to Lew, her palm still resting on his bare arm. He was staring at her with a perplexed expression. "What the hell is wrong with you?" he demanded.

She pulled her hand back, her heart racing now. "Nothing. I'm sorry. I . . . uh, I'll get back to work."

She quickly returned to her desk.

The despair she'd felt lingered. The old curmudgeon wasn't retiring. He was dying.

Emotion burned behind her eyes. That poor man.

And she had somehow tapped into his memory of getting the bad news, had experienced it as if it were her own. She remembered that moment when she'd knelt on the pavement beside the dead woman, how she'd seen the car barreling at her, felt the lightning flash of impact, the dizzying sensation of flying through the air. Right after that, she'd experienced firsthand Mac's blinding fear when he'd thought she'd been the one hit.

That made three . . . she didn't know what to call them. Visions? No, they were more than that, like an out-of-body experience.

She'd always been sensitive to the feelings of the people around her, often absorbing their doom and gloom as if they were her own. Her grandmother had called it "empathy." But she'd never experienced anything as visceral and real as Lew's despair and Mac's fear or anything as physically jarring as the hit-and-run.

Somehow, her empathy had become supercharged.

CHAPTER **FOUR**

He clicked off the TV news and tapped the remote against his temple.

Fuck, fuck, *fuck*.

The phone rang. Great, here it comes. The story of my life.

Bracing, he picked it up.

"You screwed up. Again."

No "Hello, how've you been?" Succinct. Cold. He should be used to it by now, but it still chafed. After everything he'd done. "Yeah, I know."

"What're you going to do about it?"

"I'll fix it."

"If you hadn't screwed up in the first place, it wouldn't need fixing."

"I know." That was his standard response these days. I know. I'm a class-A fuckup. I know, I know. *I know*. Jesus.

"Take care of it. Soon."

"I will."

The phone clicked in his ear, and his hand tightened on the phone. So how was your day? Stressful? Yeah, mine, too. I became a killer today. Again. And I'm still not done.

He fired the phone at the wall.

CHAPTER **FIVE**

Charlie drove home automatically after a long day at work, her mind flitting between her odd visions and the woman she'd watched die. That woman had a name now, according to the police: Laurette Atkins. She'd probably gotten up this morning, just like any other morning. Showered. Dressed. Drunk her orange juice. Eaten a muffin. And left the Royal Palm Inn, which she'd checked in to just the night before, fully expecting to return later in the day to a maid-straightened room and clean towels.

And now she was dead. Unable to do whatever it was that she'd intended to do with her life. Such as be the journalist who could actually make a difference, if not in the world, then at least in this small town.

For the first time, Charlie realized—or, rather, for the first time she *acknowledged*—that no matter how hard she fought, she couldn't be the journalist she wanted to be in Lake Avalon, not when important news stories went unreported for fear of angering advertisers, or the powerful movers and shakers who also happened to be good friends with her father. The Dick's story wasn't the first one suppressed, and it wouldn't be the last.

All Charlie had ever wanted was a job fighting the good fight, pursuing justice, helping those who had no voice. Investigative journalists seemed to be a dying breed these days. In Lake Avalon, the breed had been dead and buried a long time ago.

Maybe her older sister had known exactly what she was doing when she'd fled Florida right after high school. Maybe

Sam had somehow known that the secret to happiness was looking for it somewhere else.

Charlie fished her cell phone out of her bag and called the newspaper. Tonight was David Adams's last night on the copy desk at the *LAG*. He'd passed the bar exam a month ago and planned to start his own law practice.

"David, hi, it's Charlie."

"Well, hey. Didn't you just give me a big good-bye hug half an hour ago?"

"I was missing you already."

His laugh was heartier and easier than she'd ever heard it. All because he was facing a fresh start. "Yeah, right," he said. "So what's up?"

"I have a proposition for you."

CHAPTER **SIX**

Chicago police detective Noah Lassiter parked in front of Charlie Trudeau's small, peach stucco house on Avalon Street and killed the rental car's engine. The driveway was empty, so he settled back in the driver's seat to wait for her to come home.

Laurette's sister Jewel had called him this morning to tell him about the accident that had claimed his friend's life, had begged him to go to Lake Avalon to look into it. He didn't tell her Florida was way outside of his jurisdiction. He'd listened to her broken voice and hadn't been able to say no. So now here he was, camped out in front of Charlie Trudeau's home, waiting. He'd heard on the radio that she was the only witness to the hit-and-run. A huge break, considering she was also the woman Laurette had come to Lake Avalon to see. He hoped like hell she'd have something to offer that hadn't been reported. Otherwise, he'd be forced to approach local law enforcement.

He put the Mustang's top down, despite the temperature hovering in the midsixties, and leaned his head back to gaze up at the sky. Stars were so bright and dense that they formed a pattern blown like dust over a midnight blue backdrop.

Awe swept through him. He'd never seen such brilliant stars in Chicago, probably because of the city lights. Not that he would have noticed, since staring up at the nighttime sky wasn't his thing. Laurette had chided him about that not too long ago after he'd called on her to help him pry a confession out of a killer. She'd listened to the slimeball's spiel, nodding and looking sympathetic, even after shooting Noah her "yep, he did it" look.

He readily admitted that her gift, her ability to *know*, had scared the shit out of him. Not because he feared the unknown or supernatural, but because he feared what she might see in him. His soul was black, sullied by years of neglect.

But Laurette didn't seem to notice. The night they'd nailed their last killer, she'd suggested they clear their heads, and warm up, by checking out the view from the ninety-fourth-floor observatory of the John Hancock Building, but Noah hadn't been in the mood to mingle with tourists.

"You need to stop and look around yourself once in a while," Laurette had said. "To the left, the right, up at the sky."

He feigned a scowl at her. "You want me to stop and smell the goddamned roses, too?"

Her laugh was light as she linked her arm through his. "Noah, Noah, Noah. Why do you act like such a hard-ass when you're not?"

He chuckled at that. She didn't know him at all. "Yeah, I'm just a marshmallow on the inside."

"Crusty on the outside, soft and sweet on the inside. I wouldn't have you any other way."

A warm feeling had flowed through him on that chilly night. Well-being. Acceptance. Camaraderie. He'd felt some hope that maybe he could change. Maybe he could make up for what he'd done.

The memory broke off when a small SUV turned into Charlie Trudeau's driveway. Not wanting to spook her by approaching her outside after dark, he stayed put while a slim woman in khaki slacks and a light green polo shirt got out. He couldn't make out her features as she opened the back door and retrieved a laptop case, but her skin was pale in the moon-light, her long dark hair captured in a ponytail that had all but come loose. He'd give her ten minutes to get inside and get settled before knocking on her door and introducing himself.

In the meantime, he took in the nighttime sky some more,

wishing he'd made the effort to get closer to Laurette. He'd suspected she was interested in more than just friendship, but he'd resisted the idea, certain a man like him wasn't worthy of a woman like her.

Too bad life didn't offer do-overs.

Charlie slipped her key into the lock and pushed open the door into the house that had belonged to her father's mother. The house still smelled like Nana, like lemons and soap, and she paused on the threshold to remember what it had been like to walk in when her grandmother had been alive. Nana would be standing at the sink, washing a potato to peel for dinner and smiling at her as if the sun had just come out on a dark day.

Closing the door behind her, Charlie dropped her laptop bag on a kitchen chair just as a large black and white cat ambled in from the living room with the gait of Eeyore. Oh, bother.

"Well, hello, Atticus."

The cat rubbed against her pant leg, softly purring.

"How was your day?" she asked, bending to give his head a quick scratch. "Did you get a lot done?"

After checking his bowls to make sure he had adequate food and water, she stopped in her office to e-mail the auto dealer story to David at the paper. Her hand shook a little as she used the mouse to click the "send" button. It was done.

Resigned to being unemployed in the morning and having a very pissed-off father, she headed for her bedroom and the shower. As she walked, she shed her T-shirt and unbuttoned her pants. In the bedroom, she toed out of her shoes, kicking them toward the closet, and turned to toss her polo at the hamper. She'd stepped out of her khakis when a rustling sound near the closet startled her. Then she relaxed.

"Atticus, you silly cat—"

She broke off when a presence bigger than the cat came at her from behind. She'd barely managed to take half a step toward the door when a cord looped around her neck and cinched, jerking her back. Shocked, choking, she stumbled, ramming into the body of her attacker, who bumped against the closet door with a grunt. She tried to dig her fingers under the cord biting into her throat, but all she did was gouge her fingernails into her own flesh.

Bright lights began to explode in her head, and she twisted desperately, trying to loosen the noose. The attacker held tight to the ends of the cord, silent and still behind her, seeming to know that all he had to do was wait for the air in her lungs to run its course. As the strength drained out of her legs, she dropped to her knees with a lurch, a sickening black wave building inside her head. Oh, God, oh, God, she was going to die.

The sudden move must have unbalanced the attacker, because the cord slackened, and Charlie heaved in a jagged, burning breath, at the same time grabbing at the cord to yank it away from her throat. She expelled her second gulp of air with an eardrum-shattering scream as she wrenched around and crabbed backward, out of the bedroom and into the hall toward the living room and the way out.

The intruder, in one of those black ninja masks with only a slit for the eyes, came at her in a blur. Latex-gloved hands lunged for her throat, but Charlie frantically scooted back until her shoulder blades hit the side of the sofa and she struggled to her feet. The ninja, in loose black pants and a black long-sleeved T-shirt, kept coming, and Charlie lashed out wildly with one fist, making bone-jarring contact with the cloth-covered skull. The ninja jerked back with a pained gasp, but before Charlie could do anything more than scream again, he drove forward, smacking her in the forehead with a blinding head-butt. Her head reeled, and she slumped sideways to the carpet, fighting the black hole that spun up at her. No, don't let go, hang on, *come on.*

The ninja grabbed her shoulder, wrestled her easily onto her back and fell on her. A forearm braced across her throat, and Charlie grabbed at it, clawing, her head spinning, her strength fading. She thought she heard a loud, repeated banging noise and muffled shouting, before darkness began to spread from the edges of her vision and her oxygen-starved lungs convulsed.

And then she could breathe. She sensed rather than saw the ninja leap up and tear toward the kitchen. The back door slammed open and shut, and Charlie felt a warm night breeze wash over her nearly naked skin. She was alive. Somehow.

Rolling onto her side, she curled into a tight, protective ball and began to cough uncontrollably. When a big, warm hand lightly squeezed her upper arm, she unfolded onto her back, ready to fight even as images of furiously kicking in a closed door filled her head.

The hand pressed her shoulder to the floor, easily but gently pinning her in place. "It's okay. I'm a police officer." The voice above her was deep and soothing. "I've called for help, but I need to check the house for other intruders."

She blinked up at the man who belonged to the voice, saw a lined, rugged face, messy blond hair and striking green eyes. She had no idea who he was, but she felt immediately safe.

"You can breathe okay?" he asked.

She tried to say yes but ended up coughing. Chills quickly followed, and she curled onto her side again, coughing and shivering.

The blond man rose, and she sensed him standing over her, looking down at her in contemplative silence while her coughing settled down. She was all but naked yet couldn't bring herself to try to cover up. She didn't have anything to cover herself with anyway, but it seemed she should at least make the effort. Better yet, she should get up. There was a strange man in her house. Someone, a freaking ninja, for the love of Pete, had just tried to kill her. But she couldn't seem to move, and she felt she had to concentrate just to breathe in, breathe out. Perhaps this was a dream. What a relief that would be.

Instead of waking up, she heard the stranger who'd said he was a cop walk away. She let her eyes drift closed. Maybe when she woke, everything would be fine.

Footsteps forced her eyes open again. The cop was returning. God, he was huge. Muscled thighs filled out faded jeans that would have looked baggy on a regular man. Broad shoulders stretched a white T-shirt taut across sharply defined pecs, and short sleeves molded to upper arms that were muscled but not too bulky. It took her a moment to notice that Nana's afghan, the one she'd always tucked around her legs in the rocking chair, hung from his large hands.

He draped it over her shivering body. "Hang in there. I hear the sirens already."

He had a soothing voice, but she sensed that in other circumstances it might boom so loud it would vibrate the floor under her feet.

"I'm going to take a look around, okay?"

Sure, fine, whatever.

She didn't try to speak, or even move, instead focusing what little strength she had on breathing. Her throat felt bruised from the inside out, swollen. What would happen if it swelled shut?

Don't think about that. Just breathe.

The shivering gradually abated, as though the throw carried leftover warmth from spending so much time on Nana's lap. She wanted to get up, wrap the afghan completely around her, sit on the sofa and look at least halfway alert when the Lake Avalon police arrived. But her muscles refused to obey her brain's get up commands.

She heard the front door bang open and the running footsteps of at least two men. "Police!"

The man who'd covered her with the blanket calmly spoke from somewhere behind her: "I'm a cop. My badge is in my back pocket."

Then Detective John Logan was on his knees beside her. "Charlie? Charlie!" He turned his head away and yelled behind him, "Get the paramedics in here!"

Oh, good. Logan was here. He'd take care of everything.

She closed her eyes and toppled into the dark.

CHAPTER **SEVEN**

"So you just happened to be sitting out front when she was attacked?"

Noah returned the Lake Avalon cop's belligerent stare, telling himself the guy was just freaked about the attack. Not that Noah could blame him. He was still shaken, too, but that might have been from how much Charlie Trudeau resembled her cousin Laurette. Same long, rich, reddish brown hair. Same tiny birthmark on her cheek where a dimple would be. Charlie, though, was the more feminine one, all curves and smooth skin and long, graceful legs. Even in the intensity of the moment, he'd have to be dead not to notice that she was nearly naked. He remembered how her lace panties had matched the delicate material that clung to round, palm-sized breasts . . .

Christ, he needed to stop thinking about that. She'd been helpless and vulnerable, and he should have immediately gone to get the blanket to cover her. But he'd been so shocked at how much like Laurette she looked, and yet how different, how . . . female. He remembered the moment when she'd started to shiver, how her nipples had hardened under that tasty-looking white lace, and guilt sliced through him for letting her get cold. He was such a jerk. Apparently, a horny jerk. But surely no man could have stopped himself from looking, from appreciating. A woman shaped like that—

"Hello? Are you going to stare me down all night or answer the damn question?"

Noah focused on the burly police detective. They were probably about the same size, but John Logan had a tanned, unlined face and tidy haircut that made Noah feel like a shaggy, pale old grandpa.

"We're on the same side, Detective Logan."

Logan squared his linebacker shoulders and hooked his thumbs in his belt, a practiced stance that Noah was familiar with. It made any cop look bigger and badder. "Look," Logan said, "I'm not in the mood for any shit. Just tell me why I shouldn't haul your ass in for assault."

Noah tamped down his temper. He'd be an asshole, too, if someone he cared about had been hurt. Besides, he had nothing to hide here. "I'm a friend of Laurette Atkins and, like I said, a Chicago police detective." He spoke slowly and calmly, sticking to the facts. "Laurette's sister asked me to look into the hit-and-run. I came to see Charlie Trudeau because she was the only witness."

"Why were you sitting in your car instead of knocking on her door?"

"She'd just gotten home, and I didn't want to frighten her by approaching her outside."

"So you lurked out front instead."

"I didn't lurk." Noah kept his tone mild, deciding the cop was going to get a few more minutes to settle down before this got ugly.

"So what happened next?"

"I heard her scream."

"All the way out there in your car?"

"It was a loud scream."

"So you came running and what?"

Noah gestured at the front door, whose wooden frame had splintered under his ferocious assault. "I let myself in."

Noah was sure he saw a flicker of approval in the other detective's expression before Logan speared him with his I'm-a-hard-ass glare. "You busted down the door and then what?"

"Miss Trudeau was on the floor right over there," he said, gesturing. "She'd been choked. I found an extension cord in the bedroom, so I assume the attack began there."

"So, what, you were conducting your own investigation before we got here?"

Noah, his patience about gone, began to count to ten in his head. He wasn't one to throw punches, but he'd done nothing to earn such attitude.

The tense silence must have tipped Logan off, because when he spoke again, he sounded less accusing. "Did you see who attacked her?"

"No. He ran out through the kitchen. I heard the screen door slam."

"Why didn't you go after him?"

"I wanted to make sure Miss Trudeau was breathing okay, and I didn't know whether there were other intruders in the house."

Logan gave a grudging nod. "Good move."

Good, Noah thought. Apparently that meant they could be friends now. "What did the paramedics say?" he asked.

Logan looked away and rubbed the back of his neck. "She was shocky and had some grade-A bruises on her throat, a couple of scratches. But she'll be okay."

"She's a good friend?"

Logan nodded. "Yeah."

"Any idea why someone would attack her?"

"There've been some break-ins in the area. She probably surprised a burglar."

"A burglar who tried to strangle her with an extension cord?"

Logan's forehead creased, as though he had already thought it didn't add up. "Maybe he panicked."

"Where I come from, a panicked burglar runs out the door." Noah didn't wait for a response before plunging ahead. "Any chance the attacker could have been the same person who ran down Laurette Atkins?"

Logan's brows arched. "Why would you think that?"

"Miss Trudeau is the only witness to the hit-and-run. She was quoted on the news as saying she heard the car accelerate."

"We're still looking into that."

The cop was holding out on him, Noah decided. Something about the hit-and-run hadn't been reported. Something significant. "What kind of evidence do you have?" Noah asked casually.

Logan hesitated for a few seconds before taking a breath. "We haven't been able to establish a connection between Laurette Atkins and anyone in Lake Avalon or at the hotel. So far, there's no motive."

So the detective didn't know Charlie and Laurette were cousins. Interesting. "What about after she arrived? She didn't show up in Lake Avalon in a vacuum."

"She had minimal contact, mostly with hotel employees," Logan said. "No one knows anything, that they're sharing anyway."

"Any sign of the car?"

"It's the proverbial needle in a haystack. You know how many Sebring convertibles there are around this town? It's the rental car of choice among the tourists."

"This one must be visibly damaged, though. Dents, broken headlight, cracked windshield, blood. Something."

"We're doing the best we can. If you've got suggestions, I'm listening."

That surprised Noah. A small-town cop who didn't get bent out of shape when a detective from the big city started asking questions? "I'd like to talk to Miss Trudeau."

Logan straightened as though he'd been poked with a stick. "I questioned her myself."

"But you just said you're a good friend."

"What does that have to—"

"You're not objective."

Logan didn't bother to hide his irritation. "I can't stop you from talking to her, but I can stop you from interfering in an official investigation."

"You mean the investigation that you just implied is already at a dead end?"

Logan scowled. "I'm going to keep an eye on you, Lassiter. It'd be best if you didn't piss me off."

So they weren't going to be friends after all. It'd make Noah's task tougher, but he could deal with it. "Okay then. If you're done with me here, I'm going to take off."

"I'd tell you to hang around Lake Avalon, but I'm not sure that's a good idea."

"That's too bad, because I'm not going anywhere until I find answers."

CHAPTER **EIGHT**

After a shower, Charlie stood in front of the bathroom mirror and took stock of the damage. A thin, unbroken line of stark purple bruises circled her neck where the cord had bitten into her flesh. Vertical scratches showed where she'd dug at the cord with her own fingernails. A fainter bruise the diameter of a large orange colored the right side of her forehead where the ninja had head-butted her.

A ninja. If the attack hadn't been so frightening, she might have laughed at the idea that a *ninja* had broken into her house. As it was, the last thing she wanted to do was laugh.

When Logan asked her who might want to hurt her, she'd hesitated. She was a journalist, after all. She knew things in this town that other people, *bad people*, didn't want the public to know. Where to begin?

The married mayor traded sexual favors with an alderman for projects that benefited the alderman's district.

A home builder price-gouged customers daily while taking kickbacks from a supplier.

The company building a beach-access road bypassing downtown used illegal immigrants to keep costs down.

An auto dealer swapped sales contracts with lease contracts at the last minute. At least that one was busted.

Oh, yeah, and don't forget the blackmail scheme targeting high-profile residents. She'd love to get her hands on *those* details. If only her source weren't such a skittish butthead.

Sighing, she sank onto the edge of the bed. The truth was, during her career at the *Lake Avalon Gazette*, there'd always been someone who would have loved to cinch a cord around her neck until she stopped breathing.

She closed her eyes against a wave of nausea. She needed to focus on something else, such as the fact that she'd survived. Thanks to a tall, imposing, shaggy-haired police detective. Logan said his name was Noah Lassiter, a detective from Chicago. Despite her semiconscious state when she'd seen him, she knew she would recognize him the instant she saw him again. His appearance—broad shoulders, narrow waist, intense green eyes, careworn features—had been imprinted on her brain at a very basic level. And his voice . . . deep and resonant, oh so soothing.

She could use some more of that brand of soothing.

After pulling on shorts and a short-sleeved turtleneck, she checked the phone, which she'd muted before she went to bed. Caller ID listed five calls: two from Mac at work, as she expected; two unknown name/unknown numbers; and one from her sister Alex.

She called Alex back first, and her kid sister answered as though she'd pounced on the phone. "Charlie, thank God. Are you okay? Logan said you surprised a burglar."

"I'm fine. Just some bruises. That's all."

"That's all?" Alex's voice rose at the end, evidence that she was losing her cool. "Logan said the bastard tried to kill you. I can't believe no one in the newsroom heard about this on the scanner last night. That jerk Steve must have turned the damn thing down again. I'm going to kill—"

"Alex," Charlie said firmly.

Alex took a breath, let it out. "What?"

"I'm all right. I promise. I didn't call you because I knew you were out on a photo assignment, and I didn't want to worry you."

"You're sure you're all right? You sound tired."

"I didn't sleep very well," Charlie admitted. "Logan stayed with me, so that helped."

"He mentioned that."

"On the couch," Charlie added. "Just FYI."

"Why would that matter?"

Charlie laughed softly. Her sister was so transparent where that hunky cop was concerned. "No reason."

Alex blew out a breath. "Whatever. So I'm coming over. Do you need anything?"

"You don't have to—"

"Yes, I do. I need a shower first, though. And then I'll be there to make you some chocolate chip pancakes. No arguments."

Alex hung up on her before she could protest further.

Charlie put down the phone, smiling for the first time in what felt like days. At least there was Alex.

CHAPTER **NINE**

Noah knocked on Charlie Trudeau's front door, impressed that he couldn't tell that he'd busted it down just the night before. Whoever'd fixed it up had done a bang-up job.

Detective John Logan opened the door, and Noah was relieved to see a familiar face. It would save him from having to explain why he was here.

"Good morning," he said, reaching out to shake Logan's hand. He planned to make nice today. The more ass he kissed, the sooner he could get answers from Charlie Trudeau. Assuming she even had the answers he needed.

"Morning," Logan said, already looking fiercely protective.

When Logan just stood there, Noah asked, "Mind if I come in? I'd like to talk to Charlie."

"She's not—"

"Who is it, Logan?" Charlie asked from behind the detective.

Noah stepped to the side so he could see around the bulky cop. Charlie was walking toward the door, and the sight of her knocked the breath from his lungs. In khaki shorts that showed off long, sleek legs and a white short-sleeved turtleneck that emphasized the definition in her arms, she looked . . . edible. He hadn't thought she could be any more appealing than she'd been the night before, vulnerable in her lacy underwear. But it turned out that a put-together Charlie Trudeau, with her silky hair pulled back in a loose ponytail, that beauty mark where a dimple would be and light brown eyes flecked with gold, was just as sexy. Maybe more so.

When she spotted him, she paused in midstep, her eyes

widening and her lips parting. She stared at him for a few seconds before pink color suffused her face and she stepped forward. "Detective Lassiter," she said. "Please, come in."

Logan moved aside so Noah could enter. "I hope it's okay that I stopped by without calling first," Noah said.

"I'm glad you did," Charlie said. "Detective Logan told me what you did last night. I . . . thank you."

"Just doing my job," he said. He was impressed at her poise. If he hadn't known that the turtleneck hid bruises and artful work with makeup disguised the mark on her forehead, he never would have guessed what she'd gone through the night before. She was resilient, he thought. Strong. And beautiful with that dark hair that sharply contrasted flawless, pale skin with a hint of rose in her cheeks.

The ringing phone jolted him, and he realized he'd been staring.

"I'll take care of that," Logan said, and strode out of the room.

Noah cleared his throat and extended his hand. "Since we haven't officially met, I'm Noah Lassiter."

She glanced down at his outstretched hand. Just when he thought she wasn't going to take it, she put her fingers in his. Either her hand was chilled, or he had an inferno in his palm. When he felt her tense, he let go, thinking he'd been so distracted by how soft her skin was against his own calluses that he'd clasped too tight. "Oops, sorry."

She didn't respond, and he was thinking, What the hell? when he noticed that her golden brown eyes looked weird, as though she'd spaced out. Then she blinked, drew in a shaky breath and looked at him with a sorrowful, compassionate gaze that arrowed straight to his heart. He told himself she couldn't possibly know exactly how sad, and pissed, he was about Laurette's death.

She gestured toward the sofa. "Please, have a seat."

Charlie lowered herself to an ancient rocking chair across from the couch. "I'm sorry about Miss Atkins. You were very close."

Noah wondered how she knew. But, then, he was here, wasn't he?

"Yes," he said as he moved to the sofa. "We worked together in Chicago. She helped me on certain cases." He paused, cocked his head. "I'm sorry for you, too."

She nodded, running the tips of her fingers over the neat hair above her right ear, as though to tuck away stray strands that weren't there. So much like Laurette. Yet, Laurette's skin hadn't glowed like Charlie's. And he was dead certain that he'd never noticed Laurette's mouth the way he couldn't stop staring at Charlie's. But it was hard to look away when the tip of her tongue glanced off her bottom lip just before her teeth caught that full, nicely shaped lip, briefly worried it then let it go. His heart thudded once, twice. He had never, ever looked at Laurette's mouth and thought of sex. Ever.

One of Charlie's eyebrows ticked up slightly, and he realized she waited for him to get this show on the road.

"I know you've already gone through this with the police, but I'd like to hear your answers for myself."

"Okay."

"Can you describe what happened?"

"Miss Atkins walked into the crosswalk, and a white Sebring convertible hit her."

He blinked, surprised at her precision. "You heard it accelerate?"

"Yes."

"See the driver?"

"No."

"License plate?"

"It happened too fast."

"Did she say anything before she died?"

Charlie hesitated.

Here we go, he thought, and sat forward. She stiffened at his sudden move, tipping him off to her nerves. She appeared calm on the surface, but the tension in her shoulders and the turbulence simmering in her eyes bothered him more than they should have. He rarely met relaxed people in his line of work, yet something about this one's coiled anxiety made him wish his people skills were better.

When she still said nothing, he tried another tack. "What if I reminded you that I saved your life last night?"

Her eyes widened at first, then narrowed. "So I owe you."

"If you want to look at it like that, yes. And, like I said, Laurette was my friend. I would think that you would want to do everything you could to help find the person who ran down your cousin."

Her eyebrows arched sharply. "Cousin? She wasn't my cousin."

Huh? "You are Charlotte Trudeau, aren't you?"

"Yes, but I don't have any cousins."

Ah, fuck, he'd stumbled headlong into a family secret. Jewel had said her mother and Charlie's mother had been estranged for many years. Their offspring had never met, and now it appeared Charlie hadn't known she had an aunt, let alone two cousins. Great. That meant Charlie didn't know she'd watched her own cousin die.

Okay, how to do this. Ease into it or just blurt it out? She'd already proved with her concise answers that she had no tolerance for pussyfooting. He took a breath, held it. Here goes.

"Laurette came to Lake Avalon about a matter involving her mother's estranged sister. Your mother."

Her eyes flickered, as though a memory had nudged her. "I don't know what you want me to say. My mother doesn't have a sister."

But he could tell he'd struck a nerve. Her fingers threaded together and squeezed, released, squeezed, and her shoulders had tightened further. "I don't suppose you'd be willing to share your mother's contact information with me."

"I don't think I would be, no."

He almost smiled. So cool, so composed, except for those busy, nervous hands. "All I want to do is confirm her only-child status."

"I don't see what that has to do with Laurette's hit-and-run."

"Perhaps someone didn't want Laurette meeting with cousins who know nothing about her and the rest of her family."

"Which might be a valid theory if my mother had a sister, but she doesn't. In fact, her parents died before I was born."

"So you know every last detail about your mother."

A glint of anger showed in her narrowing eyes. "That wasn't a question."

Another nerve struck. Damn—he suddenly realized he enjoyed provoking her, watching the sparks fly out of her eyes. Pushed to the wall, she'd be fiery. Maybe out of control. Exciting. He was a bad, bad man. "I can find the information I need without your help, so why delay the inevitable?"

"The inevitable would be you finding out that you wasted your time."

"I don't doubt that you believe that, but I'm beginning to suspect I might know more about your family than you do."

She got to her feet, all graceful composure and unflappable cool. "We're done here. I'm sorry I couldn't be more help."

He pushed himself up out of the sofa's grasping cushions, trying not to be distracted by the flush in her cheeks. But he couldn't help it. He wanted to crank her anger up a notch, just to see what she'd do. "Perhaps you'd like to talk to someone in Laurette's family before you close the book on this. You look quite a bit like her."

She faltered, and her fingers brushed the tiny beauty mark on her cheek. Ah, so she'd noticed the resemblance.

He dropped the hook with the last of his bait. "I have her sister's number." He paused a beat. "If you're interested."

Her jaw clenched, a muscle working at her temple. "Or perhaps I'll just wait for her to contact me."

Damn, but the woman could think on her feet. "I wouldn't count on that. She and Laurette weren't on the same page about meeting with you. Seems there's a good deal of dissension throughout your family tree. Any idea why?"

"Charlie?"

The appearance of the woman in the arched doorway between the living room and kitchen startled Charlie as much as it did him. She flinched at the sound of her name, her gaze flying away from him almost guiltily. Her surprise faded quickly, though, and she smiled at the other woman.

"Oh, hey, Alex," Charlie said. "I didn't hear you come in."

"Logan let me in. He said Mac called."

Charlie's features clouded before she nodded an acknowledgment then gestured at Noah. "This is Detective Noah Lassiter. He's a friend of the woman who died in the accident yesterday. Detective, my sister Alex."

He stepped forward to shake the hand of the other woman, who wore white cropped pants and a red-and-white-striped shirt. She had the same ivory complexion as Charlie, but her hair, more auburn than reddish brown, was shorter and curlier. Her eyes were much darker, more curious than suspicious, and not nearly as mesmerizing. No beauty mark, either. The differences weren't particularly striking, and it surprised Noah that he'd managed to identify so many so quickly. He reminded himself that that's what he did. He was a cop. Nothing to do with Charlie Trudeau and the way she made his blood flow faster. Nuh-uh.

"I'm sorry for your loss," Alex said.

Noah nodded his gratitude, feeling like a dick for lusting after Charlie Trudeau when Laurette was dead.

Alex's gaze shifted to Charlie and seemed to carefully assess her sister's mood. "What's going on?"

Charlie shook her head, and even Noah could tell she forced her smile. "Nothing to worry about. The detective was simply asking me about the accident."

So she didn't want her sister to know about the cousin angle. Either she was protective or she knew something she didn't want her sister to know.

Figuring he'd gotten as much from Charlie as he was going to for now, he pulled his wallet out of his back pocket and slipped out a business card. "If you remember anything more about the hit-and-run or . . . anything else we talked about, please call my cell. I'm staying at the Royal Palm. Room number's written on the back."

She took the card and gazed down at it.

As he watched the top of her head, he silently inhaled her scent and decided coconut might be the sexiest fragrance on the planet. She glanced up at him, catching his scrutiny, and his breath stopped briefly. Christ, this woman. If she'd been the one doing the questioning, he would have told her whatever she wanted, as long as she wet her lips like that again, with just the tip of her tongue.

"Is there anything else?" she asked.

Her voice had dropped an octave, and his hopes soared. She felt the pull, too, that deep-down, sexual tug that made the air seem thinner, the head feel lighter and the blood in certain, down-there areas feel thicker.

"Detective Lassiter?"

He forced his gaze up to her eyes, realizing he'd focused on her full, moist lips for far too long. Again. Thinking about sex. Again. Inappropriate behavior for a detective? Uh, yeah.

He smiled awkwardly. A total, horny dickhead. "Nothing. For now."

CHAPTER **TEN**

While Alex whipped up pancakes and bantered with Logan in the kitchen, Charlie took the phone and unopened newspaper and stepped out onto the concrete slab that served as her patio. The banyan tree that arched overhead provided shade that would last all day, and she turned her face into the fresh morning breeze that flowed over her, breathing it in, letting it slow the rapid beat of her heart.

Green grass stretched back several dozen feet, dotted with squat royal palms and ficus bushes. The thick grass needed mowing, and weeds had gleefully taken over the garden that occupied one corner of the yard. She'd promised to maintain the garden after Nana died but hadn't found the time. Or, *made* the time.

Before the regret could take hold—she was so *sick* of regret—she settled onto a black wrought-iron chair that still held a slight chill from the evening and opened the newspaper.

Her heart jumped. There it was, stripped across the top just like she and David had talked about. The headline blared "CAR BUYERS SAY AUTO DEALER PULLS CON-TRACT SWITCHEROO" by Charlie Trudeau, *Lake Avalon Gazette* staff writer.

She'd done it. She'd made her point. No going back now.

If she still had a job, she could fill the next week's worth of papers with even more headline-worthy stories. Sex scandals and kickbacks and secret lives, oh my. The kind of stuff that would make papers fly out of the racks. Well, it was good to dream.

Sighing, she dialed Mac at work. Time to face the consequences. At least she could count on Mac to understand that
she'd been making a statement and that she'd deliberately kept
him out of the loop to protect him.

"Mac Hunter."

"Hey."

Silence.

"Mac?" Her heart started to race faster.

"Congratulations," he said.

Confusion. "What?"

"Your dad's been raging around the newsroom, out for
blood. So, good job. Did you do it to get back at me?"

"What are you talking about? Get back at you for what?"

"I never thought you were that vindictive."

"It didn't have anything to do with you. I was—"

"It has everything to do with me! I didn't think it did at
first, but then I called and Logan answered your phone and
it all clicked. You're pissed at me because I took the job over
you."

"Wait, what does Logan answering my phone have to do
with this?"

"Jesus, Charlie, I'm not that stupid. You acted like everything was fine, like it was A-okay, with the good wishes and
way-to-gos, but, really, you were ticked that I was more concerned about my sister's future than fucking you."

She winced. Okay, well, ow, that hurt. A lot. "Uh, I
didn't—"

"Well, you can do a little dance of celebration. You won.
The paper's going down, and I'm going down with it. We all
are."

Her already aching head began to spin in earnest. "Would
you just slow down? What do you mean the paper's—"

"Advertisers are pulling their ads. Your dad said it's going
to kill us. And, hell, maybe that's what you had in mind when
you engineered this stunt. Take down the two men in your life
you hate."

"I don't hate—"

"Wait, make that three. Your dad canned Lew. That means no retirement benefits. It's a Charlie Trudeau trifecta."

The air left her lungs, and everything snapped into crystal perspective. "Lew was *fired*? He didn't have anything to do with it."

"Somebody's got to take the fall."

"But I'm taking the fall. I'm the one—" The rest of what he'd said hit her. No retirement benefits for Lew. That meant no health insurance. Oh, no. No, no, no. "Lew is sick," she said. "He needs his health insurance."

"Do you think it matters to your father what happens to Lew while we're hemorrhaging advertising revenue?"

"But that doesn't make sense. I can see Dick's pulling their ads, but the others—"

"They're sticking together."

"But the story is true. Every word of it. That's got to count for—"

"It doesn't matter, Charlie! That's what I'm telling you."

She struggled to think, to sort through it all. Mac's anger rattled her. No benefit of the doubt. He believed the worst—she was vengeful. Closing her eyes, she forced herself to focus on what was more important right now. "Lew needs his insurance, Mac."

"There are bigger problems than that."

"You're not *listening*. Lew is *sick*."

"Whatever. Your dad wants to see you at the house when you're done fucking around with Logan."

He hung up on her before she could respond.

Lowering the phone, she stared out at Nana's backyard. This isn't happening, she thought. One story, one *true* story, couldn't possibly destroy the newspaper. And Logan? Mac thought she and *Logan* . . . Which didn't even make sense. Mac had made his choice.

Frustration and hurt and confusion twisted and turned inside her chest. She had to do something or she was going to explode.

Shoving up out of the chair, she strode out to Nana's garden, conscious of the thick blades of grass crunching under her bare feet, the sun hot on the top of her head. The thick and unruly mass of weeds in the twelve-by-twelve square seemed to taunt her: Look at the promise you broke. For shame, for shame.

Charlie lowered herself to her knees and began pulling at them, unearthing wads of sandy dirt that she tossed aside. As she tore at the weeds, hot tears brimmed in her eyes, but she refused to blink, refused to let them fall. Crying was pointless.

"Charlie!"

She glanced over her shoulder to see Alex with her hands on her hips and her dark brown eyes narrowed with concern.

"Hey," Charlie said, sitting back on her heels. She hoped her eyes didn't give away the emotion churning through her. A show of sympathy might undo her.

"What the hell are you doing?" Alex asked.

Charlie squinted at the two-foot-square patch of dirt that her furious activity had revealed. "I'm weeding."

"Why?"

"I promised Nana I would keep up her garden, and I haven't."

"So naturally now is the time to start. What's going on with you?"

Charlie pushed to her feet. Mac was wrong, she thought. He had to be. He was overreacting. That auto dealer story couldn't possibly sink the entire newspaper.

Alex folded her arms under her breasts. "I think it's time you tell me what the hot detective said that's got you so bothered."

"I'm not bothered." Which wasn't true. She was bothered on so many levels, not to mention by what she'd learned from Mac. Noah's suggestion that her mother had a sister she'd never acknowledged didn't surprise Charlie. She'd known for quite some time that her mother had a secret, would never forget the day she'd stumbled onto the evidence by accident.

And there was the fact that Laurette Atkins had called

her Charlotte. Only her mother called her that. Until Charlie knew more, though, she didn't plan to involve Alex. She knew from experience that poking around where their mother was sensitive didn't lead to hugs and kisses.

"Okay, not bothered, but what about hot?" Alex pressed. "Because I would be if that guy had been looking at me as intensely as he was looking at you. In fact, you were giving it right back to him. It was an interesting thing to watch."

Charlie forced herself to focus on her sister. "How long were you standing there?"

"Long enough to soak up the vibe."

"We were talking about a woman's death. Of course it was intense."

"I don't know, but there was something about the way you were looking at each other. Something . . . I don't know. Sweaty."

"That sounds . . . ick."

"I don't mean gross sweaty. I mean sexy sweaty. Rip-his-clothes-off sweaty."

Charlie had to laugh. She couldn't argue with that, actually. Her head had definitely taken a side-trip down that road about the time he'd started staring at her mouth like she was a tall glass of lemonade and he was a dehydrated man. Her heart stumbled a bit at the memory.

"Ah, so you thought about it."

Charlie glanced at her sister, having lost the thread of their conversation amid images of Noah slipping big, warm hands under her shirt and sliding them up. "What?"

"Sex and Noah Lassiter. You thought about it. You're thinking about it right now."

Yep, she was, but she also had bigger things to think about. Much bigger things. She tried to smile to reassure Alex. She'd spent a lifetime working on that smile, but it didn't come as easily this time. "I have to go talk to Dad."

Surprise arched Alex's brows. "Now? But the pancakes are ready."

"You and Logan can eat them." Charlie reached out on

impulse and hugged her sister. In the next instant, she was holding on to the counter in Alex's kitchen, rubbing the top of her head while white dots danced before her eyes. Damn, that *hurt*.

"Charlie?"

She blinked, surprised to see they were in her backyard, not next to the open dishwasher in Alex's kitchen. Yet, the fresh, bleachy scent of Cascade still teased her nose, and she swore she could still feel the heat of steam rising off of freshly washed dishes. Her head throbbed from where it had smacked into the cupboard door.

"Are you okay?" Alex asked.

Charlie nodded. Another damn . . . what to call it? Flash? Vision? It happened every time she made skin-on-skin contact with someone. Damn it, she had to stop touching people.

"Charlie, come on. You're really freaking me out here."

"I'm fine. Honest."

But Alex wasn't the only one feeling freaked out. Somehow, Charlie was going to have to get a handle on what was happening to her. But, first, she had to see her father.

CHAPTER **ELEVEN**

Noah Lassiter pulled off the side street and fell into place a few car lengths behind Charlie Trudeau's royal blue Escape. He had no idea if following her would lead anywhere, but he needed to know what she was hiding about Laurette's hit-and-run. Maybe nothing significant, but he sensed something was off, had seen Charlie hesitate when he'd asked her if Laurette had said anything before she died. That split second had told him that Laurette *had* said something. Something that could lead to her killer. And that's why Noah was here—to find a killer.

He'd already questioned as many guests as possible at the Royal Palm Inn. Before coming to see Charlie, he'd hit the continental breakfast, the workout room and the lobby. When he'd spotted the police officers making the rounds with their own questions, he'd had no choice but to abandon his quest. Not that he'd learned anything. The encounters Laurette had had with other guests had been the "hello, it's a nice day" kind in the hall or elevator. The only hint he'd gotten that all had not been normal with Laurette was from Charlie Trudeau. Whatever Laurette said to her before she died was the key.

And, he had to admit, he couldn't stop thinking about Charlie. She was so much like Laurette at first glance, yet so much not like her. When he looked at Charlie, he didn't see a woman he wanted to be friends with. He saw a woman he wanted to seduce.

Seduction. Hmm. Something he hadn't thought about in years. Sex, of course. He thought about sex all the time, had had plenty of the meaningless kind to relieve tension, to forget his troubles for a while and just feel. He had certain female friends who seemed more than happy to respond to his booty calls. Sure, they dropped the usual hints about commitment, but he'd made an art out of acting clueless. Truth be told, he'd never thought he'd look into a woman's eyes and feel the desire to touch her in a way that wasn't intended to lead to getting them both off. But when he looked at Charlie Trudeau, he imagined trailing fingertips over skin and glorying in the silken friction. He pictured framing her face with gentle hands and letting no more than their breathing connect.

Sappy stuff, really. For him, anyway. The king of no-strings, don't-call-me-I'll-call-you hookups. Yet, thinking about it, thinking about resting his forehead against hers and doing no more than nuzzling her cheek with his nose, had him growing heavy and hard.

Okay, he thought. Get a grip, buddy. You're working here. Focus.

CHAPTER **TWELVE**

Charlie rang her parents' doorbell and waited until her mother, wearing a simple, white cotton dress that contrasted with her dark hair and eyes, silently gestured her inside, her expression flat. Her father wasn't the only one pissed off.

Charlie swallowed hard. No fear. "Hello, Mother."

"Your father is in his office."

Charlie paused in the foyer, breathing in the white linen air freshener. Everything in Elise Trudeau's house was white and brand-new. Carpet, walls, furniture. Three months ago, the color of choice had been a buttery yellow. A year before that, off-white. Always understated, like her simple diamond jewelry and expensive strappy sandals, and never more than a year old. Redecorating had become Elise Trudeau's vocation once she'd finished trying her damnedest to raise three proper daughters who, unfortunately for her, had very strong minds of their own.

"He's waiting."

Charlie took a fortifying breath and turned. Might as well go for it. "I don't suppose you have a sister you've never mentioned before."

Elise stepped back, her lips parting in shock and her dark eyes widening. "What on earth—"

"The woman who was hit by the car near the newspaper told a friend that she was coming to Lake Avalon to meet family she didn't know. Us."

"That's . . ." she trailed off, shook her head. "That's absurd."

Yet her pale cheeks and slim neck flamed red, tightening

the knot in Charlie's stomach. She knew the signs. She'd been pushing her mother's buttons for years, damning the consequences. The woman was going to blow, and part of Charlie enjoyed watching it happen. It felt powerful. All it took was another tiny nudge.

"It's a simple question. Yes or no would suffice."

Elise lashed out with an open palm.

Fury and fear rage equally inside my skull. She can't know. How could she know? All these years, so many, long, lonely years. No one can find out. They'll hate me, know once and for all who I really am. I strike out blindly, without thinking. Rena. Oh, God, Rena. What have I done?

Charlie came back to herself to find her eyes watering from the sting. She thought she'd been braced, but the slap carried more power than usual. And this time, taunting her mother had paid off in an unexpected way. She had a name now. Rena. Would that be *Aunt* Rena?

At the same time, the flash into her mother's head had shown her that Elise wasn't simply unreasonably angry all the time. She was afraid, too. They'll know once and for all who I really am? What the hell did that mean?

"Don't ever speak to me of this again, Charlotte," Elise said, her voice shaking. "Do you understand?"

Putting a hand to the heat on her face, Charlie managed a small, humorless smile. "A simple 'no' would have been just as effective."

Elise stepped forward, and the threat of more violence forced Charlie back automatically. Old habits. Her hip bumped the table near the door, stopping her retreat, and then her mother was nose to nose with her and hissing. "I'll warn you only once. If you mention this in front of your father, I'll . . ." She clenched her hands at her sides.

"What?" Charlie prodded. "Hit me again? You might want to use your fist next time. You've always hit like a girl."

Elise's dark brown eyes narrowed dangerously, but before she could strike out again, Reed Trudeau walked into the foyer behind her.

"Elise."

Charlie's mother stiffened at the sound of his voice, and her eyes clashed with Charlie's, issuing a silent warning, before she moved back.

"Charlie?" her father said.

She edged out from between her mother and the wall, careful to avoid Elise's glittering glare, and glanced at her father, noting the tightness in his jaw. From the fire back into the frying pan. He gestured in the direction of his office before turning away. As she fell in step behind him, she sensed her mother's eyes boring into her back and told herself she didn't care. Yeah, right. That hadn't worked her whole life.

In his office, her father stood with his back to her, silently staring out the window behind his desk while she closed the door. He'd shed his suit jacket and tie but not his trademark red suspenders. As he turned to look at her, she braced, expecting him to start yelling any second. Instead, he compressed his lips into a thin line and reached into his pocket to pull out a pristine handkerchief.

Charlie stood frozen as he walked around the edge of his desk and approached her. Gently, he grasped her chin, and she slid helplessly into his memory.

The story with Charlie's name on it tightens my gut around a starburst of pain. I fumble for a Rolaids and breathe through the rage making everything feel like it's vibrating. The anger quickly yields to something bigger: regret. Thirty-eight years of working my ass off, of sacrificing every minute with my family, of being known as The Beast, and this is how it ends.

She blinked back into the present, slightly dizzy, and looked into her father's eyes as he dabbed at her cheek with a corner of his hanky. "Looks like she nicked you with a fingernail," he said softly.

Her throat thickened with the familiar yearning for him to be her hero again, her Atticus Finch in *To Kill a Mockingbird*, the tall, handsome man who fought the good fight and protected his children from evil. He'd been that man until her mother started lashing out, and her hero let her down.

He sighed, and the scent of liquor that washed over her surprised and worried her. This man didn't drink while the sun was up.

"Why do you insist on goading her?" he asked.

She tried to smile, to get a grip. "It's more fun that way."

He pocketed the hanky while he returned to his leather desk chair and sat down heavily. A sigh that seemed to come from the tips of his toes huffed through his lips.

His calm made Charlie uneasy. She'd never known him to be so composed before tearing into her or anyone else.

He ran a finger over the newspaper spread out on his desk, over the headline that told all of Lake Avalon that a crook operated in their midst.

"It's a good story," he said. "Tight, well-sourced. It sticks to the facts, avoids sensationalism. Like something I would have burned to write in my younger days."

Charlie stared at him. A compliment? "I . . . thank you."

"How did you do it?"

She took a breath, confused but relieved that he wasn't screaming at her. "Last night was David Adams's last shift on the copy desk. He's leaving the paper to be a lawyer."

He nodded and pursed his lips. "When I first saw it, I was livid." He turned the chair so he could look outside at the rippling, sun-glistened surface of the river. "I stomped around, slammed some doors, yelled at a few people, and then I came home and sat down right here, looked outside and saw it all slipping away, everything I'd worked so hard to maintain for nearly forty years. But then I realized that it's okay that it's over. I've grown tired of the fight."

His wording alarmed her. It's over? It couldn't be over. "It's only one story."

He twisted the chair toward her with a squeak of leather. "We've been struggling for quite some time. Your mother and I took out a second mortgage on the house last year to shore up the paper's financials. The loss of even one advertiser would have done us in. Unfortunately, that crook Dick's is our largest. We'll be lucky if we're able to publish on Monday."

Charlie opened her mouth to respond but found no words as the consequences of what she'd done crashed into her. She'd killed the paper, single-handedly. Killed her father's legacy. Cost Lew his health insurance when he needed it most. Cost countless co-workers their jobs.

"I should have told you, instead of trying to shield you from the worry," her father said. "I just never thought you'd . . ." Shaking his head, he opened the center drawer of the desk to withdraw a roll of Rolaids. He popped two antacids into his mouth, and the crunch of them between his teeth vibrated inside Charlie's head.

How many jobs? How many *people* were screwed? "I'm sorry," she whispered. So inadequate, so lame. So stupid. Why hadn't this occurred to her? "I'm so sorry."

"Everything's gone," he said, still chewing. "The pension fund, everyone's retirement funds. Everything. I thought I could put it all back before anyone missed it. Ironic, isn't it? You're so much like me. Idealistic to the point of being foolish."

Her head started to spin. "There's nothing left? For anyone? Not even their own money?"

"We probably won't be able to make Friday's payroll."

She sat forward, refusing to let this happen. She'd fix it, take away his reason to drink during the day. "Fire me. Make it public. I'll apologize to Dick's, in front of the whole town. I'll take the story back, say I made it up. You can say I had a psychotic break or something. Whatever it takes."

His eyes met hers, cool and dark and sad. "You didn't make it up."

"But isn't the livelihood of everyone who works at the *LAG* more important than a few screwed customers at Dick's? Those people should really be carefully reading what they're signing. They're idiots."

A bitter smile curved his lips. "The good of the many outweighs the good of the few?"

"Yes," she said emphatically. "Yes."

"Now you're thinking like me, and that's what got us right where we are."

"Dad, come on. Don't give up."

He pushed up out of the chair and turned to stare outside as the wind blew through the palms and jacaranda trees. "It's over, Charlie. We have to live with it."

"Lew is sick. He needs health insurance."

He nodded without turning. "I already let him know he isn't fired. But this time next week, none of us will have health insurance."

"Dad—"

"You can go," he cut in softly. "Try not to provoke your mother on the way out."

CHAPTER **THIRTEEN**

Charlie gripped the steering wheel with white-knuckled hands and fought the tears thickening her throat. Don't cry, *act*. Somehow, she had to fix the mess she'd made before her parents lost everything. And they weren't the only ones. Everyone at the *LAG*—friends, co-workers, people she'd known her entire life, people she loved—their lives were about to be turned upside down, *ruined*, because of her.

She couldn't sit back and let it all fall apart. She just couldn't.

Ten minutes later, she pulled into the parking lot of Dick's Auto Sales.

Harsh, high-noon sunlight glinted on the chrome and shiny surfaces of new cars and trucks artfully parked in the glass-enclosed showroom. The smell of new rubber and window cleaner hung heavy in the air, and a Muzak version of "Stairway to Heaven" played through tinny speakers while salesmen loitered around the showroom's perimeter. No customers meant they had nothing to do.

At the information desk, Lucy Sheridan, a middle-aged woman with curly black hair and a deep tan so even it couldn't have been fake, tapped away on a keyboard. She looked up as Charlie approached, and her face registered her shock.

"I'm here to see Dick," Charlie said with a friendly smile. Just pretend we don't know each other.

Lucy pasted on an answering smile and reached for the phone near her hand. "Shall I tell him who's calling?"

"Charlie Trudeau."

Lucy's finger trembled as she pushed the phone's buttons, and her gaze stayed down the entire time she spoke into it.

A moment later, Dick Wallace strolled out of his office. He was a big man, bordering on fat but still able to suck his gut in enough that it didn't hang over the waistband of his crisp, new Levi's. He had thick, silvery hair combed back from his face and a wide, let's-make-a-deal grin that could charm or intimidate, depending on his sales pitch.

He looked Charlie up and down, his shrewd, blue eyes cold above a feral, I'm-going-to-enjoy-kicking-your-ass grin. "Charlie Trudeau. You have a lot of nerve showing your face here."

She straightened her spine, not about to back down, not with so many livelihoods at stake. "Dragging everyone else into our problem isn't the way to resolve this."

"Gee, I'm real sorry about that, but you told your story, then I told mine to my many loyal Lake Avalon business friends. Guess we all just have to live with the consequences."

"The *LAG* is the main advertising outlet here. You can't reach the majority of the public without it."

"You mean the public that's suing my ass for fraud? Or the public that's canceling deals that were all but signed and sealed? The public that hasn't stepped foot in my business all day?"

Charlie swallowed. "We can work something out. I'll do another story. You can apologize and promise not to jerk people around anymore."

He laughed heartily. "Oh, that's rich."

Desperation tightened the band of anxiety around her chest. "I'll take the story back. Say I made it up."

"The damage is already done. The lawsuits are piling up."

"Then what's it going to take?"

"I want to know who ratted me out."

Oh, crap. Not that. "I don't reveal my sources."

"I know it was someone who works for me. Customers don't know the details that you shared. Who was it?"

"I don't—"

He moved like lightning and grabbed her by the throat—

I rip the newspaper in half and heave the pieces across the desk at the moron standing there. He flinches back but makes no effort to catch the paper with its damning story. "How did this happen?" I shout at him. "How did you let *this happen?" Whirling away, I bellow my rage. "I'm going to kill that bitch!"*

She came back to herself plastered against a glass wall, the back of her head throbbing. Dick was in her face, spittle flying through thin lips. ". . . with me, Charlie Trudeau. I want to know who ratted me out or I'm going to snap your neck right here and now."

A softly spoken "Excuse me" had the brute backing off so fast Charlie's knees almost buckled at the sudden lack of support. Putting a hand to her already abused throat, she stared in shock at Noah Lassiter looming in the doorway.

Dick's face flushed redder. "Who the hell are you?"

Noah gave him a polite smile. "If that's how you speak to potential customers, I'll shop somewhere else." He shifted his steady gaze to Charlie. "Perhaps you'd like to join me?"

She slipped out from between Dick and the wall and preceded Noah outside, her legs far more unsteady than she ever would have admitted.

At her Escape, Noah looked down at her with a mixture of concern and censure. "Want to tell me what that was about?"

She massaged her aching throat. Bad guy was trying to kill me—Hello? "You tell me first how you happened to be here when—" She broke off, startled by what she'd almost said.

"When you needed me?" he asked, his eyes teasing and, oddly, a little bit searching.

The fine hair on her arms stood on end, the leftover electricity of watching her life flash before her eyes for the second time in two days. Or maybe it was the memory of the inside of Dick Wallace's head when he'd vowed to kill "that bitch," more than likely her. The energy in the air had nothing to do with Noah Lassiter. Right?

"I had it under control," she said.

"I could tell."

Squinting her eyes against sunlight that seemed brighter than before, she opened her car door and got in. A steady throb began in her temples. "Well, thanks. I appreciate the help."

His lips quirked as he angled his body between the door and the frame to keep her from closing it. "What's the story? Why'd he want to snap your neck?"

She shrugged. "All in a day's work."

"He's the guy you wrote about in the paper today. You come back to rub some salt in his wounds?"

Temper flashed. "*His* wounds? He screwed over a lot of people."

"So you know he's pissed and you come over here to harass him some more? Maybe I shouldn't have interrupted. Maybe you're one of those annoying dog-with-a-bone reporters. You get slammed up against the wall often by the people you write about?"

"Writing the truth about a crook is hardly harassment." She was so *sick* of journalists being considered the bad guy for doing their jobs. "Now, if you wouldn't mind . . ." She pulled the door so that it bumped against his arm.

He stepped back and raised his hands.

She slammed the door and started the truck, but before she could back out, the passenger door opened and Noah Lassiter and all his muscles plopped into the seat next to her. "You probably should have locked that," he said with a grin.

She jammed the truck back into park. "What are you doing?"

"I wasn't done talking to you."

"I wasn't harassing that guy. He's a dick."

His green eyes twinkled as he glanced at the sign above the entrance. "Yep, that's his name."

"I meant the other kind."

He tilted his head, amused. "I know. I'm just wondering why you were trying to bargain with someone who's such a dick."

"It's complicated."

"Try me."

"I'd rather go home."

"So a guy pins you to the wall by the throat and you just give up?"

"Are you making fun of me?"

"A little."

"Well, stop."

"It just kind of makes me laugh when little people like you try to take on guys like Dick."

"*Little* people?" She couldn't help but bristle. Apparently, the guy had a big-city attitude.

"I meant in stature. Would you prefer 'small'?" He looked her over, an appreciative glint in his eye. "You're too well-proportioned to be called skinny."

Her face started to burn. She should have been irked at the once-over, but she was more irked at the pleasure that arced through her that he'd noticed. God, she was an idiot. "Whatever."

"He has to have at least a hundred pounds on you."

"I had my knee well-positioned."

"I had my eye on your knee, and it looked shaky to me."

He had that right, which just made her all the more surly. "What's your point? I have somewhere to be."

"My point is that if I hadn't happened by, you'd probably be on the floor of that guy's office puking your guts up."

"I already said I appreciate what you did. Thank you, again. Now please get out."

He grinned. "My charm appears to be failing me."

She snorted. "Charm. Right."

He settled back in the seat and propped his elbow on the console between the seats. "So where to now?"

She shot a glance at him out of the corner of her eye. "Excuse me?"

"You obviously need a guardian angel, and I happen to be free. So let's go. I'm game for anything. How about the beach? I haven't been there yet. Perhaps you could give me a tour."

"I don't think so."

"Okay, you decide. Like I said, I'm free."

"Don't you have a car here?"

"I'll pick it up later."

She studied him for a long moment. What the hell did he want from her?

He arched an inquisitive brow. "So what'd your mom have to say when you asked her about her sister?"

Ah. Rolling her eyes, she put the truck in drive. Maybe she could drop him in the middle of nowhere. "How do you know I asked her already?"

"You don't strike me as the kind to sit on vital information. You want answers and you want them now. Am I right?"

She shrugged as she pulled into traffic on Lake Avalon's main thoroughfare. "Maybe."

"So what'd she say?"

She almost told him her mother tried to slap the crap out of her and had a mini-meltdown in her head before her father intervened. But that would probably make him all the more determined to dissect her screwed-up family. "She denied it."

"Hmm. What do you suppose she's hiding?"

"Maybe she's not hiding anything. Maybe she simply doesn't have a sister." Rena could be anybody, really. A cat.

"Are you calling my friend, *your cousin*, a liar?"

"Maybe *your friend* was misinformed."

"She looked a lot like you."

"Brown hair and brown eyes are so exotic."

"You're not a very good liar."

She glanced at him. "What?"

"You narrow your eyes when you lie."

"The sun is bright, and I've got a headache." One that was growing by the second.

"Doesn't change your tell. When you lie, your eyes get squinty. It's a trend."

"And you're an expert at spotting liars."

"Want to see my badge?"

"Why would I lie about that?"

"That's easy. To protect your mother, of course. It's what we do as humans when someone we love is threatened."

Charlie braked for a stoplight and closed her eyes. Pain squeezed at her temples, flashing light across her vision every few moments. Nausea began to churn through her stomach. She'd never had a migraine, but she recognized the classic symptoms. Perfect.

Beside her, Noah slapped a palm onto his knee. "You know what I'd like to do? Meet the parents."

Charlie swerved to the side of the road and stopped.

Noah looked around in surprise. "Hey, you don't have to kick me out."

She ignored him as she opened her car door, stumbled a few yards away from the car and threw up at the base of a palm tree. Bracing a hand on the trunk for balance, she swallowed several times while her eyes watered and her pounding head spun. Her knees shook, and she prayed they wouldn't buckle.

"You okay?"

She sensed him standing behind her, probably too squeamish to get too close to the barfing woman. She closed her eyes tighter. "I'm fine."

"Right." He waited a minute while she swallowed some more then quietly asked, "Done?"

She nodded, humiliated and miserable. This had to be in the top five worst days of her life. "I think so."

He took her arm, his touch surprisingly gentle. "Let's get you back into the car, shall we?"

She let him lead her to the Escape and didn't complain when he opened the passenger door for her. She wasn't in any shape to drive. Considering how much her legs still shook, she wasn't even sure she'd be able to walk soon.

When he settled behind the steering wheel, he adjusted the seat to accommodate his long legs then put the car in gear. "Which way home?" he asked.

She let her head fall against the headrest, wishing it would explode and get it over with, and managed to point.

He didn't speak as he drove, as though he knew she no longer had the ability to communicate coherently. After parking in the driveway, he walked around to her side and helped her out, steadying her when she swayed. He found the key on her key ring that opened the front door and led her inside and down the hall to her bedroom. By the time she collapsed onto her bed, the migraine had reached full status, blinding her with agonizing flashes of light. If she'd been alone, or with Alex, she would have been groaning big-time.

"Just lie back," Noah said, bending to lift her feet onto the bed.

She obeyed, not having the energy to argue or tell him to get lost. Her first priority was simple: die now to escape the pain.

When Noah sat on the edge of the bed beside her, she opened her eyes to mere slits to look at him. Surely he was going to leave now.

Instead, he asked, "Do you take migraine medication?"

She let her lids drop closed. "No." She didn't have the energy to tell him that this was her first.

He got up and left the room, and Charlie relaxed, her body feeling strangely leaden. It would take a crane to budge her. A moment later, she heard him return but didn't bother to look at him. Maybe she couldn't have if she'd tried. Then she felt the cool, damp cloth settle over her eyes and put her hand up. Her fingers encountered his wrist, and she started at the spark of awareness.

"Sometimes this helps," he said. "Just relax. Breathe and relax."

She focused on a few deep breaths, embarrassed when a hot tear squeezed out of one eye and tracked back into her hair. Oh, God, she was such a freaking wuss. But the pain, God, it was killing her.

Noah got up and she heard the telltale sound of the blinds being closed. And then she sensed she was alone.

She let the tears she'd been suppressing all day go.

CHAPTER **FOURTEEN**

Noah stood in Charlie Trudeau's living room and did a slow turn, taking it in. It hadn't been her house first, he decided. The furniture was too old, the décor too old-fashioned.

At the shelving unit that held the TV, he glanced over the photographs in mismatched frames. Some looked a hundred years old, but the more recent ones showed a family in varying degrees of age. One of an older woman and Charlie outside caught his eye, and he picked it up. Charlie looked happy, and young, maybe sixteen. She had her arms thrown around the neck and shoulders of a woman who looked about sixty. Noah wondered if that sparkle in Charlie's eyes had dimmed because she'd gotten older or because of something else. Life tended to do that to some people. Beat out the light in their eyes.

Setting aside the photo, he glanced back down the hall toward Charlie's closed bedroom door. He debated checking on her but held back. He knew from experience that any little sound during a migraine could make the top of your head feel like it was going to blow off. Instead, he explored, telling himself he wasn't breaking any laws without a search warrant. He'd been invited in, more or less. Besides, he wasn't looking for evidence. Well, not criminal evidence.

He started in the second bedroom, which he was surprised to see was the master bedroom. The old woman's bedroom. She must have died recently, he realized, because it smelled like lilacs and not the least bit stale. The wrought-iron bed was big and neatly made, a homemade quilt in pastels folded at the foot. Feeling slightly guilty, he drew open the bottom drawer of the huge, oak bureau. That's where many people kept their secrets, he'd learned over the years. Bottom drawers.

The drawer held personal papers. Tax forms with the name Lillian Trudeau at the top. A copy of her will. Mortgage papers. Medical bills. He shuffled through the pile, not interested in snooping into the details of Lillian Trudeau's life. He wanted something, anything, that would tell him why Charlie would be so hesitant to tell him the truth about her mother. What the hell difference did it make if she admitted the woman had a sister?

His fingers found something thicker in the pile of papers, and he sifted through the old bills and receipts to locate it. Finally, it slid into his hand. An envelope of photos, the kind that developed on the spot.

He sat back on his heels and pushed up the flap to slide out about five stacked Polaroids. His heart thudded to a stop when he saw the first one.

Oh, fuck.

CHAPTER **FIFTEEN**

He sat in the big truck and watched the front of her house. The blond guy was still in there. And it didn't look like he was leaving any time soon, considering he'd left his car at the dealership.

Damn it, how was he supposed to clean up this mess when that muscle-bound oaf hung around?

His cell phone started to trill, and he rolled his eyes. Here we go again.

"Yeah?"

"Did you do it?"

"I'm trying, all right? Maybe you should just lighten up."

Silence.

Shit. Time to backpedal. "I'm sorry. I didn't mean to snap. I'm just as frustrated as you are."

"She knows. That bitch told her."

"And I took care of her. We don't have to worry about her anymore."

"When will it be done?"

"I don't know. Tonight's not looking good. That guy is hanging around."

"What guy?"

"That blond guy with all the muscles. He's not from around here. He might be a problem."

"You need to get it done. Do you realize what she can do to us?"

"Yes." He played it over and over in his head every damn second of every damn minute of every damn hour. "But I can't charge in there when that guy is there. And I don't think it's especially smart to be sitting around here all night. People will get suspicious."

"*Now* you're thinking? After everything that's happened, you choose *now* to think."

He stiffened. When had it gotten like this between them? It used to be so good.

A gusty, disappointed sigh blew through the phone. "Forget it. Just let me know when it's done. And don't let me down again."

He held the phone to his ear long after the call-ending click and imagined what it'd be like to drive out of Lake Avalon and never look back.

CHAPTER **SIXTEEN**

Charlie woke, aware first of the warm body curled up next to her. She trailed her fingers over soft fur and stared into the dark, disoriented. What time was it? Hell, what day was it?

Beside her, Atticus rose and arched his back. She enjoyed the moment when he snuggled his head into the palm of her hand and started to purr. Unconditional love rocked.

It took her another few moments of scratching his ears and then his belly before she remembered how she'd ended up in bed. Dick Wallace. Migraine. Noah Lassiter.

Crap.

She sat up, moving stiffly. She felt like she'd been beaten head to foot. At least the migraine was gone. Her head still ached, but nothing like it had. Must have been stress, she thought. Though it had come on so suddenly and violently. Could it be related to the sudden, inexplicable visions?

She wished, as she did every morning, that Nana were still alive. She'd know just what to say, how to explain the weird stuff happening to her.

Help me, Nana, she thought. Help me figure this out.

And then she remembered a conversation they'd had only a few short weeks before Nana died. They'd sat in the kitchen drinking coffee after consuming a breakfast of pancakes, eggs and sausage. Nana had cleared her throat in her I'm-about-to-impart-some-worldly-advice way.

"If you or your sisters ever need guidance and I'm not around, I want you to go see a good friend of mine. Don't hesitate."

Fear had flipped Charlie's stomach. "Nana? Are you—"

"I'm just saying. There might come a day when you need me and I'm not here. Now hush up and listen. Her name is AnnaCoreen Tesch." She waggled an arthritis-gnarled finger at a pink notepad on the other side of the table next to the phone. "Write it down now."

Charlie pulled the notepad over and snagged the pen before it could roll off the curved edge of the table.

"She lives over on Sandy Beach Way. 1237 Sandy Beach Way. You can go see her any time. Alex and Sam, too. Tell her you're my granddaughters, and she'll give you what you need."

"Give us what we need? Like a million dollars?"

"Write it down, child."

Shrugging, Charlie jotted the information on the pink paper. When she was done, Nana said, "Now, put it somewhere where you won't lose it."

That pink slip of paper was still stuck to the refrigerator door by a Metamucil magnet.

As Charlie sat up, her fingers encountered the damp cloth, and she remembered how Noah had placed it over her eyes before he'd left her alone. She glanced at the closed bedroom door, her heart starting to beat faster. He couldn't possibly still be here.

First stop, bathroom. There, she discovered her complexion was almost gray, and dark circles made her eyes look hollow. The last time she'd looked this bad, she'd had a killer flu.

Flu, hmm. Maybe that was what hit her so fast. That would explain the barfing and lethargy.

And then she saw that it was the middle of the night. No way would Noah still be here.

After splashing water on her face and brushing her teeth, she ventured out of the bedroom. Dead silence and moonlight filled the house, and she began to think she was indeed alone when she heard a soft snore. She saw him sprawled on her sofa, and her breath stopped.

Noah Lassiter slept without his shirt on, and holy God, what a sight. Moonlight worshipped the ridges, valleys and flat, smooth plains of his chest. One big hand splayed over his lower belly, his fingers relaxed in sleep. The back of his other hand rested over his eyes, as though he'd had to block the moonlight to sleep.

Was it warm in here?

It must be. Why else would he take off his shirt?

It hit her then that he had stayed here all day while she'd slept. What had he done for all those hours? And why? He could easily have called Logan and let him deal with getting someone to stay with her. Not that she'd needed a babysitter, but still.

Hunger nudged her, and she reluctantly turned away from Noah's naked chest. Not that kind of hunger, she told herself as she padded into the kitchen and debated turning on the light. Not wanting to wake him, she left the light off and pulled open the refrigerator. A few pieces of cheese and some crackers, and she'd be good to go. But she paused, block of cheese in hand, surprised to see something unfamiliar in her fridge. A casserole dish covered in foil.

She flicked the foil aside, and her mouth immediately began to water.

"It's spinach lasagna."

She jerked in surprise, barely missing ramming her head into the freezer door as she pulled her head out and turned.

Noah leaned in the kitchen doorway, his thumb hooked in the waistband of his jeans, still beautifully shirtless.

Charlie swallowed as she deposited the cheese she'd liberated from the fridge on the counter. "Uh, hi."

He smiled, cocked his head. "Hello to you. Feeling better?"

She swallowed again, told herself she was drooling because of the lasagna, not because he looked so absolutely freaking hot in the moonlight. Glittery green eyes, shaggy hair and cut chest. Gulp. "Yes, thank you. Uh, you cooked?"

He padded across the tile, and she glanced down, surprised that he was barefoot. Something in her stomach clutched hard. A beautiful man barefoot in her kitchen . . . how odd.

She stepped back, out of his way, as he slid the casserole dish out of the fridge and set it on the counter. "It's not cooked yet," he said. "I didn't want the smell to disturb you. Migraines and food smells don't mix." He reached over and cranked the dial on the oven. "I don't know about you, but I'm starving."

She didn't mention that it was the middle of the night. She was busy looking at the lasagna's evenly sprinkled mozzarella and parmesan and thinking, The man *cooks*. Can I keep him?

A moment later, he flicked on the overhead light. Charlie blinked at him, belatedly realizing she wore no makeup and looked like hell.

He gazed at her with a weird, half smile as he went to work on the cork of a bottle of red wine that she knew for a fact he hadn't found in her house. In fact, she'd had no lasagna ingredients, either.

"You went shopping?" she asked. Nice throaty growl there, Chuck, she thought, as her cheeks flooded with heat.

His half grin turned full. "Did you miss me?"

She shrugged. "Hardly knew you were gone."

He opened a cupboard door and retrieved wineglasses. He already knew his way around her kitchen. The clutch in her gut did its thing again, and she cleared her throat. "So, you didn't have to stay."

"I didn't have anywhere else to be." He splashed wine into the glasses, set aside the bottle and handed her one of the glasses. Then he clinked his own against hers. "Here's to lasagna at two A.M."

The wine tasted tart and earthy, and she savored that first tingle. As warmth spread through her stomach, she remembered how empty it was. She should probably have an appetizer, she thought.

As if reading her mind, Noah reached for the hunk of cheese at the same time, and their hands connected.

Shock zings through me like a head rush as I stare down at the photo. Oh, fuck. Oh, fuck. Someone hit Charlie. More than once. With fists. That son of a bitch. Son of a bitch. I flip through the other Polaroids, nausea growing with each new angle of Charlie's bruised and swollen face. Who did this to her? I'll tear the fucker apart.

"Charlie? You okay?"

She blinked back into her own kitchen to find Noah watching her with concern in his eyes. She pulled her hand away from his, the wine souring in her stomach. "You were snooping?"

His brows arched sharply. "What?"

"While I was sleeping, you snooped. You had no right to do that."

He shook his head, clearly baffled. "How—"

She backed away from him, shame and embarrassment dogging the heels of anger. "You need to go."

"Charlie—"

"I want you to go!"

He raised his hands, placating. "Just calm down. Let's talk about this."

Oh, God, tears were welling. She was such a wuss. But it was anger, she thought. She cried when she was pissed. "There's nothing to talk about. Now, *please*, get the hell out."

She pivoted and walked out of the kitchen into the backyard, not knowing where she was going. Just away. From him. From everything. From her screwed-up life.

Noah didn't follow her outside, and she stood on the cement slab patio and rubbed her arms against the cool night air. Jesus, how did he find those damn pictures? She hadn't even known Nana still had them. But, of course, it made sense. Nana was all about insurance. Protecting those she loved.

She heard the door open behind her and tensed, swiping at her eyes before the tears could spill. Get a grip already.

"I put the lasagna in. It'll be ready in about forty-five minutes."

She closed her eyes, swallowed. "I asked you to go."

"I heard you."

And yet he didn't move. He'd brought her home when she'd been sick and put her to bed, then stuck around and cooked for her while she'd slept.

Don't forget the snooping. A cop doing cop things. Without his shirt.

She shook her head and wondered what else he'd found. Maybe stuff she didn't even know about. She really should have cleaned out Nana's room by now, but she hadn't had the strength. It still smelled like her in there. Like lilacs.

She angrily knocked away a tear that fought free of her lashes and spilled down her cheek. Cut it out. Don't be so f-ing weak.

Catching movement out of the corner of her eye, she turned her head to see Noah's hand outstretched, her glass of wine dangling from his fingers. She debated ignoring him until he went away. She didn't need this on top of everything else. But then he gently tapped the side of her arm with the glass, and she caved, knowing as she did so that she'd given in too easily.

While the wrought-iron deck chair behind her creaked with Noah's weight, she drank down a healthy swallow of wine. Self-medication had its merits, and she anticipated the moment when warmth would suffuse her limbs. Should be any minute.

Noah said nothing, and that disconcerted her. He was a cop. Shouldn't he be asking cop questions?

Would your mother kill to protect her secret?

Well, she thought, draining the last of her wine, maybe.

CHAPTER **SEVENTEEN**

Noah sat quietly, watching Charlie's back and listening to the whir of Florida bugs and distant chirps of birds. It took several minutes before her rigid shoulders began to relax incrementally. Probably the wine. And silence. Other than the nighttime activity of bugs and birds, the night was still. So different from Chicago, where sirens and honking horns and the shouts of angry, often-drunken strangers never stopped. Except when it snowed, but that was probably because of the sound-deadening effects of snow rather than any kind of peace. Not like here. He'd never known such peace. Such stillness.

He leaned his head back, took in the brilliance of the stars. It struck him just like before. Total, mind-blowing awe. He thought about Laurette, smiled sadly. Check it out, sweetie. I'm taking it all in, just like you wanted.

"It's not what you think."

He raised his head to see that Charlie still faced the yard. The moonlight glinted on her hair, limned her pale hand as she tucked dark strands behind her ear. How she even knew that he'd found the pictures perplexed him. But, then, maybe she'd only suspected, and his reaction to her "you were snooping?" gave him away.

"And what *do* I think?" he asked.

She sighed almost silently. "It's just not."

Okay, so it wasn't a boyfriend. Father? Rage curled in his gut all over again. Some men were such brutal bastards. "How long ago?"

She didn't respond for a long moment, and he thought he'd

pushed too soon. But, damn it, he didn't know how to talk to someone he wasn't interrogating. He didn't know how to talk to *her*, this woman he somehow already cared about.

"I was sixteen," she said. "I was looking for a . . . slip. It was my sister Sam's graduation day, and I don't normally wear dresses." She paused, looked down into her empty glass.

He got up and reached around her to refill it. She kept her eyes averted, but he noticed the hand holding the glass trembled.

He returned to the chair, knowing she needed distance or she wouldn't talk.

"I found a photo album I'd never seen before. She walked in while I was looking at it."

She?

"I was excited," she said, and laughed softly, ruefully. "I'd never seen pictures of my mother as a child. There were people in the pictures I'd never met, and I wanted to know who they were, where they were, why we never saw them." She paused, wet her lips. "Something inside her snapped. Sometimes I think I actually heard it break."

Jesus Christ, her *mother* did that to her. Noah didn't know what to say, probably couldn't have spoken if he'd tried.

"I moved in with my grandmother afterward. Kept an eagle eye on my younger sister for signs of . . ." She trailed off, cleared her throat. "Sam took off right after graduation. Alex always seemed okay. Too immersed in taking care of the neighborhood strays to be distracted by family tension. Mom was colder, more distant, even more tightly controlled. She feared losing it again." She swallowed some wine. "I made it my personal crusade to goad her. I wanted her to hit me again. Figured one more good punch was all it would take to get Dad to leave her. I wanted him to leave her so badly. Wanted her to hurt."

She looked over her shoulder at him and smiled, her eyes glittering in the moonlight. "I got good at it. I could trip her trigger with a look. Not like that first time. But I could make her slip, make her lash out. She'd get this cornered look in her eyes that scared the crap out of me. At the same time, I'd be thrilled that I could do that to her. It felt powerful. Sick, huh?"

"I've heard worse," he said softly, no longer shocked at the damage that people who supposedly loved each other could do.

"I suppose you have," she replied, turning her back to him again and drinking some more.

He wondered how many blows Charlie had taken before it sank in that Mom was more important to Dad than violence and bruises. Or if it had.

"It's your turn," she said.

He blinked to see that she'd turned to face him, one arm wrapped around her middle. "Pardon?" he asked.

"You snooped through my past, now I get to snoop through yours."

He would have preferred to talk about the people in the photos she'd seen, the people she'd never met. But he also got that he needed to take his time with her. Time and patience. He never felt like he had enough of either, but he would dig deep for her.

He rearranged himself in the deck chair. "Dad died when I was a kid. Mom had been a housewife all her life, but she had a pretty good singing voice. So she loaded us all into an old school bus, and we hit the road as a band."

Charlie snorted. "You're so full of shit."

"I was pretty jealous of my older brother. He got all the chicks."

"So you were the annoying but precocious redhead?"

"Nope. Shy one on drums."

"Ah." She lowered herself into the chair next to his and leaned her head back. "Not fair."

He swallowed against the sudden tightness in his throat as he took in the slim column of her neck, the pale skin bisected by the thin bruise left by the extension cord just visible above the edge of the turtleneck. Rage hammered him in the gut with the force of a prizefighter's fist. In his line of work, he'd seen plenty of bruises on women, had felt sick and angry every time. But something about this one . . .

"The real story would bore you, trust me," he said.

"Maybe I'm in the mood for a little boredom. I've had an exciting couple of days."

He refilled her glass with the rest of the wine. "Drink up."

"You're trying to get me drunk."

"Didn't have far to go, really. You're a lightweight."

She sipped, swallowed. "You got what you wanted. Now give me what I want."

He wouldn't say he'd gotten what he wanted. Not even close. He wanted *her*. And she was just pliable enough now that he was sure he could have her if he tried. He could tell her the tragic story of his first partner and the violence that followed. Make her feel real sorry for him, maybe even make her cry, then make his move. He'd be sinking into her within the hour, take a break for some spinach lasagna, then sink into her some more. A lot of pleasure to take the edge off, for both of them. The thought of all that heat tightened his groin.

Time to think about something else.

"So the people in your mother's photos . . ." He trailed off, hoping she'd pick it up. Her defenses were down, after all.

"You first."

He sighed. Maybe she wasn't as drunk as he thought. "Mom was a teacher. Sixth grade. Dad was a cop. The clean kind. The good kind."

"Sad that you feel like you have to say that, isn't it?"

He'd never thought about it, but yeah. It was damn sad. His own kid, if he ever had one, wouldn't be able to say the same. "They were good parents. Good to each other. Good to me. When they retired, they bought a motor home and traveled the USA. Died a couple of years ago from carbon monoxide poisoning."

"Oh, God. Suicide?"

"Faulty space heater."

"Oh." She sighed. "I'm sorry."

He finished his wine and stared into the bottom of the glass, wishing he'd picked up more than one bottle. Glancing over at Charlie, he saw that she sat with her head back, her eyes closed, the wineglass clasped by limp fingers in her lap. She looked relaxed, zoned.

He wanted to ask her again about the mystery people in her mother's photos. Could one have been a sister? Perhaps a sister her mother wanted so badly to keep hidden that she'd kill? But he hesitated, unable to bring himself to disturb how peaceful she looked. A few more minutes, he decided, then he'd ask.

The timer in the kitchen started to beep.

"Lasagna's done," Charlie murmured.

CHAPTER **EIGHTEEN**

Noah lounged in the chair that he'd come to think of as his in the lobby of the Royal Palm Inn, a shaft of morning sunlight creating prisms at his feet. From here, he could see the hotel entrance, the registration desk, the elevators and the door to the stairwell. Every guest he spotted he'd already questioned about Laurette the day before or earlier this morning, before he'd met John Logan at the morgue. Logan had handed over an envelope of Laurette's belongings and told him he could pick up the rest of her things at the hotel before taking him to ID Laurette's body.

She'd been so still and pale on the cold steel table. It had shocked him seeing her like that, and *that* unnerved him. He'd seen so much in his career as a cop. But this was *Laurette*, dead at the hand of an unknown assailant.

His options were dwindling, and he'd gathered no significant information on what she was doing before she died. Most of the Royal Palm's guests were regulars, and they noticed the people who weren't, such as Laurette. So far, he'd heard about her rolling her suitcase down the hall, getting hot tea and a bagel at breakfast, retrieving ice from the machine at the end of the hall. Nothing unusual, nothing indicating that she would be the victim of a hit-and-run within a matter of minutes.

He had nothing to go on except Laurette's whole purpose for coming to Lake Avalon. To reunite her mother with Charlie Trudeau's mother, a woman who was so desperate to hide her secrets that she'd hurt her own child. Jesus, would she try to *kill* her own child? He knew from too much experience that sick people inhabited this world.

He could kick himself for not forcing himself to quiz Charlie more about her family secrets the night before. But it would have felt too much like taking advantage when she was vulnerable—a mind-set that was unlike him, really. He was all about finding what made someone vulnerable and using it against them to get what he wanted. But she wasn't a perp who needed to pay for a crime. She wasn't even just a woman, not the kind he could pleasure and take pleasure in, simply and with no strings attached. But she'd become too important for only that. He had no idea how, but she had.

So, after dinner and small, safe talk, he'd taken a cab to Dick's Auto Sales to get his car and go back to the hotel for some sleep. But he hadn't been able to sleep. His heart had beaten too fast, as though being near Charlie had given him an adrenaline surge.

"Excuse me, young man?"

He looked up to see a tall, elderly woman with short, pure white hair and silver wire-framed glasses perched on the end of her nose. "Yes, ma'am?"

"You're the one who knew the young woman who was hit by the car?"

He nodded, his heart skipping a beat. "Yes. Her name was Laurette."

"I sure wish I'd known about the accident sooner. My Harry and I spent the day yesterday on Marco Island, so we didn't hear about the tragedy until we returned last night."

Realizing he should ask her to sit, he sprang to his feet and gestured toward his chair. "Please."

She waved a dismissive hand. "No, no, if I sit down I won't want to get back up."

"So you remember Laurette?"

"Yes, yes. We didn't speak, I'm afraid. And I'm not sure I can offer you anything that you don't already know."

"Anything you have would be helpful, Mrs. . . ."

"Dillard. Mary Dillard."

He extended his hand. "Noah Lassiter."

Her hand as she clasped his was cool and dry. "Down from Chicago, hm?"

He chuckled. "Must be the accent."

She beamed. "It's a game I like to play, trying to figure out where people hail from."

"I'm sure you get to play that game a lot around here."

"Oh, yes, oh, yes."

"So where exactly did you see Laurette?"

"I was sitting right here, in fact, drinking my morning coffee and eating a banana nut muffin. That's my morning ritual here. Coffee and a muffin, mostly banana nut, sometimes blueberry, and I people-watch while I wait for Harry to get his cranky old butt in gear. I do love to watch people, especially the characters around here. Don't even get me started."

He didn't plan to, unless it had to do with Laurette. "You saw Laurette at breakfast?"

"No, I saw her come out of the stairwell. Right over there."

He turned his head to look at the door marked STAIRS.

"I noticed because she was so young and pretty. Most of the guests here are old geezers, as you've probably noticed."

"Did she look upset or anything?" he asked, trying to keep her on track.

"Distracted, really. She walked through that door and paused to search through her bag for a minute. Then she looked around, as though trying to decide whether to turn around and go back. Clearly indecisive."

Noah rubbed at his chin. So she'd forgotten something in her room. Was that significant? "Did anyone come through the door behind her?"

"Not that I saw, but that doesn't mean no one did. Harry finally showed up, and we left for Marco." She reached out and patted his arm. "I'm so sorry about your friend, Mr. Lassiter."

"Thank you. I appreciate the information. If you think of anything else"—he slipped a business card out of his back pocket and handed it to her—"please don't hesitate to call me."

A few minutes later, he was taking in the fresh coat of shiny gray paint that slathered the walls of Stairwell Number One and wishing he knew what the hell he was looking for.

He was about to give up when the door opened, and a maintenance guy backed through pulling a wheeled bucket with a mop.

"Hello," Noah said, not wanting to startle the guy.

He flinched anyway and turned to look at him with wide, dark brown eyes. The guy's youth surprised Noah, who'd been expecting the usual old fart. But then he realized: Maintenance guys saw stuff, noticed details, that other people didn't. He took a step forward, extending his hand. "I'm—"

He broke off when a tall, thin woman pushed through the stairwell door and stopped when she saw them. She had unnaturally blond hair and wore high-heeled sandals and a white skirt that showed off slim, deeply tanned legs. Her blue and white horizontally striped shirt scooped into a low V, displaying rounded, sun-worn cleavage.

She glanced at the maintenance guy. "The guests in three-twelve are having trouble with their Internet connection, Skip. Can you check it out?"

He nodded and wheeled the bucket behind the stairs before going on his way.

The woman, Donna Keene, Hotel Manager, according to the shiny gold name tag pinned to her shirt, turned to Noah and smiled. "Are you lost?"

He smiled back. "Just looking around." He gestured at the walls and steps. "Nice paint job. Professional?"

Sky blue eyes narrowed slightly but somehow stayed friendly. "You've been questioning my guests."

"Just making conversation."

"About a dead woman."

"She was a friend of mine."

"I'm sorry about what happened to her, but my guests are on vacation, and the police are already questioning them."

Okay, subtle charm wasn't working. Time for the big guns. He donned his best, most conciliatory smile and extended his hand. "Noah Lassiter."

Her gaze dropped briefly to his mouth before she put her hand in his. "Donna Keene."

Her chin lifted a notch when his hand engulfed hers, and he stared deeply into her eyes. Come to papa. "It's a pleasure to meet you," he said, holding her hand extra long to let her know he meant it.

She glanced away first, and he saw her swallow. Hooked.

"So you're the manager," he said, gesturing at her name tag.

"Owner, actually."

"It must be a good living. Every room seems full."

"I could do better. Bigger hotel, more rooms, higher rates."

He grinned. "Richer clientele?"

She returned his smile, but it seemed more sarcastic than warm. "Right."

"So I don't suppose you met Laurette Atkins when she was here."

Her gaze sharpened, her lips pursing. "Are you a cop?"

He kept his expression fixed, but the question alarmed him. He wasn't *that* obvious, was he? "Why would you think that?"

"You're asking questions like a cop."

Shit. Lost her already. Maybe the truth would work. "I'm a Chicago police detective, but I'm here as a friend."

She folded her arms under her fake breasts. "I suggest you leave my guests alone, Detective Lassiter, or I'll be forced to let the Lake Avalon police know what you're up to."

"I'm a man alone on vacation," he said, steering clear of any hint of threat. "I'm allowed to make friends, and I happen to like the crowd here at the Royal Palm very much."

She started to fire a retort at him but seemed to think better of it. Her lips thinned into a frosty smile. "Enjoy your stay, detective."

She stomped up the stairs, and Noah watched her go. If he'd been the least bit interested in anyone other than a certain journalist, he might have appreciated her hip-swaying indignation.

CHAPTER **NINETEEN**

Charlie coasted in slow-moving beach traffic and wondered whether it was dumb to go meet the mysterious Anna-Coreen Tesch. I mean, really, chasing after a woman whose name she just happened to remember from a conversation with Nana months ago? Maybe she was still drunk from the night before. Thinking crazy because a gorgeous, shirtless, barefoot guy had not only cooked for her but had also gotten enraged over the bruises her mother had left on her. See, Dad? That's how it's done.

Or, hell, maybe she was just trying to avoid the other stuff going on.

Such as her connection to Laurette Atkins. She needed to fess up to Noah that her mother did indeed have a sister. She would have done it last night if he'd asked, but he hadn't. Which was confusing, really. Why else had he hung around so long if not to pick her brain about Trudeau family secrets? He couldn't possibly have missed the part in her story about the photos she'd found in her mother's lingerie drawer. People she'd never met? A mother who went ape shit when she discovered her daughter with the photo album? Hello? She'd waved the red flags all over the place. Mom had a nasty secret that made her vicious. Go ahead and ask me about it.

Not that Charlie thought for a second that her mother would kill someone to try to keep that secret covered . . . well, maybe she did think it for a second. But certainly not for more than that. She was her *mother*, after all. Mothers didn't kill people. Well, not hers anyway. Sure, she could fly into a blind fury and smack the crap out of her unsuspecting kid, but kill? No way.

Charlie felt her lips twist into a sardonic smile. She'd never known she could embrace denial so wholeheartedly. She'd started off the day of denial by leaving the newspaper in its plastic wrap on the porch, too terrified to open it and find nothing but stories and photos and graphics filling page after page that should have been lousy with ads.

But now she was tired of sitting in traffic and not accomplishing anything, so she retrieved her cell phone and dialed Mac's number. He might not want to talk to her, but she'd give it a shot.

"Newsroom. Mac Hunter."

"Hey."

A pause, a breath, then, "Hey."

"Are you still hating me?" Her throat felt constricted, as though something lodged there that she couldn't swallow away. Her heart, perhaps.

"I wasn't hating you," he said, not all that convincing. "But I'm still mad, yeah. What'd you expect? It's been a whole fucking day."

God, so cold she found it difficult to remember that she'd found passion and solace in his arms just three months ago. And before that, a profound friendship that meant the world to her but now seemed so far gone she started to choke up. "I'm sorry everything's such a mess. I never intended—"

"I'll keep that in mind while I'm signing up for unemployment."

She closed her eyes against the burn. She needed to be stronger, less emotional. "I didn't do it to hurt you. I didn't do it to hurt anyone."

"Was there something you wanted or did you just call hoping I'd pat you on the back and say you did the right thing, damn the consequences?"

"Mac, come on. You know me better than that."

He sighed. "It's just going to take time, okay? Can you give me some time?"

She swallowed hard. "Okay." As if she had a choice. "I . . . is everything okay there? Do people know yet?"

"It's great, Charlie. Everything's just fucking great. No one knows a goddamn thing because your dad's not telling us shit. He hasn't been here since yesterday morning when he chewed me a new one for letting you fuck us all over."

"Mac—"

"I have to go."

The click in her ear sounded like a gunshot.

Numbly, she put the phone in a cubby in the console and blew out a long, shaky breath.

So many regrets, so little time.

CHAPTER **TWENTY**

Charlie slowed the Escape to a coast to check out 1237 Sandy Beach Way, home of Nana's mysterious friend, AnnaCoreen Tesch. It wasn't a dump, exactly. Okay, sure, the shack's warped, hot pink walls looked like they'd been beaten by several hurricanes and perhaps a tornado or two. And was that a rusty tin roof?

Even so, the place didn't necessarily stand out on this two-lane road lined with beachside hotels, surf shops, restaurants and convenience stores in pink, teal and purple. Then she spotted the neon pink and blue sign to the left of the shack and stomped on the brake. PSYCHIC READINGS, $10 FOR 10 MINUTES.

Nana had sent her to a *psychic*? She needed an expert, not Miss Cleo.

A horn sounded behind her, and she snapped out of her shock to steer the car onto the gravel shoulder.

Okay, she thought. The woman had to be on the up-and-up or Nana wouldn't have nudged her in this direction. And Charlie acknowledged it was somewhat disingenuous not to give a psychic the benefit of the doubt when she herself had her own mystical ability. But still.

She sat there and waffled. If she didn't seek the counsel of AnnaCoreen Tesch, what would she do instead? She needed advice, needed *answers*. If not AnnaCoreen Tesch, beach psychic, then who?

Resigned to at least give it a shot, she shut off the car and got out. The stone walk leading up to the shack was flanked on both sides by sparse grass peeking through white sand. Pots of all sizes held flowers that spilled over in shades of pink, purple and blue, giving off sweet scents that mixed with the salty tang of the Gulf air. Coupled with the roll and retreat of the waves on the beach about ten yards away, it was actually a pretty soothing location.

Her skepticism kicked in all over again when she saw the shack's purple door. A psychic could make a decent living off of tourists here. A *criminal* psychic could make an *indecent* living. She made a mental note to check on AnnaCoreen Tesch's business permits. Then she admonished herself for falling into her reporter's habits. Those days were over.

The door opened before she could knock, and Charlie almost burst out laughing. The petite woman standing before her wore a floor-length, red silk dress with long, draped sleeves, a gold rope belt and a hood artfully arranged around her long, wavy blond hair. A large crystal hung from a gold chain around her neck, nestled in ample cleavage.

"Welcome to AnnaCoreen's," she said, her radiant smile showing off model-like cheekbones. Her makeup consisted of red lipstick, too much blush and dark eye shadow framing eerie light blue eyes. Charlie, who could usually guess someone's age, had to settle on a range of midforties to sixty.

"Hi," Charlie said, doing her best to offer her most sincere smile. "I'm, uh, here for a reading."

AnnaCoreen stepped back and invited her in with a sweep of her arm. "Please."

The décor was hokey. Big surprise. Red scarves draped over lamps gave the dim interior a reddish glow. A round, black table sat in the center of the room, surrounded by four chairs. AnnaCoreen's must have been the one topped with a crushed red velvet cushion with gold tassels. A throne for the queen.

"Would you like some herbal tea?" AnnaCoreen asked in a lilting voice that carried a hint of a British accent.

"No, thanks." She didn't plan to stay long enough for tea.

Still smiling, AnnaCoreen pivoted to tend to a teapot on a banquet that matched the table. "I hope you won't mind if I have some."

"Of course not."

When AnnaCoreen turned with a teacup in hand, she indicated one of the chairs facing the throne. "Please have a seat."

Once Charlie was situated, AnnaCoreen lowered herself onto her chair and folded her hands on the table. Rings adorned every finger, her nails a garish, glittery red. Still, Charlie noticed, she had nice hands, grandmotherly hands.

"What brings you to AnnaCoreen today?"

Charlie blurted, "Lily sent me."

AnnaCoreen cocked her head, her blue eyes shimmering with an odd light. "Lily?"

"Lillian Trudeau. My grandmother."

AnnaCoreen sat back on her throne and smiled. "I see."

The intensity of the older woman's gaze unsettled Charlie. "She passed away three months ago," Charlie said.

"Yes, I know. I was at her funeral."

"I don't remember seeing you there."

"I stopped in only briefly to pay my respects."

The older woman's gentle smile calmed some of Charlie's anxiety. "Nana told me that if my sisters or I ever needed . . . guidance, that we should come see you."

She nodded, her smile never wavering. In fact, it hadn't wavered since Charlie had arrived. But it wasn't creepy. It was sweet, affectionate, perhaps even a little knowing. "I can't tell you how nice it is to finally meet you. Charlie, right?"

Whoa. The woman knew Charlie from her other two sisters? Well, she *was* psychic. She almost laughed. God, first her life was a mess. Now her brain was joining in on the fun. "You knew my grandmother well?"

"Not really, no. I met her only a few times. But I liked her very much."

"I don't understand why she would send me or my sisters here."

AnnaCoreen rose, every movement so fluid she seemed to float. "Let's take this conversation to the house, shall we?"

Charlie followed her out a back door and into a lush,

vibrant garden. A narrow brick path led to a small house that she hadn't noticed earlier because all her horrified attention had been focused on the pink eyesore. The beach house, the antithesis of the shack, was a fresh, sunny yellow with bright white trim. They entered through the kitchen. Red, blue and yellow touches kept the gleaming white floors, appliances and wicker furniture from being blinding.

AnnaCoreen gestured toward the front room, also white, surrounded by paned floor-to-ceiling windows. French doors led to a wraparound porch that faced the white-sand beach. Yellow-and-white-striped cushions on rocking chairs invited guests to get comfortable and rock the day away. Charlie immediately wanted to go out there and settle in with a glass of iced tea. Sweetened.

AnnaCoreen said, "Please make yourself comfortable on the porch while I change. I'll bring out some iced tea. The herbal stuff gives me a headache."

Alone on the porch, Charlie settled onto a rocking chair and looked out at the rolling waves, glistening in the late afternoon sun. Usually the expanse of the Gulf humbled her, made her problems seem so small and pointless. Not today.

When AnnaCoreen returned, she carried a tray with two tall glasses and a pitcher of ice- and lemon-laden tea. As thirsty as she was, Charlie couldn't stop staring at the woman's shocking transformation.

A simple red dress conformed to delicate curves and showed off bare legs that could have belonged to a dancer. The blond wig was gone, revealing short, reddish blond hair that had an amazing amount of body considering it had recently been flattened by a wig. She'd washed off the brassy eye makeup and lipstick and replaced them with simple foundation and a little pink blush and lip gloss. But the smile and cheekbones lived on in bold Technicolor.

While the costume had changed, her movements were the same—graceful, precise—as she set the tray on the wide porch railing and began to pour tea with a clink of ice.

"This is sweet tea, the kind my momma used to brew," she

said. A slight Southern drawl had replaced the faint British accent.

Charlie suppressed her sigh. So it was all a big fake-out. The shack, the crystal, the scarves over the lamps. While she couldn't help but be impressed at how well the woman pulled it off, she couldn't imagine that someone so adept at show business would be able to help her with her problem. Like she'd thought earlier: She needed an expert.

AnnaCoreen handed her a glass of tea, and her smile seemed to reach deep into Charlie's eyes. "You need to relax, honey. I'm all the expert you need."

Charlie felt her mouth drop open. What the?

AnnaCoreen continued to smile as she drifted down onto a rocking chair. "Let's say you start from the beginning."

Noah sat in the Mustang parked up the street from the pink shack and tapped his fingers on his knee. A psychic? Charlie Trudeau, journalist, was visiting a psychic?

Not for the first time, he wondered what the hell he was doing following her around. Laurette's death had swiped his legs out from under him. Someone killed her, and he couldn't find a damn bit of evidence as to why. Except for Charlie and her family secrets.

As much as he didn't want Charlie to be the key, he knew in his gut that she was. So he followed her and hoped she led him somewhere useful, somewhere that wouldn't somehow end up destroying her in the process.

Sighing, he glanced sideways at the seat next to him. There sat the large envelope John Logan had given him of what Laurette had had on her when she'd been hit. He'd retrieved the rest of her things at the Royal Palm's front desk, stashed the suitcase in the Mustang's trunk and put the carry-on and a clear plastic bag on the floor of the passenger side. He dreaded going through her things, smelling her scent on them, considered boxing it all up and shipping it to her sister. But he had to sort through it all, had to search for something significant.

Bracing himself, he reached for the envelope and upended its contents into the seat. The usual stuff tumbled out. A tiny clutch bag, sunglasses, the amethyst ring she always wore on her right hand, the small diamond-stud earrings. Nothing unusual or unlike Laurette. Nothing worth killing over.

He opened the clutch purse and peered inside. Cash, lipstick, a tampon, a couple of credit cards, some loose change, a card key for the Royal Palm.

Something was missing. But what?

He thought of what Mary Dillard had told him, that Laurette had paused after exiting the stairwell and gone through her bag as though she'd forgotten something.

Her cell phone. She always carried her cell phone. He'd found that funny about her. So simple yet devoted to that phone.

Leaning over, he snagged the clear plastic bag of stuff from her room. According to the woman at the front desk, it held the things Laurette had left on the vanity in the bathroom and scattered about the hotel room.

Unopened bottled water. Peanut butter snack crackers. A granola bar wrapper (Jesus, couldn't they have thrown that away?). A travel alarm clock. Umbrella.

He picked up a thin sheaf of loose papers and sifted through them. Printouts of online stories by Charlie Trudeau, *Lake Avalon Gazette* staff writer, Charlie's photo displayed next to her byline. So that's how Laurette had recognized Charlie outside the newspaper.

Then he noticed the cell phone at the bottom of the bag.

He sank back in the seat and shook his head. Now he knew why Laurette had come out of the stairwell looking indecisive. She'd forgotten her phone in her room and had debated going back for it.

If she'd gone back, maybe she'd still be alive.

CHAPTER **TWENTY-ONE**

AnnaCoreen stayed silent for several minutes after Charlie finished telling her about the hit-and-run and her subsequent paranormal experiences. The older woman, who'd listened quietly without interrupting, sipped her tea and watched the waves, a soft smile still in place before she began to nod and gently rock at the same time.

"Your experience is quite unusual indeed," she murmured. "Quite, quite unusual." She stopped rocking suddenly and pierced Charlie with an inquisitive stare. "Explain to me how these flashes feel."

Charlie took a breath, held it for a moment, then blew it slowly out. "It's like I *am* the person I'm touching at the time they experienced . . . whatever it is I relive. Sort of like an out-of-body experience."

AnnaCoreen pursed her lips and began to rock again. When she said nothing for a long moment, Charlie asked, "Have you heard of anything like it before?"

"Never," AnnaCoreen said, her blue eyes dancing in the afternoon light. She seemed more excited than perplexed, like a scientist who's realized she's on the cusp of discovering the cure for cancer. "You say this woman who was killed, Laurette Atkins, resembled you?"

"I believe she was my cousin, but getting that verified isn't as easy as it should be."

"Yes, Lily mentioned your family situation to me when we met."

When they met? Why would Charlie's family situation

have even come up when they met? "How exactly did you know my grandmother?"

AnnaCoreen began to rock again, a slow, even rhythm. "Lily came to me shortly before she died. She wanted to make sure you and your sisters had someone to turn to concerning your empathic abilities."

"You mean, my sisters . . ."

"Possibly. Lily knew only about you for certain. She explained that you come from a background of deep denial, that you and your sisters had been raised to reject such gifts."

"How could we be raised to reject something we didn't even know about?"

AnnaCoreen's smile didn't falter. "Let me rephrase. You weren't raised to *embrace* your gift."

"I'm not sure how Nana even knew I was sensitive," Charlie said. "She just asked me one day."

"She mentioned your mother's ability."

Charlie felt a moment of shock. Her *mother* was empathic?

"Lily suspected, yes," AnnaCoreen said. "She didn't know for sure, though."

Charlie gaped at the older woman. "Are you reading my mind?"

AnnaCoreen's smile deepened. "Mostly, I'm reading your face. It's very expressive."

Charlie forced her shoulders to relax. "So what would Laurette and I being related have to do with what's happened?"

"It's highly possible she also was empathic. Death is an incredibly powerful experience. Because you were holding her hand when she passed on, her energy could have mingled with yours to, as you so creatively put it earlier, supercharge your ability."

Charlie had only one concern. "Will it go away?"

"It's more likely that it will grow stronger with time."

So not what Charlie wanted to hear. "Can you explain why I'm tapping into these particular events? I mean, why aren't I just getting a . . . flash, or whatever it is, of them brushing their teeth or eating lunch?"

AnnaCoreen rose out of the rocking chair and walked over to the porch railing. "I'm not an expert in empathic phenomena, so please keep in mind that what I'm about to say is only conjecture. I could be wrong. Very wrong."

"All right," Charlie said with a slow nod.

"Each of us is surrounded by an energy field, or in mystical terms, an aura. Sometimes it's negative and sometimes positive. The average empathic person can walk into a room and feel the energy, or current mood, of a particular person or several people at once. In the level of empathy that you're describing, it appears that the act of physically touching another person, skin-on-skin, actually breaches the energy field, gaining you access to that person's most intensely emotional memories. You're tapping into residual energy, rather than what that person's feeling at the moment, and absorbing it into yourself as if it's your own."

"Physical stuff is affecting me, too. I felt Laurette Atkins get hit by the car, and later I felt my sister bump her head."

"Each intense event, emotional or physical, carries residual energy," AnnaCoreen said. "That's why brushing one's teeth wouldn't affect you, because it wasn't intense. And why you might not feel something every time you touch someone. It's likely you'll feel only traumatic events."

Charlie had to laugh. It was either that or cry. She'd never felt so overwhelmed. Or doomed. She imagined life without ever touching another human being, and desolation seemed to expand heavily inside her like a balloon filling with water.

AnnaCoreen lowered herself to the rocking chair beside her and patted her knee. "This is a lot for you to take in. You're doing very well."

Charlie fought back the sting of tears. Great. At least she was taking it well that she was so totally screwed.

"Have you had any side effects?" AnnaCoreen asked.

"A migraine last night. I'd never had one before. I thought it might be connected, but I wasn't sure."

AnnaCoreen nodded. "I expect the experiences will physically wear you out, sometimes severely and without warning.

Especially if you have more than a few in a day. The more powerful they are, the more draining they'll be, perhaps even debilitating."

She rose and picked up the tea pitcher to refill Charlie's empty glass. "I assume you learned how to shield yourself from others' emotions before the accident?"

"Nana tried to get me to imagine a white light and a reflective shield, but it didn't work for me. I could never get into grounding exercises, balancing my chakra or waving around sticks of sage to smudge my aura. Nothing wrong with any of that. It's just not who I am."

"Nothing wrong with that, either. Is there something that works for you?"

Charlie shifted, embarrassed. "Nana told me to sing a song in my head whenever I started to feel overwhelmed."

AnnaCoreen smiled, nodded. "To focus on yourself instead of the other person. Not that it matters, but I'm curious about which song."

"Sweet Pea."

"Ah, yes." Her eyes began to sparkle, as though reminded of a past crush. "Tommy Roe."

"It was one of Nana's favorites from the sixties," Charlie said. " 'Oh, sweet pea, come on and dance with me. Come on, come on, come on and dance with meeee.' " She stopped and felt her face redden.

AnnaCoreen clapped. "That's splendid. Some people pray or have a mantra. This is your mantra. The important thing is that it works for you."

"Will it work with this supercharged empathy?" Charlie asked. "The . . . the . . . I don't even know what to call them. I've been thinking of them as flashes."

"You can call them whatever you like."

How about big-assed mind-fucks? she thought. When AnnaCoreen's lips quirked, Charlie wondered again whether the woman was reading her mind. Then she shrugged it off. Hell, maybe the woman really *was* psychic. "My point is that the flashes happen so fast that I can't imagine being able to stave them off with a song or a protective shield."

"Probably not," AnnaCoreen said with a sober nod.

"And I can't wear gloves to prevent skin-on-skin contact. This is Florida, for God's sake. So how do I deal?"

AnnaCoreen began to rock again, gently, as she gazed out over the water that glittered like diamonds in the fading sunlight. "That's something we're going to have to figure out as we go."

CHAPTER **TWENTY-TWO**

Back in her Escape, Charlie pulled into traffic and turned on the radio to distract her going-a-mile-a-minute brain. This really was happening. She really was super empathic.

And doomed.

She couldn't live with this. Every time she touched someone? Shit.

And her mother was empathic, too? How was that even possible?

She thought of her mother's reaction to her question about her sister. Not the violence, but the fear. *They'll know once and for all who I really am.*

Straightlaced, stick-to-the-facts Elise Trudeau. Empath.

No way. *No f-ing way.*

Her mother scoffed at the idea of anything supernatural. Hadn't even read fairy tales to her daughters because the ideas of fairy godmothers and children who could fly and poisoned apples were just too ridiculous. Forget about *The Wizard of Oz* or *E.T.* or even *Mary Poppins* and her magic umbrella.

Charlie remembered at her grandmother's funeral that her mother had rolled her eyes when Alex mentioned she'd had a dream so vivid that it seemed Nana had visited her overnight.

How could someone that resistant to anything slightly paranormal be empathic?

Unless that was what made her resistant. Empathy scared the bejesus out of her, so she'd run the other way as fast and as far as she could, leaving behind the only people who knew: her family.

Jesus. Was that it?

Charlie slowed to turn onto a street that only locals knew led back to Lake Avalon proper. It would take significantly longer to get home, but she was tired of the tourist traffic and wanted the time to think, to figure out her next move.

Talk to her mother?

Right. Her jaw still ached from the last time.

Glancing in her rearview, she saw that a large SUV, or maybe it was a truck, had followed her onto the back road and was gaining on her back bumper. Great. An impatient driver. Take a chill pill, people.

She slowed down to let it pass, but instead of zooming by, it slammed into her.

"Hey!"

She grabbed the jerking steering wheel with both hands, fought to keep control of the car. In the rearview, she saw the dark—black? blue? dark green?—truck or SUV bearing down on her again. What the hell?

Bam!

The Escape swerved, shimmied. Charlie fumbled for the cell phone in the console between the seats.

Bam!

The cell phone flew out of her hand, hit the windshield and broke in two, its pieces skittering over the dashboard, one landing in her lap, the other on the passenger-side floorboard.

And then the truck, a Suburban, she thought, glimpsing the Chevrolet logo on the front end, was accelerating, coming up on the driver's side of the smaller SUV. Charlie gunned it, her heart revving as hard as the engine.

But the Suburban was bigger, more powerful. Within seconds, it was beside her. She looked over, trying to see the driver through windows tinted almost entirely black. She couldn't even make out the shape of the person behind the wheel.

And then the Suburban veered into the side of the Escape, and Charlie lost control.

She saw the banyan tree, knew she was going to hit it head-on but could do nothing about it.

The world around her exploded.

CHAPTER **TWENTY-THREE**

She opened her eyes to pain, smoke and silence. As she remembered the tree, the impact, terror spiked into her brain and she jerked into brilliant awareness. Out, she needed to get out.

She shoved away the air bag, coughing at the powdery substance that puffed into the air. Her eyes started to water while she fumbled for her seat belt, her fingers frantic and clumsy. Something warm and wet trickled down the side of her face, but she was more concerned about the smoke burning her eyes, constricting her lungs.

Pain flared in her left shoulder and across her chest and abdomen as she pulled at the door handle and threw her body against the door. It seemed to jerk open on its own, and she fell sideways, tumbling out and hitting the ground with a bone-jarring thud. Breathless and aching, she clamped a hand to her shoulder and hauled herself up onto her knees. Get away from the car.

Get away, call for help, collapse. In that order.

And then a teeth-rattling blow drove her to her hands and knees as pain erupted at the side of her head. Her senses whirled, and she shook her head, tried to clear it. What the hell? Something just hit her?

A blur of movement came at her again, and she threw herself backward and tried to crab away. A black-clad body dropped onto her, driving her flat onto her back, and Charlie braced her hands against her attacker's chest to try to hold him back. Black everywhere. Black pants, black shirt, black mask. The ninja again. What the—

Gloved fingers clamped around her throat. She gagged, bright lights exploding in her head. She thought she heard someone shouting her name before she managed to get her own, desperate fingers around the ninja's throat, between the collar of his T-shirt and the edge of his face mask, skin-on-skin. And suddenly she wasn't herself.

I dodge paint cans and tools scattered across thick plastic drop cloths as I run full out. The one who ruined everything stumbles to the floor ahead of me and, scooting backward, starts to beg, a black curl falling over one eye. "Please, oh God, please, don't do this. I'm sorry. I'm so sorry. Please." The odor of wet paint fills my senses as I raise the hammer and arc it down with all of my strength. The blunt end strikes its target with a crack-thud, *and a warm spray of blood feathers my forearms and front of my shirt.*

In the next instant, Charlie was choking. Murderous rage gave way to terror, and the masked head towering above her blurred before her eyes. The scent of fresh paint faded into the acrid tang of smoke and gas fumes, and then, at the same instant that she heard frantic shouting, the ninja shoved up off of her and took off.

Coughing and gasping for air, Charlie curled onto her side in the grass. She needed to get up, move away from the car in case it was on fire. Could it explode?

A shadow loomed over her, and before she could flinch or try to protect herself, a heavy, warm hand grasped her upper arm. The world shifted.

A black-clad figure looms over Charlie on the ground and her long, pale legs kick helplessly. What the hell? The choking, gurgling sound she makes flips a switch in my head. Oh, Jesus, oh, Jesus, that guy's not helping her. Heart jackhammering, I race toward the smoking blue SUV, mindless of the uneven ground that tries to trip me. "Charlie! Charlie!"

She realized the voice was in the here and now, but she couldn't respond. Dizzy, so dizzy.

The hand gripped harder, shook her a little. "You okay? Charlie, are you okay? Talk to me."

She knew that voice. Deep, soothing, masculine. Noah.

But she couldn't see anything because of the smoke and tears burning her eyes. And, God, her head wouldn't stop spinning.

"Fuck, come on," he said. Hands grabbed her roughly by the wrists and hauled her up.

She tried to get her legs under her, tried to help him by standing on her own, but her muscles refused to cooperate, as though her brain no longer communicated with them.

The next thing she knew, she was hanging upside down, her equilibrium, the world, completely scrambled. Her bruised gut bounced against a hard shoulder and knocked her into the dark.

CHAPTER **TWENTY-FOUR**

Noah felt it the instant her body went limp against him, and his heart rammed into his throat. Shit. By the time he made it to the other side of the road, a safe distance from her smoking SUV, the black Suburban was gone. He cursed himself for not getting the license plate number, but he'd been so stunned at the sight of Charlie's mangled Escape that it hadn't even occurred to him that the other driver hadn't stopped to try to help her. His heart felt like it still hadn't restarted since he'd seen that son of a bitch on top of Charlie, choking her.

Lowering her gently to the grass, he cradled her head in the palm of his hand to keep it from falling back and striking the ground. Fuck. There was blood at her hairline. Swallowing against the nausea, he eased some of her dark hair aside to inspect the area, relieved to see that it was only a small cut.

He trailed his fingers down her cheek, fascinated at the soft texture of her skin. She looked so much like Laurette that his stomach seized. And then her eyes fluttered open, and she looked up at him with a dazed, gold-flecked gaze that wasn't anything like Laurette's.

"Hey," he said.

"What are you doing here?" she asked weakly.

He felt an idiot-sized smile spread over his face. Coherence was always a good sign. "Saving your ass again."

And it was a cute ass, too, firm and perfect under his palm when he'd been holding her steady over his shoulder. Christ, once again, he'd noticed things about her, sexy things, that shouldn't have even registered considering the circumstances. But he couldn't help himself. *Look* at her. Even dirty and smudged, her hair a tangled mess, she took his breath away. All that dark, flyaway hair contrasting with porcelain skin. Those full lips and high cheekbones . . . and, damn, blood at her temple. He needed to stop.

Grimacing and coughing, she pushed him back and tried to sit up. He helped her with a hand behind her elbow, watching her carefully for signs that she might pass out again. Sure, that'd give him the chance to hold her close again, but he wasn't a complete asshole.

Though she grimaced as she gingerly rolled her shoulder, she seemed relatively okay.

"Did you see that son of a bitch run me off the road?"

"Actually, no. I saw him trying to strangle you, though."

"Yeah, a freakin' ninja." She giggled at that, then winced and started to cough. "Ah, crap, that hurts."

Noah looked over his shoulder for the flashing lights of help, not sure what worried him more, the coughing and wincing or the giggling.

"Help me up, would you?"

He turned back to her just as she latched onto his arm and tried to pull herself up. "Uh, shouldn't you wait for someone to take a look at you?" he asked.

She shook her head, and her forehead creased. "It'd be easier if you just helped."

Sighing, he got to his feet and drew her up, steadying her when she swayed against him. He couldn't stop himself from catching her closer for just a moment, glad that she was so warm and whole, if a bit shaky. He noticed that she leaned, too, before she started brushing at the stains on her khaki shorts. When she glanced over at her totaled car, she dropped her hand to her side as though realizing how silly it was to worry about something as simple as dirt.

"Damn."

Noah's thought exactly. "Not to be an alarmist or anything, but I think someone's trying to kill you."

She turned her head to look at him, her gaze steady and faintly accusing. "And here you are."

He cocked his head and grinned. "Yes, it's been my plan all along to repeatedly knock you senseless in hopes that you'll tell me what you don't want me to know about your family."

She narrowed her eyes and put a hand to her temple. "Jesus, I couldn't even follow all that."

He grasped her chin to turn her head so he could examine the darkening bruise on her cheekbone. His stomach flipped at the thought that it could have been so much worse. "How're you doing? Dizzy?"

"No. Pissed. Look at my car. That *bastard*." Then she pulled away from him, her light eyes piercing. "I don't suppose you got a license plate number."

"No, sorry. I thought you were getting help, not getting attacked."

"But you saw the ninja, right? I'm not going nuts?"

"I think we can both agree it wasn't a real ninja. Probably someone in a Halloween costume."

"He had one of those baklava things on his head."

He looked at her blankly. Baklava? And then he laughed. "Balaclava."

"That's what I said. There was only a slit for his eyes."

"Same attacker as the other night?"

"Unless there's a band of raging ninjas on the loose." She squinted at him, obviously struck by another coincidence. "How'd you get here? This isn't a main road."

Busted. "Uh, well, I was kind of following you."

"Kind of?"

He shrugged, gave her his most sheepish smile, suddenly feeling as lame as he sounded. "You've been holding out on me."

"And you thought following me would change that?"

"I figured it was worth a shot. I don't have a whole lot to go on, you know. The guests at the hotel saw nothing and know nothing. You're all I've got."

Charlie chewed her lip for a moment, thinking, then gestured at a flat rock several steps away. "I need to sit."

As he led her to the rock, noting she wasn't quite steady

yet, he wondered where the hell the cops were. She would have been long dead by now if he hadn't been here. He could hear sirens in the distance, but it still irked him that they were so slow.

He shifted his attention to Charlie as she lowered herself to the rock with a long, shaky sigh. When she stretched her left leg out in front of her, he noticed the bruise forming on the outside of her knee. It must have hit the door on impact, like the side of her head. It made him feel a little sick.

"Are you sure you're okay?" he asked.

She glanced up at him, narrowing her eyes against the sunlight at his back. "I could use a stiff drink."

He chuckled, amazed at how well she was taking this second attempt on her life.

"It's weird, right?"

He shook his head. Focus. "What's weird?"

"I've just had an incredibly crappy couple of days, and it's like I don't even care anymore. I mean, it's ridiculous. I've f-ed up just about everything I can possibly f-up, and the sad thing is that the person who wants to kill me today is nothing compared to the multitudes of people who're going to want to kill me next week."

"You're not making much sense."

She buried her face in her hands. "I'm so screwed. You have no idea."

He knelt beside her and put a hand on her shoulder. "Just hang on. Help is coming."

"Not the kind of help I need."

"What kind do you need? Maybe I can—"

She raised her head, suspicious again. "Are you serious?"

"Well, I need something from you: your family history. Maybe I can provide the something you need."

"You're all about payback, aren't you?"

Payback. Same as revenge, right? He'd been here before, and it was a dark, dark place. But he couldn't help it. It was *Laurette*. "Yeah, I'm a firm believer in an eye for an eye. Sue me."

She considered him for a long moment. "You really cared about her."

He thought he saw tears well into her eyes before she glanced away and into the sun. The light worshipped her, flashing the red in her dark hair and washing her skin golden. He had to concentrate to draw a full breath into his lungs. "Yeah," he said. "I really did."

She sighed and dragged a hand through her hair, wincing as her fingers caught in a tangle. "You're right. My mother has a sister. I think her name is Rena."

He closed his eyes and let out a breath. Finally. A solid connection. "That's Laurette's mother's name."

"I don't know anything about her. I can't even remember anything about the photos I saw of her. And I can't ask my mother, not in a way that would be productive, anyway."

He thought of her face, bruised and swollen. Damaged by the woman who gave her life. "I want to talk to her."

"No." She shook her head, emphatic. "She's spent her whole life running from . . . whatever she's running from. I won't let you, or anyone, hurt her."

His chest ached. So protective of a woman she'd needed protection from. "A woman is dead. Maybe your mother wanted to make sure her secret stayed secret."

"She's got her issues, but she's not a killer. You're just going to have to trust me on that."

"You're not objective."

"I'm probably the most objective one sitting here, actually. You don't think I'd like to turn you loose on her, make her pay for every time she smacked me into a wall?"

"I think she's your mother, and you're a good daughter."

"I just ratted her out to you, though, didn't I? Knowing you wouldn't let it go."

"You did the right thing, Charlie. Isn't that what you do?"

"Yeah, and then people lose their jobs and health insurance and livelihoods and everyone ends up broken. Doing the right thing sucks."

Her voice cracked, and she looked away. The need to

comfort her overwhelmed him. Sighing, he rubbed her back, felt her shuddering. "Are you okay?"

She closed her eyes. "I don't think so."

Before Noah could respond, a fire truck and two cop cars arrived at the scene.

CHAPTER **TWENTY-FIVE**

D amn. Shit. *Fuck*.

He ripped the balaclava off his head and tossed it into the passenger seat. That guy clinging to Charlie Trudeau had to go. Bastard kept getting in the way. What was his deal anyway? Following her around, sticking to her like glue, showing up in the middle of nowhere right when he had his hands around her delicate little throat, popping the eyes out of her head.

Jesus, he'd gotten excited. The moment had been at hand, he was finally going to win, and he'd actually gotten a hard-on. Then that big oaf had started screaming her name and running toward them, killing the moment like a bucket of ice. Fuck.

Taking deep breaths, he eased his foot off the accelerator. A speeding ticket would make his whole goddamn week.

Time was running out. Any day now the other one's body would be discovered. And he needed Charlie Trudeau out of the picture before that happened. The minute it hit the news that that bitch was dead, Charlie Trudeau would know who and why.

And it'd all be over.

Especially for him.

CHAPTER **TWENTY-SIX**

It had to be Dick, Charlie thought. He wanted her dead. He'd thought it clear as day in her flash when he'd slammed her against the wall: *I'm going to kill that bitch.* She'd ruined him and now he wanted her dead. But something didn't fit. What was it?

She adjusted the ice pack she held to her cheek and watched Noah and Logan conversing a few yards away. Noah gestured up the street, clearly describing what he'd seen.

And then the thing that didn't fit registered. Dick couldn't have been the one who'd attacked her. The ninja was smaller, more athletic. Younger.

Dick Jr., she thought. She'd seen him in the flash at the dealership. Dick Sr. had thrown the newspaper at him and roared, "How could you let this happen?" Dick Sr. blamed his son. And now his son was fixing the problem. Her.

Hammer smashing into bone streaked across her memory. The scent of wet paint. Consuming rage. Curly black hair. *Familiar* curly black hair. How did she know that hair?

She jerked as it hit her. Lucy Sheridan, Dick's receptionist at the dealership. Charlie's source for the contract switcheroos. Dick must have figured it out by how nervous Lucy had gotten when Charlie showed up, then he'd sent his son after her. Oh, crap.

She pushed off from the tailgate of the ambulance and hurried over to Noah and Logan.

She had her mouth open, ready to tell them what she knew when it struck her that she'd sound like a nut job. She couldn't possibly explain how she knew these things. I'm super empathic. Ask me how.

Both Noah and Logan looked at her, waiting for what she'd come over to tell them.

"Uh, I think I'm ready to go," she said, and made a vague gesture at her head. "Headache."

Noah's eyes, so kind, the color of Florida pines, narrowed with concern as he reached out and trailed a finger down the side of her face. "You hit your head pretty hard," he said softly.

She shivered at his touch, resisted closing her eyes but didn't resist leaning into his touch, amazed at how easy it was. She could get used to this. Him. "Yeah, it's pounding." Not a lie.

Logan cleared his throat. "Before you go, I need a list of people who might want to hurt you."

She gave him a rueful smile. "I'm a reporter. It's a long list."

"So there are other stories you've been working on that would piss off murdering psychopaths."

"Yeah, I had a couple in the works. A local builder who's been taking kickbacks from price-gouging suppliers. Not that that story was going anywhere. The builder's a major advertiser at the *LAG*, too."

"Do the advertisers know that the *LAG* won't expose them because of their business relationship?"

"They don't now that Dick's sins have been aired."

Logan sighed, shook his head. "Fine. How about we start with the top three on the people-who-want-Charlie-Trudeau-dead list?"

"Dick Wallace would be number one."

"Any chance he was the driver of the Suburban?"

"Too small," Noah said.

Logan arched a brow at him. "You know Dick Wallace?"

"Met him earlier, when he had Charlie pinned against the wall by the throat."

Logan's eyes darkened. "Son of a bitch." His gaze swung to Charlie. "You went over there after your story hit the streets?"

Charlie almost stepped back from the menace in his face.

"He started an ad boycott against the newspaper that's probably going to kill it. I had to do something."

Noah murmured an almost inaudible "Ah" that had her glancing at him before Logan blew out an exasperated breath. "And you think you can bargain with a guy like Dick Wallace? Come on, Charlie. You're smarter than that."

"I admit it wasn't a shining moment for me, but . . . look, this is beside the point. Shouldn't you be questioning him instead of chewing me out for being an idiot?"

Logan shook his head. "Yeah, fine. You're right. I'll question him myself."

"While you're at it, you might want to see what Dick Jr. was up to when I was run off the road. His build is similar to the ninja's."

"Great," Logan said. "My boss is going to be a real happy camper when Dick calls him up to complain about his whole family being harassed."

"He's a crook, Logan," Charlie replied. "He should have been shut down years ago."

"He has connections in the community, Charlie. Solid connections. You pissed off more than Dick Wallace with that story."

"So no one is supposed to tell the truth about a guy who has connections? What, is Lake Avalon part of the Soviet Union now?"

"I'm just saying—"

"Shit," Noah said through his teeth, cutting him off. Charlie and Logan both glanced at him in surprise. And then Noah, eyes suddenly narrowed with purpose, took Charlie's arm and stepped between her and the other cop. "Look, this isn't getting us anywhere. I think we can all agree that Dick needs a good look. In the meantime, Charlie should lie low. Maybe check in at the Royal Palm until we get a handle on the threat level."

Logan put away his notebook and pen. "That's a good idea. I'll arrange the room and get you the key." He looked at Charlie. "Maybe you should take a trip to the ER to get checked out."

Charlie started to argue. "I'm fine—"

Noah's fingers tightened on her arm. "I'll take her to the ER and home to pack," he said to Logan. "Think you can have someone bring a room key by her place?"

Logan nodded. "Yeah, I can do that."

"Great, thanks." Noah steered Charlie toward his car, his movements surprisingly brusque.

She reluctantly fell into step beside him, biting down on the surge of indignation. Decisions had been made as though she had no say. And she didn't have time to go to the ER. She had things to do, such as check on Lucy Sheridan.

"Being mad is a waste of energy," Noah said as he opened the passenger door for her.

She stopped in front of him, tilted her head back to meet his eyes. "I don't like being pushed around."

He cocked his head. "Yeah? What about almost being killed? You like that? Are you one of those people who gets off on cheating death?"

"No. Of course not. I'm just—"

He backed her against the car door. "You walked into that guy's place of business, knowing he'd want a piece of you, and cornered him. What the hell were you thinking?"

"I wasn't thinking. I already admitted that. Jesus, why are you so bent about that anyway?"

"You know what I'm bent about?" He stepped closer, and her back hit the car door. That didn't stop him from getting closer, angling his head so that he was in her face, bracing his hands on the door frame to trap her. "I've been chasing my tail since I got here, trying to find something, anything, to explain why my friend was run down on a Lake Avalon street. My friend, who had no enemies, who'd pissed off no one before or after she got here, who did nothing but what normal people do when they go on vacation. I've been questioning people right and left, trying to figure it out. And you know what? It's so clear to me now. So fucking clear. Laurette wasn't the target in that hit-and-run. *You* were."

Charlie sucked in a sharp breath. "What? No, I—"

"And that pisses me off," he cut in. "Because a good woman is dead. A *really* good woman, and she's dead because you stepped on the wrong toes in your quest to do the right thing. Sometimes, doing the right thing is wrong, Charlie."

He shoved away from her and turned his back, shaking his head. "Jesus," he said under his breath.

Charlie watched his back, still stunned. *She* was the target in the hit-and-run? Was that possible? Of course it was. She and Laurette looked similar. Laurette was struck near the newspaper, an area of Lake Avalon where the killer could have assumed he'd find Charlie.

Dick must have found out about the story before it ran and tried to stop it. Oh, God. And now Lucy Sheridan, her source, might be dead, too. A hammer buried in her skull.

Noah dropped his head back and let out a long breath. "I'm sorry," he said softly. "I shouldn't have gone off on you like that."

He's sorry? Why should *he* be sorry? Everything he'd said, oh God, everything . . . "I deserved it."

He lowered his head to look at her. "You did your job."

"It wasn't worth what it cost." She drew in a shuddery breath. She'd been so blind, so stupid and stubborn and self-righteous. "It cost so much more than I ever thought it would. I'm so sorry about that. About Laurette."

He swallowed, looked away. "She was in the wrong place at the wrong time. That's not your fault."

She laughed softly, not the least bit amused. In fact, she couldn't recall a time when she'd felt worse. "I do stuff that gets people killed and fired and destroys livelihoods, and you think it's not my fault? It's *all* my fault."

He gave her a small, sympathetic smile, but instead of offering platitudes, he gestured at the car. "Let's get you to the ER."

CHAPTER **TWENTY-SEVEN**

Half an hour after Noah delivered her to her anonymous room at the Royal Palm, Charlie walked outside to the car she'd rented at the front desk. She'd showered and changed into fresh khaki shorts and a clean white tank top. Her hair was in a ponytail and stuffed under a navy baseball cap, and dark sunglasses hid her eyes. As disguises went, it wasn't much, but between the red Sebring convertible, the cap and the shades, she figured she'd blend right in with the tourists.

As she circled a few city blocks, she kept a close watch on the rearview to make sure no one followed. She knew she was taking a chance by going out, but this was something she had to do. Lucy Sheridan might be dead, and she couldn't ask anyone else to check on her without revealing that Lucy was the source on the Dick's story. She'd promised to protect Lucy's identity. Not that that mattered if she was dead, but still.

Charlie had already tried to call her home, cell and work numbers and got no answer. Unusual for Lucy, who had been at one of those numbers every time Charlie had needed to reach her about the story.

Her stomach knotted as she pulled into Lake Avalon dinner traffic. The thought of what she might find at Lucy's terrified her. She imagined a bloody hammer and the smell of fresh paint. A crushed skull.

A few minutes later, she parked the Sebring in front of Lucy's modest, blue stucco house. She got out of the car and walked across the yard, taking in Lucy's Mazda in the driveway and the lamp glowing through the curtains of the front window. On the porch, the light shining in her face, she pushed the doorbell and listened to it chime behind the door.

Nothing.

No movement beyond the curtains.

But Lucy's car was in the driveway. She had to be here.

Anxiety tightened the back of Charlie's neck as she rang the bell again, picturing drop cloths and a blood-clotted hammer on the other side of the door.

Please, God. Let me be wrong.

Still nothing.

"Are you looking for Lucy?"

Charlie started and turned, surprised to see the slightly overweight woman in baggy, faded jeans and a pink T-shirt spotted with blue paint standing at the end of the driveway. She held the leash of a large German shepherd that sniffed at the roots of a tree next to the road. A black-with-teal-accents Marlins baseball cap sat on top of shoulder-length dirty-blond hair.

"Hi," Charlie said. "Yes, I'm looking for Lucy. Do you know her?"

"We were supposed to go to a movie tonight."

Charlie had to concentrate to keep breathing as she felt again the *crunch-thud* of the hammer striking bone. "Do you know how to reach her? I haven't been able to get an answer anywhere."

"Me neither." The woman walked halfway up the driveway, the dog following, nose firmly to the ground. "She hasn't answered her door, and usually the only time she's gone and her car is here is when she goes on vacation. I always take her to the airport."

"So she's not on vacation," Charlie said.

"Not that I'm aware of," the woman said. "And I would think she'd tell me. I water her plants and get her mail while she's gone."

Charlie inspected the flower bed, hoping to spot one of those fake rocks that held a house key. "I don't suppose you know if she keeps an extra key anywhere."

The woman traversed the rest of the way up the walk, making kissing noises to get the dog to follow. "Who are you, exactly? I've never seen you around with Lucy."

Charlie put on her friendliest smile. Think fast. "I'm a real estate agent." She thrust out her hand. "Samantha Truman. You are?"

"Sandra Stuart." She clasped Charlie's hand—

"No!" Cherokee races for the road, the traffic, and I race after him. "Cherokee! Stop!" The ball bounces into the street, and the mutt bounces right after it. My heart slams into my throat while the sound of squealing tires echoes in my head. And then Cherokee's running back toward me, the red rubber ball clasped between his teeth, ears happily flapping.

"Miss Truman?"

Charlie blinked at Sandra Stuart and felt her fake smile turn genuine. Finally, a happy ending. She glanced down at the German shepherd. "Who's this guy?"

"Cherokee."

Charlie scratched the dog's ears. "Hello, Cherokee."

"You're a real estate agent? I didn't know Lucy was thinking about selling."

"She's only exploring her options at this point. The thing is, she owes me some paperwork. She must have forgotten to drop it off before she left."

"Oh." Sandra cast an uncertain look at the front of Lucy's house.

"If you know where there's a key, I could slip in and grab the paperwork. Lucy will be so disappointed when she realizes she forgot to get it to me, and, well, it'd save my bacon, too. I kind of promised my boss . . ." She shrugged in her best I'm-a-screwup-please-save-me imitation.

Sandra nodded at the potted ficus on the corner of the porch. "There's a key under there."

Score! Charlie had to resist the urge to tell the woman not to trust strangers so easily. Especially lying ones. "Oh, thank you," she gushed instead. "I can't tell you how much I appreciate this." She tipped up the pot and slid the key out from underneath. Her fingers started to tremble as she straightened. The prospect of finding Lucy with her skull smashed in twisted in her stomach.

Sandra clicked her tongue at Cherokee. "Good luck," she said as she started backing away with the dog. "If you hear from Lucy, could you ask her to give me a call? I'm worried about her."

Charlie nodded and waved. She waited until Sandra was half a block up before she turned to Lucy's front door and slid the key into the lock. Her hands shook in earnest now, her knees joining in. Please, God, no blood and guts.

Opening the door, she stepped inside, holding her breath, dreading that first whiff of wet paint. Or death.

But when she finally allowed herself a breath, she smelled vanilla air freshener.

A walk through the house told her nothing about where Lucy had gone or when she planned to be back. Her plants had been watered recently, and mail with today's postmark sat unopened on the kitchen table. A check under the sink in the kitchen revealed an empty garbage can.

It appeared that Lucy had indeed gone on vacation.

Or, at least, someone had made it look that way.

CHAPTER **TWENTY-EIGHT**

Charlie squeezed the lime wedge into her Tanqueray and tonic, then tucked it down into the ice before taking a sip. The first zing of crisp, piney flavor sent a shiver through her taste buds. She figured it was probably not cool that she was at a bar alone, but she hadn't been able to handle the absolute solitude of the hotel room. There were other people in the lounge of the Royal Palm Inn, so she wasn't being a twit. Safety in numbers, after all.

The indoor bar where she sat had been made to look like a tiki hut. A thatch roof hung over the display of liquor bottles like an awning, and tiki torches with flickering lamps instead of flames dotted the lounge and the patio outside. A Bob Marley tune played low and rhythmic, while the scents of tanning oil and fried food hung in heavy, almost electric air.

Before she'd come down to the bar, Logan had told her over the phone that Dick Sr. and Dick Jr. both had solid alibis for the break-in and the car accident. She'd pointed out that that didn't mean they couldn't have hired someone to take her out.

"Hey, darlin', what's your sign?"

She glanced sideways, startled out of her thoughts by the deep, resonant voice. Noah leaned against the bar with a wide smile. He wore new khaki safari shorts and an olive green "Save the Florida Panther" T-shirt. He smelled of soap and rain, his hair swept back from his face as though he'd finger-combed it after a shower rather than using an actual comb. A bottle of Bud Light dangled from one hand.

When she didn't say anything, he arched a questioning brow, his green eyes glittering in the dim light.

"Do Not Enter," she said, and turned her attention back to her ice-cold drink, so like reality. Why was he even talking to her? He should hate her for causing Laurette's death. Just looking at him made her ache for what had been lost because of her.

With a chuckle, he plopped onto the stool next to her. "I was hoping for Yield."

"Wrong Way," she countered, though she had a feeling this man could rub her the right way.

She sensed him considering her and suddenly felt self-conscious in her shorts and tank top. "Soft Shoulders," he murmured.

She looked at him, careful to keep her expression neutral despite the bemusement threatening to quirk her lips. That apparently wasn't his first Bud Light. "Gator Crossing."

He laughed at that then tipped up his beer for a long swallow. She couldn't help but notice the way his throat worked. Kind of sexy, really. As was the day's growth of beard that shadowed his jaw, making him look slightly, chill-inducingly, dangerous. A bad boy. She'd never understood women who went for his type . . . until now.

Tamping down a rush of something that tweaked her tension, she went back to her drink. Couldn't be lust. She didn't do lust.

"Gator Crossing," he repeated, and chuckled again. "We don't have that one where I'm from."

She sipped from her drink and hoped the liquor would ease the tense knot at the base of her skull soon. She was tired of the steady throb of the headache and unanswered questions that whirled in her head like a cyclone.

"Dollar-fifty for your thoughts."

She looked sideways at Noah, saw from the look on his face that he'd been lame on purpose. Trying to charm her. But why? In his shoes, she'd be angry. Hell, she was angry in her own shoes. She never should have tried to defy the status quo. If she'd been the good little journalist and done what she was told, everything would be so different. No one would be dead. No one would want to kill her. The *LAG* would go on publishing next week.

She wouldn't be super empathic.

Draining what was left of the alcohol in her glass, she put it down. "Sorry, but dollar-fifty's not going to cover it."

"Those are some pricey thoughts." He signaled the bartender to set them both up with fresh drinks then grabbed a handful of nuts from the bowl on the bar. "I don't suppose you came to the bar looking for me."

She laughed at that. "Wow, that's . . . well, that's just . . . wow."

"You're flustered. I'll take that as a good sign."

"A good sign of what?"

"You like me," he said, grinning as he popped a peanut into his mouth.

She felt her face flush warm. "You're a flirt."

"I don't flirt. I'm naturally charming."

She snorted. "Right." But he kind of was, damn him. And sexy. The facial hair that darkened his jaw and eyes made her mouth water.

"While you were out, I did some exploring."

She shot a glance at him. "While I was out?"

He grinned. "Thought you'd pull a fast one, huh? You forget who you're dealing with. Big-city cops aren't so easy to fool."

She knew for a fact that no one had followed her to Lucy's. "So where'd I go?"

"I didn't say I followed you. I just know you went out."

"Ah. You knocked on my door."

"Yep, no answer. So where'd you go?"

"Maybe I'm a sound sleeper."

"I don't think so. Where'd you go?" Same tone, same dogged question.

She shrugged. "An errand."

"Logan'd be pissed."

"Yeah? How's he going to find out?"

"I'm going to tell him."

"Big-city cops are big on tattling, huh?"

"Oh, yeah." His teeth flashed white. "So?"

"Let's just say I visited a friend."

He leaned an elbow on the bar. "A boyfriend?"

She let her lips quirk, foolishly pleased at the rasp in his voice and that he was asking. "No."

His grin returned. "Good." He reached for the fresh beer left by the bartender. "I visited an old restaurant up the block that the front desk recommended. Mama Mo's. Fried chicken, collard greens and mac-and-cheese. I'm still feeling like I should go to confession."

The image of him in a confessional amused her for some reason. Maybe because he struck her as so . . . sinful.

"You can't picture me in a church, can you?"

She blinked at him, and started to smile. "Nope."

"That's okay. Before today, I couldn't picture you going to a psychic."

Damn it, that's right. Then, he *had* been following her. "You must have been so disappointed."

"Intrigued is more like it. What do you ask your psychic when you visit her?"

"Why do you assume my psychic is a woman?"

"Right, don't pull that gender-bias crap on me."

"I'm not. His name is George."

He finished swallowing a gulp of beer before he laughed. "No shit."

"Today I asked him what he saw in my future with a shaggy-haired Chicago cop who can't seem to leave me alone."

"And what did George say?"

"He told me to come to this bar tonight at this time and wait for Shaggy to show."

"Ah, so this meeting was predestined."

She shrugged and sipped her drink. "According to George."

Noah leaned in close and lowered his voice. "Did George mention what would happen after the bar?"

She shivered, unable to resist the urge to shift back from him.

He raised his head to look into her eyes. "Oops, I invaded your space. Funny, because I would think *this* would be invading your space." He casually trailed his index finger over her forearm, the touch featherlight and startling.

My fist slams into the wall. Pain explodes, and grief knots in my gut like clenched fingers aching to be unfurled. Wrong place, wrong time, wrong fucking woman. It shouldn't have been her. It shouldn't have been Laurette.

She returned to herself, her head still spinning from the surge of his sorrow and rage, to find Noah looking at her expectantly, waiting for a response. Guilt billowed up inside her. He was right. It shouldn't have been Laurette. It should have been her.

He cocked his head. "What?"

She looked down at his hand, saw his bruised knuckles. Why couldn't her superpower be the ability to turn back time? She'd go back and change places with Laurette, make things the way they should have been, the way that would spare this man so much grief and pain.

She raised her gaze to his. "I'm sorry about Laurette. You really loved her."

His head jerked back, and he slid back a few inches on the bar stool, putting some extra space between them. "Well, I missed the segue on that one."

"How long did you know her?"

He began to pick at the label on his beer, the teasing in his demeanor fading away. "About a year. She told me a while back that her mother is sick. Cancer."

Charlie set down her drink a little harder than she'd intended. Oh, God. "That's why she came to Lake Avalon?"

"She wanted to reunite your mothers before her own died."

No good deed goes unpunished. F-ing universe. "I know

it sounds cold, but it's probably best that they don't see each other again. My mother has spent her life denying who she is. I don't imagine she'll be willing to let go of that very easily."

"Isn't that a decision that she should make?"

If he'd been talking about anyone else's mother, she would have agreed. But this was Elise Trudeau, the glacier of Southwest Florida. Not just frozen but layered with years of grit.

Noah cleared his throat. "Look, I know this isn't easy for you, but a good friend of mine died while trying to do this thing for her mother, this thing that was important to her. It would mean a lot to me if we could somehow get it done. For Laurette."

Charlie had to blink away the moisture in her eyes. So sweet, so devoted to his friend. And he had no idea who he was dealing with—a coward. A cynic. He was heroic, and she was weak. "I'm sorry, but I think you're going to have to let it go."

His jaw hardened. "If our positions were reversed, if your sister Alex, say, died like Laurette did, trying to do what Laurette was trying to do, would you let it go?"

Intensity radiated off of him, out of his eyes, sending a shiver up her spine. In that moment, she couldn't have lied to him if the fate of the world depended on it. "No, I wouldn't."

"Then you'll help me."

"I don't know how—"

"Talk to your mother, tell her about Rena being sick. I'll be there with you."

She flinched. That's right, he knew. "What, to protect me? That's not—"

"If you won't do it, I will. And Mom might not like being blindsided by a cop."

He had her cornered. She hated being cornered. Yet she knew in her heart it was the right thing to do, for Laurette. But, oh, God, the fabric holding together her family was already so threadbare. This was going to rip them apart. "I'll see what I can do."

He smiled in a way that hit her in the stomach—or was that lower?—like a firm tap.

Sliding off the bar stool, she said, "I'm going to turn in for the night."

To her surprise, he stood and fell in step beside her. "I'll walk you to your room."

She wanted to refuse but could see no way to do so politely. So they walked side by side in silence to the elevator. They reached for the call button at the same time, and their hands collided. Charlie jerked hers back, shocked by the energy that seemed to arc between them.

He cast a sidelong look at her. "You need to relax," he said.

Yeah, but no way was that going to happen with him standing so close.

They stepped onto the elevator together, and the doors slid closed. "We're on the same floor," he said as he hit the appropriate button.

This elevator had to be the slowest one on the planet, Charlie thought. It hadn't even lifted off yet when Noah said, "Thank you, by the way. I appreciate what you're doing. I know it's not easy."

"You're welcome."

He faced her just as the elevator started to rise. "I'm curious about something."

Great, now what? "Yes?"

Instead of responding, he stepped toward her and bent his head. His lips closed over hers before she could take a breath. The shock of the kiss shook her, loosened her knees, and she automatically clutched at his biceps for balance. His arm went around her waist, lending support as his free hand came up to gently cup the back of her head. His tongue grazed the insides of her lips before glancing off of her tongue. He tasted like mocha, rich and dark and sweet. Which was impossible, because he'd just been drinking beer.

Her head started to spin, lazy and sensual, and she felt her body relax against him, safe and secure in his arms as his lips trailed over her jaw.

"I love the way you smell," he murmured. "Like coconut and citrus."

Her breath hitched as it registered that she'd only recently met this man. But her head was whirling, her heart beating so hard it seemed to knock against her ribs. She couldn't breathe and she didn't care. As long as he kept holding her like this.

She must have made a sound of encouragement, because suddenly he was backing her against the wall, kissing her again, more insistent this time, almost desperate. She knew the feeling as she worked a hand under his shirt and slid her palm over the six-pack abs she'd longed to touch. Oh, God, they were so firm and ridged, his skin silky smooth and hot. She could have explored them all day, mapping the terrain with her fingertips.

His stomach sucked in as she stroked her fingers above his hip. Ah, she'd found a sweet spot. Pressing against him, she threaded the fingers of her free hand into the soft hair at the nape of his neck and kissed him back, tangling her tongue with his. She felt the thud of his heart against her breasts, and then she felt his stiffening arousal just before he angled his hips away from her.

He broke off the kiss and took a quick step back before jamming a hand through his hair. "Whoa, wow, that was . . . hmm, well, I guess that answers that question."

The elevator door slid open, and he all but ran out. "Uh, my room is this way," he said, gesturing vaguely.

Charlie watched him retreat, feeling lost and abandoned, her heart racing and her insides clutching with desire. She wanted more than a few heated kisses. She wanted all of him—how much shocked her. It was unlike her to be so overwhelmed by the sensations, and desires, of her body. She thought with her head. Always. Well, almost always.

Shaking her head, she went to her own room and let herself in. In the bathroom, she braced her hands on the vanity and peered into her own eyes. They looked fever bright and dazed, her cheeks flushed pink, her lips swollen from his kisses. Her heart had yet to slow its frantic beat. That had come out of nowhere. Hadn't it?

Not that she could do anything about it. He was a cop from out of town. As soon as he solved his case, he would leave Lake Avalon, and she would be alone. Again.

CHAPTER **TWENTY-NINE**

While gasoline pumped into the Mustang, Noah turned his face to the sun. He could get used to this. Sunshine and seventy degrees in the middle of March. Why would anyone choose to live in Chicago when there were places like Lake Avalon? Okay, so there were hurricanes, but the Midwest had tornadoes and blizzards. And he could get into living with sunshine almost every damn day of the week. People here seemed happier, too, for the most part anyway, less tense. Probably all the vitamin D from the sun. But, shit, even Lake Avalon itself seemed cheerful. The small parking garage across the street was painted a jovial pink, for Christ's sake.

And there was Charlie. He'd thought his libido had taken a hike, but he'd discovered last night in the elevator that it had simply been in hibernation. One kiss from Charlie and he'd been sprouting wood like a fucking teenager. And then he'd all but run away from her. Smooth, idiot. But, Jesus, he was hungry. Ravenous, actually, wanting, needing, to bury himself in her and find salvation. He hadn't trusted himself to control the need.

And it wasn't just physical. Oh, sure, she was hot. All that rich brown hair, smooth skin and exotic eyes. She was as sexy as sin with zero intention. Supremely fuckable . . .

Better still, she was strong. Strong and stubborn and quick on her feet. He didn't care for women who backed down when they were challenged. He used to think that was why he was still single. Submissive women turned him off, and so many women these days were like that, especially the ones who threw themselves at him. Not that he hadn't let himself succumb to the charms of several. He wasn't a dolt, after all. But even when he'd met someone he could fall for—such as Laurette—he hadn't gone for it. Mostly, he'd felt too much like an unworthy mate, but she also hadn't fascinated him as much as Charlie did. Now there was a woman who could make a bad man change.

The gas nozzle clicked, and he turned to take it out. Sudden pain drilled along his temple, snapping his head back. He thought, Fuck, aneurysm? And then his knees buckled, and he slumped against the side of the car and slid down. His left knee hit the asphalt while a rainbow of lights swirled with the pungent fumes of gasoline inside his head. Something spattered his hand, and he glanced down.

Blood.

CHAPTER **THIRTY**

S o you didn't see *anything*?"

Noah glared at Detective John Logan, barely preventing a full-blown "you're a butthead" scowl. He had to remind himself the guy was doing his job. Noah would be asking the same annoying questions if the roles had been switched.

"Like I said before," he said carefully, "I was pumping gas and the next thing I knew, I was on my knees, bleeding."

He gingerly brushed his fingers over the burning furrow in his scalp. The wiseass doctor who'd cleaned it up had joked that the scar would leave a new part in his hair. At least it would be hidden, unless he shed his hair like his dad had, and then he'd be screwed in more ways than one.

"You're lucky the sniper was a lousy shot," Logan said.

Noah let his pounding head fall against the pillow at his back and took a long, deep breath. Getting shot in the head, okay, *grazed*, sucked, but Logan was right. The shooter's bad aim had saved his life.

"Looks like he used an old .22 hunting rifle."

"A .22? That's a lousy choice for that distance."

"Yep," Logan said, hooking his thumbs in his belt loops. "So you've been in Lake Avalon, what, two days?"

"Something like that."

"You make enemies quick."

"I'm guessing by your attitude that you found no evidence at the scene."

Logan smiled slightly, as though he'd decided to take Noah's rudeness as a sign that they were buddies. "Obviously, we found the bullet or I wouldn't have been able to tell you what kind of gun it was. So other than that and blood all over your fancy ride, nope."

"Any idea where the shot came from?"

"Parking structure across the street. Sorry, no security cameras."

Noah closed his eyes for a moment. He could have used a beer. No, something harder. Bourbon. Or something softer. Charlie. "Witnesses?"

"No one other than the gas station clerk who saw you go down and called 911." Logan paused. "Snipers aren't something we've seen here in LA."

LA. That struck Noah as funny. Probably because Lake Avalon wasn't like LA in even a tiny way. Well, there were palm trees. "Are you suggesting I brought this guy with me from Chicago?"

"You have a better idea?"

"Someone in Lake Avalon doesn't like Chicago cops?"

"See, that's the thing. It takes a lot to get Lake Avalon residents riled."

"So snipers and fatal hit-and-runs and journalists getting run off the road and strangled are the norm around here?"

Logan scratched his chin as if stroking an imaginary goatee. "You have a point. So you think someone took a potshot at you because you're asking around about the hit-and-run?"

"No. I think someone took a potshot at me because I've been hanging around Charlie, and some asshole wants her dead. I've interfered twice now."

Logan's eyes widened, but before he could respond, his cell phone started to ring. "Sorry, I need to take this." He stepped away to answer it. "Logan."

Noah dropped his head back and stared at the ceiling. Thinking hurt, but he couldn't stop. Someone wanted Charlie dead bad enough to try to take him out. Whoever was after her was getting desperate, and that scared the crap out of him.

Logan sheathed his phone. "We've got a situation. I have to go."

Noah raised his head, noting the other detective looked unnaturally pale. "What's going on?"

"Body discovered. A woman. Looks like murder."

Noah's heart just about stopped. "Where's Charlie?"

Logan paused, his complexion going paler. "Isn't she at the Royal Palm?"

"Have you talked to her today?"

"No. Have you?"

"No." Noah swung his legs over the side of the bed and stood up. His head whirled like crazy, and his stomach flipped, but he clenched his teeth against both and stayed on his feet. "I'm coming with you."

Logan cocked his head, then gave Noah's shoulder a light shove. Noah reeled back. His butt hitting the bed kept him from landing on his ass on the floor.

"Yeah, I didn't think so. I'll send someone to check on Charlie," Logan said before he turned and left.

It was no longer a secret that he had no innate talent as a sniper. He hadn't even known what kind of gun to use. Not that he'd had access to a sniper rifle. Stupid hunting rifle that used to be his dad's was it.

Maybe the police department had been right when it had rejected his application. He was an idiot. And he was sure he would hear all about his idiotness as soon as word got out that he'd fucked up. Again.

Christ, he should put the goddamn gun to his own head and put himself out of his misery. He would never win. Never.

No matter how hard he tried, he'd fuck up every time.

Okay, he thought. I can do this. I can save it.

Maybe the cop would get the hint. Or at least be incapacitated enough to stay away from Charlie Trudeau long enough for him to take her out.

There was money on the line. Lots and lots of money.

And pride. And self-respect. He needed them both back—bad. Or he'd never be able to get it up again.

All he had to do: find Charlie Trudeau.

And kill her.

CHAPTER **THIRTY-ONE**

Charlie felt groggy from a sleepless night as she walked to the elevator, her head still aching. At least she'd managed to cover her black eye with makeup. Hell, she had on so much makeup it felt like a mask. But she preferred to think of it as another part of her disguise, a supplement to the cheery straw beach hat that hid her hair and the sundress she'd picked up in the gift shop. Charlie Trudeau in a bright yellow sundress was about as incongruous as grilled grouper with a slab of melted Velveeta on top.

She had no idea what she would say to her mother, but she wanted to talk to her without Noah being there. Maybe her mother would be more inclined to be honest. She could hope.

The elevator door slid open, and she stepped on, casting only a brief glance at the rumpled man huddled in the corner. She did a double take at the same moment that she smelled booze and sex. *Mac*.

He straightened away from the wall. And wobbled.

She couldn't speak, too shocked to form words. He was *drunk*. Mac, the guy who feared becoming an alcoholic more than losing his hair. What the hell was he doing? And who had he been with? Not that it mattered. Just last night she'd been smooching Noah Lassiter in this very elevator. Clearly, they'd both moved on.

"Hey," she said and faced the closing doors.

He didn't respond, and her heart sank. So he wasn't going to talk to her.

And then he spoke, disbelief lacing his tone: "Charlie?"

Her shoulders relaxed some as she realized her disguise worked at first glance. "Yep."

"What—"

"Long story," she cut in, then looked him up and down. "You?"

"Longer story."

Silence. This was turning into a long ride down.

He sighed, shook his head. "Look, I'm sorry. I said . . . some things . . ."

Her throat closed as relief rushed in. "It's okay."

"It's not okay. I screwed up. I didn't mean to . . . hurt you." He leaned his head back and banged it a few times against the wall. "Jesus, it seems all I've done lately is hurt you."

She looked sideways at him, the muscles in her chest wrenching at what they'd lost. They'd been best friends before Nana died, before she'd turned to him for comfort and they'd fallen into each other's arms. Fools. "We both made mistakes," she said.

"Yeah, but mine aren't the kind we can recover from, are they?" He roughly scrubbed his hands over his face then sighed heavily. "I made the wrong choice, Charlie." He dropped his arms to his sides and peered at her with intense, reddened eyes. "I don't want that damn job. I want you."

She took a stunned step back. "What?"

"I'll get a different job, whatever it takes. Just let me make it up to you."

Oh, right, he was trashed. He had no idea what he was saying. She shook her head and looked away. "You're drunk."

"And thinking clearly for the first time in months. I'm dead serious."

"It's too late, Mac."

"How can it be too late?"

She thought of Noah and their kiss last night, how she'd felt it to the soles of her feet. It was *way* too late. "It just is. And, besides, it's awfully easy to give up a job that you think might not be around this time next week."

"You think I'm saying this because I know the newspaper's about to go down in flames?"

"Why not? You can't have your first choice, so you'll settle for your second."

"That's so fucking unfair, Charlie."

He crowded her into the corner, but she shoved him back harder than she'd intended. "You're pouring your heart out to me while you reek of another woman. What the hell is wrong with you?"

He dropped back from her as if she'd slapped him. Turning away, he faced the elevator door and dropped his head back. "You're right. I've been drinking all night. I'm too wasted for this right now."

She clenched her jaw. "It's over. We didn't make it past our first challenge as a couple. Let's just leave it at that."

He said nothing, didn't look at her, and she studied the side of his face, saw the muscles working in his jaw.

The elevator dinged its arrival at the lobby level, and he waited for her to walk out ahead of him. Pissed off and loaded but still a gentleman.

Sighing, she turned to him. "You're not planning to drive, are you?"

"No time to sober up. Duty calls."

She caught his shirtsleeve before he could brush by her. "I'll drive you." She couldn't let him get into his car in this condition. He could have an accident and get injured, or injure someone else. She'd never forgive herself. And it worried her that he was willing to chance it. Also not like the all-about-responsibility Mac she knew.

"All I need is coffee," he said.

"We'll stop and get some on the way."

He hesitated, and before he could respond, she said, "I'm not taking no for an answer. Either you sober up before you go or I drive you. Which is it going to be?"

"Fine," he grumbled, and gestured for her to lead the way.

He didn't speak again until they were in her rental car.

"What's with the car?" he asked.

"I had a little accident yesterday."

He tensed beside her. "You're okay?"

"I'm fine. Just some bruises."

"So were you at the Royal Palm with Logan?"

"What? No."

"I mean, it's you and him now, right? That's why you won't give me a second chance."

She choked off the urge to scream. "There's nothing between Logan and me. He was at my place the other day when you called because someone broke into the house. He stayed overnight because I was . . . scared."

"Big of him."

She swallowed down the hurt that surged into her throat. She'd had a break-in and a car accident in a matter of days, and all he could come up with was a snide remark? It didn't matter that he didn't know she'd almost died both times, that someone was actually trying to kill her. If he truly cared, he should have been able to do better than that.

He sighed as he looked out the passenger-side window. "I like it here, you know. In Lake Avalon."

The change of subject threw her. Okaaay. "There's a lot to like about it."

"It's been my haven. My sister's haven. It was tough to pick up and leave Philly, to talk her into leaving behind her friends. But it's grown on her. I think she's finally happy. I mean, she has her moments. Skipping school, mostly. But she's better now, better than she was after Mom died and Dad . . ."

He didn't have to finish. She already knew what came next: After their father drank himself to death and left Mac in charge of his younger sister. Yet he'd spent the night drinking. Not that she feared one night would turn him into an alcoholic, but he'd always been so careful about how much he drank, limiting himself to one beer or glass of wine no matter the situation. And never going for the hard stuff. She'd admired his discipline, his absolute devotion to making his sister's life better.

"You've done a great job, Mac," Charlie said. "Jennifer's lucky to have you."

"If I lose my job, we'll have to start all over again somewhere else."

Her heart dropped into the pit of her stomach. Oh, crap. Suddenly she got why he had been so unreasonably angry at her. She hadn't even thought about what it would mean if he had to leave Lake Avalon for another job.

"Do you know how hard that's going to be for her?" he asked. "She's a senior in high school. At least when we moved here she was a freshman. She was the new kid, but everyone in her class was new to high school. If we have to move, she'll have to leave her friends behind all over again. Be the new kid all over again, only this time it'll be worse, because she'll be arriving where everyone else has already formed their bonds."

"I'm sorry, Mac," Charlie said. "I'm so sorry. I didn't know—"

"I know you didn't. It doesn't change the complete shittiness of the situation, though, does it?"

She didn't know what to say as she slowed for a stoplight. She'd screwed up on so many levels that she might have set a record.

Mac's cell phone started to ring, and he pulled it out and checked the caller ID screen. Flipping it open, he didn't bother with a greeting. "I'm on my way, all right? Keep your damn pants on. I don't know what—" He broke off and listened. "Shit, are you kidding? Where?" Another pause, this one almost a minute long. The more seconds that ticked by, the straighter he sat in his seat, then, "We need to get someone over there right now. Who've we got? . . . Jesus, that's it? . . . Fine, send her. She wanted a shot, so this is it."

He snapped the phone closed and dropped his head back against the headrest. "Fuck."

"What's going on?"

"Scanner traffic's been going nuts this morning. First, some guy got shot at a gas station, and now we've got a body at a house on Tarpon Bay Street. A woman bludgeoned to death with a hammer."

A white light burst inside Charlie's head, followed by the scent of wet paint and the memory of the blunt end of a hammer smashing into skull.

"Christ," Mac mumbled. "It's going to be a long fucking day."

CHAPTER **THIRTY-TWO**

Charlie turned onto Tarpon Bay Street, in a middle-class area of Lake Avalon, and followed its palm-tree-lined curves until she found the house with all the cop cars out front. Neighbors and other gawkers milled around across the street from the small, yellow stucco house that had had no reason to stand out before it became the site of murder. She parked the Sebring up the block and walked back to the growing crowd.

"What's going on?" she asked the first person she encountered, an elderly man wearing a white-and-green-striped golf shirt, matching shorts and black socks with sandals. His gleaming bald head seemed to redden in the sun as Charlie watched. Must be new to the area, she thought, if he didn't know to sunscreen the top of his head.

"Just moved here from Detroit and already got a dead neighbor. Property values are dropping as we speak."

She bit back the urge to get sarcastic. Yeah, dead people really suck for the rest of us. "What happened?"

He looked her up and down, his faded blue eyes suspicious behind black-rimmed glasses. "Who the hell are you?"

She gave him a polite smile and moved on. She knew a man who couldn't be charmed when she saw one. She was about to strike up a conversation with a young woman who had a baby on her hip when she spotted Sara Jansen, the obits writer from the *LAG*, wandering around like a kid who'd lost her mother in the grocery store.

Charlie strode over to her. "Sara?"

Sara turned toward her, long, red hair flying as relief

flooded her freckled face. "Charlie, hey. Thank God you're here. I have no idea what I'm doing."

Charlie took in the reporter's notebook clutched in the girl's hand and felt a moment of shock. This inexperienced girl was so young that she still had baby fat rounding out her face, yet Mac had sent her to cover a murder scene. What the hell?

"Have you talked to any of the cops yet?" Charlie asked.

"I tried, but they keep blowing me off."

Of course they did. They had no idea who she was. "Follow me," Charlie said, and headed for the front door of the house. Over her shoulder, she said, "You have to act like you belong here. You'd be surprised what they'll let you get away with if they think you know where you're going."

Sara nodded and made a note in her notebook, pen grasped by fingers tipped with stubby, orange-painted fingernails. Under normal circumstances, Charlie would have laughed, but her heart was knocking against her ribs as she walked through the open front door and inside. The first thing that hit her was the smell. Not wet paint as she expected. Death.

And then she saw the body. Or, rather, the top of the body's head. Curly black hair matted with blood and bits of something white. Oh, God, bone?

She stopped in midstep, still on the entryway's square of tile, only vaguely aware of Sara bumping into her from behind. She heard Sara gasp and gag, sensed the girl whirl away and run back outside.

Charlie stood, riveted, as a police officer draped a white sheet over the body, hiding it from view. She blinked and tore her gaze away to take in the modest living room with its well-used gray carpeting and nondescript furniture. The most striking thing about the room, besides the corpse in the center of it, were the plants. Spider plants, ficus trees, philodendrons, aloe plants, jade plants. They were everywhere, on every available surface, crowding every corner. Verdant life amidst pale death.

And it seemed wrong, so wrong.

A hand closed around her arm—

Bile surges into my throat as I take in the gore. Oh, Christ, that chunky gray shit is brains. And then I see the maggots. I whirl away and slap a hand over my mouth.

In the next instant, the hand steered her outside into the shocking bright light of the sun. She blinked in surprise, saw Logan glaring down at her.

"I don't think anyone gave you permission to be in there," he growled, drawing her off the walk and into the grass, out of the way of the coroner's gurney.

She swallowed against the nausea churning in her gut. She'd seen that woman killed in her head. *Lived* it. And then it hit her. No fresh paint. No drop cloths. No tools scattered around. The woman wasn't killed here.

Logan tightened his hand on her arm and gave her a quick shake. "What the hell are you doing here? You're supposed to be lying low."

"Uh, I was with Mac . . . he said . . ." She trailed off, glancing back toward the house and thinking of familiar black hair. Was it Lucy Sheridan? "Who is she?"

"You know I can't tell you that until we've notified next of kin."

"How about a hint?" When his lips tightened, she knew she'd pushed him enough. "Can you at least tell me when it happened?"

"Coroner says she's been dead since at least Monday." He tilted his head, considering her. "I had the impression you weren't working for the *LAG* anymore."

Damn. "Uh, right." She gestured vaguely over her shoulder. "I told Sara I'd help her out. She's new at this."

"That redhead barfing in the bushes?"

She turned to see Sara holding her hair back while she spit and flailed her free hand in the universal "ew, gross" gesture. "Yeah, that's her."

"Can't blame her," he said grimly. "I tossed my cookies, too."

"In your defense, you saw brain matter and bugs."

She realized at the same instant that his lips parted in surprise that she'd made a reference to something she shouldn't have known. "I saw them, too," she said quickly.

"I didn't think you got that close."

"Well, I did."

He shook his head, disgusted. "You and the new girl need to stay out of there. You'll contaminate the scene." He sighed. "Which you already know, Charlie. What's the deal?"

"I . . . sorry, I guess I wasn't thinking. Murder in Lake Avalon . . . that's new to me."

"Yeah, us, too. The chief'll make a statement later."

"Okay. Thanks."

She'd taken a step in Sara's direction when Logan said, "Oh, hey, Charlie."

She turned back to him. "Yes?"

"Do you suppose you could look in on Noah Lassiter later?"

A funny feeling slid through her lower belly. Anticipation maybe? But then, at the serious expression on Logan's face, it morphed into trepidation. "Why? What happened?"

"I wouldn't ask except I'm going to be tied up here the rest of the day, and I don't think the guy has anyone to check on him. And you two seemed . . . friendly earlier."

The top of her head grew warm, and she had to resist the urge to grab the detective by the front of his shirt and shake him. Just tell me! "What happened to him?"

"He was shot this morning."

CHAPTER **THIRTY-THREE**

Noah flipped through the TV channels for the millionth time, hoping for something, anything, to take his mind off the throbbing, itching, burning streak marching across the right side of his skull. But typical of hotel cable, the offerings were limited to sixteen, unless he wanted to pay extra for porn. Which, actually, might not be a bad idea. A little pleasure to deaden the pain. An image of Charlie Trudeau in lacy underwear popped into his head.

A knock at the door brought his head around too fast, and he swore under his breath when the scalp wound gave a painful tug. Fuck!

Snatching his Glock out of the holster dangling from the desk chair, he eased up to the side of the door. "Who is it?"

"Charlie."

His breath caught. Logan had let him know she was okay, but that hadn't stopped him from worrying. Or wanting her. Glancing down at the twitch of longing in his gray gym shorts, he murmured, "Down, boy." Louder, he called, "Give me a sex—sec." He shook his head hard. *Damn* it. "I need a second," he ground out.

"All right."

He thought he heard a soft laugh as he walked in bare feet over to the desk chair, where he holstered his weapon then grabbed his shirt and drew it on. Leaving it hanging open because he lacked the dexterity at the moment to shove small buttons through smaller holes, he went to the door and pulled it open.

Charlie's gaze landed squarely on his bare chest, and she

stared for a full three seconds before she raised her exotic, gold-flecked eyes to his and smiled. "Hi."

"Hi." He grinned, stupidly happy to see her.

"Logan told me what happened. Are you okay?"

He gave a macho shrug. "Oh, that. Sure, I'm fine. I was just grazed."

"Do you need anything?" she asked. "I could pick up something for you to eat, if you . . ."

She trailed off, and he realized he was staring at her too intently. But he couldn't stop himself. In a yellow sundress that made her smooth, pale legs look long and supple, she looked good enough to back against the wall. He liked that she had some meat on her. Slim with curves. Sinking into her would be absolute fucking heaven.

He cleared his throat. He should have been surprised at the need burning inside him. It was unlike him to feel so edgy, so desperate, but he couldn't help it. The past several years had been dark and scary, and the sun hadn't truly come out again until he'd arrived in Lake Avalon and looked at Charlie Trudeau for the first time. Yet that seemed so simplistic, not to mention unfair to Laurette. How sick was it that he would see light at the end of the tunnel so soon after she'd lost her life?

"Such dark thoughts."

He raised his gaze to Charlie's, surprised at how much like Laurette she'd sounded. That was the crux of it right there, he realized. She looked and sounded like Laurette, so he felt as though he knew her. Yet he hadn't wanted to back Laurette against the wall and dive in. He'd thought about it, sure, but that was about it. When he thought about it with Charlie, heat shot into all the right places and it seemed the only place to find relief was in her eyes.

Okay, he told himself, swallowing hard, just get her the fuck in the room and go from there. "I could use some company," he said, stepping back and gesturing for her to come in.

She hesitated. "Are you sure? You're probably not feeling that—"

"It's okay," he cut in. "Please, come in." Please, please, *please*.

As she passed by him, he breathed in her coconut scent. He wanted to drown in that wake. "Can I get you anything?" he asked as he shut the door and flipped the dead bolt.

Charlie faced him. "The idea was for me to get *you* something."

He indicated the ice bucket on the desk, filled to the brim with cubes and a bottle of cheap vodka, his own personal pain killer. "Think I'm covered. Drink?"

She grimaced before she shook her head. "No, thanks. I don't take my Vladdy straight."

Grinning, he whipped open the mini fridge under the desk and produced a small carton of OJ. "Me neither."

As he poured orange juice and vodka into two glasses, heavy on the Vladdy for himself, he watched Charlie out of the corner of his eye. She seemed on edge as she glanced around the hotel room. Crap, she'd probably noticed the way he'd been looking at her, like she held the map to paradise for a man who'd lost his way.

After swirling the contents of their glasses to mix them, he handed the juicier one to her and clinked his glass against hers. "Here's to a Chicago cop getting sniped in Florida."

Her response was more of a wince than a smile as she gingerly took a sip.

He gestured at the bed that was still made. "Want to have a seat?"

While he settled on the bed he'd been lounging on, she perched on the edge of its twin so tensely that he doubted the mattress held her full weight. She had something on her mind, but instead of telling him about it, she drank again, swallowed, then ran the pink tip of her tongue along the inner edge of her top lip.

Aw, man. Was there ever a more sexy thing for a woman to do with her tongue? But then he thought about it and decided, well, fuck, *yeah*. "So," he said, startling himself with the abruptness and volume of the word.

Charlie also started but quickly covered by saying, "Do you have any idea who would shoot at you?"

"I think you've made someone nervous, and I've been sticking too close to you."

She raised her brows. "You mean you got hurt because of me?"

He shook his head, frustrated. He didn't want to talk about this. He wanted to touch her. He couldn't think for wanting to touch her. Leaning forward, he started to put his hand on her bare knee but froze when she jerked back so violently that orange juice and vodka sloshed out of her glass and spattered the front of her dress.

"Oh, hey," he said, raising his hands, palms out. "I didn't mean to startle you."

She released an embarrassed laugh and brushed at the wet spot. "It's not your fault I'm a klutz."

Rising, he took the glass from her and set it on the desk on his way to the bathroom. "I'll get you a towel."

He returned with a dampened washcloth and held it out to her. She took it carefully with two fingers, deliberately avoiding contact with him. Okay, that's just weird.

"I guess I'm kind of jumpy," she said. "The break-in and getting run off the road . . . everything's such a . . . mess."

Christ, he was a child to think that every little thing she did had to do with him. Sitting across from her, he watched her wipe at the wet stain that covered nearly half of her left breast. Her nipple was poking at the material. If she hadn't been wearing a bra, he might have been able to see the shadowy outline of something really luscious.

"You're not the only one off your game," he said quickly, to distract himself from lusty thoughts. "I haven't been on mine since I got here."

She lowered the washcloth and met his gaze. Awareness flared in her eyes, and in the next instant, she was on her feet. "I should go. You're exhausted, and . . . so am I."

When she headed for the door, he followed close behind, not wanting her to go. Not wanting her to ever go. He almost reached for her arm but stopped himself. Then he thought, Fuck it, and reached for her anyway.

The instant his fingers closed around her forearm, she stiffened. He heard a sharp gasp as she staggered backward, against his chest. And then she was sliding down his front as though her bones had turned to spaghetti. He caught her under the arms, but the awkwardness of their positions off balanced him, and he ended up landing butt-first on the floor with Charlie sprawled in his lap.

He sat there, bone-jarring pain zinging into his skull, and stared down at her in shock. Her head lolled back over the crook in his elbow, her eyes open and staring at nothing. Fear seized his gut. Holy mother of God, was she dead?

Then she blinked and sucked in a ragged breath as though she'd been held underwater for too long and her head had just broken the surface.

What the hell? What the *hell*?

When she raised her head and moved as though to get up, he put his arms around her and gathered her firmly to him. "Wait," he said, surprised at how gruff he sounded. How scared.

She stilled and relaxed, closing her eyes.

He wanted to ask her if she was okay, what the hell just happened, but he couldn't speak, his heart still thundering at the shock of seeing her blank eyes and thinking she was dead. The thought of losing her when he'd just found her . . .

"I'm okay," she said, and awkwardly patted the arm he'd crossed over her chest to hold her in place.

She might have been okay, but other than that awkward pat, she didn't move. Her complexion was ashen, her breathing deep and measured, as though she were concentrating. He could feel the fast trot of her heart against his arm. Had she had a seizure?

After several moments, she looked up at him. She didn't move for a long time, just stared into him as if she could read exactly who he was in his eyes, as if she somehow *understood* everything about him. He felt the urge to squirm under that steady gaze, as though his secrets were exposed and he was powerless to hide.

And then she looked away, and said, "I'm really okay. I can get up now."

He didn't let go, sensing that the minute he did, she'd flee without explanation. Yet she did seem okay. She was still pale, but her eyes were clear, their light brown somehow darker against her pallor. "What just happened?" he asked.

"Please, I'd like to get up now."

She put a hand against his chest for leverage and started to move off of him. The change in position made her ass grind right against his crotch. He jerked in a breath, shocked at how quickly blood rushed to that spot. Fuck, he was getting hard. "Uh, you might want to be still."

She froze, her gaze flying up to his. Color flooded her face. "Oh, God, I'm sorry."

He had to laugh. *She* was apologizing for his inability to control himself.

"What should I do?" she asked, her voice lower now, hoarse.

He groaned and closed his eyes. It was as though the raspy words had stroked right over his most sensitive spot. Throbbing began in earnest, his length already so hard he desperately needed to reposition himself to ease some of the pressure. Yet if he moved, he would end up rubbing against her more fully, and that would make things worse. Christ, just thinking about it was making things worse. He wasn't going to be able to will this away. Hell, a cold shower might not take care of it. He was such an asshole. A sex-starved asshole.

"Just give me a minute," he muttered, eyes tightly closed. A minute? More like an hour. He breathed in slowly, evenly, only to have the tropical scent of her hair swim through his senses. *Je*sus.

Her hand left his chest, and the tiny amount of friction the movement caused against his crotch made stars burst in his head. Another possible embarrassment roared into his brain. If she moved like that again, he might come like a damn teenager. Holy shit, he was pathetic. And more turned-on than he'd ever been. For a crazy moment, he considered suggesting it'd be a shame to let this raging erection go to waste. But instead he clenched his teeth together and began to count to twenty. He lost his train of thought at fifteen when he felt her breath caress his lips.

And then her soft mouth touched his, and his eyes snapped open.

CHAPTER **THIRTY-FOUR**

Noah sprang to life under her, his hands flying up to plunge into her hair and hold the sides of her head while his mouth devoured hers. His tongue, both seeking and bold, took her breath, and he was rising with her in his arms, shifting her as if she weighed nothing until her legs could wrap around his waist. She moaned a little when the dress hiked up and her center settled against his rigid length. Oh, God, what had she started?

Oh, God, don't let it stop.

When he'd grasped her arm, she'd lived those seconds when he'd been hit by the bullet, lived his moments of fear, regret and pain. He'd thought he was going to die, and she'd felt his anguished disappointment that he hadn't done more with his life, *been* more. He'd thought about his parents, wishing he'd made more effort to be there for them when they got older. He'd thought of the sister he hadn't seen in years, the nephew he never tried to get close to. He'd thought of a young man, a close friend, in a pool of blood and gore while blinding shame tore through him. And he'd thought of Laurette and how he'd let her down, first by not being a better man and second by not finding her killer before his own death.

Charlie didn't know how she'd managed to feel all of this in the seconds she was inside his head. Maybe the intensity of his emotions when he'd been shot had ramped up the intensity of her experience. Whatever the case, she now knew Noah Lassiter in a way she had known no other person. He was troubled, passionate, flawed. He craved connection. He feared love. He wanted to *live*.

So when she'd been sitting on his lap, watching his fierce concentration as he'd tried to control his body's response to her, it had seemed like the most natural thing in the world for her to press her lips to his, to give him what he craved and receive what she craved in return. Connection.

Now, he pitched forward onto the bed and came down on top of her, the movement driving him hard against the aching spot between her legs. She jolted at the incredible sensation, her gasp swallowed by his mouth covering hers. His hands were everywhere, undoing the front of the dress, sliding under her bra, cupping her breasts. She didn't know when he'd unhooked her bra, but he laid it open and his mouth went to work on her right nipple. His tongue rolled, and his lips sucked so hard that stabbing need arched her up off the bed.

And then he had the dress completely off, and his fingers were sliding into her panties, oh, God, driving her to heaven. She wanted to tell him to slow down. She hadn't even had a chance to touch him, but his hunger was overwhelming and before she could even squeak out a suggestion, he was stripping away her underwear and nudging her thighs farther apart. She raised her head to say something, she didn't know what, but the words turned into a moan of astonished pleasure when he plunged his tongue into her heat. She grabbed at the sheets beneath her to keep from bucking him off.

She peaked fast, choking back a cry, and just when she thought he was going to let her catch her breath and perhaps let her return the favor, he was kissing his way up her belly, stopping to explore her navel with his tongue, and then each nipple, laving and sucking and nipping. By the time he got to her mouth, she was still panting. Her head swirled with shock at what he'd just done to her, and how quickly, and prayers that he wasn't finished with her yet.

"That's better," he murmured as he spread light kisses along the underside of her chin.

She released a soft laugh, her head spinning with his heady, musky scent. He was so large that she felt small, even fragile, beside him. His hand cupped her breast, and she glanced down, gasping as he caught her nipple between two large fingers and gently squeezed.

"Your nipples are so sensitive," he said, and bent his head to take the other one into his mouth.

She let her head fall back, shifting restlessly under this new assault. She ran her hands up his arms, marveling at the sharp definition of his tensed muscles, then up around his neck and into the thick hair at the back of his neck. Everything about him was big and hard, yet smooth and satiny. And she wanted him naked, wanted him inside her with an urgency that stunned her. In fact, everything about this moment was stunning. Before doubts could temper her bliss, she moved her hand to the waistband of his shorts, slid her fingers under.

The tight muscles under her hand contracted, and Noah's breathing deepened. "You don't have to do that," he said.

She paused, confused. He didn't want her to touch him?

"Trust me," he said. "I want you so much it's killing me, but I'm not so sure this is what you want."

She raised her gaze to his, almost laughed. "Are you nuts?"

He chuckled, the sound vibrating his chest against her arm. "I hear myself saying it, and in my head, I'm telling myself to shut the hell up."

"I'll say it, too. Shut the hell up and let me—"

His fingers closed over her wrist before she could claim the prize. "If you were someone else, I'd already be inside you," he said, his voice guttural.

Frustration at the image that loomed in her head made her groan, and she looked up into his green eyes. "Like who? Who would I have to be?"

He smiled, though it looked strained. "Anyone but you."

Huh? "I'm not sure how to take that."

He sighed, lightly skimming his hand over her left breast until her nipple stabbed at his palm. She swallowed at the ache his touch sent spiraling down to her center. He was right there, hard as steel and ready for the taking, caressing her almost reverently, yet he was holding back. It had to be painful.

"This is exactly where I wanted you," he said, "the minute you walked through that door tonight, but I don't think you're thinking on all cylinders. And I'm not the kind of guy to take advantage. At least not with you."

He lowered his head and kissed her. The stroke of his tongue against hers wiped her brain clean of questions and insecurity. When he raised his head, she was breathless and achy and wondering whether she could wrestle him onto his back and take him against his will.

She looked up into his eyes as she glided a hand from his cheek down to the front of his broad, hair-free chest. The pad of her thumb found his right nipple, and she pressed and wiggled it, still holding his gaze. His breath sucked in, and he muttered, "Oh, hell, who am I kidding?" before his mouth came down on hers again, hot and insistent.

She arched against him, so relieved she laughed against his lips. "Thank God."

With an answering laugh, he rolled on top of her and settled between her legs. "Thank God indeed."

Eager to have him fill her, she worked her hand between them and stroked her fingers over the front of his gym shorts. He was so thick and hard and hot that her mouth watered with anticipation.

"Someone needs to come out and play," she whispered as she caught his earlobe between her teeth.

He shuddered, then braced above her on his hands to grant her free access. She smoothed her hands down his flanks, loving the hard ripples of muscle, then moved her hands over his hips, sliding his shorts down to his thighs. His cock sprang free of its constraints and bobbed above her, its tip glistening with evidence that it was more than ready for action.

"Wow," she breathed, fascinated and a little afraid. He was never going to fit, yet she couldn't wait to try him on.

His chuckle had an edge. "It's not too late to change your mind."

She reached for him, closing her hand over hot velvet skin that encased unyielding iron. "It's way too late," she said, and reared up to capture his lips.

He settled onto her with a groan, catching his hands in her hair. She shifted eagerly to center him.

"Wait," he choked, the slight thrust of his hips bumping his cock against her heat.

"Now what?" she gasped, ready to scream with frustration.

"Condom?"

"Pill."

He swallowed hard, positioned right at her entrance, his tip applying only slight but maddening pressure. "I'm clean," he said.

"Me, too."

"Is that a turnoff?"

"That you're clean?"

"No, that I brought it up now."

She nipped at his chin, reveling at the scrape of his whiskers. "Not at all." Then she kissed him hard, telling him with her tongue what she wanted him to do. Now.

But instead of plunging, he grasped her hands and pinned them to either side of her head. His cock was so rigid that he didn't have to guide himself to her. He just eased into her an inch and groaned, the cords in his neck standing out. "You're so tight."

She let out a breathless laugh but couldn't form words to respond. The pressure was almost as overwhelming as the pleasure as he eased in another inch. Impossibly, she felt herself building to another climax and he wasn't even halfway in.

He lowered his head, concentration tightening the muscles in his face as he rotated his hips in a way that wrung a moan from her throat. She was almost there, reaching, straining.

"I'm not going to last," he gasped. "You feel too good."

She moved against him, trying to take more of him, wanting all of him before it was too late. "Hurry, please, hurry."

He answered her with a short thrust. She bowed back, sucking in a harsh breath. Oh, God, he was huge, stretching her, filling her. When he began to withdraw, the heavy dragging sensation against the center of her world sent her head back into the pillow. His lips pressed to her arched throat before he thrust again, harder this time, filling her with more, more, until he rocked against the spot that made her world implode.

She cried out, pulling her hands free and grabbing his hips to hang on as he surged into her, again, again, again, his powerful thrusts drawing out her orgasm until she couldn't breathe, couldn't think, could do nothing but mindlessly ride the waves crashing into her.

And then he stiffened, throwing his head back and groaning through clenched teeth as he came. He kept thrusting, as though he couldn't stop himself, thrusting and coming and groaning.

In the next instant, everything in Charlie's head transformed with a dizzying jerk. A shuddering sensation like she'd never known surged up from the center of her body, and she felt herself drive forward into soft, wet heat, thrusting, thrusting as a dark bliss clamped down on all sides, engulfing her, sucking at her, squeezing. A freight train roared in her head. Oh, God, oh, God, so tight, so hot, not enough, it's not enough. And then every muscle went rigid and suddenly she was gushing, spurting, rocketing. Charlie. Oh, God, oh, Jesus. *Charlie.*

She came back to herself with a harsh inhalation, aware first of Noah collapsed beside her, one big hand splayed possessively over her belly as he struggled for breath. Once his breathing calmed, he kissed her, his lips and tongue languid and gentle, serene. The depth of the kiss brought tears to her eyes. He settled back beside her but kept running his hand over her breasts, her abdomen, up over her chest and throat, as though he couldn't get enough of touching her, caressing her.

As her heart dropped out of overdrive, she replayed what

just happened. That last orgasm had been so different, so unusual . . . as though she had somehow been turned inside out—

Her heart rate kicked back into high gear as it hit her.

That wasn't her climax. It was *his*.

CHAPTER **THIRTY-FIVE**

Charlie let herself into her hotel room, her heart still racing, her whole body feeling flushed and languid. Noah, Noah, Noah. Heat suffused her face as she chanted his name in her head. A mixture of elation and incredulity flowed through her that she'd connected with him in a way that even now seemed impossible. And who knew it would be so incredible? Who knew she would get the added bonus of popping into his head and experiencing *his* shattering orgasm?

God, her body still seemed to hum with energy. Maybe it was adrenaline, but she preferred to think of it as life. She'd been dying a little every day for the past month, ever since she and Mac had split, stressed and unhappy and even a little desperate. Noah had reawakened her. *Noah.*

She'd left him snoring, slipping out the door with her bra jammed in her purse, too wired to sleep and not wanting to disturb him. Besides, she needed some time to think.

Sighing, she dropped onto the edge of the closest bed and picked up the phone to check her voice mail at home. A message from her dad, surprisingly, and three messages from Alex, not surprisingly, each one sounding more concerned than the last. Crap, she should have called her sister a long time ago, but she hadn't wanted to worry her. Instead, she'd probably worried her even more. Geez, she couldn't seem to get anything right these days. Except sex with Noah. Now *that* had been about as right as anything could get.

Releasing a shuddery sigh at the memories, she listened to her last message.

"Yes, hello, Simon Walker of Walker Media calling, and

I fear I'm about to leave you a highly disorganized message, as is my habit. I just arrived in your fair city and I'm a bit taken aback by how simply splendid the weather is here. I flew in from New York, where the jet had to be deiced before we could take off. It's a frightening thing, sitting there and watching them spray that pink foam on the wings. You have to worry about whether they're being thorough enough." He stopped, took an audible breath and chuckled warmly. "Ah, yes, why I called. Word on the street is that the Java Bean has excellent coffee. I do hope you'll meet me there, Charlie Trudeau. I have a proposition for you, of the journalism kind. How about seven P.M.? I do hope to see you there."

Click.

She lowered the phone, stunned. Billionaire newspaper magnate Simon Walker wanted to meet with the woman soon to be famous for single-handedly killing a community newspaper? He probably wanted to know how to prevent stunts like hers from occurring at his hundreds of daily newspapers across the nation. Great. More salt for her wounds.

She checked her watch. Almost a quarter of seven. Should she bother or pretend she didn't get the message? Except it was Simon Walker. If she ever wanted to work in journalism again, she probably shouldn't dis the biggest cheese.

Sighing, she tried Alex's number at work.

"Alex Trudeau."

"It's me."

"Where the hell are you?" Alex shouted into the phone. "I've been worried sick. Logan said you've checked in at the Royal Palm, but he wouldn't tell me what's going on. He said that was up to you. Bastard. Makes me want to take his head right off."

Charlie couldn't help but chuckle. "If I'd known Logan's life was at stake . . ."

"It's not funny, you bitch."

She heard the joking, and relief, in Alex's tone but sobered anyway. "I'm sorry. I didn't mean to worry you."

"What room are you in? I'm coming over there after work."

"You don't have to—"

"Yes, I do. You're going to tell me what's going on with you if I have to sit on you and force it out."

"What about the menagerie?" Charlie asked. Alex had a second career taking in stray dogs in her neighborhood.

"I'll check in on them before I come by. So stop arguing already."

"Fine, fine. I'm in 514."

"I'll bring the margarita mix."

After a quick shower and a change into khaki slacks and a red polo, Charlie walked into the Java Bean at five to seven and paused to scan the customers, having no idea what Simon Walker looked like. The usual suspects were here. Three teen girls huddled on a sofa, giggling as they took turns casting longing glances at a table of two hunky but apparently clue-less guys. At least four patrons sat alone at small tables, their attention fixed on the laptops opened before them. A young couple, tan and beautiful, sat across from each other, hold-ing hands as they alternately sipped coffee and gazed into each others' eyes. Charlie thought of Noah and enjoyed the tingle that ran up her spine, and through other, private, areas. Maybe she'd have time to visit him again before Alex showed up tonight.

The tempting scents of coffee and warm chocolate filled her head, and her stomach growled to remind her she hadn't had dinner. Seeing as how no one had acknowledged her entrance, she assumed Simon Walker wasn't here yet. She was about to approach the counter to get a snack to hold her over, perhaps one of those big-ass chocolate chip cookies the Bean was famous for, when the door behind her opened. She turned to see an older man with thinning salt-and-pepper hair and craggy features amble in.

His face split into a huge grin when he saw her. "Oh, I do hope you're Charlie Trudeau."

She couldn't help but return his welcoming smile. "Hi. Simon Walker?"

"One and only," he said, clasping her hand in both of his big, soft mitts and pumping it up and down before she had a chance to brace herself. When nothing more than a feeling of warmth and well-being infused her, she relaxed.

He was only a few inches taller than her five-five, and judging from his wrinkles, she put him in the ballpark of sixty. His kind, blue eyes were the color of well-worn denim and crinkled at the corners as though he'd spent his entire life smiling. A feeling of familiarity nudged her, as though she'd known him forever.

He grinned, rocking back on his heels. "Oh, you are absolutely lovely." Then he gave her a fatherly pat on the arm and handed her his briefcase. "Why don't you take this and get us a table outside while I place our order? What would you like?"

"Uh." She couldn't think. The most powerful man in the newspaper industry was beaming at her, and she couldn't think. Real professional. "Whatever you're having is fine."

"Now the pressure is on," Simon said with a wink. "I'll meet you outside."

Feeling dazed, she walked out into the cooling dusk, found an empty table set back from the street, set Simon Walker's briefcase next to a black wrought-iron chair then sat down in the one next to it with her back to the building. Sitting out in the open like this, knowing someone wanted her dead, was probably at the top of her list of stupid things she'd done this week. But she wasn't going to be sitting here alone for long, and if anyone tried to kill her now, there'd be plenty of witnesses.

When Simon Walker elbowed his way through the door of the Bean, his arms were laden with bagels, muffins, cookies and two Big Gulp-sized cups. She rose to help him distribute the goodies on the table and wondered whether he'd left

anything in the display cases. Then she spotted her favorite—
chocolate-filled croissants—and didn't care.

"Everything looked so good I couldn't decide," he said,
chuckling. "I hope you've got an appetite."

"I'm starved, actually," she said, sitting back down as he
handed her a tall stack of napkins. "And it looks like I can be
messy, too."

His chuckle turned to a belly laugh. As he sat across from
her, he reached for one of the huge cups. "Iced mocha cappuccino," he said, before clamping his mouth around the fat straw.

Charlie caught herself smiling as she watched his weath-
ered cheeks go concave while he tried to suck the thick slush
through the straw. Oh, to be that enthusiastic about something
as simple as a frozen coffee drink.

Finally getting a mouthful, he swirled it around as though
tasting a fine wine, then swallowed and smiled his approval.
"Ah, that's refreshing. I would never have dreamed of having
an iced cappuccino in March, but here we are. Sitting outside
even. What's the temperature, do you suppose? Seventy? Oh,
wait, I remember, the pilot said it was seventy-two." He drew
in a big breath, leaned back in his springy chair and took in
their surroundings. "It's a beautiful, *beautiful* evening."

"It is," Charlie said, tearing into a chocolate croissant.
She was certain her companion would approve of her lack of
shyness.

"Such a wonderful town, Lake Avalon. All these art deco
buildings are breathtaking, are they not? You can just *feel* the
history." He leaned forward. "I bet you're wondering why I've
swept into your life this evening, Charlie Trudeau."

Her mouth too full to speak, she nodded.

"My career in newspapers started many, many years ago.
Think *His Girl Friday*, though I was far more debonair than
Cary Grant and wore a much better hat. And my Rosalind,
well, she didn't speak nearly as fast and while she didn't have
the legs of a Rockette, I loved her just the same. But I digress.
My point is that when I started I was fresh out of college and
ready to change the world."

"I know that feeling," Charlie said.

Simon grinned. "I thought you would." He dropped his voice to a conspiratorial whisper. "I have to admit that I'm not pleased with how the business has evolved. What about you?"

"Uh . . ."

"My sentiments exactly. Every damn newspaper across this great nation is chock-full of news supported by information taken from press releases and Web sites like it's the word of God. Reporters are quoting experts right and left and no one is saying a good goddamn thing. When someone, a politician perhaps, tells a bald-faced lie to the American public, do our nation's journalists call him or her on it? No. Oh, sure, there might be some bitching and moaning on the editorial pages, but who reads those editorial pages anyway? Meanwhile, there on page one, the page everyone sees all day long in the newspaper racks on every street corner, sits the lie in all its glory with nary a counterpoint. I ask you: What good does that do the American people?"

Before Charlie could form a response, he plunged ahead. "The industry has become about selling cornflakes."

She nodded helplessly. Cornflakes? Huh?

He thudded an index finger against the latticed tabletop. "It doesn't matter what's *in* the newspaper. What's important is what it *looks* like. The theory is that if it looks good, readers will buy it. And, I'll admit, there is some truth to that. But it's not just about the packaging. It's about what's being *packaged*. Now, don't get me wrong. I'm proud of all of my newspapers and their Web sites. Some of them do a decent job of balancing the cornflakes with the heavy-duty fiber, if you know what I mean. But the smallest ones, the ones at the community level . . . well, you know all about what happens at the community level, don't you, Charlie Trudeau."

She did, but she didn't say anything, figuring he didn't plan to pause long enough to allow her to anyway.

"What happens at the community level, my dear girl, is reporters like yourself get hamstrung. You're forced to stay away from certain stories, because certain stories might anger certain revenue-generating customers and losing those revenue-generating customers would be very bad for business. Am I right?"

When he peered at her, apparently expecting a response this time, she gave an enthusiastic nod. "Yes."

"Yes!" He slapped an open palm on the table, making bagels and muffins and croissants jump. "Yes, I'm right. I *love* being right. But, then, who doesn't?"

She laughed, a bit overwhelmed by his exuberance.

He picked up his iced cappuccino and tapped the plastic rim against her cup. "I like you, Charlie Trudeau. I especially like saying your name, in case you haven't noticed. It's a good reporter's name. Charlie Trudeau. I'm impressed that you don't use your full name, like some reporters. You might know a man as Dave Brown, but his byline is David Michael Edwin Brown III. It's downright odd, if you ask me. But tell me, what is your full name, Charlie Trudeau?"

"Charlotte Meredith."

"Ah, a lovely name for sure. But Charlotte Meredith Trudeau just doesn't have the same dog-with-a-bone journalistic cachet as Charlie Trudeau. Don't you agree?"

"Wholeheartedly."

His blue eyes twinkled. "I suppose I should get to why I've come to see you." He scooted back his chair, propped his briefcase on his lap and popped it open. When he pulled out Tuesday's *Lake Avalon Gazette* with the damning auto dealer headline, her heart thumped harder. Oh, no.

"I have a friend who retired here to Lake Avalon," he said. "My best lifelong friend, you might say. Avid newspaper reader. Sharp as a fox and just as cagey. He called me the other morning and read your crooked auto dealer story to me over the phone." He spread out the paper and tapped his finger on her byline. "This is good work, Charlie Trudeau."

Pride swelled through her for a change. "Thank you."

"I've heard it cost you."

Surprise lifted her brows.

"I tried to call you at the *Gazette* yesterday," he said, "but was curtly told you were no longer employed there."

Her cheeks started to burn. Good-bye, pride. Hello, shame. "Yes, that's true."

"You were fired?"

"I planned to quit anyway."

"Why?"

He fired the question at her so sharply that she stuttered at first. "Well, I—I—" She stopped, took a breath. "Like you, I'm disappointed in the direction of the news business today."

His grin returned full blown. "You're an idealist."

"I suppose I am."

"I am, too. Which is precisely why I'm here. I want you to work for me."

That set her back. "In New York?"

"Anywhere. You pick the newspaper. I have them all over, you know. California, Colorado, Illinois, Pennsylvania, even here in Florida. You name a state, I'll give you a list."

"Oh, well, I don't know—"

"Yes, yes, I know it's sudden. I'm prepared to give you time to think about it, of course."

Reality quickly followed the first rush of excitement. Any other newspaper would have the same issues as the *LAG*. Advertisers ruled, period. "I've pretty much decided to leave the news business."

"And do what?"

"I don't know yet."

"Because there is nothing else. You're a journalist to the bone, and you've got something that many journalists today lack. Do you know what that is?"

"An unrealistic idea of what my job should be?"

He threw back his head and guffawed. "I like that, but it's not what I was getting at. You've got guts, Charlie Trudeau. And balls. Pardon my French, which is a silly saying, because what I said was not French at all. It was English, but perhaps also French because the French also have balls. But I'm off track once again. What I'm trying to say is that you saw a good story and you went after it. Your boss told you no and his or her boss probably also told you no, and what did you do? You wrote it anyway and then you conspired to get it onto the front page. And what happened?"

"I lost my job."

"What else?"

"I pissed off my father."

"Oh, dear. Daddy owns the newspaper here?"

"Yes."

"Hot damn, my dear, you've got even more balls than I thought. What else happened?"

"My co-workers are going to want to kill me when they find out the newspaper could collapse financially."

He nodded, still grinning. "What else?"

She looked back at him, out of ideas.

He turned the newspaper on the table so she could clearly see the headline. When he spoke again, his voice was soft, almost reverent: "You made a difference."

Her gaze swept up to meet his.

He nodded, arching one dark, silver-streaked brow, his smile never wavering. "You let a community of thousands know that Dick's Auto Sales can't be trusted. That, young lady, is what newspapering is supposed to be about."

"Except that's not what it *is* about."

"Come to work for me, and we'll change that. Together. One newspaper at a time."

"What?"

"You heard me. I want to change the world. Just like you. And we can do it."

"You don't need me to do that."

"Of course, I don't. But it would be so much more fun to have you on my side. You're Charlie Trudeau, the journalist who spat in the eye of powerful advertisers to print the truth. Imagine that. The *truth*. We could spread it everywhere. Politicians, crooked businessmen and bad guys across the nation beware."

"But if you don't cater to your advertisers, how will you make money?"

"Not all advertisers are crooked."

"Of course not. But many are loyal to each other. They band together like unions."

"And to them, I say, pshaw. I'm a billionaire. In the beginning, we need only enough revenue to break even. Once we've changed the industry, the sky is the limit. What do you say? You and me against the world."

She couldn't help but laugh. Pshaw? You and me against the world? This guy was a hoot. Or crazy as a loon. And she wanted to say yes. Desperately wanted to say yes. But that would be foolish, and she was tired of being foolish. "I'll think about it."

He beamed at her. "Brilliant."

He shoved open his car door and got out to pace, unable to sit still another stupid fucking second and stare at Charlie Trudeau's stupid fucking house.

Where the fuck was she? How the fuck was he supposed to kill her when she didn't fucking come home? It's like she'd disappeared off the face of the fucking planet.

He curled his fingers into fists at his sides, wished they were wrapped around her stupid fucking neck. Imagined choking her almost unconscious then letting up, letting her catch her breath, only to choke her almost unconscious all over again. He was in the mood for some hard-core torture now. Long, drawn-out, scream-inducing torture.

Because of her, he'd been racing around this godforsaken shithole of a town like a chicken with his nuts cut off. Trying to find Charlie Trudeau, to kill Charlie Trudeau. Stupid fucking bitch was killing *him* instead.

Hearing his cell phone, he ducked his head through the driver's side window and snatched it up. Time to get his head chewed off for the millionth time this week for fucking up.

"Yeah."

"They found Louisa."

He swallowed hard, closed his eyes. Fuck, fuck, *fuck*. "Yeah, I heard."

"They haven't released her name to the public yet. We still have some time."

"Uh-huh."

"And I have good news for you."

He opened his eyes. "What is it?"

"I know where Charlie Trudeau is, and I know how you can kill her."

CHAPTER **THIRTY-SIX**

Charlie hung up the phone, frustrated. She'd tried all of Lucy's numbers again and gotten no answer. No voice mail, either, which meant she couldn't even leave a message. Maddening.

She'd also gone online to check the address of the house on Tarpon Bay Street against directory assistance to try to get a name. She'd found a listing for L. Alvarez, but the name meant nothing to her.

She lay back on the bed and groaned aloud. By now, the police had to know that the woman with curly black hair hadn't been killed where her body was found. But would they know the crime scene they sought had been freshly painted? Could she somehow let them know that without raising a bunch of questions about how she knew? Perhaps an anonymous tip. Except with technology these days, tips were rarely anonymous anymore.

Closing her eyes, she thought about Simon Walker and his too-good-to-be-true offer. Fresh starts didn't get much fresher. She could have what she'd always wanted, *be* what she'd always wanted—an investigative journalist with no restraints. So tempting. But could she abandon Lake Avalon, her father, after making such a mess? Shouldn't she do something to clean that up first?

A soft knock on the door had her sitting up and looking at her watch. Must be Alex.

When she opened the door, Alex looked Charlie up and down, her auburn curls bouncing. "Holy crap. You had sex."

Charlie's laugh sounded breathless to her own ears. Oh,

yeah, that. And it wasn't *just* sex, but something much, *much* better. "Don't say stuff like that out in the hall. Get in here."

Alex walked in and turned, crossing her arms under her breasts. "Who did you have sex with?"

Charlie laughed again, embarrassed. Alex wasn't going to let her avoid her questions, but she stalled for more time by standing in front of the mirror and pulling her hair back from her face to secure it in a ponytail. Despite the puffiness of her bruised cheek, it didn't take a genius to know by looking at her what she'd been up to. Her lips were swollen, her cheeks and neck slightly red from whisker burn. Her eyes seemed to shine. The glimmer of life.

"Who were you with?" Alex asked again.

Charlie drew in a steadying breath, her gaze fixed on her own eyes in the mirror. "Noah."

"The detective from the other day? The one who got shot at today? You *slept* with him?" Alex asked, incredulous.

Charlie smiled, still holding her own gaze. She felt different. Confident. She'd turned a man on so intensely he'd thought her name not once, but twice, while his world had exploded. Her insides fluttered low in her belly, and she smoothed a hand over her lower abdomen, remembering what it was like to experience his release, so different, so—

"Charlie?"

She focused on the reflection of Alex's baffled expression. "We didn't sleep," she said.

Alex's mouth dropped open. "What the fuck, Chuck?"

Charlie turned away from the mirror. "I think I need to figure some stuff out before we go there."

"Oh my God, you're going to deny your sister details?"

"Looks like. Sorry."

"You are *such* a bitch." But Alex was smiling. "He was good for you. You're actually glowing. So is it too much to tell me how you left things? I mean, you're going to see him again, aren't you?"

Charlie shrugged, feeling her cheeks heat all over again. "I kind of slipped out while he was sleeping."

"What?" Alex nearly shouted it.

"I guess I wigged out a little and bolted."

"Go back." Alex lunged at her, turned her by the shoulders toward the door and gave her a hard nudge. "He's probably still snoring. He'll never know you left."

Laughing, Charlie sat at the foot of the double bed closest to the door and toed off her shoes. Her muscles felt limber, as though well-lubricated by Noah's attention.

She felt Alex silently watching her, assessing, and didn't mind. She'd be scrutinizing, too, if their roles had been switched.

"Oh, all right. Shut me out." But instead of being mad, Alex just sounded amused. "That's pretty much your MO anyway. I mean, you had a car accident yesterday and you didn't call me. I thought I'd made myself clear after the break-in."

She shrugged. "The accident was minor."

"Not according to Logan. Your Escape is totaled."

He apparently hadn't mentioned the murderous ninja. Thank you, Logan. "Don't I look okay to you?"

Alex tilted her head, her gaze shrewd. "You tried something with makeup that isn't quite working." She pursed her lips. "And there's that sneaky stuff with the Dick's story. Why didn't you mention you were planning that?"

"It was kind of a last-minute thing. And I didn't want anyone to think you had anything to do with it."

"No. I just ended up looking like the sister Charlie doesn't trust to confide in."

"Alex—"

"You'll be happy to know that David's doing cartwheels. On day one of his new law firm, he had screwed customers from Dick's lining up."

"That's great. Good for him."

"Yes, good for him. But you and me, we need to get something straight."

Uh-oh. "Okay."

"I know something serious is up. You checked into the Royal Palm, for God's sake. You're scared."

"Maybe a little."

"So the car accident wasn't really an accident, right? Logan hedged all over the freaking place when he told me about it."

Charlie nodded. Time to come clean. "I was run off the road."

Alex sank onto the bed next to her. "Damn. I was afraid of that."

"But Logan set me up here, and it's safe. I've been using the back entrance. No one outside of you guys and Mac knows I'm here. And, get this, when I went out earlier today, I disguised myself by wearing a dress."

Alex laughed heartily at that. "Charlie Trudeau in a *dress*? I wish I'd seen that."

"It was kind of pretty, really." And especially fun when Noah peeled it off.

"Mom would be so proud."

Charlie rolled her eyes. Refusing to wear dresses had been one of her sillier acts of defiance. "She would have thought she finally won."

"So you were out sneaking around, huh? I bet Logan didn't know about that."

"Actually, he does. He kind of caught me in the act."

"That's my Logan. You can't get much past that guy."

Charlie grinned at her. "Your Logan, huh?"

Alex waved a dismissive hand. "A figure of speech. So what else did you do since we talked? Besides screw Noah Lassiter's brains out."

Ah, tingles again. So very . . . delicious. She cleared her throat. Focusing now. "I met with Simon Walker."

Alex tilted her head. "Why does that name sound so familiar?"

"The newspaper god."

"*That* Simon Walker? You *met* with him? What the hell?"

Charlie laughed at Alex's excitement. She wondered when she'd lost her ability to get that excited about anything. "He offered me a job."

"You're kidding. What job? Where?"

"Anywhere I want."

Alex blinked and shook her head. "My head is spinning. Help me."

"He said I could pick any newspaper I wanted."

"Wow." Alex laughed. "Wow."

"I know. Weird, huh?"

"Hell, no. Not weird. Amazing. And you deserve it, Charlie. You worked so hard to make the *LAG* better and just kept running into brick walls."

Charlie gave her sister a sad smile. "I might have killed it."

Alex's excitement dimmed. "I know. I've heard the rumors."

"They're not just rumors. Dad told me what I did was a deathblow."

"I kind of figured as much since he's been avoiding the newsroom. Have you talked to him?"

"Amazingly, he didn't seem all that mad."

"You're kidding."

"He said it was a good story."

Alex held her palm up for a high five. "Way to go, Charlie."

Charlie halfheartedly smacked her hand. "It was heartbreaking seeing him like that. Giving up."

"He's a big boy. He can take care of himself. Let's talk about where you're going to go to work for Simon Walker."

Charlie shook her head. "It's kind of unfair, isn't it?"

"What?"

"I kill the *LAG*, and then I get to go on to this fabulous new opportunity while everyone else loses their jobs."

"You *made* that opportunity, Charlie. The rest of those bozos sat around with their thumbs up their butts and smiled and nodded and did what they were told. You bucked the system, defied them all. You're a freaking visionary."

Charlie laughed at that. How many visionaries got called that after doing something with blinders firmly strapped on? "I have to say, you're taking this pretty well. You're going to be unemployed, too."

"I don't know. This could be my chance at a fresh start. You know I've never been as married to newspapers as you are."

That was true. Alex had always been far more interested in animals. The woman had six dogs and always seemed to be taking in another stray, the go-to expert any time a *LAG* co-worker had a pet problem. Charlie had expected her to become a veterinarian rather than a photographer at the newspaper.

Alex said, "I'd rather talk about Simon Walker. He came *looking* for you. That means he's going to do whatever it takes to make you happy. You could change the whole industry."

"I doubt that."

"You're not thinking big. What's up with that? You've always thought big." Alex grinned. "You know what we need to do? Celebrate."

"That might be a bit premature. I haven't said yes."

"You'll say yes tomorrow. Tonight, we celebrate. And, by the way, I'm staying the night."

"That's not—"

"I know it's not necessary, but I am anyway. Let me big-sister you for a change."

Charlie smiled, touched. "But you're not the big sister."

"We'll fake it." Alex stood up and put her hands on her hips as she looked around. "Does this place have a minibar?"

CHAPTER **THIRTY-SEVEN**

Noah rolled over, expecting, anticipating contact with Charlie. If she was sleeping, he had a few ideas about how to wake her up, all of which involved her screaming his name as she came.

But he was alone in the bed, and the sheets on her side were cool.

He sat up, closing his eyes against the tug of pain in his scalp, and looked around the dark hotel room. The light-blocking curtains prevented him from knowing the time. A glance at the clock gave him a time, but it could be A.M. or P.M. for all he knew.

Sighing, he shoved aside the covers and sat on the side of the bed. Must be morning, he thought. He had to have slept several hours or he wouldn't have felt so good, better than he'd felt in weeks. Maybe years.

Charlie, Charlie, Charlie.

He smiled as he scrubbed his hands over his face. Jesus, she'd blown his mind. Who would have thought a woman so laid-back and levelheaded could be so passionate once you stripped away her clothes? He still smelled like her, like coconuts and the musk of very hot, very messy sex.

His groin started to tighten at the memories, and he pushed off from the bed and headed for the shower. As he twisted the water on and waited for it to warm up, he considered where this, with Charlie, could lead. He had a job in Chicago. Not a life, though. Just a job that had been his life. A job that had bruised and bloodied his soul over the years. Could he leave it behind? Yeah, he could. In a heartbeat.

Of course, all of this could be premature. One night of hot sex didn't make a long-term relationship. But, Jesus, Charlie Trudeau. Just thinking her name made his heart kick like a baby in a womb, eager for rebirth.

He'd have to tell her.

Sighing, he braced his hands on the tile and let the water hit him square in the face, careful to angle his head so the spot where the bullet grazed his scalp was protected.

Charlie was all about the truth, doing the right thing. He'd have no choice but to tell her.

"You're all about payback, aren't you?"

In one shot, she'd pegged him.

The guilt boiled up inside him like rolling lava. Not because he'd exacted bloody, satisfying revenge on someone who deserved it, but because he didn't feel bad about it. He'd do it again without a second thought, and afterward he would celebrate. Raise a glass to the heavens, knowing the bad guys were in hell for what they'd done.

Charlie Trudeau stood for truth, and Noah Lassiter stood for justice.

The question now was: Would Charlie accept Noah's idea of justice?

CHAPTER **THIRTY-EIGHT**

Charlie woke thinking about Noah. She'd slept fitfully, probably in part because she and Alex had downed a couple
of coconut rum shots and snacked on pretzels before falling
into bed, but mostly because she kept dreaming about Noah.
A throb of desire echoed the direction of her thoughts, and
she squeezed her thighs together to try to prolong it. She
wondered what he was doing now, whether he was still sleeping, whether he woke with a morning erection. She imagined
sneaking down to his room before Alex woke, pictured what
it would be like to slip into bed with him while he slept and
wake him with her mouth on his—

"Yeah, I want to order breakfast."

Charlie opened her eyes and raised her head. Alex was sitting up in the other bed with the room-service menu opened
on her knees, the phone pressed to her ear. She smiled and
winked at Charlie as she rattled off her order. "Buttermilk
pancakes, French toast, scrambled eggs, two sides of bacon,
the fruit plate, two large glasses of orange juice and coffee
for two."

Once she hung up, Charlie said, "You must be starved."

"Yep, and I remember you mentioning while we chowed
down on pretzels that you had a chocolate croissant for dinner
last night."

Charlie smiled and sighed. "You take better care of me
than a mom."

"Yeah, I noticed you didn't say 'our mom.'"

While Alex laughed, Charlie pushed aside the covers and
got out of bed. Her muscles felt stiff as she stretched, probably

because Noah had given them such a workout. Thinking about him, and what they'd done together, made her flush. God, would she ever be able to remember it without getting hot all over again? "Mind if I jump in the shower before the food gets here?"

"Go right ahead," Alex said as she grabbed the remote and turned on the TV. "Make it a cold one. You did some very suspicious moaning in your sleep last night."

Charlie was laughing, and blushing furiously, as she gathered clean clothes, then went into the bathroom and shut the door. She took a fast shower, her stomach growling the entire time. Hopefully by the time she got out, the food would be there.

She was already dressed in khaki shorts and a white tank top, reaching for the extra product that helped prevent her hair from frizzing in the humidity, when she heard a knock at the hotel room door. Room service already? That was fast. She quickly ran the goop through her hair, then washed and dried her hands. She couldn't wait for coffee.

She heard Alex open the door with a cheery "Good morning!" and then a sharp, puzzling crack. Charlie reached for the knob, then jerked her hand away when something— fingernails?—grazed the other side of the door, followed by a heavy thud.

"Alex?"

Charlie swung open the bathroom door, expecting to see a room service cart laden with breakfast. But instead she saw Alex on the floor at her feet, her body jerking spasmodically.

"Alex!"

Alex's eyes were wild with pain and fear, and she was making a choking, gurgling sound. Charlie smelled the blood at the same time that it registered on her stunned brain that it was bubbling from Alex's chest above her right breast.

"Oh my God!" Charlie dropped to her knees and planted both hands over the wound.

A hammer blow of force in the chest drives me back. My butt hits the carpet with a bone-jarring thud, and as I reel back in what seems like slow motion, I meet the dark eyes of the slight, all-in-black ninja standing in the doorway, a gun clasped in one shaking hand. Gun? Gun? And then I'm staring up at the ceiling. What the hell just happened? Why can't I breathe? A razor blade of pain slices through my chest, and I try to suck in air. Something thick like syrup bubbles into my throat. I begin to choke.

Charlie coughed, gulping in air as she shoved away the disorientation and lingering shock, and pressed her hands harder on Alex's bloody chest.

"Someone call 911!" she shouted toward the open room door, not knowing if anyone was even within yelling distance. "911! We need 911!" She kept shouting it, knowing she couldn't afford to take the pressure off the wound—Alex might bleed to death. Finally, someone came running. She heard a gasp, an "Oh, my Lord," and more running feet but didn't raise her head, her focus intent on her sister.

"Stay with me, Alex, stay with me." Her dark brown eyes rolled back anyway, and Charlie swallowed down rising terror and started shouting again. "Alex. Alex! Come on, come on."

Blood was streaming between her fingers despite the pressure she applied. She didn't know what else to do, how else to stop it.

A voice came from somewhere above her, an older woman: "The ambulance is on its way. What can I do?"

"Towels," Charlie croaked. "I need towels."

And then she heard heavier footsteps and a familiar voice: "Holy Christ."

She looked up, saw Noah, a gun in one hand, his face absolutely white.

Sobs began to claw their way up her throat.

CHAPTER **THIRTY-NINE**

Noah pushed open the door to the ER's exam room two, and his heart clattered to a stop when he saw Charlie sitting on the edge of the bed, looking pale and sick, clutching a blanket wrapped around her shoulders. When her eyes focused on him, their depths were dark and anguished. He walked over to her and put his arms around her. Neither of them spoke as he held her, but he felt her trembling, and it broke his heart.

"She's still in surgery," he said. "The nurse said the doctor's optimistic. Says she's healthy and young, strong."

"It's my fault," she said in a low, raw voice.

He drew back and gazed down at her, his heart wrenching when he saw the tears streaking her cheeks. He wanted to kiss away her tears, her pain. "How can it be your fault?"

Her fingers tangled in the front of his T-shirt. "I knew I was a target, and I let her stay with me. I let her open my door. It should have been me."

He pulled her to him again, a bit more forcefully than he'd intended, but he couldn't help it when his entire insides jerked at the thought of it being her in the OR getting a bullet removed from her lung.

"You thought you were safe," he said, stroking her hair, pressing his lips to her temple. He wanted to absorb her into him and serve as her allover bulletproof vest.

"But I wasn't safe. How could that guy know where to find me?"

Her breath hitched, and she let go of the blanket to wrap her arms around him and hug him tight, burying her face against his neck. He felt the gasping puffs of air against his skin, felt the tension in her body, and knew she was weeping but trying to hold it in. It made him ache all the more.

After a few minutes, she eased back from him and swiped at her face. Her eyes were red, her nose running. He reached over and plucked the box of Kleenex off the tray table beside the bed, then waited while she took one, blew her nose and wiped her eyes.

"I'm sorry," she said, her voice strained.

He could tell she had more crying to do but was doing her damnedest to control it. He stroked a hand over her hair, then curled his fingers around the back of her neck and squeezed. He wasn't surprised that she'd fight so hard to be brave. "It's okay. Take as much time as you need."

She gave him a tremulous smile. "You're kind of amazing, aren't you?"

He returned her smile, felt emotion, and dread, tighten his throat. "Yeah, I'm amazing."

She swallowed, nodded, closed her eyes and sat still for a long moment, breathing deeply. He caught himself matching the rhythm of her long breaths, yet his heart thrashed each time he thought, It could have been her. She could have been the one who'd opened that door. He didn't wish harm on anyone else, but he was damn grateful it hadn't been Charlie.

A light knock on the door preceded John Logan pushing it open and sticking his head into the room. "Charlie? You up to a statement?"

She nodded and wiped at her eyes. "Yes, come in."

Logan's usually neat, sandy hair looked as though he'd repeatedly run his hand through it. Dark circles rimmed his eyes below the lines of stress in his forehead. "You okay?" he asked, darting a questioning glance at Noah.

Noah had to bite down to keep his frustrated sarcasm to himself. Of course she's not okay, you nitwit.

"I'm sorry to put you through this," Logan said to Charlie, "but it's important to do it while . . ." His voice gave out, and he paused to swallow several times. "While the . . . incident . . . is still fresh."

Noah studied the cop and wondered whether he should be on the case at all. Clearly, Alex's shooting had shaken him. But Charlie nodded, sniffled. "I understand. It's okay."

He pulled a small notebook out of his breast pocket and flipped it open with shaking hands, then removed a pen from the same pocket. "Tell me what happened."

Charlie drew in an audible breath. "It was the same guy who attacked me at home and ran me off the road. Same ridiculous ninja outfit and everything."

When she shivered, Noah scooted closer, putting his arm around her shoulders and drawing her tight against his side. She reached for his hand, and he folded her icy fingers into the shelter of his palm, hoping his warmth would seep into her.

"Let's start at the beginning," Logan said. "Everything you can remember."

"I was in the bathroom. I'd just showered and was getting ready to dry my hair. I heard the knock at the door, assumed it was room service. I heard Alex open the door, and then a . . . loud crack or pop. I guess it was the gunshot. Then a thump, like someone had fallen. I opened the door and Alex was . . ." She paused, swallowed. "She was on the floor. Bleeding."

Logan, paler than before, stared down at his notebook for several seconds. Gathering his thoughts or gathering his control, Noah wasn't sure. He started to say perhaps Logan should take a break when the cop raised his gaze to Charlie's face.

"And the . . . person who shot her?" he asked through clenched teeth. "Where was he?"

"Gone. I tried to stop the bleeding and yelled for someone to call 911."

Noah realized what she'd said at the same time that Logan's tense expression turned to puzzlement.

Noah cleared his throat. "Let's go through it again, Charlie. And take your time. *Exactly* what happened."

"I was in the bathroom. I heard the gunshot, opened the door and saw Alex on the floor."

"And where was the shooter?" Logan asked.

"I told you. He was already gone."

"You saw him running away?" Noah asked.

"No, all I saw was Alex." She dragged a hand through her hair. "It happened fast, within seconds."

Logan tucked away his notebook then looked at Noah and angled his head toward the door. "Could we talk in the hall?"

"Sure." Noah was reluctant to leave Charlie alone, but he also wanted to hear what Logan had to say. To Charlie, he said, "I'll be right back."

In the hall, after the door was firmly closed, Logan said, "I'm worried about her. She seems confused."

She seemed adamant to Noah, but he couldn't argue with Logan. At least not logically. "She said it happened very fast."

"She *had* to have seen the shooter to know it was the same person from the other incidents."

"The trauma of what happened could be messing with her memory," Noah said.

"But when did she see the shooter? She was very specific that the shooting happened while she was behind a closed door. I can't imagine any potential killer being stupid enough to shoot someone in the chest and then stand there, in a public place, for a few moments afterward."

"Did anyone at the hotel see the perp run away?"

Logan shook his head. "Charlie's room is at the end of the hall. The shooter most likely took off down the stairs."

"What about the exit to the stairwell? The shooter would have had to leave the stairwell when he got to the bottom."

"He could have gotten off at any of the four floors below Charlie's, ditched the disguise, and walked out like any other guest."

"Security cameras?" Noah asked.

"I've already had the recordings pulled. Another detective's going over them, but I don't know how much help they'll be. Donna Keene, the hotel's owner, said the elevators tend to run slow, so it's not unusual for first- and second-floor guests to use the stairs. Plus, a lot of the employees use the stairs to avoid holding up the elevators."

"Christ," Noah muttered.

Logan hooked his thumbs in his belt loops, but instead of squaring his shoulders, they rounded as though weighed down. Vertical lines on either side of his mouth deepened. "I'm going to need to question her further."

"Maybe that could wait until things with Alex settle down. She's obviously not thinking straight right now." He paused. "And you seem a bit emotionally involved."

Logan ran his hand behind his neck. "I want to find that bastard who shot Alex and take his fucking head off."

Noah could relate. "You don't have to worry about Charlie. I'll take care of her."

Logan nodded. "I figured. So you're planning to stick around for a while?"

"Yeah," Noah said. "I'm sticking around."

CHAPTER **FORTY**

Charlie couldn't stop shuddering. And smelling blood. Alex's blood. Her brain seemed to spin in circles around the fact that her sister had been shot instead of her, unable to make sense of it yet unable to rebuff the horror of it. Alex might die. She didn't think she could live with herself if that happened. Maybe she wouldn't be able to live with herself if it didn't.

Noah stepped into the room and gave her a reassuring smile. "Do you need anything?" he asked. "Another blanket?"

Realizing her shivering was visible, she clasped the blanket more securely around her shoulders and tried to quell the chills. "I don't think adding layers will help."

Noah sat beside her on the bed and slid his arm snugly around her shoulders. "Maybe body heat will."

She relaxed against him, leaned her aching head on his shoulder. She felt weak and dizzy, as though she'd lost as much blood as Alex had. Alex, oh, God, Alex. She searched for something to say to Noah. If she didn't focus on something else, she was going to dissolve. "What were you and Logan talking about in the hall?"

Noah rested his chin on the top of her head, idly threading his fingers through her hair. "We can talk about that later."

"I'd rather do it now. Is there a problem?"

He sighed. "You're not going to let it drop, are you?"

"I need to know if there's a problem."

He didn't respond right away, and his hand stopped stroking. "Your story is a little off," he said.

"Story?" She stiffened and pulled away from him so she could see his face. She expected to see doubt when he released her, but his green gaze didn't waver from hers. And she didn't see one scintilla of uncertainty. "What's off about it?" she asked.

"I can't help thinking it's best that we don't do this right now. You're too shaky."

"I'm not too shaky to help the police find the son of a bitch who just shot my sister. Tell me what's off."

He got off the bed and leaned against the wall across from her, as though he needed the distance. "You're able to identify the shooter, yet the sequence of events you described makes that seem impossible."

"I saw him, Noah. He wore the same black shirt and pants as he did the other times. He had on the ninja mask with no opening for the mouth. Exactly like the other times. I know what I saw."

"I believe you. I'm just wondering when you saw it."

She opened her mouth to protest further but stopped when the disconnect in her story clicked. She'd seen the shooter through *Alex's* eyes, not her own. "Oh."

Noah straightened from the wall. "What?"

She stared at him, baffled about how to proceed. He'd think she was crazy if she told him the truth. And, yet, did she have a choice?

"I can't help you if you don't tell me what you're thinking."

She began to shiver in earnest, a chill in every cell. She tried to reconfigure the shooting in her head, tried to find a spot where she could say, Oh, yeah, I saw the shooter when I came out of the bathroom. But then they'd probably want to know more specifics, such as which way the guy ran, and she had no idea. If she fed them details that were wrong, she could throw off the investigation. Oh, God, now what?

"Charlie," Noah said, his tone firm. "Please tell me what you're thinking."

She rubbed at her temple. Thinking hurt. Trying to figure out how to lie hurt.

When she didn't respond, he approached the bed. She

straightened as he braced his hands on either side of her thighs and looked deep into her eyes. "I need you to tell me. It's important."

She closed her eyes against the caress of his breath against her lips. She could smell his soap—Dial, the same she'd used this morning at the hotel—yet his body chemistry seemed to give it a musky twist that teased her senses.

"I'm not thinking anything," she said, hearing the tremor in her voice.

"Open your eyes and look at me, Charlie."

She did as he said, immediately pierced by a gaze as hard and bright as emeralds. He no longer looked like the man who'd made her come multiple times last night. He looked unyielding and a little scary.

"I'm a cop. I know when people are lying. And when people lie, it's because they have something to hide, some involvement in the crime."

Her whole body tensed. "You don't mean—"

"A lying witness," he cut in, his gaze level, "goes at the top of my suspect list."

She raised her chin. "Trying to intimidate me isn't going to work."

"I'm not trying to intimidate you. I'm telling you how cops operate. Logan knows you pretty well, so he's not going to put you at the top of his suspect list until he has a damn good reason. But the way your story doesn't add up is going to make it tough for him."

She let her shoulders sag, the effort to keep them square too much. "I don't know how to explain it. I saw the shooter. My memory is fuzzy about when, so you're going to have to take my word for it."

"That's enough for me. The question is whether it's enough for Logan."

"It has to be. That's all I have." She shivered as the chills returned, ramping up the throbbing in her head.

"Do you think hot coffee would help?" Noah asked.

"Only if I can go with you to get it. I don't know why they

want me in here anyway. There's nothing wrong with me."
Not that a doctor could cure, anyway.

"Then let's go." He held out his hand for her to take it, and
she eased off the bed and shed the blanket, leaving it in the
middle of the bed in a heap.

"Jesus."

At his harsh exhalation, she looked at him. He was staring
in white-faced shock at the front of her tank top. She glanced
down at herself as she remembered. Even so, her stomach
flipped at the sight of white cotton thick with dried blood.

"Wait here while I get you something clean to put on,"
Noah said, then left her alone.

Noah paused outside her door and took several deep breaths.
He'd seen plenty of blood in his career. Blood, guts, and
other gore he didn't want to think about. But he hadn't seen
it on someone he cared about since his first partner had been
killed.

Hearing raised voices, he looked up to see John Logan
at the nurses' station having an intense conversation with
another man in wrinkled khakis and a royal blue dress shirt
that showed large sweat stains under the arms. Noah thought
he heard Charlie's name and started in that direction just
as the man whirled away from Logan and slammed his fist
into the yellow concrete wall. Logan grabbed the guy's arm
and levered him back against the wall and started speaking to
him in a low, urgent voice.

Noah decided to focus on getting Charlie something clean
to put on. Then, once they heard the all clear on Alex, he'd
take her somewhere safe and never let her out of his sight.
He'd make love to her for hours on end to make her forget seeing her sister bloody and on the brink of death.

A nurse set him up with some pale green scrubs. On the
way back to Charlie, he noted that the sweaty guy was leaning against the wall now, his head down and nodding, under
control, as Logan talked to him.

Noah pushed through the door and found Charlie standing in the center of the room with her back to him. She turned to face him, and his gut flinched. She was crying again. God, it ripped at him when she cried.

"Scrubs," he said, indicating the folded pile in his hands.

She wiped the wetness from her cheeks, but other than that she didn't move, staring at him as though her world had been destroyed and she had no idea how to put it back together. Her eyes seemed to ask him, Where do I start? What do I do?

Setting the scrubs on the bed, he went to her and folded his arms around her. "Try not to expect the worst," he murmured.

He felt her fist rap weakly against his shoulder. "I feel so helpless," she whispered.

He rubbed his hands up and down her back, knowing exactly how she felt. His helplessness wasn't focused on Alex, though. Setting her back from him, he said, "Let's get you into the scrubs, okay? Maybe by the time we get back from having coffee, there'll be some good news." He grasped the hem of her blood-crusted tank top. "Raise your arms."

She glanced up at him in surprise, and he smiled. "Yes, I'm going to help you change."

Her damp eyes darkened. "Someone could walk in."

He took two steps backward, drawing her with him, until his body was against the door, serving as a backstop. "Raise your arms," he said again.

She held his gaze as she obeyed, and he drew the tank over her head and tossed it toward the bed. She wasn't wearing a bra, and he stared down at her breasts, wanting to touch, to caress, but knowing the timing wasn't appropriate. But, God, he wanted to. They were so perfectly shaped, like succulent peaches tipped with rosy nipples that invited a taste. His mouth watered, and he swallowed.

As he watched, those nipples hardened, and his breathing went shallow. Blood seemed to geyser into his cock, pressing suddenly aching flesh against the fly of his jeans. He couldn't stop himself from touching her, just a soft stroke of his hand up her rib cage to the underside of her right breast, his thumb pausing just beneath the nipple he desperately wanted to stroke.

"So soft," he murmured.

She caught his hand, but instead of pulling it away, she moved it so that he covered her, her nipple nudging against his palm. He raised his other hand and did the same, and her head dropped back on a sharp intake of breath.

The sight of the long column of her throat made his belly erupt with fire. He stepped closer and switched their positions, backed her against the door and lowered his lips to her exposed throat. She moaned, and her arms slipped around him, her hands sliding down to grasp his butt. Everything left his head but Charlie and throbbing need. He reached down with both hands and grasped the backs of her thighs, hiking her up so she could wrap her legs around him and he could fit his erection to the vee in her thighs. She tensed, and her breath stopped, then shuddered out when he pressed harder.

Oh, God, he wanted to fuck her until she screamed. He wanted to fuck her for eternity, be this close to her forever. He thrust against her again, fierce and frustrated by the barrier of clothing between them.

"Is this wrong?" she whispered.

He stilled. Shit, was he being a completely selfish bastard? "Does it feel wrong?"

"It feels right. Everything about you feels right."

Thank God! "Then it can't be wrong," he said, and caught her earlobe between his lips. "I want to be inside you right now," he murmured. "I'm so hard it hurts."

She shuddered again, moaning at his next driving thrust. He buried his mouth on hers and swallowed the moan, turned-on even more by the vibration of her voice against his tongue. He shifted, wanting to touch her, to feel her wet and ready against his fingers, and used one hand to undo the button on her shorts. She leaned back, her breathing uneven as she let her legs fall open farther to allow him easier access, and watched as he slowly lowered the zipper. Then he worked his hand into her khaki shorts, sliding a finger against the crotch of her panties.

She gasped, quivered, arched her head back. "Oh!"

She was so aroused he could smell it, and his head swam with her sexy scent. He moved his fingers, eager for more than dampening panties. He wanted flesh. He wanted to make her forget, just for a while. He deftly angled his fingers around the material of her underwear, found what he was looking for and sank his middle finger into her.

She went rigid around his hand and pressed down. The shift in position sent his finger deeper, his other fingers spreading her until he felt the heated slide of soft, wet satin against the pads on his palm, his one finger still deeply embedded inside her. He flexed that finger, curled it, pressed it against an unyielding spot that he thought might be *the* spot and began to rub.

She came with a whimper, her head back, her legs spasming on either side of him before they slid a few inches down his thighs as though she no longer had the strength to hold onto him. He angled his head so he could watch her face, fascinated by the roll of ecstasy that tightened her features, her body. He'd never made the effort to watch a lover climax before, and not only did it make his heart feel like it inflated, but it made him burn to be inside her, to feel the clutch of those hot inner muscles around his cock.

But he was also painfully aware that the door wasn't locked, and even though they had it blocked, someone might try to come in at any moment.

He lowered his head and kissed her parted lips, easing a few inches away from the door and lifting her. She slid down his body, coming to rest on top of his hardened dick, and he held her suspended there, wishing like hell they were naked. He'd be slipping into her right now, and she'd be riding him, clamped around him like a tight, wet fist.

The knock he dreaded killed the moment, and they both jerked to awareness.

"Oh, no," Charlie breathed.

Noah stepped back, letting her feet touch the floor, and grabbed the scrubs top off the bed. He thrust it into her hands, then drew her behind him and turned to shield her just as the door opened.

The sweaty guy he'd seen talking to Logan earlier stopped in midstride, eyes widening as they landed on Noah. "Who the hell are you?" the guy demanded.

Noah opened his mouth to ask the same question when, behind him, Charlie said, "Mac?"

The guy's narrowed eyes cleared. "Charlie, thank God."

She stepped out from behind Noah, fully dressed and dragging both hands through her hair. She was flushed and much less shaky than she'd been a few minutes ago.

"Noah, this is Mac Hunter," she said. "Managing editor at the newspaper."

The muscles in Hunter's face clenched as though she'd just hurled a terrible insult at him. Then he looked at Noah with fire in his eyes, not extending his hand in the customary friendly gesture.

Noah was glad. He didn't want to shake hands. He'd just had his fingers inside Charlie, and he wasn't interested in sharing. He rubbed their tips together at his side, noted they were still slightly damp, and resisted the urge to lift them to his nose. He was still hard, aching and heavy with unfulfilled need.

Hunter moved to Charlie's side, stepping closer than Noah would have preferred, and lowered his head as though to speak to her privately. "Logan told me about Alex. I'm so sorry," he said, his voice gruff. "You weren't hurt?"

She shook her head but didn't look at him. Easing away, she rested her hip against the bed. She hadn't put a tremendous amount of distance between them, but to Noah the message was clear: Back off. Hunter didn't get the hint, or ignored it. He leaned toward her, placing his hand over hers braced on the bed. She flinched, and her eyes glazed over for an instant before she gasped and pulled her hand away like she'd been stung.

Noah moved quickly, seizing Hunter by the arm and shoving him face-first against the wall and pinning him there with his arm cranked up between his shoulder blades. "Are you okay?" he asked Charlie. "What'd he do?"

Hunter jerked against his grip. "What the fuck are you doing? Let me go!"

Charlie shot off the bed and grabbed Noah's arm. "No, don't! He didn't hurt me."

"Then what the hell happened?"

"Please, let him go."

Noah reluctantly released Hunter, who turned and leaned back against the wall. He massaged his shoulder. "Jesus, you're trigger-happy."

Noah ignored him, watching Charlie as she first rubbed at the knuckles of her right hand, then grasped Hunter's right hand. She turned it palm down and examined his bloodied knuckles.

"You punched the wall," she said.

Noah felt a shaft of surprise. How did she know how he'd hurt his hand?

"Yeah," Hunter said. "I'm so mature." His fingers curled to grip hers. "I heard about the shooting, and I thought it was you."

Noah watched them, feeling like an outsider and at the same time wanting to surge forward and rip Hunter's head off. Instead, he stayed put. She was obviously close to this guy.

As she gave the other man a soft, sad look, doubt wormed its way through Noah's belly. Just how close were these two?

"I couldn't breathe," Hunter went on. "I couldn't breathe thinking I'd lost you."

"Mac—"

"I've been such an incredible ass," he cut in. "I want it back, Charlie. I want *us* back."

Noah stiffened when Hunter pulled her to him. Mine, he thought as a roar of possession gathered in his gut. But then Charlie's dark eyes met his over Hunter's shoulder, and she held his gaze without blinking. Noah took that as reassurance and forced himself to chill.

Charlie drew back first, and Hunter seemed reluctant to release her, but he did. Then she sank onto the edge of the bed, looking pale and shaky, her forehead furrowed. Noah went to her, placing himself deliberately between her and Hunter.

"You okay?" he asked for her ears only.

"Headache," she said, her lips barely moving.

He tipped her head up with a finger under her chin and studied the gold-flecked depths of her eyes. They looked glassy, almost feverish. Like they had the day after he'd stepped between her and Dick Wallace at the dealership.

"Maybe I can get some Tylenol," she said.

Tylenol wasn't going to do it, he thought.

Hunter cleared his throat. "So what's the deal here? What am I missing?"

Charlie raised her voice and said, "Noah came to Lake Avalon to investigate Laurette Atkins's hit-and-run."

Noah turned to face Hunter. "I'm a Chicago police detective."

"Lassiter? Didn't someone take a shot at you yesterday?" Hunter asked.

Noah nodded. "I was grazed by a bullet, yes."

"You recover fast."

"It was minor."

"It didn't feel minor to me," Charlie said.

Noah glanced at her sharply while Hunter voiced the word ringing in his head. "What?"

Charlie looked up, blushed. "I . . . was just imagining what it would be like . . ."

Even if she'd finished the sentence, Noah wouldn't have heard it. He was thinking about that moment when he'd snatched at her hand in his hotel room, how she'd reacted so violently, how she'd gone catatonic for several frightening instants. She'd gotten the same look, though far more briefly, just now when Hunter had touched her without warning. And then she'd rubbed her hand, as though her knuckles hurt, before inspecting Hunter's bloody fingers. She'd *known* he'd slammed his fist into the wall.

It didn't feel minor to me.

She'd known Noah was close to Laurette after they'd clasped hands the first time.

After the incident in his hotel room, she'd looked into his eyes as if seeing him clearly, as if understanding everything about him.

It didn't feel *minor to me.*

Noah jolted.

She'd *felt* the bullet graze his head. She'd *felt* Hunter punch the wall. Just as Laurette had *felt* it when a suspect was lying.

Charlie was empathic.

CHAPTER **FORTY-ONE**

The surgery went well," Dr. Shane McKee said as he ran a hand through his short, sweat-darkened hair. He still wore scrubs, which made him look doctorly despite his dimpled baby face. "She'll be in recovery for several hours before being transferred to the ICU for a day or two. It will take some time, but I expect a full recovery."

Charlie hung back as her mother shook the surgeon's hand and her father clapped him on the back. Her knees felt weak, and she leaned against Noah, conscious of his hand at the nape of her neck, lightly massaging. She didn't want to touch the doctor, to experience whatever recent trauma he might have suffered. She'd already been floored four times in the past several hours.

First, by Mac slamming his fist into the wall. Then two more times when her parents blustered into the ER waiting room. Her father had hugged her tight, and her mother had briefly touched her arm. The skin-on-skin contact meant Charlie lived in quick succession their horrified moments when Logan had told them Alex had been gunned down. The anguish, the fear, the grief.

When Logan had walked into the waiting room, a friend of the family now rather than a cop investigating a shooting, he'd hugged her even tighter than her father had. And his fear for her sister, his absolute, gut-wrenching terror, tore through her in a numbing wave.

After Mac reluctantly left for work, and the rest of them sat in silence and waited for word about Alex, Charlie's headache grew to near-migraine status, a disorienting dizziness whirling through her senses for several moments at a time.

Now, she listened to the doctor give a full accounting of Alex's injuries, growing dizzier and more nauseated with every word.

"You okay?" Noah asked near her ear.

She nodded, then braced herself and clasped the doctor's large, warm hand.

Terror explodes in my head as I fly through the air, everything around me glittering like the sharp points of broken glass. And then I hit those points and go under, gulping in air and salty water at the same time. My head breaks the surface, and I look wildly around, choking and sputtering as I turn in the water toward the sailboat and spot the reason I ended up in the water. The boom jerks to and fro, the main sail flapping wildly, its busted rope whipping through the air.

Charlie blinked, realizing the doctor had released her and now Noah stood in front of her, worry etched in the lines of his forehead. "Charlie?"

She raised her eyes to his. Alex was going to be okay. And like that, the waves of terror in her brain parted and one coherent thought blasted through: Dick did this.

She was going to kill Dick.

With the taste of salt water still on her tongue, she pivoted toward the door. "I have something to do."

Noah fell in step beside her. "Uh, where are you going? Don't you want to wait to see Alex?"

"This won't take long."

She heard her father call her name but didn't acknowledge it as she burst through the doors of the ER into the Florida sun. She paused, squinting into the parking lot, then turned to Noah and thrust out her hand, palm up. "Keys."

He tilted his head, his eyes narrowed. "No."

She lunged forward, shoved at him. "Give me your fucking keys!"

He grabbed her wrists and brought her up flush against him. "Why? Where do you want to go?"

"That son of a bitch Dick shot my sister. I'm going to end this once and for all." She jerked at her wrists, maddened by her inability to free herself. She was trapped. Always trapped.

Noah held tight. "You need to take a breath, Charlie."

"A *breath*? You think that's going to do *anything*?"

He didn't respond this time, just held tight to her wrists.

She felt herself shaking, felt the heat of the sun beating on top of her head. Her legs felt as though they were treading water, weightless and insubstantial. And then light popped in her head, washing her vision white, and pain smashed into her right hand, as though she'd just slammed her fist into a wall. She blinked, and she was standing in front of Noah. He watched her expectantly, warily, waiting for what she did next.

Light flashed, lightning inside her brain, followed by agony razoring through her chest and the sensation of blood gurgling into her throat. Then it was gone, and she was outside. The setting sun served as the backdrop to a parking lot dotted with medians of lush grass and palm trees.

A starburst behind her eyes preceded a wave of gut-wrenching fear for the life of a precious daughter, a woman so young, so vital. When she came back to herself, her stomach heaved, and she tried to push Noah away and pull free.

He tightened his grip. "What is it? What's going on?"

"I'm going to be sick," she mumbled. He released her, and she managed to stumble away, onto the nearest median, before gagging. Nothing came up.

Noah knelt beside her on the grass, his hand on her back, rubbing in circles, while she took deep, ragged breaths. "That's it," he soothed. "Just breathe, just breathe."

Light exploded, like the flash on a camera blinding her, and she was airborne. She hit cool salt water and went under, the terror crushing. In the next instant, she was back with Noah, on her knees in the grass. Her stomach twisted a second time. Again, nothing came up.

Noah rose beside her, keeping his hand on her shoulder.

"Let's go back inside and let them look at you," he said, his voice low and shaky.

"No," she said, panting, so dizzy she didn't think she could stand up by herself. Whatever was going on was supernatural. A regular doctor wouldn't be able to help. "I need to go see someone."

"Yeah, a doctor. You're probably dehydrated, and you haven't eaten all day."

She grasped his wrist, dug in her fingers as she braced for the next lightning burst in her head. Her skull felt as though it were splitting in two. She couldn't think, could barely remember how to string words together. If it got worse . . .

Noah seemed to growl, then bent and swung her up into his arms. She caught his shoulder for balance, had to concentrate to keep her whirling head from dropping limply back over his arm. "We're going back into the ER," he said.

"No, please." She struggled to find words. "I don't think . . . a doctor can help. I need . . . an expert."

"An expert what?" he demanded.

"If she can't . . . help, you can bring me . . . back."

"Charlie—"

She sank her fingers into the front of his shirt, swallowed several times. She was feeling stronger, her stomach calmer. The pain in her head still pounded viciously, but she could think. And the flashes of light had stopped. For the moment. "Trust me. Please? I'll tell you how to get there."

He hesitated, staring into her face with narrowed green eyes. He was scared. She could see it in his gaze, and she could relate. But there was nothing she could say to ease his fear when she didn't know how to ease her own. All she knew was that AnnaCoreen might know better how to help than an ER doctor.

"Please," she said, and managed to stroke a hand down the side of his face.

He closed his eyes at her caress, swallowed. Then, with a groan, he carried her to the car.

* * *

Noah knew he was driving too fast on the shoulder of the road, flying by the backed-up beach traffic, but he didn't care. All he cared about was getting Charlie to this so-called expert she seemed to think could help her. At the same time, he berated himself for letting her talk him into this when his instincts had screamed at him to get her ass back into the ER. As it was, she sat in the passenger seat of the Mustang, quiet except for telling him when to turn. Every few minutes, her entire body would clench, as though gripped by a terrible pain, and her breathing would go shallow and ragged. When he looked away from the road, for too long to be safe, her eyes would be blind, the way they'd been right after he'd grasped her hand in his hotel room and she'd gone briefly catatonic. Each time, the tension passed within seconds, and she'd go limp.

He assumed she was having some kind of empathic reaction to the trauma of Alex's shooting. He didn't know much about empathy, but he knew from what Laurette had told him that empaths could be bombarded by the emotions and moods of other people and that it could be devastating.

"It's on the left," Charlie said, her voice so weak she could only whisper.

He peered through the windshield, horrified. The pink shack. The fucking psychic? Oh, God, they'd wasted so much time.

"There's a house behind it."

"Charlie, come on. You need a doctor."

"Just humor me. Please."

He ground his teeth together—he had to trust she knew what she was doing—and parked in front of the shack. He got out, ran around the front of the car to Charlie's side and opened her door. She was rigid again, staring at nothing, her forehead shiny with perspiration. Tears streaked her pale face in a steady stream. Then she sagged in the seat and blinked several times, her eyes looking like they tried to roll back in their sockets.

Something snapped in Noah's head. He couldn't take it anymore. He just couldn't, scared to death that these bizarre episodes were killing her. "Forget this. We're going to the hospital."

Hearing the crunch of gravel, he turned to see a petite older woman with short reddish blond hair hurrying toward them. "Charlie?" she called. "Are you with Charlie?"

Noah didn't respond, shocked that she knew.

She pushed him aside with surprising strength and knelt in the car door. She grasped Charlie's wrist, checking her pulse, then patted her gently on the cheek with the palm of her hand. "Can you hear me, dear? Open your eyes and talk to me."

Charlie forced her eyes open, wet her lips. Noah bent down so that his head was close to the older woman's, Charlie's voice so faint that he caught only some of her words. "Flashes . . . over and over . . . can't make them stop . . . head . . . hurts."

The woman rose and turned to Noah, her features tight with worry. "Bring her inside."

He hesitated. "I'd rather take her to the ER."

Her piercing blue gaze swept up to bore into his. "You want what's best for her," she stated firmly. "Bring her inside. Now, please."

Without another word, he bundled Charlie into his arms and kicked the car door closed. She was dead weight, her head limp against his shoulder, as he followed the woman over a stone path through a garden buzzing with insects. He could hear the wash of Gulf waves in the distance, smell salt in the air.

Inside the house, the woman gestured and said, "On the sofa in there," as she thrust a teapot under the kitchen faucet and ran water.

He walked through the pristine kitchen into a clutter-free living room that contained a yellow floral-print overstuffed sofa, two matching chairs and a glass coffee table whose base looked like it had been carved from driftwood. The light was low and soothing, and Noah lowered himself to the sofa cushions and cradled Charlie on his lap. She had begun to shiver, so he gathered her close, stroking her hair, her arms, his heart pounding with fear. She no longer seemed to be with him, as though trapped in some recess of her own mind, her body clenching every few minutes, becoming infused with that terrible tension, then sagging against him as tears spilled from her eyes. He hoped to God this psychic woman could make it stop, that he hadn't made a fatal mistake by bringing her here.

The psychic walked into the living room then with a tray that she set on the coffee table before perching on the edge of the sofa in front of where Charlie's legs stretched out.

"I'm going to give her a tranquilizer," she said, plucking an orange plastic pill bottle off the tray and shaking three small white discs into her palm. After dropping the pills into a cup filled with reddish liquid, she stirred with a spoon to help them dissolve.

"What is it?" Noah asked, tightening his arms around Charlie. No way was he letting this woman pour something weird down her throat.

"Ativan."

"And that?" He jutted his chin toward the cup.

"Herbal tea. Apple cinnamon. Can't you smell it?"

He did then, and relaxed some. Herbal tea and Ativan. Nothing exotic or smacking of hocus-pocus. He could live with that.

"It's going to put her out," the woman said. "She needs to sleep so healing can begin."

Fear spiked right into his brain. "Healing?"

"I'll explain later." She picked up the cup and tapped Charlie's cheek until she roused some. "Charlie, dear, you need to drink this. It's tea and a sedative. I made sure it's not too hot."

Noah took the cup, his hand shaking, and held it to her lips. He tipped it back slowly until she drank it all.

"That's good," the woman said, stroking her fingers over Charlie's forehead and down the side of her face. "You're going to feel better soon. I promise."

It took twenty minutes before Charlie's muscles ceased their ritual of contracting and releasing, before the tears stopped coursing down her face. She relaxed in his arms, her eyes fluttering. Her lips moved, as though she tried to speak but didn't have the strength. Noah's heart clutched, and he lowered his lips to hers and kissed her softly to reassure her.

"It's okay to let go," he said. "I'll be here when you wake up."

Another ten minutes passed before he felt the moment she dropped out of consciousness into a deep sleep. The psychic did, too, because she rose, her hands clasped restlessly before her as she breathed an unsteady sigh. "Well, then, I think we're going to be okay."

Noah looked up at her and had to fight down the urge to bellow, or cry. Now that Charlie had stopped trembling, he had started. "What the hell was that?"

She gestured down the hall. "Let's get our girl tucked into bed, and then we can talk."

CHAPTER **FORTY-TWO**

"Can I get you something to drink?" the psychic asked as she walked out onto the wraparound porch.

Noah glanced at her from where he'd collapsed onto a rocking chair facing an expanse of light sand that ended at the jagged line of dark water. "Scotch?"

She paused before him, looking him over, then extended her delicate, manicured hand. "AnnaCoreen Tesch."

He clasped her hand, a bit unnerved by the shrewdness of her gaze. What was she seeing? "Noah Lassiter."

"From Chicago," she said.

He arched a brow, then realized that Charlie must have mentioned him to her. That made him stupidly happy for a moment.

AnnaCoreen's lips curved. "I know accents. Sorry to disappoint you."

He didn't react, deciding he'd let her think his disappointment was because he'd thought she had psychically known where he was from.

Her smile grew before she turned to go. "I'll be back shortly."

He settled back in the rocking chair and stared out at the water illuminated by a full moon. Lights in the distance suggested a small cruise ship or other vessel slowly chugging across the horizon. A faint clang sounded in the distance every fifteen seconds or so, almost drowned out by the energy of the waves racing ashore then retreating.

He should have started to relax, but he couldn't. He'd sat on the side of Charlie's bed for a long time, watching her for signs of restlessness. When she didn't move other than to breathe deeply, her lips slightly parted, he'd lightly kissed her then left, closing the door behind him.

AnnaCoreen returned with another tray, this one stocked with small plates, Italian bread, chunks of cheese, olives, sliced fruit and two glasses of amber liquid. She set the tray on a small table between his chair and another one and picked up one of the glasses.

"Thanks," he said, accepting it. When he took a gulp, he tasted iced tea loaded with sugar.

AnnaCoreen settled onto the other chair and began to pile food on one of the plates. Apparently, she was hungry, he thought, just before she handed him the plate.

He dug in, suddenly starving. "So you said you'd explain," he said around the bread and cheese in his mouth.

She sat back and began to gently rock. "I assume you already know that Charlie is empathic."

"Yes, but I don't know the details. I mean, I know . . . knew a woman who was empathic, but it was different."

"Charlie's gift is unfamiliar to me as well, and perhaps to most others. I've done some research, consulted some friends, and no one I've talked with has heard of this particular type of empathy. That doesn't mean it's never happened before, just that the people I've consulted have never heard of it, which makes it very unusual."

"I think I need an overview," he said. "I'm aware of her empathy, but . . . well, we haven't discussed it."

AnnaCoreen stopped rocking and studied him. "You're new in her life."

He couldn't help the swell of defensiveness. "Is that a crime?"

"Of course not. You care deeply for her."

He nodded, his heart rate kicking into a higher gear. "Deeply" might be an understatement considering how much he'd wanted to destroy something when she'd been in pain. "Yeah, I do."

"It happened fast."

He stopped himself from rolling his eyes at how each "question" was a statement. Maybe she *was* a damn psychic, but he was too tired and emotionally wrung out to play this game. "If you already know all this, why are you asking me?"

"Why does it frustrate you?"

"I'm not frustrated."

"You are. And angry. Why?"

"What, are you a therapist on top of being psychic?"

"I care about her, too."

She said it so simply that he almost didn't catch the subtle change in her tone. Was she warning him? He felt the first clutch of fear that she really could see through him, straight to his soul. "I'm not going to hurt her." He said it as much to assure her as himself. He *wasn't*, damn it. He'd die first.

AnnaCoreen held his gaze for several beats, her expression unreadable. "There's darkness inside you that concerns me, Noah Lassiter," she said softly. And then she turned her face toward the water and began to rock again.

Realizing he was holding his breath, Noah drew in a long stream of air. She was messing with him. No way could she know anything about where he'd been or what he'd done. It just wasn't possible. And, regardless, his prime concern right now was Charlie.

"So are you going to give me the lowdown on Charlie's empathy so I'm prepared the next time she needs help or are you going to keep me in the dark?"

She glanced at him and smiled. He thought he saw a flicker of approval in her blue eyes, or maybe that was wishful thinking.

She rocked some more, as though thinking carefully before she started speaking. "Charlie described it as feeling as though she's inside the other person's head during a recent traumatic event. She feels what they felt, hears what they heard, sees what they saw."

"Holy Christ," he breathed, setting aside his plate of food.

"It's triggered by contact," she said. "A skin-to-skin transfer of energy that carries the other person's memory."

He thought of that frightening moment in his hotel room when he'd touched her, how afterward she'd looked up at him as though she'd understood everything about him. Later, she'd said his shooting "didn't feel minor." He'd assumed she'd somehow absorbed his experience, but it hadn't occurred to him that she'd actually *lived* it. Fuck, he thought. *Fuck.*

"Yes, it's a little much to take in," AnnaCoreen murmured.

He glanced at her. Had he spoken aloud?

She said, "I saw coverage of this morning's shooting on television. The last broadcast said Charlie's sister was in stable condition."

"Yes," he said, struggling to stay focused. "The doctor thinks she'll be fine."

"That's good news." She paused. "Charlie was there when she was shot?"

Noah's stomach turned. It so easily could have been Charlie. And then he remembered skidding to a stop in the doorway of her hotel room. She'd had her blood-covered hands on Alex's chest. It struck him now how she had been able to describe the shooter. She'd *seen* the shooter from Alex's point of view, had probably felt the bullet rip through her chest.

He sat forward, bracing his elbows on his knees and lowering his head. He felt sick, stunned. A grinding queasiness slithered through his stomach. Oh, God, Charlie.

AnnaCoreen cleared her throat. "Judging from the shape she was in when you arrived, I'm assuming she'd had repeated contact with multiple emotional people in the aftermath."

"Yes. Her parents. Detective Logan. Some other guy named Mac."

"I assume that Charlie was jolted by the shooting," she said, "then everything she felt after that added up. As you might imagine, taking on other people's pain and emotion, especially when it's that intense, tends to wear a person out."

He raised his head, glanced at her. She looked pale yet serene in the dim light. "Like her circuits became fried?"

She smiled slightly. "Yes. If she were a computer, we would describe it as a system crash. Sleep should repair the damage."

Noah's heart leapt with alarm. "Damage?"

"I'm speaking metaphorically, of course. I assume what we're dealing with is an extreme form of fatigue. Her system was unable to absorb any further shocks and began to recycle the ones it had already sustained in a sort of endless loop. Sedation stopped the loop, so she should wake up as good as new."

"How can you be sure?"

"I can't be. All we can do is wait and see."

Noah eased into the dimly lit guest bedroom and shut the door as quietly as possible. In the bed, Charlie didn't stir, but he could hear her breathing, even and deep, relaxed. Now if only he could relax, but he didn't think he would until she opened her eyes and looked at him, spoke to him, smiled at him. Everything AnnaCoreen told him whipped around his head like a crisp sheet on a laundry line in high winds.

Worry for Charlie had clenched his stomach, and exhaustion burned his eyes. As a cop, he'd witnessed plenty of anguish in his career. He couldn't imagine what it would be like to have to actually *feel* it as intensely as the person bearing it. How could Charlie possibly survive being forced to repeatedly relive other people's pain? Was she strong enough? Was *anyone* strong enough?

Sitting on the side of the bed, he braced an arm on the other side of her hip. Her dark hair was spread over the pillow, a frame to her pale, peaceful face, a sharp contrast to the earlier strain and torment of repeated flashes.

His heart swelled as he gazed down at her. There was much he didn't know about her ability, much about it that frightened him. How much did she see when she touched him? How much did she know about who he was, who he'd been?

He knew only one thing for certain: Fate had brought them together, and he wasn't going to blow this shot at a second chance.

He paced the length of his work area, his shoes scraping against the gritty concrete, his heart thundering, his mouth dry with fear. It was all falling apart, and he couldn't stop it. He'd failed. Again. Almost killed the wrong woman. Jesus fucking Christ, he was so screwed.

It was Charlie Trudeau's fault. The woman had a fucking guardian angel looking out for her.

He curled his hands into fists, imagined them around her delicate throat, remembered what it had felt like the last time, the absolute, incredible sexual thrill.

He'd gotten so turned-on, so hot, because he'd been so close to finally getting it done, to saving everything for . . . *her.*

Except *she* wanted that other guy. What the hell? He'd done everything for her, been everything to her, let her do things to him, dominate him, manipulate him. He'd *killed* for her. And then he'd watched her turn around and give herself to that other guy.

Fuck.

He knew why, too. That other guy was smart. Educated. No dirt under his fingernails. A white-collar bastard with a white-collar paycheck. And that's what she wanted. That's what every woman wanted.

All she wanted from him was for him to do her dirty work. She didn't want to get her hands bloody, so she'd screwed him senseless until he'd begged to do whatever she wanted, just as long as she kept touching him, sucking him.

God.

And now everything was fucked. He hadn't been able to get it up since that moment he'd gotten hard while strangling Charlie Trudeau. That moment had startled him, frightened him. He didn't like being that man, being that *freak*. Violence didn't get him off, damn it. Violence had *never* gotten him off.

At least it hadn't *before*.

Before she'd fucked with his head, turned him into a killer.

Goddamn her.

CHAPTER **FORTY-THREE**

Charlie opened her eyes to the shimmery shadows of water-reflected sunlight on an unfamiliar ceiling. Soft, warm sheets and a white down comforter laced with the scent of fabric softener enveloped her. While she didn't immediately know where she was, she felt snuggly and relaxed. There was nothing to fear here, and she let her thoughts unfurl lazily.

The last thing she remembered was Noah violently swearing at a red light. The flashes had veered out of control, had indeed become big-assed mind-fucks, paired with excruciating pain that had gripped her skull in razor-tipped talons. Thank God, the pain was gone. Now, her head felt balloon light, free of anxiety. She sighed softly, letting her eyes drift closed. She was so very tired.

Alex.

Charlie's eyes popped open, and she sat up straight in the bed, fear jacking up her heart rate. Oh, God, Alex. Was she okay? How much time had passed?

Shoving aside the comforter and sheets, she got out of bed but paused beside it when she realized she wore nothing but the scrubs shirt and underwear.

The door opened behind her, and she turned to see Noah walk in. He was even less dressed than she was. He had a white towel slung around his waist and was rubbing another over his shaggy, wet hair. If she hadn't been terrified about the condition of her sister, she might have taken a moment to appreciate the exquisite grace of his perfectly formed male torso with its sharply defined muscles and tantalizing ridges. Instead, she had only one concern at the moment.

"Alex?"

He lowered the towel and snapped his head up. He looked her up and down, his eyes searching. When he met her gaze, his shoulders relaxed, and he smiled. "She's doing well. I talked to your dad before I hopped in the shower. She's still in intensive care, but her doctors are pleased with her progress. She's going to be fine."

Charlie's legs went wobbly, and she sank onto the edge of the bed, speechless with relief.

"How do *you* feel?" Noah asked as he approached the bed.

She noted that he'd shaved. She'd never seen his face without stubble, and took a long moment to appreciate the smooth, flawless skin of his angular jaw before dropping her gaze. He was naked under that towel, and her mouth watered with a hunger that surprised her with its intensity. What better way to celebrate that her sister was alive and well?

He lifted her chin with one finger, and she stiffened.

Terror infused every nerve as I stomped on the brake for another frustrating red light. This can't be happening, don't let it happen, don't let it happen. I'll be a better person. I'll be whatever you want me to be. Just, please, please, don't do this to her.

She came back to herself, shaken by the depth of his fear. He was a cop, no stranger to emergencies, yet—

"Charlie?" Noah was searching her eyes. "How do you feel?" he asked again.

She released a cleansing breath, letting go of his lingering despair, and smiled up at him. "Good. Rested."

"And your head?"

"Like new." She placed her palm against his abdomen, pleased by the way his muscles jumped and his breath sucked in. Her own breathing went shallow, her heart beginning to thud. "What about you?"

His eyes narrowed, darkened. A muscle flexed at his temple. "Relieved that you're no longer catatonic."

She slid her hand down, palm flat, to just under his navel. Soft hair so blond it was invisible against his skin tickled her palm, and she felt her inner muscles clutch with anticipation. "I feel good, Noah. Energized." She smiled slowly, hooking her middle finger under the edge of the towel. "Is the door closed?"

He swallowed. "Yes, but I think we need to talk."

"Let's talk later." She tugged, and the towel dropped from his hips. She gazed down at his semierect cock, watched in fascination as it thickened and lengthened, rising up before her eyes. Her breath caught at the beauty of it, and she slid her tongue over her bottom lip, holding back from diving in. Wow.

She was so enthralled that she didn't realize Noah had moved until his hand slid into the hair against the side of her neck and he bent to catch her lips with his. She tilted her head back, welcoming his tongue, his taste. The flavor of mint toothpaste and the scent of Dial soap washed through her senses.

He moved to ease her back on the bed, but she stopped him with her hands on his hips and broke the seal of their lips. "Wait," she whispered. "Not yet."

He groaned deep in his throat but backed off, his hair falling over his forehead in damp tendrils. She nudged him back another step and knelt before him, sliding her hands around to his firm butt, then down the sides of his thighs. She felt his legs quiver with anticipation and smiled up at him as she grasped his twitching cock and closed her mouth around him.

He dropped his chin to his chest, his fingers sinking into the tops of her shoulders. "Oh, Christ," he breathed, his gaze steady on hers.

She skimmed her tongue over his silken head, felt the spasmodic reaction of his hard flesh and did it again and again until the salty taste of his arousal teased her tongue. When she delved her tongue firmly into the tender slit at the top, he bucked against her, driving himself against the back of her throat. She relaxed, took all of him, and sucked. He seemed to grow larger and hotter as she tightened her fingers around his hard length. She pumped her hand up and down, dragging her lips slowly over his shaft until the head popped out of her mouth, glistening, then taking him in all over again. She repeated the process with varying degrees of speed, fast and firm, then slow and teasing, her tongue exploring all his ridges and veins.

"Jesus, Charlie," he groaned. "You have to stop. I'm not going to last."

She didn't want him to. She wanted to feel him explode in her mouth. She wanted to taste him, swallow him. He plunged his hands into her hair, tightened his grip on her head to try to halt her intensifying assault.

"Stop," he said, his voice gruff, the subtle thrust of his hips belying the command. "I want to be inside you when I come."

She grasped his wrist with one hand to still him, focused entirely on the part of him pulsing with heat and vitality between her lips. She hummed her satisfaction at how big and hard he was, her inner thighs dampening with anticipation for the moment when this part of him would be driving into her, taking her beyond the stars. She loved the way his body went rigid and swept her eyes open and up so she could watch him in the throes of his release. He threw his head back, the cords in his neck standing out in sharp relief, his pecs gleaming with a fine sheen of perspiration. He was a god towering above her, ripped and huge, so beautiful her insides clenched with an almost desperate want.

He came with a ragged groan, his cock jerking in her mouth.

And then the world shifted.

Soft wet heat clamps and swirls and sucks at the only part of me that matters at the moment. I'm fighting the rising geyser, not wanting this bliss to end so soon, it's too damn soon. But control is gone, and pleasure sends me soaring with the speed and force of a jet leaving the ground. I'm flying, rocketing, gushing, coming, knees threatening to buckle with the sheer joy of it. God, Charlie. Don't let it end. I love this woman.

She blinked, dizzy and breathless and disoriented. It took her a second to realize she was on the floor, cradled against Noah's damp, naked chest. They were both fighting for air, her head spinning from the intensity of his climax. Or was it what he'd thought? He loved her. Holy crap, he *loved* her. Was that even possible so soon?

Noah raised his head to look down at her, his eyes dazed. "What happened at the end there? Were you . . . did you . . ."

She grinned and rested her chin on his chest, running the tip of her finger over his cheek to stop a trickle of sweat. "Yep."

He stroked his hand over her hair, tucking some of it behind her ear. "But I didn't . . ." He trailed off, clearly amazed and confused at the same time, and then a little chagrined. "I never even touched you."

"I was touching *you*," she said.

"I've heard of women who get off on that, but your response seemed a little intense."

Her smile grew as she idly trailed her fingertips over his left nipple, enjoying the way his breath whistled in through his teeth. "I assume you spoke with AnnaCoreen about me," she said.

"She explained some stuff while you were out of it. Which was damn scary, by the way." He caressed her cheek with his knuckles.

She tilted her head into his tender, almost reverent touch. "I'm okay now. So she must have told you what happens when I touch someone who's experienced something dramatic."

"Sure, but—" He broke off, his eyes widening. "Oh. You mean you . . . you felt me . . ."

"Uh-huh."

"That's . . . incredible."

She couldn't help but laugh at his wonder. It still amazed her, too. But she wouldn't dream of complaining of this particular side effect of her new ability. At least there was a bright side. A *very* bright side. Warmth and well-being spread through her. Noah loved her. Except . . . maybe he'd thought that because he was coming. Who knew what men thought at that critical moment? Did the timing discount the sentiment?

He sat up, drawing her with him and onto his lap. His arms surrounded her, holding her close as he nuzzled her hair. "God, you smell so good." He kissed the side of her neck. "You should eat something," he murmured. "You've got to be starving."

Touched at how thoroughly he took care of her, she turned her head into his kiss, claiming his lips with hers and telling him with her tongue that food could wait.

Groaning, he deepened the kiss and slid a hand under her scrubs top. Her nipple hardened before his fingers even rolled it. He spent a full minute kissing her lips, stroking her breasts, rolling and gently pinching her nipples, until she was restless in his arms, aching, nearly ready to beg. Experiencing his orgasm had been a nice appetizer, but her body ached for the real thing.

"Maybe we should move to the bed," he said.

Before she could agree, he rose, lifting her in his arms. He laid her on the bed and drew her scrubs shirt over her head and tossed it aside. He kissed her again, his tongue sliding over the crease in her lips, then entering, demanding, plunging. He stroked his fingers down her ribs and into the waistband of her panties, which he eased down her legs and off. Bracing above her, he nudged her legs farther apart with his hand, letting his fingers feather the inside of her thigh.

She moaned, wanting him to go faster, to get inside her. But he took his time caressing her everywhere—the backs of her knees, her ankles, the arches of her feet, back to the insides of her thighs—everywhere but where she wanted it most. When she couldn't stand it anymore, she shoved at his shoulders and rolled so that she straddled his hips, her hands braced on his chest, her hair hanging down.

He grasped her waist with a chuckle. "In a hurry, are you?"

"You have no idea," she said as she tossed her hair over her shoulder and settled her mouth on his. She nipped at his lips with her teeth, and he made a sound in his throat that sounded like a growl.

When she came up for air, he adjusted his position under her so that his rigid cock was right at her entrance. "Jesus, you're so wet I can smell it."

She smiled into green eyes burning with desire. "Does it turn you on?"

He bumped his hips up, his hard, hot cock nudging against her. "What do you think?"

She began to lower herself slowly, taking him in an inch at a time, sucking in a shuddering breath. His hands tightened on her waist, then, without warning, he rolled her under him and plunged. She gasped and arched, shocked and thrilled at the abrupt invasion. He withdrew and plunged again, sinking into her to the hilt, stretching, filling. Sliding his arms under her thighs, he drew her legs up, opening her farther, withdrew and glided home again.

"I'm not going to last," he rasped. "You're so tight and hot. I get inside you, and I can't control myself."

"Go ahead and lose control."

Instead of beginning the final, desperate thrusts that preceded his orgasm, he unexpectedly withdrew and paused, braced on his arms, his breathing harsh but controlled.

He gave her a determined, albeit pained grin, a trickle of sweat tracking the side of his face. "Not yet," he said. "You're going to have to wait for it right along with me."

She started to protest but instead gasped when he lowered his head and his hot, wet mouth sucked in her left nipple. His tongue rolled it against the roof of his mouth before catching it gently between his teeth and tugging, tugging. She arched off the bed at the stab of longing between her legs. He did the same to the other nipple, then suckled it hard, his tongue circling and pressing and flicking.

She grasped his head, unable to stop the raspy moan that escaped her throat. His breath was warm and moist as he moved down, pausing to taste the skin above her navel, then sweeping his tongue into that little indentation. His teeth nipped at her flesh, burning a trail straight to her throbbing center. And then he was there, right there, and she raised her head to watch him, surprised when he got off the bed, grasped her by the ankles and pulled her toward the foot. He knelt before her then, his eyes on hers as he flattened his tongue fully against her heat. She just about shot off the bed, but he held her still, his hands firm on her thighs, keeping her open so he could sink his tongue into her. Just when she thought he was going to go slow and torture her, he took her fast, his tongue flicking and plunging and probing until the rocketing waves built and began to crash into her over and over, building higher and higher.

He left her at the crest of one of those waves, but before she could protest, he rose over her, grasped her thighs, dragged her forward and plunged, impaling her with his rigid cock.

She gasped, bucked, shocked to be filled at the height of orgasm. He held still while she pulsed around him, the pleasure drawn out by the pressure of his unyielding flesh inside her. When she began to relax, he drew her up into his arms, his cock still firmly embedded, and put his knee on the bed. He came down on top of her with a grunt, and she arched, stunned that he was able to slide in another inch.

Breathing hard, gasping, desperate for more of him, she grasped his butt and arched her hips, encouraging him to move, to thrust. He was so hard, so hot, and the pleasure was a throbbing ache that required only a tiny amount of friction to bloom and flood yet again.

He groaned, his chest rumbling against her breasts. "If I move, I'm done. I can't help it."

She answered him with a flex of her inner muscles, and he gasped. "Christ, you're evil."

She laughed, and he growled. And then he braced above her and moved only his hips, withdrawing and plunging, again and again, while she held on to his forearms and looked up at his face, so tight with concentration, his eyes on hers.

The cords in his neck were taut, his jaw set, as his thrusts became short and jerking, desperate, before he came with a harsh groan.

She flashed on his orgasm at the same time that her own crashed through her, the sensation so violently extraordinary that stars burst behind her eyes. She couldn't think, couldn't see, couldn't hear. All she could do was feel, her mouth open against his shoulder in a silent scream as pleasure, intense, fantastic, staggering pleasure, roared through her body, tightening muscles so taut they felt they could snap.

When it was over, she couldn't move, couldn't breathe, stunned beyond thought as nerves she hadn't known existed sparked with incredible, jolting aftershocks.

Noah cupped her face and kissed her, gentle, tender, loving. "You're going to have to tell me about that one," he murmured, "when you're able to think again."

She released a sound, a short laugh, tried to draw a steady breath and couldn't. Simultaneous orgasms, his and hers, had scrambled her brain. And she didn't care if she had a coherent thought ever again.

Noah loved her.

CHAPTER **FORTY-FOUR**

Charlie walked into AnnaCoreen's kitchen feeling energized and relaxed, flushed and sated. Reaching for the coffee carafe, she remembered how Noah had taken her yet again against the wall in the shower, whispering in her ear how unbelievably turned-on he was by the knowledge that each time he came, she relived the blissful moment. He drew their lovemaking out until the water ran cold, slowing his thrusts just before she crested until she was digging her nails into his back and begging him to tip her over. And then he timed his climax perfectly, letting himself loose moments before she began to convulse in his arms, so that while her own pleasure rolled through her, his unfurled right on top of it, blinding and deafening her to everything but the shattering rapture that hurtled through her body.

Afterward, she was so limp that he had to tell her to hang onto him while he lathered her hair, rinsed it, then soaped her up all over. When he slipped his hand between her thighs yet again, she'd weakly shaken her head. Chuckling, he'd backed her against the wall and kissed her deeply, his tongue and lips and teeth working her up to the point where she was ready for his hand to go back to where it wanted to go. But then he'd turned off the water and began to towel her off, his hands lingering on her breasts, stroking, caressing, as though he'd become obsessed with touching her and couldn't stop himself.

When she'd gotten dressed in a pair of khaki shorts and an airy white linen blouse on loan from AnnaCoreen, Noah watched every move. Then he mumbled that he needed to get back into the cold shower and would join her and AnnaCoreen in a few minutes.

Hearing AnnaCoreen's approach behind her, Charlie turned. "Good morning."

AnnaCoreen tilted her head, smiled. "My, my, but you're looking mighty . . . refreshed."

Charlie laughed as her face grew warm. "I am, thanks. I had a great night's sleep."

"Among other things," AnnaCoreen said, then shooed her toward the door that led to the front room. "You go outside. I'll bring you some coffee and breakfast."

"You don't have to—"

"Don't be silly, girl. Of course I don't have to."

"Thank you," Charlie blurted. "For last night. I . . . don't know what would have happened if you hadn't been here."

AnnaCoreen's movements were fluid as she filled the coffee carafe with water. "You would have gone to the emergency room. They would have assumed you were having seizures and injected you with Ativan, which would have worked more quickly than how I gave it to you." She glanced at Charlie, smiled slightly. "For future reference. Now, go relax on the porch. I'll join you in a few minutes."

Charlie did as she was told, fearing she would insult her hostess if she refused. On the porch, she settled into a rocking chair and breathed in the salty air. The Gulf, sparkling under the morning sun, looked restless, whitecaps forming on waves that weren't normally so robust. She supposed she should be unsettled, too. Someone—it had to be Dick Wallace—had tried to kill her again, had almost killed Alex. But she felt safe here, protected. She figured this calm feeling wouldn't last. Granted, Alex was going to be okay, but Charlie felt anger that someone, Dick, had hurt her sister simmering deep inside her, working its way toward the surface.

AnnaCoreen appeared by her side, bearing a cup of steaming coffee and a plate with a sliced banana and a bagel smeared with cream cheese. She set the plate on the table beside Charlie and handed her the cup of caramel-colored joe.

"Thank you," Charlie said, wondering how AnnaCoreen had known she liked milk in her coffee, let alone that a bagel and a banana were part of her breakfast routine. She took a sip of coffee, further surprised that it was sweet.

"How did you—" She broke off, smiled. "Duh. Psychic."

AnnaCoreen released a rich laugh as she settled onto the chair next to Charlie's. "I just made it the way I like it, honey."

Charlie watched her, fascinated by this woman she felt so close to yet had met only a few days ago. When the breeze blew a lock of wispy blond hair across AnnaCoreen's cheek, she tucked it aside with a hand whose age spots and blue veins contradicted the illusion of youth that exquisite bone structure and good skin gave her face. Charlie thought of Nana and felt a pang of grief. And guilt. Nana's garden sat untended at home, weeds no doubt already overtaking the area she'd cleared the other day.

AnnaCoreen began to rock next to her. "Your friend is very attached to you," she said.

Charlie smiled, glad to think about Noah instead of sadness. "I know."

"He's a good man."

Charlie leaned her head back, sighed. "Is he?"

"Unfortunately, he has many demons."

"Don't we all?"

"His are particularly . . . dark."

"He's a police detective. I'm sure he's seen things that no human being should ever have to see."

"I understand that you care for him deeply, but you would be wise to proceed cautiously."

Charlie started to ask what in particular made her feel that way, but then Noah sauntered onto the porch in jeans and no shirt, his hair damp from his shower. He was idly scratching his rock-hard belly, and Charlie's mind went blank at the sight of that large hand against the backdrop of rippling abdomen. That hand, those ridges, that *man* . . . as exhausted as she was from all that they had already done, she wanted him all over again. God, she thought, maybe she was in love with him.

He met her eyes then, and his gaze darkened with heat.

AnnaCoreen's voice interrupted the direction of her thoughts. "Would you like some coffee, Noah?" She was already out of her chair and headed for the door.

"I can get it," Noah said, not very convincingly.

AnnaCoreen waved over her shoulder. "Be right back."

Alone with Noah, Charlie leaned her head against the wooden slats of the rocking chair, content to do nothing but drink in the glory of his naked chest. Her heart began a sensuous thud, as though her body recognized and responded to its mate.

He ambled over to her, a secret smile teasing his mouth as he leaned down to kiss her. He eased her coffee cup from her hands just before his lips brushed hers. At contact, she was transported back to the shower.

The water rains down on my back, ice-cold and a sharp contrast to the heat of the silk-sheathed steel grasped in my fisted hand. The rising pleasure pulses as I pump, my free hand splayed against slick, water-drenched tile for support. I imagine Charlie in bed, silky hair spread over a crisp, white pillow, the tip of her tongue tracing her upper lip. Oh, yeah. I come with a grinding groan, jetting into my hand as my body spasms helplessly with the violence of release.

She returned to herself gasping and found Noah, who'd braced one hand on the arm of the chair while he sipped her coffee, hovering over her with a self-satisfied grin.

She released a breathless, shaky laugh, her heart thumping, her body humming.

Noah straightened as AnnaCoreen returned and handed him a cup. "Thanks," he said as he set Charlie's on the table next to her chair and drank from his own. "Ah, black just like I like it."

Charlie blinked up at him, still struggling to focus. Was it possible for too much pleasure to turn your brain to mush?

AnnaCoreen's chair creaked as she sat down. "I'm not one to rain on parades, but until we know more about Charlie's flash fatigue, you two should probably . . . take it down a notch."

Charlie tore her gaze away from Noah's, a rush of blood making her face burn. "I'm sorry?"

AnnaCoreen smiled, her eyes twinkling. "You've discovered a rather lovely benefit of your ability. It's natural to want to explore the possibilities, but you know what they say about too much of a good thing."

Charlie tried to think of a response other than uhhhh.

Noah obviously wasn't the least bit embarrassed, because he switched gears smoothly, without even a hint of blushing. "Flash fatigue?" he asked. "What happened to Charlie last night has a name?"

"Not officially," AnnaCoreen said. "But I'm fairly certain it's something we'll have to deal with again. It's best to be prepared for the next time."

Charlie's brain finally engaged, triggered by a potentially disturbing realization. "Can we back up a minute?"

AnnaCoreen's knowing expression seemed to say, Welcome back from the land of bliss. "Of course."

"This . . . lovely benefit . . . is that going to happen when I touch other people?"

Noah released a belly laugh, and Charlie shot him a chastising glance. "It's not funny."

"No, but it could be a hell of a lot of fun."

"Leave it to a guy to think so."

Chuckling, AnnaCoreen asked, "Have you experienced it with anyone besides Noah?"

"Not so far."

"Then it's likely that your deep, emotional connection to him enhances your ability to tap into his energy. That ability could heighten further as your relationship grows."

A growing relationship? Deep, emotional connection? Holy crap. She *did* love him.

"Hmm," Noah mused, "the idea of being able to get you off with a mere phone call has a certain appeal."

"Noah," Charlie gasped, horrified.

AnnaCoreen laughed again. "I don't know about the remote possibilities, but it's certainly a theory you could test."

Noah got up and headed for the door. "I have a call to make."

Charlie had to laugh. "Get back here, ya big horndog."

He returned, grinning, and she thought the most amazing thing in the world was seeing him smile. She sensed he hadn't smiled nearly enough in his life and vowed to change that. If she got the chance. Who knew what would happen once he had to return to Chicago? The thought of a long-distance relationship did not sound appealing.

As he sat back down, she reached over and grasped his hand, pleased by the way his eyes flared with awareness as he squeezed her fingers.

She had to force herself to turn her attention back to Anna-Coreen. "So, about what happened last night. You called it flash fatigue."

AnnaCoreen nodded as she began to rock. "Can you tell me how you were feeling before the flashes began cycling?"

"Mainly, I had a headache. A migraine. I kept seeing flashes of light that got more intense before each vision."

"Would regular migraine medication hold off the cycle?" Noah asked. "Or perhaps Charlie could take a tranquilizer as soon as the headache starts?"

"It would be best for a doctor to determine the appropriate course," AnnaCoreen said.

Charlie was skeptical. "How do I explain what's happening to a doctor? He or she would think I'm nuts."

"There's a doctor from Fort Myers who visits me regularly," AnnaCoreen said. "She has an open mind, and I'm sure I can arrange for you to see her. I also think it'd be a good idea for her to do a brain scan."

"A brain scan?" Noah asked, alarmed. "Why?"

"We would be remiss not to keep an eye on what's happening physically as well as emotionally," AnnaCoreen said. "We don't know exactly what we're dealing with. If these flashes are having a physical impact of any kind, other than the obvious, we need to be on top of that."

Noah's complexion had gone bone white. "What kind of physical impact?"

"It's just a precaution," AnnaCoreen said. "We don't want any nasty surprises down the line."

Noah pulled his hand away from Charlie and sat forward to brace his elbows on his knees.

Charlie skimmed her hand over his bare back. "Relax, Noah. I'm—" She broke off when she saw the scar on his lower back. She'd felt it before, when they'd been tangled together and sweating, but what had caused it had never occurred to her until she was looking at it, up close and personal. Her mouth dry, she traced the circle of pale, puckered flesh with the tip of her finger. "Is this from a bullet?"

He straightened, catching the wrist of her exploring hand and drawing her palm up for a feathery kiss. "It's nothing to worry about."

Charlie wanted to protest, wanted to know how and why he'd been shot. The thought of him in pain, bleeding, made her head feel heavy and full, achy. And, for the first time, it sank in how little she knew about this man. Yes, she'd been inside his head, had experienced firsthand his doubts and regrets, had connected with him on the most visceral level. She knew him so intimately that being with him felt absolutely right, as though the piece that had been missing from her life had locked right into its predetermined place.

But she knew little *about* him. AnnaCoreen's voice echoed in her head: *He has many demons . . . you would be wise to proceed cautiously.*

AnnaCoreen rising from her rocking chair jarred her from her thoughts. "I have an appointment in half an hour. Perhaps while I'm gone, you two could focus on who's trying to kill our girl and what we're going to do about it."

CHAPTER **FORTY-FIVE**

Noah watched AnnaCoreen walk into the house, then looked at Charlie and grinned. "I like her."

She smiled back at him. "Kind of freaky sometimes, though, isn't she?"

"Well, she is psychic."

She dropped her head back against the chair and laughed. "That she is."

Noah settled back in his own chair and propped his right ankle on his left knee. "So you think it's Dick."

Charlie sighed as though the mention of the man's name made her want to jump off a tall bridge. "It seems so obvious that it's probably not. I mean, Logan's right. The guy would have to be a complete idiot to go after me. And, much as I hate to admit it, he's not an idiot. He's been screwing over customers and getting away with it for years." She took a breath, held it. "There's something I have to tell you."

He tried to stop himself from stiffening, but he didn't like her doomed expression. He also didn't like the thought that he'd probably look the same way when he told her his own secret. And she might not be able to get over his walk on the dark side. He cleared his throat. "Okay."

"When the guy attacked me after running me off the road, I got an empathic flash off of him. I saw him kill someone else."

He sat straighter, disbelief surging through him. "Why the hell didn't you tell me this before?"

"Would you have believed me?"

"Hell, yes. I worked with Laurette for a year. I know all about empathy. Jesus, Charlie."

"I didn't know that at the time. I thought you'd be . . . well, I thought you'd be like I'd be in your shoes. Skeptical."

"Fine, fine. I get it, and you're right. When Laurette first told me, I didn't believe it. But then I saw her in action." He rubbed at his forehead, thinking. "Her ability wasn't like yours, though. She sensed things. She didn't relive them." He paused. "Who did you see him kill?"

"A woman with curly black hair. I recognized the hair, but I can't place the woman. You know how you see an actor in something and you know you've seen them before but you can't place where? That's how it is. I have no clue how I know her. Part of me thinks she might be Lucy Sheridan, the receptionist at Dick's."

"And why do you think she'd be murdered?"

"She was the anonymous source on my story. She was terrified he would find out and kill her."

"That'd be awfully obvious, too, don't you think?"

"Well, yeah. But I haven't been able to reach her. I went to her house, and it's like she went on vacation."

"Or went into hiding."

She nodded. "Then, yesterday, you know the woman who was bludgeoned with a hammer? I went to where they found her body at a house on Tarpon Bay Street. All I saw was the top of her head. She had curly black hair."

Noah bit back the urge to jump all over her for exploring crime scenes without protection but instead got to his feet. "There's something in the paper about that today." He went inside to retrieve the paper then returned and handed it to Charlie. "She was identified late last night as Louisa Alvarez."

Charlie released a gust of breath. "Not Lucy then. Thank God. But I don't know a Louisa Alvarez." She bent her head to read the story.

When she went still, Noah knew something had clicked. "What is it?"

She looked up at him, her complexion ashen as she raised the paper and pointed at the snapshot of the woman accompanying the story. "I know her. But not as Louisa Alvarez."

Charlie scanned the news story about Louisa Alvarez. The police had confirmed the murder weapon, a ball-peen hammer, and determined that Alvarez had been killed somewhere else and moved to her home. Her breath locked in her lungs when she read what Louisa did for a living.

"Oh."

Noah hovered over her shoulder. "What?"

"She was a maid at the Royal Palm Inn."

"So?"

She raised her head to look at him. "About three weeks ago, this same woman, she said her name was Maria, asked me to meet her. It was very clandestine, kind of silly, really. Over-the-top covert in the back of a dark bar on the not-as-nice side of town. She told me she had information about a blackmail scheme at one of the local hotels. A businessman or politician or some other high-powered, wealthy person would meet his or her lover, or sometimes a prostitute, at this hotel and someone would take pictures. Blackmail pictures."

"Why are some rich people so insanely stupid?"

Charlie gave him a wry smile. "Sex and power make the world go round."

He chuckled. "Well, sex with you makes my world go round, but back to the naughty story."

"So the pictures would be sent to them, and they'd pay to get the disc."

"Classic blackmail."

"And expensive. It's a small town. Lots of people would like to know what mischief the mayor and her aldermen are up to in the wee hours of the morning."

"The mayor is a woman?" Noah said, incredulous.

"I hope your disbelief is because she's a cheating idiot, not because she's a woman."

He grinned. "Well, yeah, of course. I always thought women were smarter than that."

She punched him in the shoulder. "Yeah, right."

"Go on."

"So Louisa aka Maria said she'd tell me the name of the hotel and the people behind the scheme, for a price."

"But you don't pay for information."

"Right. Plus, she wouldn't tell me who she was or how she knew this stuff. She wanted to remain completely anonymous."

"Wait, what about Lucy? You used her as an anonymous source."

"I know her real identity, know her connection to the story. I know how she got the information she shared with me, and she gave me paperwork to back up her claims. Louisa wasn't offering any of that."

"So, what, you told her to forget it? A story like *that*? You had to be beside yourself."

"Yes, but I also know some people will do anything to get back at people they're mad at."

"Such as make shit up."

"Exactly."

"So you never knew which hotel it was or who was behind the blackmail."

"Right. Except now I know there's a good chance it's happening at the Royal Palm, since Louisa was a maid there. And whoever's behind the blackmail must have found out she talked to me and killed her. And then they came after me."

"But if she never told you anything useful . . ."

"Her killer doesn't know that. He might think she told me everything. Or maybe she told him she told me everything, maybe to try to prevent him from killing her. Her version of evidence in a safe-deposit box."

"But all she did was set you up as the next target."

She reached out and grabbed his arm. "We have to go back to the Royal Palm."

"What? No way. The killer found you there."

"Exactly my point."

He pulled away and stood up, backing away. "No way. No fucking way. You're not going back there as bait. I won't let you."

The muscles in her chest expanded at the wild fear that darkened his eyes. He really did love her. God, how cool was that? But instead of letting herself sink into the joy, she forced herself to focus. There'd be time for joy later. "It's the only way."

"We'll find some other way. We'll go to Logan. You can tell him what you told me."

"Do you think he'll believe any of it? How do we explain how I know anything?"

"It's simple. Louisa came to you about a blackmail scheme and now she's dead. You don't have to tell him anything about the empathy. He doesn't have to know that you saw her get killed."

"We have no idea who's behind the blackmail. It could be anybody."

"If it's at the Royal Palm, the police can narrow it down pretty quick, starting with the people who work there."

"But the people who work there might not have anything to do with it. It could be anyone who stays there or has access. And as soon as the police show up asking questions, they'll know we're onto them and flee. We may never know who it was."

"We find the rooms they used and the equipment, we'll have fingerprints, DNA, you name it. Charlie, I do this shit for a living. You have to trust me."

"And what if the fingerprints and DNA don't lead to anyone? What if they're not in the system? What if these are amateurs who let things get out of hand? Obviously, the guy trying to kill me isn't the brightest ninja of his clan, considering how often he's failed."

He jammed a hand through his hair, scrubbed his palms over his face, then looked at her with a new idea. "What about going at it from the angle of the people who were blackmailed? Maybe one of them would have an idea who's doing it."

"And how are we going to get any of those people to admit they were that stupid? They obviously don't even talk to each other or this blackmail thing wouldn't have legs."

He turned his back and stared out at the waves, his hands wrapped tight around the railing. "Damn it, Charlie. I have no right to tell you this, but no. Absolutely, positively no."

"You're right. You have no right to tell me that. But these people almost killed Alex. You turn around and look me in the eye and tell me you wouldn't try to go after them if the same thing happened to someone you care about."

He turned his head toward her but didn't meet her eyes. "You're talking about revenge."

"I don't want to kill anybody, Noah. I want to catch them and make sure they pay for what they've done. I'm talking about justice."

CHAPTER **FORTY-SIX**

Noah forced himself to loosen his grip on the railing before he could rip it away from the porch with his bare hands and beat the ground with it. He didn't like it. God, more than that. He *hated* it. She would get herself killed. He couldn't live if anything happened to her.

But who the hell was he to try to stand in her way? He was the king of justice. And not the neat, tidy kind that she sought, the kind that ended with the bad guys in cuffs perp-walked to prison. His brand of justice involved blood and guts and screaming death. In fact, he didn't have the right to call what he'd done justice. Revenge, plain and simple, served cold. Justice just happened to be a side dish.

He focused on a buoy bobbing among the Gulf's white-tipped waves. That'd been him before he met Charlie. Laurette had managed to start reeling him in, but Charlie sliced through the rope binding him to the anchor resting on the sandy floor. Charlie freed him, and he couldn't help wanting to cling to her for dear life.

"Noah?" Charlie asked.

"I don't think I have to tell you that I don't like it," he said over his shoulder. "And I don't even know what you want to do."

"Frankly, I have no idea. I was hoping you could help me with that part. You're the expert."

He wanted to tell her no fucking way again, yell it at her. Walking back into that hotel was stupid, reckless. But he tamped down that response. He needed to be rational or she wouldn't listen. Emotion had no place here. Only logic. Doing anything except letting Logan deal with it could mean death. Logic.

Turning toward her, he leaned back against the railing and crossed his arms. "In my expert opinion, going back to the Royal Palm without any idea of who's after you would be stupid."

"He's already tried to kill me three times and failed. He's got to be frustrated by now. Frustration makes people sloppy."

His stomach flip-flopped all over the place. "Charlie—"

"I'll start asking questions about Louisa," she cut in. "I'll make it clear I know about the blackmail, maybe hint I know more than I do."

No way, no way. Damn it, no way. He clenched his jaw against the protests in his gut. "I want to be there, too."

"That would be impossible to explain."

"You can tell people I'm your bodyguard."

"And you think I can flush this guy out while I'm walking around with a bodyguard? Come on, Noah." She rose and walked over to him, pausing in front of him to caress the side of his face. Her gaze was soft, loving, as she looked into his eyes and gently smiled. "Especially when the bodyguard looks as badass as you do."

He couldn't stop himself from angling his head into her touch, before forcing himself to step to the side, breaking the contact so he could think. One touch and every cell in his brain zeroed in on how much he wanted to touch her, hold her, love her. Save her. "Don't try to joke your way around me on this. I'm not letting you walk into a potentially dangerous situation without protection."

Charlie dropped her hand. "I don't want to argue about this, but I'm not going to sit around and wait for him to come after me again." Her light brown eyes darkened. "He shot my sister."

He grasped her by the arms, barely resisting the urge to shake her. "This killer is desperate. It's monumentally stupid to make yourself accessible to a homicidal maniac."

"If I hide, this could go on forever. Someone else could get hurt."

"Yeah, like you. The smart thing to do is to approach this methodically, like any other investigation. We question every-one at the hotel, check every room, find the equipment and the method of the blackmail and that will lead us to the bad guy."

"Meanwhile, the bad guy is packing up his stuff and mov-ing to another town so he can do the same thing all over again. Seems to me that dangling the bait he's been after all along is the most efficient way to get this resolved."

"I'm not letting you do this alone. That's all there is to it."

"You can't stop me."

"I can sure as hell try."

"How?"

"Well, first of all, I'd give your buddy Logan a call and tell him what you're up to. I can probably talk him into placing you in protective custody."

"You wouldn't."

"Or he could arrest you for obstruction."

"Obstruction? How?"

"You've withheld information that's important to an ongo-ing investigation."

"Noah, come on."

"No, *you* come on. I just found you. No way in hell am I letting you use yourself as bait. I couldn't live if something happened to you."

Starting to smile, she slipped her arms around his waist and kissed his chest before hugging him close. "You couldn't live, huh?"

He closed his eyes and held her against him. "I'm not kidding."

"I know," she murmured, snuggling her head under his chin. "I feel the same way."

He let out his held breath and stroked a hand over her back, up into her hair. "It's a little crazy, isn't it? How fast . . ."

She smiled up at him. "Which is crazier? That I'm super empathic or that we fell for each other in a week?"

He chuckled, then kissed her slowly, deeply, before resting his forehead against hers. "This Mac Hunter guy. You and he . . ."

She drew back and studied his face. "Don't worry about him. That's over."

"He seemed pretty adamant that he wanted you back."

"He can't have me."

"But you loved him at one time, didn't you? The way you looked at him . . ."

"Mac and I have a history. But that's all it is. History."

Relieved, he nuzzled the curve of her neck. Her skin smelled like salvation. "Before I met you, I wasted a lot of time being an idiot. I'm done with that."

"Thank God," she said, kissing him again.

He lifted her onto the porch railing and nudged her legs apart so he could stand between them, then smoothed his hands over the material of her shorts, his thumbs lightly massaging toward the vee of her thighs. "This is where I want to be."

"Woo-hoo for me," she said, grinning.

He pressed his lips to her throat, and she dropped her head back, hanging onto his shoulders. She smelled of soap and Gulf air, and he breathed in her now-familiar scent, not surprised in the least when blood and heat rushed to his groin.

He gathered her off the railing into his arms, and she wrapped her legs around his waist, settling against his growing erection. A shuddery moan slipped through her lips as she twined her arms around his neck and buried her mouth on his. He headed for the door that led inside.

In the bedroom, he kicked the door shut and lowered her onto the bed, his hands diving for the bare skin under her blouse.

She cupped his face and looked into his eyes. "What if I wear a wire?"

He paused with her left breast under his palm, her nipple

hardening against his skin. What the hell was she talking about? "What?"

She wriggled so that she was centered under the bulge in his pants. "You could sit in your room or in the lobby and listen to what's going on." She arched her hips to press firmly against him. "If I run into trouble, you'd be right . . ." her breath hitched, "there."

He closed his eyes, groaned. "This isn't the right time for this conversation."

She reached between them, undid the button of his jeans and worked her hand inside. "Oh, wow, you're not wearing underwear."

"AnnaCoreen's weren't a good fit," he said through his teeth as her fingers slid over his cock, rubbed. "Oh, God." He stopped being able to think, shocked at how damn good her hand felt stroking the most sensitive, most vulnerable part of him.

"It's the perfect setup," she murmured, kissing his chin, his jaw, teasing his earlobe with her tongue. "I can do what I need to do, and you can be right there, doing what you need to do."

He lifted his hips back, breathing hard, ready to tear her clothes off but holding himself in check. "Let's get something straight, shall we?"

She gave him a feline smile, flexed her fingers around him. "Sure."

He dropped his forehead against hers, concentrated on taking deep, calming breaths. "Please, stop."

"Stop?"

His hips bucked, driving himself against her warm palm. Christ, he already wanted to come. "Yes, stop. Now."

Her fingers paused in their stroking, but she didn't withdraw her hand. Thank God. He swallowed, tried to think straight. No matter how often or how forcefully he refused to help her with her plan, she'd find a way. Wouldn't it be better to be there, ready to crush anyone who tried to harm her, than tempt her to try to go it alone? "We'd have to have a code word."

"Code word?"

"Yes, so that if you got into trouble, all you'd have to do is say the word, or phrase, and I'd come running."

"Just say the words and you'd come?"

He groaned, so desperate to thrust that his head felt light and heavy at the same time. "I'm trying to be serious here."

"So," she moved her fingers in a feathery stroke, "just so we're understanding each other. If I wear a wire while I set myself up as bait, you won't try to stand in my way."

He kissed her temple, her nose, her lips. "You're going to find a way to do it no matter what I say, aren't you?"

She smiled. "Yes."

"Then I'm going to be there every step of the way."

Her smile grew, and she reared up to nip his chin. "I already know what the code phrase can be."

He had to laugh, but it ended on a choked moan when her fingers resumed their assault. "You'd better tell me now before I lose it."

She pressed her lips to his ear and whispered, "Take me."

CHAPTER **FORTY-SEVEN**

Charlie started shaking all over again when she saw all the tubes hooked up to Alex. Noah's hand resting lightly at the back of her neck under her hair kept her grounded, and she focused on that, found strength in his presence.

"The doctor said she'll be okay," he murmured near her ear.

She took a breath and let it slowly out. Right.

They found her parents in a waiting room that must not have been redecorated since the 1980s, considering the square wooden chairs sporting orange seat cushions and the ratty, orange-and-green-striped sofa.

Reed and Elise Trudeau sat on opposite sides of the room, and Charlie marveled that near-tragedy, which usually brought people closer together, seemed to have driven her parents further apart.

Her father, looking exhausted beyond words, rose and walked over to her and Noah. His dark eyes were kind as they looked into Charlie's, his hand steady as he caressed the side of her face. She tensed for a blast of the inside of his head, but all she felt was extreme exhaustion, grinding fear and a burning, twisting pain in the center of her gut.

His voice drew her back to the moment. "You doing okay, Squirt?"

She almost burst into tears on the spot. He hadn't called her Squirt since she'd actually been one. "Hanging in. And you, Dad? How are you?"

He shrugged, cast a weary glance over his shoulder at her mother. "It's been rough."

"How is she?"

He shrugged again. "What can I say? Withdrawn, as usual. Barely holding it together."

"Why do you—" She broke off when Noah's fingers tightened on her skin.

Reed cleared his throat and stood a bit straighter, as though he knew the rest of her question and was relieved he didn't have to answer. "I'm going to make the official announcement tomorrow, but the Sunday newspaper will be the last issue of the *Lake Avalon Gazette*."

She fought to control her spiraling emotion. This is it. He's giving up for good. "I would have thought the recent crime spree would be good for business."

He nodded. "It has been, actually. Nearly all the advertisers have come back, and then some. They know better than to pass up the numbers we're selling. But I'm afraid it's not enough to prop us back up on the edge of the cliff."

And then she did something she hadn't let herself do since she was a teenager: She threw herself into her father's arms. "God, Dad, I'm sorry. I'm so, so sorry."

He stroked her back, her hair, pressed a kiss to the top of her head. "It's not your fault, honey. It was only a matter of time." He set her back from him and smiled down at her. "I heard you got an offer you can't refuse from Simon Walker."

"How do you know about that?"

"He called me. Wanted to make sure he wasn't stepping on my toes in his run at you. I told him to go for it. In fact, I told him not to take no for an answer. It'll be good for you, Charlie. What you've always wanted but I couldn't give you."

Shame swept through her that she hadn't believed in him, that her lack of faith had cost him everything. "You did the best you could, Dad."

"Not quite. I should have done better." He glanced at her mother again, and sadness and regret seemed to settle over him like a heavy wool blanket. "On many levels." Shaking his head, he looked back at her with a sad smile. "At any rate, it's my turn to visit with Alex."

She reached up and kissed his cheek. "I love you," she whispered in his ear.

He hugged her to him. "Love you, too, Squirt."

He started to pull away, but she stopped him with her hands on his arms. "Promise me something."

He tilted his head. "What?"

"That pain in your stomach? You need to get it checked."

His eyes widened. "How—"

"Just trust me, okay? It could be serious."

He cleared his throat, nodded. "I saw the doctor yesterday, actually. It's an ulcer, but we caught it before it got too serious, so don't worry." Then he smiled, a wondering kind of expression crossing his features. "You always surprise me, Charlie."

As he walked away, she noticed for the first time that his gait was that of an old man. She glanced away, toward Noah but not really looking at him. "I broke my father," she said softly.

Noah turned her to face him. "He seems like a pretty strong guy to me."

She cupped his face, kissed him on the mouth. "I'm going to tell my mother about Rena now, okay? You might want to take a hike."

"Are you sure it's the right time?"

"Yep. Her guard might be down. Unlike you, I'm not too noble to take advantage."

"Good luck."

After he walked out of the waiting room, leaving only Charlie and her mother in the room with burnt orange accents, she sat down in the chair next to Elise's. "Hi."

Elise didn't look up from the hands clasping and unclasping in her lap. "Charlotte."

Charlie drew in a breath and looked at the side of her mother's face. "Why do you call me that?"

"It's your name."

"I'm not Charlotte. I'm Charlie."

"Fine. If it'll make you happy, I'll call you Charlie."

Charlie laughed softly. "So all it took for you to want to make me happy was for Alex to be on her deathbed."

Elise stiffened. "This is an inappropriate time to try to agitate me."

Charlie nodded and chewed briefly on her bottom lip. "I know about Rena."

Elise said nothing, but her hands stopped twisting. "Who?"

"Your sister, Mother. Your sister Rena. I know all about her, so there's no point in denying it any longer."

"You can't know," Elise said, her voice low and hoarse. "You can't possibly know."

"You're not the only one who can see inside other people's heads."

"I don't know what you're talking about, and I suggest you shut your mouth before your father returns."

"I'm not going to tell him, Mother. That's your job."

Elise pushed up out of the chair and paced away, her arms wrapped around her middle.

"And just for the record," Charlie said, "I don't think he'd hold it against you. He has plenty of other reasons to leave you, and he hasn't."

Elise stopped pacing and glared at her. "Your sister is in intensive care, hanging onto life by a thread, and all you can do is taunt me."

"I'm not trying to hurt you or taunt you or make you miserable. I'm just trying to talk to you. Can't we just talk?"

"Not about . . . that."

"Why not? Why can't we talk about the truth? What's so horrible about it?"

"It's evil," she breathed. "It's unnatural."

"Evil? Who told you that?"

"No one had to tell me. I figured it out all by myself, and then I ran away and never looked back. I'm not like them. I never want to be like them again."

Charlie stood and went to her mother. "Are there others? Do you have other sisters?"

Elise turned her back, dropped her head back and stared at the ceiling as though beseeching the heavens. "I vowed I would never talk about them. They're not a part of me. Not anymore."

"Rena is sick, Mother."

Elise whirled to face her, horror widening her eyes. "What?"

"She has cancer."

Elise slapped her—

Rena, oh, God, not Rena! All this time. Wasted.

Charlie dropped out of her mother's shock and back into the moment with her ears ringing and her cheek stinging. The same old pain.

Her mother glared at her with fiery eyes. "Do *not* try to manipulate me like that ever again. Ever. Again. I will take your head off. Do you understand?"

Charlie curled her hands into fists at her sides. "I understand that you've wasted a lot of time denying who you are and what you are, and it's made you a very unhappy, very angry woman. Now your sister is dying. You have an opportunity to return to her, to see her before she's gone. What you do with that opportunity is up to you." She took a step toward her mother, forcing her back for a change. "And if you *ever* hit me again, I will hit you back. Do *you* understand?"

Instead of responding, Elise turned on her heel and stalked out of the waiting room.

Charlie's shoulders sagged, and she lowered herself to the closest chair. Could that have gone worse?

God, she missed Alex. And Sam. Where the hell was Sam?

Charlie had left her older sister a message with the latest cell phone Sam had sent her, preprogrammed like the older models before it with a masked phone number that went right to voice mail. While Sam never answered the phone, she always returned Charlie's calls. Sometimes not for a few days, though. And their conversations were always short and to the point. "Nana died in her sleep. Just so you know." No sisterly small talk here.

Charlie tried not to be annoyed with her sister's mysterious absentee act, sometimes wondering if Sam had gone into witness protection without telling any of them. That'd be just like her. And would make sense, considering Sam hadn't returned to Lake Avalon once since she'd fled, not for visits, not for holidays, not even for Nana's funeral. Charlie wondered if she would have come for Alex's funeral.

"You did the best you could."

She raised her head to meet Noah's eyes, surprised to see him standing before her. She struggled to focus on the moment. Oh, yes, she'd failed yet again to get her mother to act like a human being. "Were you listening?"

He nodded. "Just outside the door." He gave her a tight smile. "Wanted to charge the room when she slapped you."

"It's good that you didn't. I needed to handle that."

"I know."

She sighed. "I'm sorry I couldn't do better. For Laurette."

"Hey, you got her to stop denying the connection. That's huge, isn't it?"

She nodded. "Yeah, I guess it is."

He took her hand and drew her to her feet. "If we're going to kick some Royal Palm butt, we need to get going. But, first, there are a few things I'd like to do to you."

CHAPTER **FORTY-EIGHT**

We're good and screwed now. Charlie Trudeau has probably already told the cops everything she knows about Louisa and what we've been up to."

"Then why haven't we been arrested?" he asked, his hand tightening on the phone. The thought of prison terrified him. Everyone knew what happened to young men in prison.

"I have no clue. Maybe with Louisa dead, they want to catch us in the act. They're probably setting up a sting operation as we speak."

"So we take a break, let it all blow over."

She scoffed in his ear, her voice harsh. "You're so young and stupid. It's not going to blow over until they've nailed us. Especially with Charlie Trudeau on the story. You saw what she did to Dick's. That was the point from the start. *Silence* Charlie Trudeau before Louisa's body was discovered. If you'd dumped Louisa in the river instead of taking her home and trying to make it look like a fucking break-in, we'd have been fine. Fucking amateur."

"Well, I'm sorry I let you down with the way I handled my first homicide. But I *am* a fucking amateur. I didn't sign up for murder."

"I don't appreciate your tone."

"You don't appreciate my tone?" His temper slipped a dangerous notch. "Give me a fucking break! I'm so sick of your condescension. I gave you everything. Did everything you wanted. I became a killer—" He strained to turn down the flame of his rage. "You know what? Maybe I'll go to the police myself and tell them all about you, about how you seduced me to get me to do your dirty work. How about that?"

Silence.

Oh, fuck, what had he just done?

When she finally responded, her voice was cold steel. "You were a willing participant."

"I was putty in your hands," he countered.

"Very hard, eager putty."

Rage rushed to the top of his head. Murderous rage. She'd used him, turned sex into an act of manipulation and domination, and then she'd turned around and slept with that other guy, like what they had meant *nothing*.

She laughed in his ear, that low, sexy laugh that used to instantly get him hard. "You enjoyed yourself, and you've reaped the other benefits as well. You have exactly what you wanted. Cold, hard cash."

What good was cold, hard cash when he was at the mercy of this psycho bitch? She'd used sex to turn him into a killer. Fucked him over in so many ways that the last time he'd even been able to get it up was when he'd had his hands wrapped around Charlie Trudeau's throat.

"Are you there?" she purred. "Are you thinking about my mouth on your—"

He slammed the phone down.

CHAPTER **FORTY-NINE**

Noah had her pinned and desperate, her nails digging into his back while her inner muscles clamped around him, eager and primed for release.

"Please."

The thunder of an approaching storm shook the house, as though backing her demand, but he held still, stronger and heavier, able to impose his will on her, if not out of bed, then in. Most definitely in.

She hooked her ankles over his lower back and tried to lift her hips, to get him to move, to finish. Inside, where she was deliciously tight and hot and wet, he felt her flex around his cock, trying to coax him to lose control. Jesus, he wanted to lose control, he was so close. But he enjoyed torturing her, enjoyed making her beg. Hearing his name on her lips in that guttural, frantic moan . . . it undid him.

Slowly, keeping her still with his greater weight, he bracketed the fine bones of her wrists with his long fingers and drew her hands above her head. He flattened them to the bed and sank his fingers between hers, reveling in the hitches in her breath, its uneven rasp in her ears.

"Please, Noah."

More thunder as he closed his eyes, focused. Not yet, not yet. He wanted to live in this moment as long as possible. Charlie open under him. His flesh deep, deep inside her. Connected in the most basic way.

He'd never felt like this before. Never took his time like this. Sex had been about getting off, releasing tension, having a good time. Here, with Charlie, it was so much more than that.

He loved her. The thought of losing her . . .

He rested his forehead against hers, regulating his breathing, waiting for the perfect moment. Until he'd slowed down, stopped just before she peaked for the second time, their lovemaking had been fast and furious, as frenzied as the storm that grew outside. He'd felt desperation riding his heels, fear that this might be the last time. Once he told her . . . she might not want him anymore.

Oh, God, please. He'd shrivel up and die.

Lightning flashed, thunder boomed, Charlie moaned.

"Noah, God, you're killing me here."

Her voice was choked, beyond desperate. And he smiled, pleased that he could do that to her.

He moved, one slow, dragging withdrawal, until his cock popped free and cool air washed over his heat. She whimpered out a protest that slashed straight to his gut. Hold on, baby. Just hold on.

He couldn't remember ever being this hard, this ready to explode. It took all his willpower to hold back. It helped not being inside her, surrounded by all that hot, wet friction.

He shifted his hands, trapping her wrists in one and moving the other down between their sweat-slicked bodies. She moved restlessly, tugging at her hands, groaning at her inability to escape. He held fast, knowing if he let her touch him, it'd be over. And he wasn't done yet.

He grasped his cock and rubbed the tip against her center, knowing exactly where to focus his attention and gritting his teeth at the exquisite sensation. She pushed up with her hips, seeking more.

"In," she gasped. "I want you inside me when I come."

"Are you close?" he asked, and released a strained laugh, because he knew damn well how close she was.

She groaned and reared up to nip at his chin. "Now!"

He responded with a deep, grinding thrust, and as she

started to come, he let himself go, fighting to focus, to watch her come while he came. He wanted to see what his orgasm did to her.

Every muscle in her body went taut under him. He released her hands, and she grabbed his hips as she convulsed, her head arching up off the pillow, the cords in her neck standing out in sharp relief. He thrust and thrust, going deeper, trying to drive himself as deep inside her as he could, and while her head tossed on the pillow and his name burst from her lips, he blasted off.

The world turned white, and he had to fight the need to throw his head back and shout her name, fight to keep his eyes open and on her face, on her expression. He rocked against her as the mind-shattering pleasure rocketed through him, braced above her, looking down and watching, anticipating. God, he couldn't wait. It was going to be a sight to see.

He felt the briefest pause in her body, before what had just blown his mind blew hers.

Her mouth opened,. but no sound came out as her dazed eyes locked on his. For a long moment, her every muscle went taut, her entire body frozen in his moment of blinding, stunning ecstasy. Her head fell back to the pillow, but the rest of her, the rest of her shuddered uncontrollably against him, and he felt her inner muscles tighten and clutch at him all over again, as though experiencing his orgasm had triggered another of hers.

Amazing, he thought, breathing hard, gasping for air. Unfuckingbelievably amazing.

And then her eyes rolled back in her head, and her whole body went limp.

Noah jerked in surprise, scrambled up onto his knees. "Charlie?"

She blinked up at him in the next instant. "Hey."

He leaned over her, studying her dazed and dark eyes. "Did you, uh, did you just black out?"

Her smile grew, and she stretched languidly, groaning. "No. I got seriously light-headed, though."

He sat back on his heels, his heart still trying to ram a hole through his rib cage.

She pushed herself up and leaned forward to kiss him. She tensed when their lips first touched, but then she sucked his bottom lip into her mouth, stroked it with her tongue before letting it go. When she drew back, she grinned at him, her eyes twinkling. "You think you're wielding a lethal weapon, huh?"

He stared at her, realizing that that first moment of tension when she'd kissed him had been a quick trip into his head, into that moment when he'd thought she'd lost consciousness.

She started to laugh, her head thrown back, her whole body shaking.

Seeing her laugh so heartily, so carefree . . . so beautifully naked, snapped him out of his shock. He grabbed her to him and rolled her under his body while she shrieked, then buried his mouth on hers. Her laughter died in her throat, and she met his tongue with the same desperate need that he felt. He smoothed his palm over her breast, unbelievably pleased when her nipple instantly hardened against his skin and she moaned all over again.

He grinned against her mouth, teased her with his tongue. "On the brink of death only a moment ago and you're already begging for more."

Her soft laugh puffed air into his mouth. "I wasn't kidding when I said you were killing me."

"Guess it was just too much of a good thing."

"Oh, there can never be too much of that."

Settling down next to her, he stroked his hand over her hair, tucked a sweat-dampened curl behind her ear, then trailed the tip of his finger over her lips. She nipped at it and smiled so that this heart turned over in his chest. He needed to tell her before one of those trips she took inside his mind told her.

"What are you thinking?" she asked, threading her fingers through the hair above his right ear. "You know I wasn't really in any danger just now, right?"

Sighing, he rolled onto his back and stared up at the ceiling. Outside, the rain finally began to fall in great, slashing sheets.

He took a breath, held it. "There's something I have to tell you."

CHAPTER **FIFTY**

Charlie sat up next to him, no longer surprised at her lack of inhibition with him. Her body felt languid and relaxed, like it did after an hour of yoga. Except for the throb between her legs, the throb in her heart, reminding her what Noah was able to do to her over and over. She had to stop herself from touching him again, closing her hand over the part of him that now lay limp and exhausted against his belly. She'd give him ten more minutes, she thought, and then put her life in his hands again. Assuming he was done telling her whatever he wanted to tell her.

But then he sat up and swung his legs over the edge of the bed. In the next moment, he was standing and pulling on his pants.

"Noah?"

He left his pants unbuttoned, God, so sexy, and drew on his T-shirt, hiding his gorgeous body. Disappointment arced through her. Surely they could take a little more time to play before getting to work. The blackmailing murderers weren't going anywhere, were they? And wasn't he the one who didn't want her to be bait, anyway?

Yeah, so she was stalling. Get over it.

He cocked his head, his expression deadly serious. "I can't focus when you look like that."

She glanced down at her naked self, then grinned back up at him. "Good. My plan is working."

He bent, plucked her underwear off the floor and held it out to her. "Please."

Sighing, she got out of bed. While she dressed, he left the bedroom.

A few minutes later, she found him in the kitchen making coffee. Tension had stiffened his shoulders.

"Are you okay?" she asked. "You're starting to scare me."

He gestured at the table. "Let's sit."

She did as he asked, pressing her hands between her knees to hide the sudden tremble in them. Was it over already? Was he going to tell her he was returning to Chicago, that they were through? She'd already checked on how many newspapers Simon Walker owned in Illinois. Three. One right in a Chicago suburb, as luck would have it. If Noah wanted her to, all she had to do was pack.

Except the thought of leaving Lake Avalon, Alex, her father . . . could she do it? Lake Avalon was her home, her heart. She would have left it a long time ago if she didn't truly love it, didn't truly belong here.

Noah pulled a chair over so that it faced hers. He sat so that their knees nearly touched. She would have scooted forward so that they did, but he seemed to want the distance.

All the easier to leave her.

He bowed his head, as though saying a prayer, before raising it and meeting her eyes. The pain in his gaze shocked her, but when she reached out to grasp his hand, he pulled back. "Just let me . . ." He trailed off, shook his head. "Damn, this is harder than I thought it'd be."

Okay, now he *really* was scaring her. And the nurturing part of her wanted to make it easier for him. "Hey, it's no sweat. We've had a good time, right? Nothing wrong with that."

His eyes narrowed. "What are you talking about?"

"It's over, right? That's what this is about? You're trying to tell me you're going back to Chicago and long-distance relationships are too difficult to deal with, yada, yada, yada. I understand. I've thought about it myself."

"Yada, yada, yada?" he asked, his voice dangerously low.

She shook her head, rolled her eyes. "Come on, Noah.

We're both adults. Did you think I'd be so in love with you already that you'd crush me by leaving? Come on. We're more mature than that. I mean, it's silly to think that this week has been about love anyway. It's way too soon for that. What we've had is good sex. *Great* sex. Wow, it's going to be tough to live without that, isn't it?" She hoped he didn't notice the crack in her voice that gave away how much what she'd just said hurt, how much she hadn't meant a word of it.

He scooted back the chair and stood, paced away. "Well, okay, guess I was . . ."

"Making a big deal about nothing?"

He stopped and faced her, then tilted his head to study her. "That's all bullshit, right? Everything you just said."

She pursed her lips. Wow, he was good. She must have been squinting all over the place. He'd said that was her give-away when she lied. "Uh, well . . ."

He started to grin. "Okay, whew. You freaked me out a little there. What were you doing? Trying to make leaving you easier or something? What the hell?"

"I, uh, well, I thought, you know, that's kind of what I do. Make things easier for other people."

"Well, don't do that with me. Ever. Okay? I mean, yeah, I'll have to leave eventually. I have a job. But not right away. I have several weeks of unused vacation saved up over the years. And even then I don't plan to walk away from you, from this. We'll work something out, okay?"

She heaved out a relieved breath. "Thank God."

His answering grin faded after a few moments, though. "Of course, you're going to want to hear what I have to tell you before you decide you're willing to keep me around awhile longer."

She shrugged, tucked hair behind her ear. "Go ahead. Just try and turn me off."

He sat down again, and she thought for a second that she saw tears in his eyes. Her heart gave an ominous thud. He was scared. She knew better than to reach out to him this time and kept her hands to herself.

He cleared his throat, craned his neck one direction and then the other as though popping kinks. When he finally spoke, his voice was low, shaky. "When I first became a cop, I was paired with another rookie. A few years older than me, but still a rookie. He was also a new father."

She watched his face, alarmed when his complexion washed pale and his anxiety rolled over her in a wave. She moved her hands under her thighs, sitting on them to keep from touching him.

"We'd been partners for about six months when we answered a noise complaint and walked into the middle of a drug deal."

Charlie captured her tongue between her teeth to stifle her gasp. Oh, no. Oh, God, no.

"When all hell broke loose, Brendan took the first hit. He went down while he was calling for backup, and . . ."

His breathing went deep and fast, and sitting on her hands suddenly didn't seem like such a great idea. She started to reach for him. "Noah—"

"I turned to run," he cut in, his tone harsh. "They shot me in the back."

She leaned back in the chair, her heart skipping through several beats. She thought of the scar, the small, circular pucker of flesh on his lower back. He'd been shot. *Shot.* Her head started to spin.

"Have you ever seen that *RoboCop* movie from the eighties?" he asked.

She swallowed against a surge of nausea. "I couldn't make it through the beginning."

"That's what those bastards did to Brendan. Two held him down, and the third used a shotgun to shoot off his hands, one at a time."

She closed her eyes, gripped the seat of the chair with perspiring hands.

"Then his feet. I can still hear him screaming. Begging. And all I could do was lay there and watch, knowing that I was next. Knowing that instead of helping him, I tried to run. Lucky for me, our backup arrived before it was my turn."

He got up abruptly, knocking the chair back a foot, and turned his back to her, bracing his hands on the counter as though he needed the support to keep from folding. "After I got out of the hospital, I found out that the guys who did it were informants on a huge investigation involving the DEA, FBI, ATF, you name it. In other words, they couldn't be touched. So I hunted them down myself and . . . I killed them. Every one of them. Made it look like they killed each other, and then I walked away and never looked back."

Charlie stared at his back, shocked.

He faced her, his green eyes piercing. "That's the man I am, Charlie. I didn't trust the justice system to work, and I didn't even give it a chance. I wanted them to pay, clear and simple. And I made them pay. I don't feel bad about it. If anything, I feel bad that I don't feel bad. What I did was wrong. I defied everything I stand for as a cop. I did the *wrong* thing, and I'm not sure you can live with that."

She flinched back, shocked further. "You think I—"

"I think you stand for truth and justice and doing the right thing. I'm the dirty cop you write a page-one story about and win a Pulitzer."

She said nothing for a long moment. So he'd already decided how she would react. Did he really think things in her head were that black-and-white, no room for shades of gray? That he'd tell her what happened, and she'd instantly condemn him?

Mac hadn't given her the benefit of the doubt, either. And her mother assumed she was trying to hurt her when she'd told her about Rena's cancer. What was it about her that made others think she was so cold?

"Please say something."

She shifted her gaze to Noah's. He looked absolutely terrified of what she would say or do next, as though any moment she would yank the lever that dropped the floor out from under his feet and left him dangling from the noose. And that made her feel sick inside. He expected harsh judgment from her. And oh, it hurt.

"I . . ." She hesitated, shook her head. Lost—she was so lost. "I don't know what to say."

He nodded, his lips tightening into a thin line. "That's okay. Uh, maybe we should take some time . . . you know, think about things."

If that's what he needed . . . Oh, God, she didn't want that. She wanted *him*. Forever and always. Faced with losing him, it hit her like a mallet between the eyes: She loved this man. She didn't want to live without him. But could she live with what he'd done? A part of her could understand why, but he was at least partially right. If she'd discovered Logan had done something similar, it'd be a big story about a vigilante cop and justice run amok.

"Charlie?"

She focused on him. He was waiting for her to agree to the we-should-take-some-time thing. And maybe that was the answer. Time. She gave a halfhearted nod. "Okay, sure."

He gestured lamely toward the hall. "I'm going to hop in the shower, then I'll run out and get the stuff we'll need to wire you up before we go to the Royal Palm."

She nodded again. Don't go. Please don't go yet. "Okay."

He gave her a tight smile, his eyes miserable, then walked out.

Charlie's shoulders sagged, and she looked down at her hands tangled on her knees. That hadn't gone well. And she had no idea what to do about it.

She heard the shower come on, and her heart felt leaden. She shouldn't have let him walk away like that, but she didn't know what else to do. She couldn't look him in the eye and tell him she thought it was okay that he'd killed three men in cold blood. It wasn't okay. No matter how much she might understand what had driven him.

It wasn't okay.

Regardless, she loved him.

Pushing up out of the chair, she headed toward the bathroom.

She shed her clothes outside the door then eased inside. Steam rose in clouds, parting for her as she opened the shower door and stepped inside. Noah, who had his hands braced on the wall, the water hitting him full in the face, turned toward her just as she slid her arms around his waist and pressed a kiss to his bare chest. His eyes were wide as he looked down at her. Hopeful.

She smiled up at him, holding his gaze, as she kissed his chest then ran a tongue around his nipple until his breathing quickened and his desire for her nudged against her belly. His hands caught in her hair, and groaning, he backed her against the wall, lifting her until her legs wrapped around his waist.

He sank into her with a sigh.

CHAPTER **FIFTY-ONE**

"Can you hear me now?"

Charlie turned her back to the mostly empty lobby and lifted a hand to her right ear. The earbud tucked inside was more comfortable than she'd expected, and Noah had said the microphone he'd tucked inside her cleavage under her tank top was sensitive enough to pick up the sound of her heartbeat.

"Yes, just like I could hear you three minutes ago," she said, careful to speak normally as he'd instructed.

Strain laced his chuckle inside her head, uncertainty. He didn't know where they stood, and she couldn't blame him. She didn't know, either. "Where are you?" he asked, all business.

She swallowed against the ache in her throat. Just focus and get this over with. Deal with relationship stuff later. "Being visible in the lobby before I go snooping through supply closets."

"It's unlikely that you'll find any damning evidence that easily."

"I know that. All I want is for the bad guy to find me snooping and freak out."

He groaned in her ear.

"Okay, not *freak out*, really. What I meant was 'get sloppy.' Are you comfortable where you are?"

"Oh, yeah. Sitting at the bar with a rum-free Coke in front of me. You can join me anytime and we can go upstairs."

As if sex would fix what was wrong. They'd already tried that, and while it had still been mind-blowingly amazing, surrounded by the steam of hot water, cool tile against her back and the hot, muscular length of Noah against her front, they weren't fixed. Their easy camaraderie had cooled like the water in the shower. Banter felt forced. She didn't even know how to respond to his teasing suggestion. Oh, God, was this it? Was it already over?

She closed her eyes and pressed her lips together. Way to focus, Chuck.

Noah's voice hummed in her ear: "What're you doing now?" More strained now. She hadn't responded to his teasing, and he wasn't taking it well.

She cleared her throat. "I'm standing here talking to myself."

"Where's here?"

"Still the lobby."

"Okay, well, as soon as you change floors, you need to let me know so I can position myself where I can get to you quickly."

She breathed out a sigh. "This is a dumb idea, isn't it? You're just humoring me with this microphone business."

"You never know. It might work."

"So if you were a blackmailing murderer, where would your center of operations be?"

"The basement."

"This is Florida. We don't have basements."

"Really?"

"The ground's too soft and wet."

"Hmm, I like the sound of that."

Her stomach clenched at the rasp in his voice. He could so easily turn her on. His voice in her head, his hum in her ear, the thought of him listening to her heartbeat. "Focus, please," she said, for his sake as well as hers.

"So if there's no basement, where's the boiler room and air-conditioning?"

"Probably in a back room somewhere. You know, that's not a bad idea. I'll find the boiler room." She lowered her voice. "Breaker one-nine, birdie's leaving her nest. Repeat, birdie's leaving her nest. Approaching Stairwell Number One. Charlie, out."

His chuckle was warm, easy in her ear, sounding like it had before he confessed his sins. "Don't mock law enforcement, missy. You won't like the consequences."

She laughed softly, her shoulders finally relaxing. Okay, they were back. "Oh, I bet I'll like them very much indeed if you're the one—" She broke off as she pushed through the door marked STAIRS.

"Charlie? What is it?"

She stood in the stairwell, surrounded by freshly painted walls the same gray as the dots dancing all over her vision. The wet-paint smell overwhelmed her senses, and she saw again the blunt end of a hammer smashing into skull.

"Charlie? Answer me."

The alarm in his voice snapped back the dots. "I'm okay, I'm okay."

"What just happened?"

"I know where Louisa Alvarez was killed."

And then she saw the body.

CHAPTER **FIFTY-TWO**

harlie? Answer me, damn it!"

He could hear her heart racing—or was that his heart?—as he tore out of the bar and through the lobby. Hotel guests either stopped in their tracks to stare at him or stumbled out of his way.

He burst through the door marked STAIRS and looked wildly around. Where the fuck was she? "Charlie!"

A few steps in, and he turned his head to the left and saw her kneeling under the stairs where he'd seen the maintenance guy stash his bucket and mop the day the hotel manager had reamed his ass for questioning her guests.

Charlie wasn't moving, just sitting there on her knees in her white tank top and khaki shorts, staring at something on the floor.

"Charlie?"

He was at her side in three long strides, and froze when he saw what she was looking at. The hotel manager. Donna Keene. With a gun in her hand and the top of her head blown off.

And then he saw Charlie's hand on the woman's wrist, saw that she was *touching* her.

"Are you crazy?!?"

He surged forward, but before he could grab her and haul her back from the corpse, she scrambled away from him. In the next instant, she pressed back against the wall opposite the stairs, her knees up to her chest and her eyes wild.

Noah lowered himself to his knees in front of her, his frantic heart tearing up the inside of his chest. He raised his hands in front of him, placating, and they shook like those of a drug addict long overdue for a hit. "It's okay, it's okay. I'm sorry. I didn't mean to grab you like that."

She blinked, shook her head in slow motion, then focused on him.

So pale, he thought. So pale and tired and scared. "Are you okay?"

She closed her eyes and swallowed, nodded.

Acutely aware of the dead woman just behind him, he kept his gaze on Charlie, gauging, assessing. What had she seen? From the glimpse he'd had of the body, Donna Keene had been there several hours. He could smell the blood, and other things, but it wasn't horrible yet, and the stairwell was cool, air-conditioned, still heavily scented by fresh paint. Anyone using these stairs probably wouldn't have thought much about the dead-person smell for at least a few more hours.

Had Charlie seen the way she died? Lived her final moments?

She drew in a shuddery breath, let it slowly out. Any hint of color had yet to return to her cheeks.

"Can you stand?" Noah asked, reaching out a hand.

She looked at his hand but didn't take it, and he knew why. He lowered it and got to his feet, taking a step back as she used the wall to push herself up and stand on her own. Her fingers trembled as she tucked her hair behind her ear.

Noah gestured at the door. "I'll call Logan from the lobby."

She nodded and preceded him through the door into the jungle of the lobby with its multitude of green plants and guests milling around as they returned from dinner or got ready to go. Some of them cast curious looks at Noah and Charlie, probably because Charlie wasn't walking especially steady and Noah was behind her, his hand hovering just behind her elbow, ready to reach out and catch her if her knees gave way. In his earbud, her heart beat fast and erratic.

Once she was safely seated in a wicker chair, her back to the stairwell door, Noah fished out his cell phone and called

Logan. In this position, he could keep one eye on Charlie and the other on the door to the stairs in case anyone decided now would be a good time to get some cardio rather than take the elevator.

"Logan."

"Yeah, it's Noah Lassiter. I'm at the Royal Palm. We've got a body in a stairwell."

"What? Are you kidding me?"

"Nope. Looks like suicide. Hotel manager. She's been there at least a few hours."

"I'm on my way."

Noah flipped the phone closed and stashed it, then knelt before Charlie, still careful not to touch her. She had her eyes tightly closed and her arms wrapped around her middle, visibly shivering. When he stripped off his T-shirt and draped it around her shoulders, she opened her eyes and quirked an eyebrow at him.

God, he wanted to touch her so much. And he wanted to shake her. What the hell had she been thinking? Touching a dead woman. Jesus!

A tremulous smile curved her lips. "Hi."

He smiled back, relieved to see her eyes had cleared, and some pink replaced the gray in her complexion. "Hi."

"You want to kick my ass."

His smile widened. Well, duh. "Yeah, kind of." And then he turned serious. "But I wouldn't. You know that, right?"

She tilted her head to one side and back, swallowing convulsively. "Yes. I . . . you just startled me."

He clenched his fist on his knee to keep from reaching for her. "Probably as much as you startled me. What were you thinking?"

"I guess I wasn't. I just thought . . ."

"What? What did you think?"

She shook her head, dropping her gaze to his bare chest, where it stayed fixed, though not with the heightened awareness she'd shown in the past, or that he would have preferred. "I don't know," she murmured. "Curious, I guess."

"Jesus, Charlie." He smoothed his palms over his thighs. Get a grip. Be a cop. "Logan's on his way." As if she hadn't been sitting there while he'd made the call.

"I didn't see anything," she said softly.

He sat back on his heels and dragged a hand through his hair. Son of a bitch. Son of a *bitch*.

"Maybe she's been dead too long." Shuddering, she hunched her shoulders under his shirt. "She was cold."

He thought of how she'd reacted when she'd relived his shooting, how her head had snapped back and she'd gone catatonic for several moments. And that had been for a bullet that *grazed* him. He hadn't seen what had happened to her when Alex was shot, but what would it do to her to relive a bullet that blew off the top of someone's head? His stomach lurched, threatened to heave on the spot. Maybe it could kill her.

"I'm sorry," she said. "I know I shouldn't have."

He shoved to his feet and paced a few steps away, not sure he could keep himself from grabbing her and wrapping her up tight against him, waffling between absolute fucking relief and the need to shake some sense into her. *Damn it*. He shoved another hand through his hair. If he didn't vent, he was going to explode, and it wouldn't be pretty.

"You're damn right you shouldn't have," he ground out. "That was stupid, Charlie. You still don't know exactly what you're dealing with with this empathy crap, and you reach out and touch a dead woman? *Shit*."

"Nothing happened."

He turned to her, glad to hear the strength returning to her voice. Maybe his rage was good for something after all. The color in her cheeks had risen, and her eyes were bright.

"You know that *now*," he said, not willing to let it go just yet. Not until she realized how serious this was. "I could have found you dead on the floor. You realize that, right? That reliving someone *dying* could kill you?"

"It didn't."

"Not this time. Who knows what could have happened if she'd blown her head off in the past ten minutes?"

"I get it, Noah. Okay? I get it."

He dropped his head forward, took several deep breaths. Get a grip. Get a fucking grip. But he was still shaking. He couldn't help it. Losing her . . . Jesus, he couldn't even think it. "I'm sorry. I'm . . . you scared me. You scared the living shit out of me."

"I didn't mean to."

"You looked gray, Charlie. You weren't answering me."

She shuddered again. "She . . . well, the top of her head was gone." Sighing, she shook her head. "Second dead-person brains in two days."

He dropped his shoulders, drew in a long breath. Heart rate finally slowing, he dropped into the chair beside her. "Okay. I think I'm going to live now."

She smiled sideways at him. "I really am sorry."

His fingers twitched, itching to grasp her hand and squeeze. "Me, too. I kind of blew a gasket, didn't I?"

"It's okay. It's nice to know you care that much."

"You know I do, right? I'd be lost if I lost you. You already feel like a part of me."

Her smile turned soft and wry. "You fall fast."

"Never faster or harder."

"I . . . before, when you told me about your partner . . ."

He drew back a little, not wanting to go there. Never wanting to go there again, not when it drove her away from him, made her distant. "That's not—"

"I was hurt," she cut in. "And disappointed that you didn't trust me enough to understand, that you expected me to condemn you. I know you, Noah. I've been inside your head. I *know* you."

He watched her wet her lips, and his heart jerked around, unsure what to do.

"I know it seems like I see only in black-and-white," she went on, "but I understand shades of gray. I understand what it means to be human and flawed, to do terrible things without thinking because you're so driven to right a wrong. I'm guilty of that myself." She paused, took a breath. "Yes, what you did was very wrong, but I . . . I know you. I know who you are on the inside . . . and I can live with it because I love you."

He blinked, his brain stunned into white, airless silence. She loved him. She fucking loved him! He would have lunged at her and kissed her down to her soul if he'd been able to do it without forcing an unpleasant flash on her.

Smiling, as if knowing exactly what he was thinking, she held her hand out and wiggled her fingers. "Let's just get it over with."

Still, he hesitated. He wanted to protect her. Always protect her.

"What," she prodded, "you're not going to touch me now? Ever?"

He cleared his throat and his head. Tried to think of a way to spare her. "Maybe it wears off after a while."

"We're both going to have to get used to this, you know. You can't go around refusing to touch me because you're afraid of what I'll feel."

He gave her a teasing grin. "Maybe I could spend some time in the men's room replacing it with something infinitely more pleasant."

She laughed softly. "Much as I like that idea, this is quicker and easier. Give me your hand."

Reluctantly, he put his hand in hers.

She stiffened, and her eyes went blind. He tightened his fingers on hers and stood to place a soft kiss on her mouth, felt the instant she came back to herself because her lips softened under his, parted. As his tongue stroked against hers, her sigh passed through his lips.

Drawing back, he caressed the side of her face with the back of his hand. So smooth and warm and alive. He'd never get enough of touching her.

"Wow," she breathed. "You really wanted to kick my ass."

But then she opened her eyes and gave him a radiant smile that flipped his gut on the spot.

CHAPTER **FIFTY-THREE**

Logan joined them, carrying a plastic-bag-encased piece of paper covered with scrawled writing. "Donna Keene left us a suicide note."

"What does it say?" Noah asked.

"She fesses up to all kinds of bad voodoo, including murder and blackmail. Says she's been blackmailing the high-profile guests of the Royal Palm Inn. One of the maids, Louisa Alvarez, found her out and told her she blew the whistle to Charlie Trudeau. Says she killed Louisa then tried to kill Charlie to silence her before Louisa's body could be found because she feared Charlie would know why Louisa was killed. She also took a shot at Noah, because he kept getting in the way when Donna went after Charlie. Once Louisa's body was discovered, she figured it was all over and killed herself."

Charlie sank back in the chair, the shiver coursing through her making her wish she hadn't handed Noah's warm shirt back to him. "She was the ninja?"

Logan nodded. "We found the costume in her suite upstairs."

"I could have sworn the ninja was a guy," she said. "He was so strong."

Noah put his hand on the back of her neck, lightly massaged. "Donna Keene was thin, but she could have had muscle mass."

"I just . . . you'd think I would have known the attacker was a woman. You know, something . . . like I would have noticed she had breasts or something."

"She might have strapped herself down," Logan said. "Who knows what crazy people do?"

"So it's over," Charlie said. She felt lighter all of a sudden, relief a large, helium-filled balloon beneath her feet.

Noah gestured at the note in Logan's hand. "May I?"

Logan handed it over. "Coroner says she's been dead about six hours."

"Why didn't anyone hear the gunshot?" Noah asked. "It would have echoed in that stairwell like a son of a bitch."

"Good question," Logan said. "Maybe she did it during the thunderstorm. The thunder was pretty vicious."

"I can't believe she did it under the stairs," Charlie asked, unable to wrap her brain around it. "What if a kid found her?"

Logan said, "Some people are dramatic that way. They want to make an impression."

"Sometimes we just can't explain what killers are thinking when they do what they do," Noah added.

Charlie shuddered. So many lives caught in the cross fire. Laurette. Alex. Noah.

Noah handed the letter back to Logan then put his arm around Charlie's shoulders. "So I guess this means you don't have to play bait after all."

Logan's forehead creased. "Uh, bait? What's that about?"

"Nothing," Charlie said quickly. "We'll get out of your hair and let you finish up here."

"Before you go, any word on Alex?" Logan asked.

Charlie smiled at him, patted his shoulder. "She's doing really well. I'm hoping to get to talk to her when I go back to the hospital."

He smiled, his relief as palpable as hers had been. "Excellent. Tell her hi for me."

"I will."

CHAPTER **FIFTY-FOUR**

He let himself into the bastard's house through the unlocked back door. Amazing the level of trust in Lake Avalon, as though nothing bad ever happened here. If he weren't the one causing all the recent trouble, he'd have been locking and double-locking his doors at night.

Hearing the clink of glass in the kitchen, he crept across the floor in that direction.

After this, he had only one more loose end. Charlie Trudeau.

He planned to take his time with that one, expected she would provide exactly what he needed to get back on track, to get himself unfucked-up.

Killing the hotel bitch had helped. She'd actually smirked at him when he'd pointed the gun at her, smirked and laughed, said he couldn't even maintain an erection to fuck her, he certainly didn't have the balls to pull the trigger.

He showed her.

He wasn't weak. He wasn't stupid. He was strong. Ironically, because of her. She'd shown him that killing wasn't anything to be afraid of. Before he'd put her down, he'd killed twice, and no lightning bolts had shot out of the clouds.

Killing her was easy. Made him invincible. She couldn't manipulate him anymore. She couldn't make him do her dirty work anymore.

Now it was *his* dirty work.

Now all he had to do was clean up the mess, fix what was wrong with him, what she *made* wrong, and move on.

First, clean up the mess.

When she'd realized he really would pull the trigger, she'd started to babble. About the other guy. That bastard. "You think I wanted him for sex? I used him for insurance. I told him all about you. Everything you've done, everyone you've blackmailed, including me. I made sure he knew it was you and only you. If something happens to me, he'll know who and why, and he'll go to the police."

Rage had burst and burned behind his eyes like fireworks in furious, glittering red.

He'd shot her. Covered the gun with her own pretty pillow and shot her. So easy. So powerful.

And then he'd put her where someone would find her soon, somewhere where he knew she would hate to be found, a place symbolic of everything about him she held in contempt, and made it look like suicide. So easy again. The cops here were too stupid to look further once they read the suicide note.

Stopping in the kitchen door, he gazed at the guy kneeling in front of the kitchen sink. He had something cradled in his hands. What was it?

He angled his head, saw it was a bottle of booze. The guy seemed to be trying to decide whether to open it and chug.

He tightened his fingers on the handle of the pipe wrench.

Better drink fast.

CHAPTER **FIFTY-FIVE**

Charlie sat at Alex's bedside, her fingers linked with her sister's and her head down on the side of the bed near Alex's hip. God, she was tired. And her head was doing its usual clumsy tango, a steady bass line beat in her temples. Tylenol hadn't even taken the edge off. Hopefully, a little time with her head down and her eyes closed would help.

Noah had dropped her at the hospital, then took off to take care of a mysterious errand, promising he'd catch up with her at her place in a couple of hours.

She couldn't believe it was over. Just like that. Bad guy committed suicide, leaving a note packed with confessions. Anticlimactic, to say the least. Amazingly tidy, really.

She felt a bit cheated. The woman who'd shot Alex was dead, and Charlie didn't get to make her suffer for it. Inflicting some suffering would have made her feel better—or maybe not. She had no idea. She was just plain tired.

And then she jerked her head up and blinked against the bright light, disoriented and muzzy, surprised that she must have drifted off. The beeping alarm that had awakened her drew her gaze to the heart monitor. Alex's pulse had spiked to over 100.

All fogginess vanished as Charlie lunged for the door and whipped it open. "Nurse! Doctor! Somebody!"

When she saw a nurse come running, she returned to Alex's bedside. The alarm had stopped, and a glance at the monitor told her Alex's heart rate was already slowing.

Charlie took her sister's hand again, her own pulse racing

as the nurse hurried into the room and started pushing buttons on the bedside equipment.

"What happened?" Charlie asked when the nurse said nothing.

"Looks like she's waking up."

"But her heart rate . . ."

"It's okay now. Blood pressure's elevated but not dangerously. Let's just take a minute and see what happens."

Charlie fixed her gaze on Alex's face, willing her to wake up, to be okay.

Alex's lips moved, and her eyelids fluttered. She said something, but it was unintelligible.

Charlie got on her knees beside the bed and stroked Alex's cheek. "Hey, Alex, you in there?"

Alex turned her head, tried again to open her eyes. "Charlie?"

Charlie clasped her sister's hand in both of hers, not caring that tears already slipped down her cheeks. Happy tears. "Welcome back. You're okay. You're doing great. Don't worry, okay?"

"Dead woman."

Charlie leaned closer, barely able to hear the soft, raspy words. "What?"

"Dead woman . . . under stairs . . ."

A gasp escaped Charlie's lips. How did Alex know about that? "Don't worry about that. Everything's okay."

Alex moistened her lips. "Thirsty."

On cue, the nurse handed Charlie a cup with a straw. "Thanks," Charlie said to the nurse, then held it for Alex. "Here's some water."

Alex sipped some, still blinking as though trying to focus. "What happened?"

"Ninja with a gun delivered our room service," Charlie said lightly. "We won't be staying there anymore."

A small smile curved Alex's lips. "You're okay?"

"I'm great now that you're talking to me."

"Noah?"

"He's great, too."

"You like him."

Charlie laughed, and more tears slid free. "Yeah."

"Noah and Charlie sitting in a tree . . ."

"Why am I surprised that you're able to be a smart-ass even when you're only semiconscious?" She brushed at the hair on Alex's forehead. "How're you doing? Any pain?"

Alex sighed. "Good drugs." She opened her eyes wide, looked at Charlie with absolute coherence for a short moment. "You should get some . . . for that headache."

Charlie swallowed the renewed swell of emotion that clogged her throat. "You worry about you for now, okay?"

Alex's eyes drifted closed.

After a few minutes of listening to her steady breathing, Charlie looked at the nurse, who nodded. "She's going to be fine," the woman said. "But she needs her rest."

Charlie gave her a grateful smile, pressed a kiss to the top of her sister's head then walked out to deliver the good news to their parents.

She was just outside the room door when it hit her that there was no way Alex could have known about the dead hotel manager under the stairs. Or even that Charlie had a headache. Only if . . .

Charlie stopped dead and glanced down at her hand. She'd been holding Alex's when her sister had regained consciousness.

Had Alex awakened to an empathic flash?

CHAPTER **FIFTY-SIX**

Charlie let herself into her house and left the heavier door open so fresh air could come through the screen into the stuffy place. In the kitchen, she paused to listen to the silence. Atticus ambled in from the other room and sat his butt down to stare at her, looking ambivalent at her return, and perhaps a bit miffed at her prolonged absence.

"I'll make it up to you, Fur Butt," she said and dropped her bag onto a kitchen chair. "I'm sure you got plenty of attention from Mrs. Wiggs." The older woman from across the street loved to come in and hang out with Atticus when Charlie was out of town or had to work late.

She squatted beside him as he rubbed his soft, silky fur against her calf. She massaged his ears the way he loved, and purring promptly commenced.

After some quality time loving up the man of the house, Charlie opened the patio doors and a few windows to let in fresh air, then went into the office and looked up Simon Walker's number. She'd made a decision about his offer and wanted to discuss it with him. When she picked up the phone, she noticed the light blinking on Nana's old answering machine. The glowing red number on the ancient device she hadn't been able to bring herself to get rid of told her she had seven messages.

First, she had to call Simon Walker, before she lost her nerve.

When she got his voice mail, she said, "Hello, Mr. Walker, this is Charlie Trudeau. After giving your generous offer some serious thought, I have a proposition for you. Of the journalism kind."

She hung up the phone and smiled. Maybe he'd go for it, maybe he wouldn't. But she'd give it a shot and see what happened. Still smiling, and feeling like maybe, just maybe, she'd get it right this time, she pushed the "play" button on the answering machine.

First message, at 8:06 from two nights before: "Charlie, it's Mac. Could you please call me at work?" Simple, to the point, a conciliatory note in his voice. Maybe he'd finally forgiven her.

Second message, at 9:13 the same night: "Hi, Charlie, this is Lucy Sheridan. I heard from a neighbor that a woman who sounded like you was looking for me. I took one of those last-minute cruises to the Caribbean. You know, to get away from everything and refresh. I . . . well, I guess I was a little scared of what might happen, and I ran away. At any rate, I'm home now if you still need to talk to me." Well, that was a relief. Dick was still a dick, but he apparently wasn't a murderous dick.

Third message, at 10:11, still the same night: "Hey. Mac again. Just wanted to let you know I'm headed home from work now. You can reach me at home or on my cell, okay? Um, okay, well, I hope to hear from you soon. I, uh, left a message on your cell, too." He followed that up with a soft laugh, as if he'd embarrassed himself.

Fourth message, 11:03: "It's me again. Look, I know I've been a jerk. A total jerk. And I'm sorry. But I really need to talk to you. Please call me. It doesn't matter what time it is." His tone carried a hint of desperation. And he sounded like maybe he'd been drinking.

Fifth message, 12:05 A.M.: "I'm an idiot, okay?" Definitely drunk, his words slurring. "A stupid fucking idiot. I . . . when we ran into each other at the hotel, and . . . you were right. I'd been with someone. Donna Keene. I . . . I ran into her and she was lonely and I was lonely and we drank too much and . . . well, I kind of liked her, and now I find out she was a nutcase and blackmailing half of Lake Avalon and trying to kill you and now she's dead. I think she seduced me to try to find out where you were so she could go after you again. But I didn't know where you were, thank God. I didn't know. But, I mean, how fucking stupid am I? Letting you go was the dumbest thing anyone could have done on the planet. I don't know what I was thinking. I *wasn't* thinking. Well, yeah, I was thinking, but not about what it would be like not to have you beside me. I miss you, Charlie. God, I miss you so fucking much. I miss everything about us. Everything. I want to try again. I want us back. I'll fix what I did. Whatever you want, I'll do it. Just tell me what to say, what to do, and I'll do it. I . . . I need you, Charlie. You're my compass. Without you I do really stupid shit. Charlie, please—" The message cut off with a long beep.

Sixth message, at 8:39 yesterday morning: "It's me . . ." His voice paused for a long moment, and she could hear his uneven breathing. "I . . . I'm . . . damn it, I'm sorry. I got drunk, and I said some things. I mean, I meant them, I think. But, look, I'm sorry, okay? I just need to talk to you, to clear the air. I'm . . . I'm kind of not in a good place right now. Please call me. *Please*." Voice thick and sleepy but sober and probably smarting from a hangover. She felt sorry for him, wished she'd been there to take his call. She missed him, too, more than she'd expected.

She picked up the phone to call him back.

"I wouldn't bother."

She whirled toward the voice behind her, surprised and baffled to see a young man standing in the door of her office. He looked no more than twenty-two, with thick, brown hair and dark brown eyes. Slim yet muscular, like he worked out a lot or did physical labor for a living. His smile, friendly, even a little apologetic, confused her at first but calmed her initial burst of alarm. Had he entered the wrong house?

"Can I help you?" she asked. So weird to ask that of a man who'd walked in uninvited, but he didn't look threatening or sinister. He looked like one of those fresh-faced college kids selling magazines to win an exotic trip or a Mormon boy making sure all the souls in the neighborhood were in good repair.

He nodded, that friendly, amenable smile still in place. "I think you can, yes."

CHAPTER **FIFTY-SEVEN**

Noah set down his coffee. "So you think it's doable."

Logan nodded, toying with the slim plastic straw he'd used to stir his own coffee. "I don't see why not. You should probably run it by Charlie, though."

"Of course. I just—"

Logan's ringing cell phone cut him off. "Hang on." A moment later, the phone pressed to his ear, he said, "Logan." He listened for a few moments before his brow started to furrow and his eyes went dark. "Are you sure?" Another long pause. "Run it through the database and call me right back."

He snapped the phone closed and shoved back from the table, his tan already faded into an ashen hue. "Where's Charlie?"

Noah felt his head snap back in shock. "She's probably home by now. Why?"

"That was the lab. Donna Keene's body was moved after she was shot. She didn't kill herself."

Noah got to his feet, fear spiking through the top of his head as Logan raced for the door at a dead run.

Noah fumbled his cell phone out as he followed on Logan's heels. Charlie's phone was ringing in his ear when he realized something else Logan had said. "What are they running through the database?"

"Hairs inside the balaclava found in Keene's suite don't belong to her. If we're lucky, we'll get a DNA match."

"Fuck," Noah said under his breath. He shouldn't have left Charlie alone. Damn it, he shouldn't have let her out of his sight. He remembered Donna Keene's body under the stairs at the Royal Palm. There'd been no blood spatter. Why the hell hadn't he noticed that before? But he knew why. He'd been completely focused on Charlie, completely wigged out because she'd tried to get an empathic flash off of a corpse.

"Come on, Charlie, answer."

Logan didn't argue when Noah got into the squad car with him.

As the engine roared to life, Logan glanced sideways at Noah. "Anything?"

Noah shook his head. "No answer," he croaked, dread obliterating his voice.

Logan set his mouth into a grim, determined line. "Where did you see her last?"

"Hospital with Alex. She would have left by now, though. We were meeting at her house in"—he checked his watch—"half an hour."

"Call and check anyway."

Noah's hand shook as he squinted at the keypad on his phone. Don't lose it, don't lose it. "I don't know the number."

Logan rattled it off. "That's direct to Alex's room."

A minute later, a man's voice answered. "Hello?"

"Is Charlie there?" Noah asked.

"May I ask who's calling?"

He bit into his lip. Just answer the fucking question! "Noah Lassiter. Is this Mr. Trudeau?"

"Yes. Hello, Mr. Lassiter. Charlie left about half an hour ago. You can probably reach her at home by now."

"Thank you," Noah said, and clicked off the call. He felt sick. Seriously ill. "She should be home."

"Then she's in the shower," Logan said, nodding emphatically. "Let's not panic."

Noah sat back and clenched a fist on his knee, his other hand curled around the safety handle near his head as Logan yanked the squad car into a sharp turn at tire-squealing, fishtailing speed.

She's in the shower. That worked. That made sense. She'd want to wash away the stench of Donna Keene's death. They'd get to her house, and she'd be standing in the kitchen in a towel, her silky hair damp around her shoulders, droplets of water glimmering in the hollow of her pale throat. He'd have to move fast to keep Logan from getting an eyeful.

Please, God. Whatever you want, you've got it.

Logan didn't bother pulling into Charlie's driveway. He slammed on the brakes in front of her house, sending the car into a sideways skid that wasn't completely finished before Noah scrambled out and raced for her front door. He heard Logan right behind him, heard him shout something. His heart pounded, jackhammered, in his ears, nothing but white noise in his head and a desperate, desperate chant: Please, please, please. Whatever it takes.

The front door was locked. Good sign, but she didn't come running at his frantic pounding.

Logan started toward the side of the house and the back door that led into the kitchen, and Noah tore after him, nearly losing his balance in the slippery grass.

Logan had his gun out when he stopped and pressed his back to the peach stucco next to the screen door. He signaled Noah to chill, and it took all of his restraint to obey. You're a cop, act like one. Jesus. But he didn't have his gun. In shorts and a T-shirt, he'd had no way to conceal it, so he'd left it locked in its box in his hotel room. Big, stupid mistake.

His nerves jumped like sparking electrical wires as the other cop eased the screen door open and gave the inner door a push. Hinges gave an ominous creak, raising the hairs on the back of Noah's neck.

Logan went in first, gun braced. "Police!" he called.

Noah followed. "Charlie?"

No one in the kitchen. No one, it seemed, in the house, judging by the silence.

Logan moved on quiet feet toward the door that led to the rest of the house and angled his head down the hall, letting Noah know he would check the bedrooms.

Noah was looking around the living room, feeling helpless, when Logan called to him.

"Noah."

He jogged down the hall and found Logan in Charlie's office, standing stock-still and staring at something on the carpet, his complexion white.

Noah looked down, and his world contracted down to a narrow tunnel.

Blood.

CHAPTER **FIFTY-EIGHT**

Charlie opened her eyes to noise all around her and blinked several times, trying to orient herself. She was on her side, in a large room or warehouse . . . factory? As her head cleared, her brain started registering details.

The roar of machinery, almost deafening in its metallic clanging and chugging.

Darkness except for an eerie, yellow glow in the distance.

Concrete floor cold and gritty against her skin.

Hot, unmoving air choked with dust.

Hulking shadows of the noisy machines on either side of her.

Where the hell was she?

She rolled to her back and pushed up on one elbow, clenching her jaw against the swirling in her head. As she waited for the dizziness to fade, she took a physical inventory. The taste of blood in her mouth. Grit like sand between her teeth. A steady throb in her jaw.

The bastard had coldcocked her.

He'd kept smiling that pleasant, I'm-not-here-to-hurt-you smile and punched her right out.

Son of a bitch.

She'd been so *stupid*. Standing there like an idiot. Can I help you? Can I *help* you? F-ing moron. He'd just looked so damn harmless.

She started to lift a hand to explore her jaw. Resistance.

She jerked her arm, heard the clang of metal, felt the tug at her wrist. Panic turned the inside of her head white as she scrambled up onto her knees and groped around in the dark, her eyes adjusting now to the lack of decent light.

Her right wrist was handcuffed to a heavy pipe that ran vertically up the wall.

She jerked again, unable to stop herself, and cried out at the bite of pain. Cried out as it finally sank in how much trouble she was in. Serious, serious trouble.

She spent several sweaty minutes trying to squeeze her hand through the cuff to free herself. Pushing and pulling and grunting. Come on, come on. She gave up when the slickness of blood washing her hand did nothing to help.

She shifted, pressed her back against the wall and tried to breathe, to think. The roar of the machines—air conditioners? water heaters? heavy-duty washers and dryers?—seemed to press in on her, thickening the air in her lungs. Don't panic, don't panic.

Who was she kidding?

She started to scream for help.

CHAPTER **FIFTY-NINE**

Noah looked out on Charlie's backyard, everything inside him still. His brain had stalled when he'd seen the blood on the carpet. Not a lot of blood. Just a spot, really. But it was Charlie's. He was going to lose her. He could feel it in his bones.

If not to a madman, then perhaps to Mac Hunter. He and Logan had listened to the phone messages on Charlie's machine, knowing it was a stretch but desperate for a clue about what happened to her. Noah had heard the desperation in Hunter's voice. Hell, if he were Charlie and a former lover wanted him back that bad, he'd give the guy a second chance. Especially if the alternative was someone as fucked-up as Noah was.

Behind him, Logan snapped his phone closed. "Shit."

Noah turned toward the other cop. "What is it?" he asked, his lips barely moving.

"No DNA hits on the hair inside the balaclava. All we know is it's not Keene's."

"But, clearly, she was working with someone."

"Or she was set up."

"Someone at the hotel," Noah said.

Logan nodded. "Gotta be."

Noah headed for the door. "Let's go."

"And do what?"

"Search Donna Keene's suite. Maybe we'll find something that IDs her partner."

Logan hesitated, and Noah's patience stretched to the breaking point. "Do you have another idea?"

Logan shook his head. "No. Let's go."

CHAPTER **SIXTY**

Charlie let her chin rest on her chest and focused on leveling out the hitches in her breath. She had enough problems at the moment without hyperventilating.

Her throat hurt from screaming for help, but the guy who'd chained her up here had planned well. No one could hear her over the thrum of the machines. When he came back, no one would hear her screaming then, either.

She closed her eyes tight, swallowed against the surge of sickness. Don't be sick. Don't freak out. Don't hyperventilate. Think. *Think.*

The scrape of footsteps less than a yard away snapped her eyes open, and she jerked her head up to see the outline of a man coming toward her, the yellow glow at his back. She flinched, her lungs seizing, as he reached above his head and pulled a chain. Light from a bare bulb cast the hot, humid space into harsh relief.

He squatted before her, and she pressed back, turning her head against the wall as the glaring light seared her eyes. She couldn't see him, didn't want to see him, didn't want to accept that this was where she was, this was how she was going to die. Screaming where no one could hear her.

"How's it going?" he asked, his voice barely audible over the machinery. Concerned, affable. Amused, even.

She closed her eyes, prayed. Get me out of here. Please, get me out. Noah . . .

"Look at me."

She turned her head to look at him. Don't piss him off. She

knew what he could do when he was smiling. Knock her cold with one punch. What could he do while angry?

His lips curved. Nice lips, really. And teeth. So white and perfect. Not the mouth of a psycho. Not the hair. Not the eyes. A dark-eyed, dark-haired kid who could have been the lean, wiry college quarterback as much as the reserved but jovial genius on *Jeopardy!* But he wasn't either of those men. He'd kidnapped her and chained her to a pipe. He had plans for her.

She started to shudder and hated that she was so f-ing weak. Do something. Don't just sit here and shake. Don't be pathetic.

"What do you want?" she asked, voice hoarse from screaming.

"You're going to heal me," he said, and his teeth gleamed.

Heal him? What the hell did that mean?

He moved fast, and in the next instant, he had his hands clamped around her throat.

The bastard's on his knees in front of the sink, staring intently at the bottle of booze in his hands. I raise the heavy pipe wrench. Better drink fast. I swing at his head, absorbing the jarring impact that sings up my arms with a satisfied smile. Yes.

Charlie crashed back into herself, choking against the strong, steel fingers compressing her windpipe. Air. She had no air.

She tore at his wrists, sinking her nails in, gouging and tearing at his skin. Let go, let go, let go. Breathe, she had to breathe.

He released her as quickly as he'd grabbed her, and she fell against the pipe, coughing and gasping. As sweet, life-giving air rushed into her lungs, the import of the flash hit her.

Mac . . . oh, God, oh, Jesus, he'd hit *Mac* with a . . . a *wrench.*

How long ago? Was Mac *dead?* She relived the impact of the weapon, felt an answering, sympathetic burst of pain in her own skull. The son of a bitch had hit him so hard.

And then she noticed that that son of a bitch, resting on

his knees in front of her like a religious man before an altar, had his head back and an expression of pure bliss on his face. What the hell?

Everything snapped into shocking, clear focus. His hand, oh, God, his hand . . . it was pressed to the front of his navy work pants, rubbing, massaging the bulge at his crotch.

Her shoes scraped the floor as she frantically tried to back away from him. But the wall stopped her, forced her to stay right where she was, chained and helpless, with a front-row seat as this guy jacked off. And when he was done? What then?

He drew in a breath through his nose, then released it on a trembling sigh. "Do you know how long it's been since I've been hard like this?"

She didn't dare breathe, didn't dare blink. This isn't happening. It's *not* happening.

He opened his eyes, pierced her with an oddly nonthreatening glare, as though angry but not at her. "She totally fucked up my head. She made me do things in return for . . . her attention." He paused and swallowed loudly, his breathing getting rougher, uneven. He stilled his hand, forming a fist that he pressed to his thigh, and seemed to concentrate until his breathing settled. "Not yet," he said through his teeth. "I don't want to come like this. I want it to be perfect."

Charlie's aching brain stalled. She refused to imagine what would make it perfect for him. Didn't *want* to imagine. Couldn't. I'm not here. *I'm not here.*

He tilted his head, and his gaze fixed on her face: You are here, better deal with it.

His Adam's apple bobbed, and sweat gathered at his temples. "Before I killed her, I tried to fuck her, for old times' sake. I couldn't get it up. That bitch emasculated me." He paused, smiled in a way that indicated his sanity had slipped, was still slipping by slow degrees. "She was surprised that I knew that word. She called me stupid more times than I can remember. But I'm not stupid. I'm smart. A lot smarter than her, obviously, because she's the one who's dead."

He shifted toward her, all teeth again, but his friendly smile had turned psychotic. "I'm going to fuck you until I'm all better. As many times as it takes."

The threat narrowed her vision to a long tunnel, black crowding in from the edges. Helpless. Handcuffed to a pipe. No way to protect herself. No way to fight back. A part of her wanted to pass out, escape, but when he shifted toward her, she clawed back from the slippery edge of unconsciousness and pressed back, trying like hell to make herself a part of the wall, trying like hell to ignore the ballooning pain in her temples. Not a migraine now. *Please.*

She needed out. Now. Before it was too late. Before she was incapacitated.

"Please don't do this," she said. "We can work something out. Just . . . just . . ."

He grinned at her, seeming amused. "Why would I negotiate when what I want is right here, free for the taking?"

He reached for her but paused when she recoiled. He cocked his head and studied her, concerned again. "You know, this is going to be very uncomfortable for you if you don't relax."

She shuddered so hard her teeth clicked together. This can't happen. It *can't.* Somehow, some way, she wouldn't let it. She had to stall, keep him talking, distract him until . . . until someone, Noah, came for her. He had to be coming. He had to be. "I . . . I don't even know your . . . name."

Surprise raised his eyebrows. "You don't care about that."

"Of course, I do. We . . . we have a connection, don't we? Isn't—isn't that why we're . . . here?"

"Skip," he said. "It's Skip."

She almost sighed. A good sign he'd talk, a good sign she could stall. "Is that a nickname?"

His eyes narrowed, as though he doubted her interest. "It doesn't matter."

"It matters to me," she said quickly. "Like you said, I—I need to relax. Can't we talk for a while? Please?"

He shrugged one shoulder. "I was named by a nurse after my mother abandoned me in the ER."

She tried to give him a sympathetic smile, but the muscles in her face felt like stiff plastic. "I'm so sorry. That must have been hard for you growing up."

He shrugged again, sullen now. "Doesn't matter. I turned out okay."

Uh, yeah, you turned out great. Ignoring the growing ache in her temples, she tried to think. This was an interview, she told herself. She needed to know the what, why, where, when and how. Whatever it took to keep him talking. "Will you tell me why you're doing this?"

"You don't care."

"Yes, I do. I'm a reporter. I need to know the truth. It's what I do."

"There's no point. You won't be able to tell anyone."

"Please, I'm trying here. Don't you want me to know you?" Reasoning with a madman. It made no sense, but what choice did she have?

His shoulders sagged. "I loved her."

Finally. "Who?"

"Donna."

"Donna Keene? The manager of the Royal Palm." Dead now. Suicide. Or was it? Didn't he say something earlier about killing a woman?

"The first time she flirted with me, I couldn't believe it," he said. "A woman like her. Beautiful. Classy. When she invited me into her suite for a drink, I didn't dare to hope . . ."

A deep sigh rose up out of him, and he closed his eyes, dropped his head back.

Charlie kept quiet, let him talk. Talk all night, buddy.

"It was good," he breathed. "We were perfect. She was perfect. She made me feel things I'd never felt before . . . I fell in love with her. For a while, it was amazing." He opened his eyes and looked at her. "And then she told me about her idea. She knew I needed money for school, said she planned to do it on her own, but I could help her and she'd give me a cut. All I had to do was set it up and take the pictures."

Charlie felt a genuine nudge of sympathy for him. The

woman had played him, manipulated him into helping her screw over her own wealthy customers. But the sympathy didn't last long. The woman was dead because she'd tried to control a psychopath. A psychopath who was now focused on *her*.

"It worked fine for several months," he went on. "Until Louisa found the closet where I kept the equipment. Donna accused me of leaving it unlocked. I *know* I didn't." He squinted his eyes tightly closed, shook his head. "I'm sure I didn't."

Charlie knew what happened from there. Louisa contacted her, said she knew of a local blackmail scheme but wanted cash before she'd reveal her real name or provide the details.

He opened his eyes, his gaze intense on her face. "Donna wanted me to kill Louisa, to keep her quiet. I didn't want to. I'm no killer. I *wasn't* a killer. But I had no choice. Donna said I had no choice. And I knew she was right. If I wanted to keep what we had, if I wanted to keep the woman I loved, keep her safe, I had to . . . to do whatever it took to protect her. So I cornered Louisa, but before I could kill her, she said she'd already told you everything."

Ah, now it made sense, why he'd kept coming after her. He'd been told so many lies. "Louisa never told me details."

He narrowed his eyes, his lips pressing into a thin line. "She said you were going to write a story in the newspaper about what we'd done."

"She lied."

"No, she didn't. You were going to ruin everything. She *told* me."

"Look, I'm not a lawyer, but I think I can help you." She paused to wet her lips. The headache was growing, pain rolling toward her like a huge spiky steel ball down a steep hill. Soon, she wouldn't be able to focus, maybe not even speak. She had to hurry. "It's understandable what happened. Donna Keene made you fall in love with her, and then she used you, manipulated you. People will understand. You loved her, and she played you. I'll tell your story, help you with the police. I know them, you know. I work with them."

"Not anymore," he said. "It's common knowledge that you no longer work at the newspaper."

"But that's going to change. I might go back. I . . . you just have to trust me to help you."

"I don't trust anyone anymore. Only myself." A muscle in his jaw flexed. "I'm done talking now. It's time."

CHAPTER **SIXTY-ONE**

Noah slammed the desk drawer shut harder than necessary. "Just a bunch of fucking bills. You?"

Logan shook his head, his flushed face showing deepening lines of stress as he surveyed the mess they'd made going through Donna Keene's office. "There has to be *something*."

But there wasn't. They'd already ripped apart her Royal Palm suite on the top floor then moved on to her office here, behind the check-in desk. Noah dragged a hand through his hair. "What about the maids? Louisa Alvarez was a maid. Maybe she told one of the others what she knew."

"We questioned them after Keene's body was found. None of them knew anything."

Noah started to pace. Time was slipping away, damn it. Charlie was slipping away. "What about desk clerks? The bartender in the lounge? Cocktail waitresses?"

"We went through them all," Logan said. "We can do it again."

"We're wasting *time*."

Logan spread his hands. "Then what? What do we do?"

Noah swung around, wanting to punch something, anything. "Fuck. I don't know." He scrubbed his hands over his face. They needed another angle, another avenue. "What about the blackmail? How'd they do it?"

Logan clenched his jaw, swallowed. "We don't know for sure yet, but we think they targeted wealthy guests who checked into the suites on the top floor. We've cleared the guests out of those rooms for the investigation but haven't had a chance to do more."

Noah whirled toward the door. He didn't bother with the elevator. He headed for the stairwell off the lobby and took the stairs three at a time to the fifth floor, Logan right on his heels.

Their harsh breathing synchronized, they strode down the hall to the first suite door. Logan used the master key he'd gotten earlier from the desk clerk to let them in.

Noah went straight to the bedroom, decorated with a nautical theme in teak wood and a mural of a sky with myriad birds flying overhead painted on the ceiling. A large, framed picture of a sailboat floating on serene water hung above the king-size bed. Noah lifted it away from the wall, knowing it was too easy, but what the hell. Damn it. Nothing behind it but a nail for the wire.

Logan checked behind the mirror in the shape of a sailboat steering wheel above the bureau. Nothing.

Noah examined the walls, looking for peepholes, while Logan went to the window, where he drew aside curtains made to look like billowing sails and scanned the outside stucco walls.

"No cameras outside," he said. "How the hell did they do it?"

"Maybe they didn't use this room," Noah said as he tilted his head back to study the sky blue ceiling covered with wispy clouds, seagulls, pelicans and some other kind of birds.

The ceiling fan caught his eye, and he moved to stand beside the bed so he could study it. Simple, white, with five wide blades. The light kit consisted of four bulbs cupped in delicate, frosted-glass globes. In the center, a decorative bronze seagull spread its wings as though coasting on the breeze created by the blades.

"You see something?" Logan asked.

Noah shoved the bed aside, then went into the next room and grabbed a chair from the table. After placing it under the ceiling fan, he hopped up onto the seat.

"Wait," Logan snapped before he could touch anything. "Fingerprints."

Noah dropped his hands and squinted up at the belly of the seagull. Something was off about it. A reflection? Perhaps from a lens? He squinted. No, just a shiny bird belly.

He shifted his gaze to the ceiling, registered that separate tiles made up the mural, fit together like straight-edged puzzle pieces. Removable. "I'll be damned."

"What?" Logan asked. "What is it?"

"False ceiling."

Very carefully, using just the tips of his fingers, Noah lifted a three-by-three square of ceiling tile, surprised at how light it was, and moved it to overlap its neighbor. The chair wasn't tall enough, though, to allow him to see into the ceiling. "Call the front desk and get someone to get a ladder up here."

Logan picked up the phone on the bedside table while Noah jumped off the chair. His heart was pounding, raging, the clock ticking. How long would it take to get a ladder? Too fucking long.

He went to the bureau and dragged it away from the wall, straining muscles in his back and arms. Damn, but the son of a bitch weighed a ton. Then Logan, off the phone already, was at his side helping.

"Front desk said it might be a while," Logan said. "Their maintenance guy didn't show for work today."

Noah didn't respond. He had his own ladder now. He hefted himself up onto the top of the heavy furniture and stood up. The perfect height.

With his head in the ceiling, he could see the large piece of plywood overlaying the tiles to the left. Perfect size for a body to recline while snapping some dirty pictures.

Noah dropped off the bureau, landing with a jarring thud that vibrated through his knees and hips. "What's next door?"

Logan followed him out into the hall, where they stopped in front of the supply closet. Logan tried the knob. "Locked."

His master key didn't work. Before Noah had finished swearing in frustration, Logan drew his gun and shot out the lock.

Noah laughed darkly as he pushed the door inward. "I like the way you work."

Logan just smirked as they surveyed the narrow supply closet that held no supplies. It did hold a ladder, however. Open right under a trapdoor in the wall to the right, just inches from the ceiling. A bulky black bag sat on the floor between the legs of the ladder. While Logan zipped open the bag and peered inside, Noah climbed the ladder and swung open the trapdoor.

"Bingo," Logan said below him.

Noah glanced down. "Camera equipment?"

"Yep. What've you got?"

"Looks like it was set up so the guy with the camera could crawl out into the ceiling. He cut holes in the plywood that probably line up with holes in the ceiling mural, most likely in darker spots, like the shadows of the birds, so they wouldn't be noticeable."

"Jesus."

"Pretty simple and low-tech, really," Noah said.

"Who'd be able to set something like this up without drawing a bunch of attention?"

Noah got it. It made perfect sense. "Maintenance guy."

"Who didn't come in today," Logan said. "Shit."

CHAPTER **SIXTY-TWO**

When his calloused hand closed over her cuffed wrist, Charlie jerked at the contact, ignoring the answering pain as the manacle cut into her already abused skin. No, no, *no*.

"Please, don't," she said, not above begging. "I can pay you. Whatever you want."

He shook his head, *tsked* under his breath, his index finger stroking the inside of her wrist while the rest of his fingers banded the fine bones as surely as the cuffs did. "I don't need money. All I need is you." His fingers tightened. "As long as it takes."

She twisted her wrist in his grasp, and his grip slipped in her blood. He glanced down, and his flinch vibrated through her hand.

"You're bleeding," he muttered. "What did you do to yourself?"

Confused that he would care, she looked down, her vision watery and too bright. The throbbing in her head was secondary at this point, overwhelmed by the dread of what he planned to do to her. She searched for more words, anything to stall him, to *stop* him. But she couldn't think, couldn't focus. A dazzling flare of light behind her eyes, inside her head, told her time was running short.

While he dug around in his pocket for who knew what, she tried to pull away, ashamed at the whimpering sounds coming from her throat but unable to make them stop. Fight, you idiot. Fight.

She yanked her arm, felt the tendons and ligaments in her shoulder wrench, felt his calluses rasp her skin.

And then he did something she didn't see coming: He inserted a key into the cuffs and cranked. The bracelet fell away from her hand with a metallic clink.

She was free.

She didn't think. She shoved at his shoulders with all of her strength, levering up with her legs, and knocked him on his ass. Shock blanched his features as she scrambled to her feet and swayed a moment as her head swam. But then she loomed over *him*, her feet planted between his spread knees. He must have realized the vulnerability of his position in the same instant that she did, because he started a frantic crawl backward. She took her shot while she had it, maybe it'd be the only one she'd get, and kicked him as hard as she could, square in the crotch.

A wild howl erupted from his throat, and he curled onto his side, clamping his hands between his legs.

Charlie, her knees trembling, stepped over him, sickened by the viciousness of what she'd just done. She'd felt a crunch. Bone? Cartilage? Whatever it was, she'd damaged something big-time. Self-defense, she thought. He was going to rape her. And not just once. She protected herself. Still, she couldn't help the revulsion that gripped her stomach.

Disoriented, her temples pounding, she stumbled toward the way out. At least, she hoped it was the way out. She had no way of knowing. She simply followed the light. The light was salvation. A hysterical giggle caught in her throat. Old movie line. Something about souls that had lost their way. She could relate. She had no idea where she was, how to get out of wherever the hell this was. Old factory? But, no, the machines wouldn't be running if it were old. Boiler room? Hell? Did it matter?

She had to get to Mac. That crazy *bastard* had hit Mac with a wrench. Maybe killed him.

The first door she tried opened into a smaller room. Finished walls but unfinished concrete floor. Bare lightbulb blazing overhead. A tool bench against the wall to her left. Maintenance equipment lined up along the wall to her right—floor buffers, ladders, wet vacs.

And straight ahead, stuck to the wallboard surrounding another door, maybe the way out, oh, God, hundreds of glossy photos. Naked bodies in the throes of various carnal acts.

She forced her feet to move despite the urge to turn and run the other way, forced herself to approach the door, keeping her eyes averted from the intimate images.

Focus.

Get out.

Now.

Her hand shook uncontrollably, her breath noisily sawing in and out of her lungs, nausea climbing up her throat, as she grasped the knob and tried to turn it. Locked. *Damn it.*

She pivoted. Go back.

And froze.

He was behind her, crawling, reaching for her, his sweaty face pasty, his pain-filled eyes wide and crazed.

She darted around him, but he flung himself to the side, directly into her path. She couldn't stumble back fast enough to avoid the fingers he closed around her calf.

Agony erupts like a volcano, burning, searing, slamming into my gut and sending fire through my veins and to every nerve ending. In the next instant, I'm on the floor, retching, curled around myself, red like blood flashing across my vision. Air locks in my lungs. Can't breathe, can't breathe. Fuck. Fuck. Fuck!!!!

Charlie came back to herself, her cheek throbbing where it rested against the cold, sandy floor. Her body, tucked into a tight, protective ball, twitched from a phantom agony whose echoes were already fading. Every muscle trembled, the aftermath of staggering pain she'd inflicted on another. Self-defense, she thought. God help me, it was self-defense.

Focus.

Get out.

But her head, oh, God, her head. The pressure grew, expanded, like something inside her skull wanted out as badly as she did. It clawed at her temples, seeming to shred the soft tissue.

Where was he?

There, less than a yard away, on his side, groaning and breathing heavily like a horse that needed to be put out of its misery. For the moment, not a threat.

Fighting the urge to be sick, she unfurled, forcing tensed muscles to unclench, pushed up onto her knees and locked her elbows. A starburst whited out her vision, and dizziness slammed her world sideways. She closed her eyes while nausea did its queasy dance, a dull roar beginning in her ears.

Stop. Please, stop. No time.

Crawl.

She made it as far as the end of the tool bench against the wall, intending to use it to pull herself up, before the inside of her head went supernova. The detonation was so fast and vicious that it drove her back down onto her side and onto her back, where she pressed her palms to eyes that threatened to implode. Oh, God, oh, God.

It wasn't even flash fatigue. Not yet.

The prelude, though. If she was going to save herself, she had to do it *now*.

His fingers, clammy, trembling, clutched weakly at her ankle, and she kicked his hand away, more of a flick, really, and ignored him, focused entirely on forcing her reluctant body to obey the commands of her increasingly sluggish brain. Overload. Circuits fried. Consciousness circling the drain.

Twist, turn, onto your stomach, brace your elbows, lift your butt, get your legs under you, up onto your knees, grab the edge of the tool bench and pull. There, that's it. You've got it.

Only a few feet away, he was trying to get up as well, obviously in a monstrous amount of pain. Pain she caused. Incredible, sickening pain she'd felt.

Move. You have to *move*.

Light dazzled like the flashbulbs of a million cameras. Huge red spots obliterated everything in front of her, and she tried to blink them away. But they weren't going away. They hovered, splattered, spread, turned to darkness.

Blind. She was *blind*.

She heard him stir more decisively, heard shuffling followed by a ragged grunt and wheezing. "Bitch," he panted. Closer now. "You *fucking* bitch. You're going to beg me to kill you."

He crashed into her from behind, carrying her sideways, away from the tool bench and into the wall. She managed to twist in his arms, striking out at him with her fists as they both smashed into the wall and slid down it, landing in a heap. Her head bounced off the floor, sending sparks through her reeling senses.

And then his hot breath was in her face, his forearm braced across her throat.

"You really shouldn't have done that."

CHAPTER **SIXTY-THREE**

This is it!" Noah shouted. He had to brace a hand on the dashboard to keep from flying into the windshield as Logan stomped on the brake. The squad car screeched to a stop in front of the house where Skip Alteen lived on the top floor.

Logan ordered their backup to approach with sirens and lights off.

"I don't suppose you have an extra weapon," Noah said, his gaze fixed on the door at the top of the stairs.

Logan reached down and pulled a gun out of the holster strapped to his ankle. "Don't tell anyone I gave you this."

Noah glanced at the weapon, a subcompact Glock not much different from the one he used on duty. Just what the doctor ordered. "Just so you know. If this son of a bitch left one tiny mark on her, I'm taking him out."

"Get in line," Logan said in a low voice. "Ready?"

"Let's do it."

Logan kicked in the flimsy old door, shouting, "Police!" in his authoritative voice.

Noah went in behind him, the Glock braced and sweeping. He vaguely registered the three other squad cars pulling up out front as he took in the apartment.

The creep who resided here lived a spartan but apparently rewarding life. New, black leather sofa with matching recliner, the kind that looked like a first-class seat on a brand-new jumbo jet. A huge plasma-screen TV on a fancy black stand. Home theater system. Video game console with stacks of games, some still in their packaging. On the sofa, a textbook sat open, as though a student had left in the middle of studying. The place could have been the college dorm room of a filthy rich student.

A filthy rich, demented student who'd kidnapped the woman he loved.

"Charlie?" Noah called, aware that his voice sounded strained, shaky. "Charlie!"

He'd already noted that nothing moved inside the apartment. Not a peep. Not one furtive shuffle.

No one was here.

"Charlie!" Logan yelled, a hint of desperation in his voice. He sensed it, too, the utter stillness of the apartment.

Noah lowered the gun, dropped out of his stance. He'd never felt so hopeless, so lost. "She's not here."

CHAPTER **SIXTY-FOUR**

Charlie didn't open her eyes right away, aware first that everything about her head throbbed. Jaw, cheek, chin, temples. He'd hit her again, though it hadn't taken much at the time to knock her unconscious. The headache, thank God, had receded to a steady pounding without the jagged lightning edges. No blazes of light now, no freight train in her ears. Apparently, she'd been out long enough for her system to level. Good to know for future reference.

Unfortunately, he'd been busy while she'd been out. She was tied up now, sitting with her back against a wall. Her hands, bound in front of her, rested between her slightly spread knees, the thick rope binding her wrists lashed to her tightly secured ankles. She wondered vaguely why he hadn't used the cuffs again. As if it mattered, but still.

The floor under her was hard, familiar. Still the boiler room. Or whatever it was. Or maybe not. It was quieter here, the steady roar of machinery muffled, as though behind a wall. Despite the stifling heat, she started to shiver.

"I know you're awake." His voice strained. "I can tell by the way you're breathing."

She opened her eyes, blinked against the harsh light, but relieved she could see. And then not relieved. She was still in the smaller room with the tool bench and maintenance equipment. And the photos. Plastered all over an entire wall, surrounding the door that had let her down by being locked. Men and women. Men and men. Women and women. People she recognized. People she didn't. Captured during their most intimate moments.

"Nice, aren't they?"

She leaned her head back, swallowing convulsively, and slid her eyes to the man sitting gingerly on the large, upturned plastic bucket. He looked bad. Pale, almost gray, sweating profusely. His red-rimmed eyes glowed with a feral madness.

"My art," he said, his breathing uneven. "People have paid me good money for those."

He shifted, squeezed his eyes closed, grimaced. "Man, you fucked me up. I don't think I'm going to recover from this." Tears slipped out of his eyes, and he swiped at his running nose. "I may be permanently damaged."

Charlie stayed quiet. Assessing. Don't piss him off again. A tug at her hands verified the strength of her bonds. And then she noticed the pipe wrench on the floor at his feet. His weapon of choice. She knew how it felt in her hand. Heavy and powerful. Had felt him swing it at Mac's head. Oh, God, how long had it been since he'd struck Mac? He might be dead by now.

"If only I'd managed to kill you the first time," her captor said, and sniffed hard. "Everything would have been fine. She wouldn't have started hating me and calling me stupid. She wouldn't have turned to that other guy."

He must mean Mac. That's why he went after Mac, why he tried to knock his head into next week. Charlie couldn't stop the sound of distress that escaped her throat as she yanked at her hands again. She had to get away, get to Mac.

He watched her with shimmering, crazy eyes. "It should have been perfect. But now all I've got is this." He leaned down gingerly to pick up the wrench, hefted it into his hand like a baseball player gripping his lucky bat, then stiffly pushed up from the bucket with a groan.

"This will have to be perfect enough."

"No, please!" she cried, and let tears flood her eyes, let him see every quake and shudder. Reasoning didn't work. Negotiating didn't work. Maybe stark, raving fear would. He'd shown her compassion before. Maybe he hadn't used the cuffs again because she'd bloodied her wrist trying to escape. Maybe, maybe, maybe.

"Please, don't. Please. You made a mistake. Everyone makes mistakes." She was babbling now, certain this was it, that she was going to die. "Everyone does stuff they regret, that they shouldn't have. You're only human. That's all. Everyone's human. You made a mistake. We all make them. Every one of us."

Her tears, her gasping desperation, seemed to reach him, because his face softened, and he lowered the wrench again.

He was so close to her she could smell his sweat. And blood. Did she smell blood? Maybe it was her own.

Forehead furrowing, he reached out a palsied hand and stroked her hair. The man was absolutely nuts. Homicidal one second, tender, almost apologetic, the next. The tips of his fingers brushed the arch of her cheekbone.

Pain arcs through me, radiating from throbbing flesh that has swelled so much it's stretching the skin painfully tight. The bitch's face, pale and wet with perspiration and tears, angles up, eyes wide and terrified. She's going to die screaming. I'm going to make her die screaming. "You really shouldn't have done that." *Lashing out backhanded, knuckles connect with bone, the blow vibrating into my shoulder and down, down into mangled, swollen flesh. Ah, God, she killed me. She fucking killed me. I bend forward with a groan and puke like a dog. Fuck!*

". . . everything. I can't let you live." He sounded so reasonable, so *there*.

She blinked him into focus, pressed her head back against the wall to steady the wobble. Breathe, breathe. Pain escalated in her temples, an express elevator shooting to the penthouse. Not again. Please, not again.

At least the flash had provided her with another angle.

"You need help," she said, forcing strength into her weak voice, swallowing against the building nausea. "You're hurt.

You're probably bleeding internally. I can help you. Get you to the ER."

Incredulous, startled, either by the realization that he could be bleeding internally, or that she offered to help him, he stepped back, only to flinch and bend forward as though the movement had sliced through him like a knife. A long, harsh groan ground through his teeth. "This is your fault," he gasped, sweat running down his face. "You broke something inside me."

She jerked hard at her wrists. "I can't help you if you don't untie me."

He dropped to one knee with a grunt, one hand pressed to his groin, the other bracing against the floor with a clank of the wrench. "Oh, God." He retched, a horrible, wrenching sound.

"Untie me," she said, desperate now. If he fainted, or died, she could be trapped here for days. Helpless. Starving. Slowly going insane.

Light flashed across her vision, and she saw Mac kneeling in front of the sink, felt the impact of the wrench against his skull.

She came back to herself unable to breathe at first, until her lungs expanded, pulled in a hitching breath. Flash fatigue. Oh, no. No no no no no no no *no*.

"You have to untie me *now*."

He shook his head, his jaw clenched so hard she could hear teeth grinding. Then, amazingly, he shoved himself to his feet, wavered for a moment.

Camera flash, and gut-crushing pain exploded inside her, a hot rush of burning lava surging through the center of her body and into her blood, radiating like lethal ripples on a pond, spreading out to every nerve.

She came back to herself sobbing and gagging, with the vague impression that someone had cried out, maybe her. Her wrists were bleeding as though she'd thrashed, causing the ropes to abrade her skin.

Something was different. What was different?

She lifted her head, fought back the sickening whirl of dizziness. Was she alone? Where did he go?

Then she saw him. On the floor at her feet, unconscious, his complexion so pale it looked like wax. The wrench rested in his lax fingers.

It was over. He couldn't kill her now.

A brilliant burst of lightning snapped her head back, and she lost herself again in his agony.

CHAPTER **SIXTY-FIVE**

Noah, his heart raging, burst through the door into the boiler room of the Royal Palm. The woman at the front desk had said Skip had made himself an office back here, back where no one else ever went. Too dark and creepy, she'd said with a shudder.

Perfect for a hostage. Had to be. Charlie *had* to be here.

"Hang on, just hang on," he said under his breath.

Heat blasted him in the face, made the prickle of sweat crawl over his skin.

Beside him, Logan said something, but Noah didn't catch it over the thunder of various machines that cooled the air, heated the water and otherwise maintained the hotel's atmosphere.

"I'll take this way," Logan said, louder this time, jerking his head to the right.

Noah nodded and headed left, stepping slowly, easily, grateful for the glaring light of several bare bulbs. Probably one reason it was so fucking hot.

Every door he opened revealed nothing but storage. Paper products. Shelves and shelves of family-sized canned goods. Bottled water. Sheets. Towels. Blankets. Pillows. Shower curtains. Regular curtains. Cleaning supplies. Furniture.

Every damn thing on the planet but what he wanted.

Charlie. No Charlie.

His control slipped, and hope fluttered a little more out of his grasp. She'd told him she loved him, and he hadn't said it back. He should have said it back. She would never know . . .

Last door. He crashed it open with a violent, frustrated kick.

And froze in shock.

Skip Alteen on his back on the floor, unconscious.

Charlie. Not moving. Head lolling on her shoulder. Blood trickling from her nose and the corner of her mouth.

"Oh, God," Noah moaned, his knees going weak.

He shouted Logan's name, screamed it, every bit of helpless rage erupting out of him as he toed the wrench away from Alteen's hand then dropped to his knees in front of Charlie.

She was tied up, blood on her face and wrists. Broken, oozing skin at her temple. And bruises. Oh, God, bruises in the shape of fingers on her throat and arms. In the blunt shape of a fist on her jaw, her cheekbone. The rage fired his blood, made his fingers clumsy as he pressed them to the pulse point in her throat. Her skin was damp, like ice under his fingers.

Logan made a ton of noise barreling through the door, then stopped cold behind him, his heaving breath rattling to silence. "Christ. Oh, Christ! Is she—"

"I've got a pulse," Noah blurted, and a slightly hysterical laugh burst from his lips. Relief so powerful it made his head swim. "It's strong. Her pulse is strong." He grasped her chin, gently, tenderly, angled her limp head away from the wall to try to revive her. "Charlie?"

No response.

He bent his head over her hands, went to work on her bonds. First things first.

"This guy needs an ambulance," Logan said behind him. "I think he's in shock. Lucky fuck."

Noah agreed. If the bastard had been standing, or even halfway conscious, he wouldn't have stayed that way.

Logan said a few words into the radio attached to his shoulder, then moved to Noah's side. "How is she?"

"Unresponsive," Noah said through numb lips.

Then, as though his voice revived her, she jerked and gasped, her eyes flying open, wide and startled.

Noah grabbed her forearms before she could strike out at him, trying to keep his grasp light on her bruises. "Charlie, it's okay. You're okay."

She stiffened, her head arching back hard enough to bounce off the wall, and realization slammed into Noah. He released her and stumbled back, knowing it was already too late, that his touch had shot his fear and rage right into her.

Logan glanced at him in surprise. "What the hell?" He reached out to steady her himself.

Noah knocked his hand away. "No!"

As Logan stared at him like he'd lost it, Noah got to his knees and grasped the sides of Charlie's head, alarmed that her eyes looked blind, as though the flash hadn't ended.

"What's wrong?" Logan asked. "What the hell is wrong?"

She relaxed then, her head suddenly limp in his hands, her eyelids fluttering. Noah, desperate to feel her, to know she was okay, leaned forward and kissed her. He tasted her blood and closed his eyes, concentrating on the moment when her slack lips moved, responded, and her tongue met his.

In the next instant, she was there with him, her dazed eyes open and fixed on his. Clear, almost wild. Instead of diving into his arms, as he expected, as he wanted, she pushed him away with surprising strength.

"Mac," she gasped. "He hit Mac."

CHAPTER **SIXTY-SIX**

Noah didn't like it. They should be going to the ER, getting Charlie checked out. If he'd known how to get there from here, they'd already be halfway there. Instead, he steered onto another side street, following Charlie's directions to Mac Hunter's.

"The paramedics are on their way," he told her, not for the first time. "Logan, too. They'll do everything they can."

"I need to see him." She grasped his hand. "He hit him hard, Noah. I felt it—" She broke off, and her body snapped taut next to him.

He looked at her, saw the cords in her neck standing out, her teeth clenched against a scream. His heart began an erratic thud. Flash fatigue—supersized.

He'd suspected it earlier, but she'd brushed him off, told him she was fine. She *wasn't* fine. She wasn't anywhere near fine. The flashes hitting her were so much more frightening, so much more intense, than the last time she'd been in flash fatigue. What the hell was she seeing? Feeling? What did that bastard do to her?

He caught her hand, gripped her fingers tight against his palm, not knowing what else to do to help her ride it out.

When the tension left her muscles, the shuddering moan that followed, like she was in terrible, agonizing pain, ripped right through him.

"We need to go to the ER," he said, fear making his voice guttural. "Or AnnaCoreen's."

She sagged in the passenger seat, absolutely limp. "Please," she whispered. "I need Mac."

The way she said it, the crack in her voice, sparked another worry. She'd said she and Hunter were over. But he'd heard the pleading in Hunter's voice on her answering machine. He'd said he'd do anything to get her back. Would Charlie *take* him back?

Shoving away the doubt, he considered arguing with her about AnnaCoreen again but knew he wouldn't win, so instead he tried to think of how to get his hands on some tranquilizers to stop the flash fatigue. He had no desire to know what would happen if such intense flashes went untreated for too long. Then it hit him: The paramedics at Hunter's would have Ativan or some other tranquilizer among their supplies.

A red light loomed ahead.

"Please run it," Charlie said.

After slowing to make sure no cars were coming, he blew through. He spotted the flashing red lights of an ambulance and a police car before he was close enough to Hunter's blue green stucco house to steer the Mustang to the curb. Charlie opened the door and would have stumbled out while the car was still moving if he hadn't slammed on the brakes. "Jesus, Charlie!"

But she was already running for the front door.

He jammed the car into park and went after her. He caught up on the porch, followed her inside toward the activity in the kitchen. She dodged the police officer who tried to intercept her. "Mac? Mac!"

Noah shouted for Logan, who waved the cops back. He was behind Charlie again when she saw Hunter and gasped. Hunter was laid out on a gurney, a bloody white towel wrapped around his head and an oxygen mask over his nose and mouth. Charlie rushed forward. "Oh my God, Mac!"

Surprisingly, the man was conscious and turned his head toward her, raising a blood-spattered hand. Before Noah could stop her, she slid her hand into Hunter's and leaned over him. "It's okay, I'm here."

The flash on Hunter's attack buckled her knees, and Noah surged forward to catch her, but she caught herself on the side of the gurney, never letting go of Hunter's hand. Then she was stroking his forehead, talking to him. "Hang on, Mac, please hang on."

Noah moved to the other side of the gurney, his heart jackhammering, his gaze fixed on Charlie, watching her carefully. So pale and bruised, tears running unheeded down her cheeks.

Hunter raised his free hand to move aside the oxygen mask. He was trying to tell her something.

"Don't try to talk," Charlie said. "Save your strength. Promise me you'll save your strength."

His mouth curved, and he managed to get out three faint words: "I love you."

A quiet sob escaped Charlie's throat, and then she lowered her head and kissed Hunter's lips. She murmured something near his ear, too low for anyone else to hear.

Noah's heart stopped beating.

"We have to go," the second medic said. "You can follow us to the hospital."

Nodding, Charlie let go of Hunter's hand and stepped back. The medics zoomed out of the kitchen with the gurney, leaving Charlie and Noah facing each other.

She met his gaze, tears rolling freely. He didn't move, having no clue what to do. Obviously, she loved Mac Hunter. The pain lancing through him wasn't like anything he'd ever felt. He should have told her earlier, when she'd said she loved him. He'd hesitated, and now he'd lost her.

She took a faltering step toward him. "Noah . . ."

She stopped and stiffened, dazed eyes going blind.

He rushed forward to brace her, support her, whatever she needed, realizing belatedly that he hadn't thought to try to get Ativan from the medics. A hard shudder racked her body, and then her knees gave way. He lowered her carefully to the floor, and her head lolled over his arm. He waited for the moment when she'd look up at him, no longer senseless.

When she relaxed this time, though, she didn't gasp in air as though surfacing from the deep end of a pool. And she didn't open her eyes. It took him a moment to realize she'd lost consciousness.

Logan walked into the kitchen talking: "We need to secure the crime scene—"

Noah looked up at the stricken police detective, fear closing his throat. "We need another ambulance."

CHAPTER **SIXTY-SEVEN**

Noah paced the ER waiting room, hearing nothing, seeing nothing, but the double swinging doors through which the paramedics had rushed with Charlie. He'd shouted at them in the ambulance to give her a tranquilizer. While one medic questioned why when she was already unresponsive, the other commented that her heart rate was off the charts and her blood pressure was rising. Then a horrible beeping alarm had gone off, and the next thing Noah knew, the medics were diving for defibrillator paddles.

Shuddering at the memory of Charlie's heart being shocked back into rhythm, he flipped open his cell phone and started to call information to get AnnaCoreen's number before he realized he couldn't remember her last name. *Shit.*

Logan pushed through the double doors then, and Noah met him halfway, the sober look on the other cop's face stirring terror he had to struggle to contain.

"How's she doing?" Noah asked.

"They don't know what's wrong with her." Logan rubbed the back of his neck. "They're doing blood work."

"Can I see her?"

"I doubt it. They've got her in one of the back rooms. They just chased me out."

Noah wanted to scream at the way he'd been shut out, but Logan knew these people, and he didn't. "Have they given her anything? She needs a tranquilizer."

"Yeah, yeah, they gave her something to get her heart rate stabilized and blood pressure down. An alpha-blocker something or other. It seemed to be working when they made me leave."

Noah's shoulders sagged. "Okay, then. She'll be fine now." She had to be.

Logan cleared his throat. "They're thinking it was an epinephrine overdose, but it doesn't make sense. She's not taking anything like that, and they didn't give her any."

"Epinephrine is a form of adrenaline," Noah said.

"But where'd it come from?"

Her own body, Noah thought, feeling sick. The combination of flash fatigue and the attack on Hunter had overdosed her. Or, rather, she'd overdosed herself by insisting on touching the guy when she knew she was already in a vulnerable position. That's what you did when you loved someone. You put yourself at risk, blind to the consequences.

Noah sank down onto a nearby chair, seeing again the kiss she'd given the man who'd said he loved her. He hung his head, fighting down the despair gathering inside him. He was going to lose her. He knew it in his gut.

"Alteen's in surgery," Logan said, probably talking just to talk. "Ruptured testicles." He winced and paled further as he said it. "Sounds like Charlie defended herself pretty well."

"Good for her," Noah growled. He wouldn't have minded rupturing some testicles himself, but Charlie had obviously taken the fuckwad down all on her own.

The ER doors swung outward and a hulking man in blue scrubs sauntered through, one hand under his scrubs shirt lazily scratching his belly. Logan approached with his hand outstretched. "Dr. Henderson, hi. How is she?"

Henderson's bushy salt-and-pepper brows drew together as he shook the detective's hand, but he wasn't scowling. He was smiling. "Good, really good. Remarkable, really. I expect a full, though puzzling, recovery. In fact, she's already awake and asking for . . ." He trailed off, as though trying to remember the name.

Noah rose, buoyed by hope.

Dr. Henderson snapped his fingers. "Ah, yes, a fellow named Mac."

Noah felt his world deflate, his heart break.

Logan said, "Mac is the other patient back there."

"Oh, is he? Dr. Phillips is working on him. Severe head trauma. Very serious. It's been a bit touch and go, I'm afraid."

Noah turned away without hearing the rest. Charlie had regained consciousness and asked for Mac Hunter. And, really, that made sense. Hunter was the better man. Untainted by sins of the past. Worthy in a way that Noah could never be.

He also knew who killed Laurette and why, and the murderer's balls were under the knife. His work here was done.

While Logan and Henderson continued their conversation, Noah turned and walked out of the ER.

CHAPTER **SIXTY-EIGHT**

One week later

The afternoon sun warmed the back of Charlie's neck as she broke up clumps of dirt and sand with her gloved hands, smoothing out the topsoil in Nana's garden. Several small clay pots and seed packets were lined up along the edge of the garden. She planned to start seedlings in the pots, then transfer them to the garden once they'd sprouted some leaves. She'd learned from books she'd gotten from the library that she was starting her herb garden about a month late, but maybe summer would start cool this year. You never knew.

Besides, it felt good to work in the garden, good for her soul, just as Nana had professed so often when she'd been alive. When Charlie had her hands buried in the dirt, she didn't think about the ache that resided so deep inside her that she didn't think she'd ever be able to dig it out. The ache for Noah.

If Alex had her way, Charlie would have been in Chicago three days ago. But Charlie held back, sensing Noah needed time to work something out. She didn't know what, but she could be patient. For a while.

In the meantime, she focused on helping Alex deal with healing. She wasn't alone: Logan had been sticking to Alex like Velcro. So far, Alex had given no further indication that she was empathic, as Charlie had suspected after her sister had come to talking about the dead woman under the stairs. Just as well, Charlie thought. One of them with turbo empathy was enough.

Mac's recovery also was progressing nicely. He and Charlie had made their peace with each other, and though awkwardness still intruded, she knew they'd get through it. At first, he'd vowed to win her heart back from the Chicago cop. He said it shouldn't be too difficult since the dirtbag had bolted on her. She hadn't been able to argue with that. Noah *had* bolted. And at times, when she was feeling especially raw and hurt, she thought "dirtbag" was too kind a word for the man who'd stolen her vulnerable heart and shredded it.

Regardless, she and Mac had talked a lot over the past week, and he'd come to the realization that he'd been so desperate to get her back because everything else in his life had fallen apart. He'd tried to cling to her, convinced she could make things right again. That job fell to him and only him.

Now if only she could figure out what was up with Noah . . .

"I hope you're wearing sunscreen."

She looked up into the sun, her heart leaping. She had to shield her eyes to put a face on the hulking shape standing before her. Even then, his eyes were hidden by mirrored sunglasses.

"Noah," she breathed. She had to fight the simultaneous urges to jump him and scream at him. Instead, she rose gracefully, shedding the mud-caked gardening gloves, taking her time checking him out. He wore olive safari shorts and a white T-shirt that adhered so nicely to his chest that she could make out each tantalizing bulge and ripple.

She sensed him checking her out in return, sensed his gaze as it traveled from her head, where her hair was pulled back in a loose ponytail, over her face tanned from hours of working in Nana's garden, down her white, dirt-smeared tank top to the short-short navy cotton shorts she would wear only in the privacy of her own backyard.

While she couldn't see his eyes, she imagined she could feel their heat touching her. Or maybe that was wishful thinking. Maybe he'd come to tell her it was over, that he'd given it some thought and decided the best thing to do was go their separate ways. After all, he lived in Chicago. She lived in Lake Avalon. They'd fallen for each other during a stressful time. Relationships like that never lasted. But why come all this way to say something he could have said on the phone?

Hope curled in the pit of her stomach. Please, please, *please*.

He gave her an uncertain smile, shoving his hands into the back pockets of his shorts and rocking back on his heels before breaking the tense silence. "So, how's it going?"

How's it going? How's it *going*? She wanted to kick him. And then kiss him. No, *kicking* him would be so much more satisfying. But then she remembered his kisses. Now *those* were satisfying. "It's going well," she said, hating the telltale rasp in her voice. "And with you?"

He looked past her shoulder at the garden, his expression ambiguous. "You've been busy."

She turned to look at the square area that she'd completely cleared of weeds. "I promised my grandmother I'd keep up her garden. And with another week before I go back to work, I should be able to get it in good shape."

"You're going back to work at the newspaper?"

She smiled. "Yes. Simon Walker is buying it." She still couldn't believe how generous he'd been about bailing the paper and her father out of a very deep financial pit. When she'd made the audacious suggestion to the billionaire that he make the *LAG* the test site for a new kind of journalism—the kind not hampered by advertisers or politics—she'd promised to make sure it was worth every penny to him. He'd laughed his belly laugh and agreed, saying he loved a challenge.

"That's good news." He smiled, clearly pleased for her. "And you're doing okay? Last time I saw you . . ."

"I'm fine. I have alpha-blockers for the next time flash fatigue sets in. We won't know whether they'll work until it happens, but they seemed to work in the ER. In the meantime, I've been careful. No flashes for the past three days." She realized she was babbling but couldn't stop herself. "AnnaCoreen's doctor has been a godsend. According to her brain scan, I'm not in any danger of my head exploding." She paused, then added ruefully, "At the moment, anyway."

"Good, that's good." He tilted his head back, and the expanse of his long throat and corded neck muscles made her mouth water. She noticed he gazed up at the sky as though he'd never get enough of its bright blue vastness. He was stalling, she realized, and waited for him to say what he wanted to say. God help him, it had better be what she wanted to hear.

He drew in a breath, let it out. "I got your messages," he said.

All forty million of them? But instead of succumbing to sarcasm, she said, as blandly as possible, "I didn't get any of yours."

His face reddened, and he squinted behind the mirrored lenses. She wanted to rip those damn things off his face so she could see his incredible, green eyes. It'd been too long since she'd gotten to submerge in them. Her hands shook with the need.

"How's Mac?" he asked.

She arched a brow at his flat tone. Was he just being polite because he knew how deeply she cared for Mac? "He's doing well. No brain damage, and he should be good as new in a matter of months. Skip Alteen has pleaded guilty to a whole bunch of charges."

"I heard about that," he said, nodding. "Logan has kept me informed. About Alex, too. I'm glad she's doing well."

Charlie sighed, tired of the game they were playing. "What's going on, Noah? I came to in the hospital, and Logan said you took off. Now I find out he's been keeping you informed when I can't even get you to return one phone call?"

His Adam's apple bobbed. "I didn't want to get in the way."

"The way of what?"

"You and Mac."

She stared up at him, shocked. "What did Logan tell you?"

"Nothing. I . . . I saw it for myself."

"Saw what?"

"He said he loved you, and you kissed him." He paused, scowled. "Like you love him back. And then you asked for him instead of . . . well, me. I thought maybe . . . crap, Charlie. I thought maybe you might want him back. He's a good man, a *better* man. And I didn't want to get in the way of that, in case that's what you wanted. He's . . . damn it, he's better for you."

She glared at him for a full minute, fighting the urge to shove him back with both hands and tell him he was an idiot for making such a huge, asinine assumption.

Noah made a low growling sound. "So are you going to say something or what?"

"You're a nitwit."

His brows arched above his glasses. "What?"

"Mac is a dear friend. Yes, I love him. And, yes, we have a history. But that's it. *History.* Yeah, I asked for him in the ER. Last time I saw him, he looked like he was *dying.* And what's this business about him being a better man? I don't even know what you mean by that."

"He's got a clean slate, Charlie. I'm . . . flawed."

"We're *all* flawed."

"Some of us more than others."

She sighed, shook her head. "This isn't about me being able to accept what you did. I do accept it. I accept *you.* This is about you being able to forgive yourself, and I don't appreciate you pretending that it's about me and Mac when it's about your own insecurity. I mean, that's what this week has been about, isn't it? You're trying to give me an easy out. Well, I'm not taking it. I love you, Noah. *You.* Accept it or don't." She dragged a hand back through her hair and squinted into the sun, giving her eyes another excuse to water. She wasn't going to cry in front of him. Not this time. But, hell, the ball of emotion climbing up from her stomach into her throat expanded, making breathing evenly a challenge. Desperate to get away before she crumbled at his feet, she turned to walk away. Idiotic, insecure man.

"Charlie."

She stopped but didn't turn, closing her eyes. She wanted him to grab her, whirl her around and tell her he was staying. But, no. No drama, no emotion. Just a soft exhalation of her name. God, she wanted him to touch her so bad. She ached for it. Had missed it like she'd lost a piece of herself. A vital piece.

"I'm sorry," he said quietly. "You're right. I'm going to have to work on that."

She faced him, struck breathless by how gorgeous he was, the sun washing his hair with golden highlights, his green eyes even more intense. She loved this man more than she ever thought possible. Love and want gripped her heart in a tight fist that refused to let go. And she didn't want them to. Ever. "You're the one, you know."

Noah cocked his head. "The one?"

"You want me to spell it out for you?"

A grin teased the corners of his mouth. "That would be nice, yes."

"T-H-E O-N-E. You're The One." She moved toward him, intending to kiss the growing smirk off his face, but he stepped back, raising a put-on-the-brakes hand. "What?" she asked, impatient to get her hands on the pecs so enticingly outlined by his T-shirt, impatient to get her hands on *him*.

"I quit the Chicago PD," he said.

She blinked up at him. "Wow."

"I want to help you here, in Lake Avalon."

"Help me how? Do I need help?"

"Logan and I talked about it before I went back to Chicago. I wanted to get his thoughts on my idea of starting a private detective agency. You and the newspaper are going to need some experienced assistance in that area if you're going to go around exposing bad guys."

She pretended to consider that for a moment, while her heart launched into cartwheels. He was staying. *Noah was staying.* "An experienced detective could indeed be helpful."

"One other thing."

She couldn't help but tense, thinking what he was going to say next would swipe the nimble feet out from under her cartwheeling heart. "What's that?"

"I need a place to live. At least until I can find my own place."

She casually nodded, thinking she knew enough people in Lake Avalon to ensure he never found a suitable place to live. "It just so happens I have a room for rent."

"Really?" He tried to suppress his grin but didn't really succeed. "In your house here?"

"Yes. In fact, it's the master bedroom."

"Oh. Does that mean I'd have to share the bed?"

"If you have a problem with that—"

He hooked a hand around her waist and dragged her chest to chest with him. "I don't have a problem with that at all." He lowered his head, but paused with his lips an inch above hers. "Did I mention that I love you?"

"I don't think so," she said, sliding her hands over his shoulders. God, she loved his shoulders. So strong. "Was it implied?"

He grinned, still not kissing her, driving her crazy with not kissing her. "Just so we're clear: I love you."

She smiled up at him, savoring the feel of soft, smooth cotton layered over the bunched muscles in his shoulders and back. "I love you, too."

"I want to make babies with you."

She blinked, thrown, but then started to grin. She liked the sound of that. A lot. "Okay. Wow."

"When it's time, of course."

"Of course."

"And don't think I came back to you not bearing gifts."

"You brought me a present? Oh, goody. I hope it's that you're not wearing underwear."

He touched his lips to hers, and reality fell away as a flash of Noah's pleasure erupted inside her. Her head dropped back on a ragged, involuntary moan, and the voice inside her head,

Noah's voice, chanted three words over and over again. *I love you.*

Charlie shifted back into the present, disoriented and feeling oddly weightless. Noah was carrying her across the yard, toward the house. Laughing and breathless, she wrapped her arms around his neck and held on. "That was the best present ever," she murmured, then attacked his ear with her tongue.

His chuckle rumbled his chest against her body. "There's more where that came from."

Keep reading for a special preview of

TRUE COLORS

The second romantic suspense in
Joyce Lamb's **True** trilogy

Coming soon from Berkley Sensation!

CHAPTER **ONE**

The child looked up at her with wide, blue eyes, so young, so innocent, his bottom lip quivering as one tear tracked a dirt-smudged cheek. Her hand trembled, her finger poised on the trigger, her heart racing, pounding in her ears. Sweat trickled into her eyes, and she furiously blinked the stinging away. Focus. You have to focus.

The chaos around her, someone shouting, someone else—another child?—screaming, seemed distant, surreal. All that mattered was the boy staring up at her, pleading with large, terrified eyes. He couldn't have been more than six. Too thin, scraggly blond hair, dirty face and dirtier clothes. He had a scrape across the bridge of his nose, and he was desperately trying not to blubber, yet unable to stop.

And then, as she helplessly watched, the little boy's face screwed up, and he began to cry in earnest. "Daddy! Where's Daddy?"

Her finger jerked on the trigger.

The gunshot was deafening.

Alex bolted up, a scream of denial caught in her throat. Strong hands held her down, and she began to thrash. Let go, let go, let go.

"Hey! Whoa, whoa, it's okay, it's okay."

She struggled, panicking because she didn't know where she was or who had hold of her. The hands that gripped her arms gave her a firm shake. "Alex, it's okay. It was a dream."

The words finally penetrated the lingering shock and revulsion, the overwhelming guilt, and she sagged back into the sofa cushions, blinking against the light blinding her. In the distance, she heard the dogs barking frantically in the backyard.

Logan braced over her, his tanned face pale as he peered anxiously into her face.

She relaxed in slow degrees, her heartbeat still frantic, her lungs fighting for air. Everything was fine. Police Detective John Logan was here.

"Nightmare," she breathed. "I'm okay. The dogs—"

"I'll take care of them."

Before she could protest, he was striding into the kitchen. She heard him stop at the treat cabinet then open the back door and go outside. His voice, low and soothing, assured the animals that Mommy was fine, in words she couldn't make out.

She sat up from where she'd fallen asleep with her head resting on Logan's shoulder and put her feet on the floor, dragging a hand through her damp, curling hair. Her whole body felt warm and sticky, her brain fuzzy with sleep.

Dropping her head into her hands, she tried to calm her breathing as frustration, and horror, clutched at her throat. She'd shot a child in her dream. A small, helpless little boy. And it wasn't the first time. She'd had the nightmare over and over for the past two months. What did it mean?

The first time, she'd written it off as nothing more than a bad, albeit twisted, dream. But then it happened again. And again. Right about the time she'd started weaning herself off the powerful pain medication prescribed after she'd gotten shot in the chest three months ago by a psychopath gunning for her sister.

Logan ambled back into the living room. God, he was stunning. Every time she looked at him lately, she lost her breath. Blue, blue eyes, like a starburst, full of life and vitality. Short, dark brown hair that curled in the Florida humidity. Straight nose. Full lips. Strong chin shaded by razor stubble thanks to a fast-growing beard and a reluctance to shaving more than once a day. And dimples. Honest-to-God *dimples* that deepened, taking her stomach along for the ride, when he smiled.

He handed her a glass of ice water, and she took it with a grateful smile and drank down a refreshing gulp while he sat beside her.

They'd been friends for nearly two years before the shooting, ever since he'd arrived as Lake Avalon's newest detective. They'd flirted at the scenes of crimes, accidents, fires and other newsworthy events that she'd photographed for the next day's newspaper while he kept order. She'd always thought he was hot—that's what caught her eye the first time. Hot guy in a uniform, snapping orders at unruly people. Of *course* she noticed. Hello?

After she got shot, though, he started dropping by, casual as you please. In the early days of healing, when she still needed someone close by, he'd come over with a pizza on nights when her sister had other plans. Then, he'd show up with popcorn and a DVD in the middle of a Saturday afternoon to keep her company during her most restless hours. She suspected Charlie put him up to it at first, her sister's form of guilt-free bailing on keep-Alex-entertained-while-she-heals duty.

But she'd been able to take care of herself for weeks now, had even returned to her job snapping photos for the newspaper, and still Logan dropped by regularly, always with the excuse of feeding her or bringing a movie that she just had to see or catching the latest episode of *The Amazing Race* or *Seinfeld* reruns or even just channel surfing. Sometimes, like tonight, they'd fall asleep together on the sofa, like an old married couple.

She didn't mind. She enjoyed being with Logan, loved his comfortable company. But she was definitely wondering where they stood. Were they just BFFs? Or, hell, maybe this was John Logan's idea of romance. Maybe they'd been dating for weeks, and Alex hadn't even realized. She was so confused. Or perhaps clueless. Yeah, that would be just like her. She'd already spent the past fifteen years—prime dating years—so wrapped up in which wounded animal needed saving next that when she did get involved in a romance, the man invariably ended up feeling second best to her mutts and split.

Just then Logan scooted closer and put both hands on her shoulders, rolling the tight muscles with his large, gentle fingers. Through the cotton of her T-shirt, she detected a tremor in those strong fingers and turned her head to glance at him again. He looked tense, his jaw set, that something's-bothering-me muscle flexing at his temple. Well, she couldn't blame him. This wasn't the first time she'd awakened screaming in his presence. Poor guy. Lucky him, so far she'd had the nightmare only when he was on the sofa with her.

"Tell me about the dream," he said.

She shifted her shoulders under his hands, distracted by the heat of those hands through her shirt, distracted further by the heat gathering low in her belly. Just friends, she thought. Just friends.

"Is it about when you were shot?" he prodded.

She shook her head and swallowed. "No."

"Then what?"

"I . . . don't think I . . . It's too . . . horrible." Her head started to throb like it had the other times she'd had the nightmare.

"Maybe talking about it will make it stop."

Somehow, she didn't think so. Nothing would help. And it was too disturbing. Besides, she didn't want to admit she could even dream such a thing. "So . . . are we a thing?"

She blurted it without thinking. But, well, she wanted to know. And she *really* didn't want to talk about nightmares. She was far too happy a person for dark shit like that.

His gentle massage paused. "Uh . . ."

Heat flooded up her neck at his flustered reaction. "Never mind. I'm just . . . you know me . . . think before I speak . . . I mean, speak before I think . . ." Oh, God, somebody get her a paper bag to put over her head.

Logan resumed the massage. "Well, I've been—"

"It's okay if we're just friends. I mean, you've been great keeping me company. I've really enjoyed it. But, you know, I'm good now. So if you have other things to do . . ." Forget the paper bag. She needed something to clamp her lips shut. One of those giant red chip clips.

The magic fingers stopped, and this time, instead of letting his hands lightly remain on her shoulders, he removed them. "If I have other things to do?"

"Well, I know Charlie kind of dumped babysitting duty on you after I got hurt, and while I appreciate it and all . . ." Crap.

"Are you trying to tell me you want me to leave?"

"No! Of course not." With a sigh, she closed her eyes and hung her head. That paper bag would now have to be shaped like a dunce's cap. "Please tell me this is just another bad dream."

"Wish I could," he murmured, sounding hurt.

"I'm sorry," she said. "I'm a dolt. In fact, it's probably low blood sugar. I haven't eaten since . . ." She checked her watch. "It's been two hours." And she sure as hell wasn't hungry again already. Lame. *So* lame.

Instead of responding, he got up, leaving her on the sofa to watch his amazing backside disappear into her kitchen. Regret stabbed into her as sharp as one of those knives that could cut through a can. She needed to learn to keep her big mouth shut.

The headache that came from the nightmare spread down the back of her neck, sending tendrils of tension into already taut muscles. Pushing to her feet, wishing she had the coordination to actually kick herself, she headed for the kitchen. The six dogs roaming the fenced backyard were no doubt wondering when she planned to give them some chow. At least she had them to keep her company now.

In the kitchen, she froze, surprised to see Logan bent over with his head deep in her fridge, his butt very nicely filling out his faded jeans. She had to resist the urge to reach out and do a firmness check. She bet on a scale of one to ten, that sweet, muscled package would rate at least a fifteen.

Folding her arms, she leaned against the doorjamb and

waited for him to resurface, a smile curving her lips. Maybe she hadn't messed up after all. Maybe they could pretend she'd never said a word. Things could go back to the way they were. Comfortable. Friendly. Relaxed. Though she might need to seek some advice on how to deal with having such a hunky, appealing guy as just a friend.

He straightened, arms laden with a head of lettuce, a pound of bacon and a jar of Miracle Whip, and bumped the fridge door closed with one lean hip.

"How about a BLT?" he asked as he dumped his bounty on the counter and reached for a tomato sitting on the windowsill above the sink.

"Sounds good," she said. She hunted up the bread and popped two slices in the toaster.

They worked side by side, like they had dozens of times before, but this time, Alex sensed Logan's tension. He didn't tell her about his day at work. He didn't ask about hers. He didn't tease her or joke around or ask who she wanted to see in the Stanley Cup finals. As if anyone in Florida really cared about hockey. But he was a Detroit man, born and raised. At any rate, silence—a tense one—was highly unusual for them. Which just made her worry all over again that she'd ruined something really, really good.

When they sat down at the table with their sandwiches and glasses of iced tea, Alex couldn't stand the awkward silence any longer. She had to force herself to swallow her first bite. This was one of her favorite sandwiches, especially when Logan made it, yet it stuck in her throat like a chunk of dry chicken.

"I'm sorry," she finally said. "I shouldn't have said anything."

He continued to chew his bite, then washed it down with tea. "What are you doing tomorrow night?"

Alex tilted her head, baffled. "What? Why?"

He took another bite, his expression maddeningly unreadable. Once he swallowed, he said, "Do you have plans?"

"Well, no. I thought we'd order a pizza and watch a movie. You know, the usual."

"What if we go out for dinner?"

"Out? As in to a restaurant?"

The barest hint of a smile touched his lips. "Yes, out to a restaurant. And we could see a movie afterward. At the theater."

"You mean, like a date?"

He laughed, low and soft. "Yes, like a date."

She narrowed her eyes. "So . . . we *are* a thing?"

His blue eyes, so bright and beautiful, darkened with seriousness . . . and serious heat. "Alex, when we're a thing, you'll know it."

And then he grinned, and the sight of those damn sexy dimples swiped any remaining hope of a coherent response right out of her brain.

Oh, yeah.

CHAPTER **TWO**

Alex wiped her damp palms against her khaki-clad thighs, hyper-aware of the man in the driver's seat next to her— the minty freshness of his breath, the hint of sunscreen and a touch of something new . . . a light, rain-scented, fresh cologne that teased. Nerves over their date hadn't launched a full-out attack until his red Dodge Ram pickup had pulled into her driveway. Hadn't helped that he'd strolled to her front door holding a fresh bouquet of daisies, as relaxed and handsome as ever in new jeans and a white polo that emphasized his muscled, sun-tanned arms.

She'd laughed nervously while she fumbled the flowers into a vase filled with water, feeling silly, and giddy, while he'd loved up her excited pooches. He'd gotten a *haircut*, for God's sake.

She couldn't remember ever having such intense nerves over a date.

She acknowledged that everything in her life felt more intense since she technically died three months ago. A man trying to kill her sister had shot Alex by mistake. Her heart had stopped in the operating room, and it had taken three zaps from defibrillator paddles to get her back.

Ever since, she'd felt different. She figured death did that to people. Made them more aware of the people around them. Made them feel emotions—compassion, pleasure, pain—on a deeper level. Or maybe her senses just *seemed* sharper, like a head that felt lighter, and better than before, once a blinding headache faded.

Whatever the cause, she thought she might have developed

a serious crush on this man, and she couldn't stop the big, dumb smile that spread through her entire body.

Afraid he would look at her and wonder what had made her smile so goofily, she cleared her throat and noted he'd pointed the pickup toward Lake Avalon Beach.

"Where are we going for dinner?" She had a craving for the tasty steamed shrimp at Antonio's Beach Grill.

He glanced sideways at her, his lips quirking up at one corner in a way that twirled her stomach even more.

"It's a surprise," he said.

"This is weird," she said, then hated the furious blush that raced up her neck. What was with her and the blurting lately? "I mean, isn't it?"

He chuckled, low and sexy. "What's weird? That we're on a date?"

"Yeah. A date. *Us*."

"Why are you so freaked out about it?"

"I'm not freaked. Not technically. I mean . . . well, aren't you? A little? We've been friends for a long time."

"I'm not surprised in the least. This is exactly where I intended to be once the time was right."

While she appreciated a man who knew what he wanted—and the fact that he seemed to want her was a double, no, *triple* bonus—the timing puzzled her. "Why is now the right time?"

"Well, for one thing, you're healed. Which means your head is clear and you're over any of those urges to reaffirm life by jumping on the next guy who smiles at you."

She remembered a moment several weeks ago when she'd had just that urge. Logan had showed up at her door with the ingredients for hot fudge sundaes and a DVD of the quirky dog-show film *Best in Show*. She'd thought then, This is the man of my dreams.

"And another," he went on, "you noticed."

"Noticed what?"

He grinned at her, his blue eyes glittering in a way that sent shimmering waves of anticipation all through her. "You noticed me."

She felt her eyes widen in shock. "How could I not? You've been there for me."

He shrugged. "That's what friends do."

She thought about that for a long moment. Friends didn't do everything he'd done. Keeping her just busy enough to prevent insane boredom without robbing her of the energy she needed to heal. Taking six rambunctious dogs on long walks when she was too wrung out to give them the attention they deserved. Cooking elaborate, amazing meals for her (and cleaning up afterward). Mowing her yard. Watering her plants. Taking care of her garbage and recycling. Going with her to get groceries. Making her laugh on a bad day. Sitting quietly with her while she napped, probably hoping to prevent the recurring nightmare.

Her sister hadn't done even half of that, and she'd done plenty.

So "that's what friends do" was a major overstatement. But that was Logan. The most generous, kind man she'd ever known. And now they were on a date. Which made her wonder if her cluelessness had wasted precious time.

"Could we have gone on a date sooner if I'd said something?" she asked.

"Probably not. You needed to be back to a hundred percent."

"Oh." A hundred percent to go on a *date*? She'd been back to work for weeks, had even climbed a tree yesterday to get the perfect photo of a Lake Avalon resident's prizewinning flower garden.

"This is going to be intense," he added.

Her heart thudded, along with other, secret places. "*Oh*."

"Just so you know."

"Okay."

"Not to make you more nervous."

"Nervous? Me?" She shot a grin at him, relaxing for the first time since he'd arrived with such pretty, sweet flowers.

"Well, you have been squirmy since I picked you up."

"Squirmy?" Great. Perfect. No sophistication here. She was *such* a doofus. "That sounds—"

"Adorable," he cut in. "You're adorable."

She blushed again—doofus squared—and thought maybe she'd somehow suddenly become the luckiest woman on the planet. Hell, maybe Logan was her reward for surviving the shooting.

Before she could respond, he stiffened in his seat and slammed on the brakes. Alex braced a hand on the dashboard, wincing at the jerk of the seat belt across her still-tender chest . . . and watched in shock as the van in front of them tipped onto its side and began to violently roll across the oncoming lane of traffic. Miraculously, it hit no other vehicles before it rocked to a scratched-and-dented stop, upright in the ditch, its windshield a web of cracks beneath a caved-in roof.

Logan steered the truck onto the shoulder of the road, already releasing his seat belt and reaching into the cubby for his cell phone, which he handed to Alex. "Call 911," he said, his voice deadly calm.

Speechless, Alex fumbled the phone, her hands shaking. Whoever was in that van might be dead, was undoubtedly dead if they hadn't been wearing seat belts. And, oh crap, was that a trail of smoke snaking out from underneath?

Logan didn't hesitate to shove open his door and sprint over to the destroyed van, easily falling into his role as a competent police detective, while she stumbled out of the truck, her fingers clumsy as she tried twice to dial the necessary numbers.

Other cars were stopping, drivers and passengers getting out and gawking. Alex heard a man say, "I already called 911," as he walked up beside her. That allowed her to shift her attention from the damn phone to Logan as he tore open the van's driver's-side door and dragged out a screaming woman with blood pouring from a gash at her temple.

"Get my baby! Get my baby!"

"Hell," the guy next to Alex said. "Her back tire blew. I saw it explode just before the van flipped."

Alex's journalistic training snapped into gear, and she dove back into the cab of Logan's truck and dug through the camera bag she hauled around everywhere she went. Digital camera in hand, she ran back to the scene, where she started snapping photos of Logan as he delivered the hysterical woman to bystanders running up to help. Then he turned back toward the van, that, yes, was definitely smoking now. Big, black clouds, the kind that looked to Alex like a precursor to a fiery explosion.

She should help, she thought. Run over there and do something. But she couldn't move, her heart in her throat and her feet frozen to the ground as Logan jerked the bottom of his shirt up and over his mouth and nose and plunged into the billowing smoke. Oh, God, he shouldn't do that. What if he got hurt? But it was his job as a police officer to help.

She belatedly remembered her own job and snapped a picture of his disappearing back. That's what photojournalists do. They record the story. They don't get involved.

As she waited for him to reappear, counting the seconds, her eyes stinging from the acrid air, she heard sirens in the distance. It all seemed so far away, her focus having narrowed down to the spot where she'd last seen Logan. She should have been taking more pictures of the chaotic rescue scene, but fear for him had constricted her chest muscles so much she could barely breathe.

Logan, come on, come on, where are you?

And then he stumbled out of the smoke with a small child cradled in his arms.

She released her held breath on a gust of air and brought the camera up to take the picture, already knowing it would make headlines. There was nothing newspaper readers loved more than a ragged hero streaked with blood, carrying a crying, soot-smudged child away from wreckage that looked like no one should have survived. Especially a hero as good-looking as John Logan, his eyes even more blue and penetrating in a face blackened by smoke, the child looking tiny and defenseless in his large, muscled arms.

That's my guy, Alex thought, her heart swelling with pride. My hero.

He delivered the bawling child to her mother and turned toward Alex, his eyes streaming from the smoke, sweat making his hair spike. He was filthy, and she couldn't wait to get her hands on him, to feel his beating heart against her. He could have died in that van.

He stopped before her, and she looped her camera strap around her neck so she could put her arms around him and hug him. He tried to hold her off with a laugh. "I'm a mess."

"I don't care." She stood on tiptoe to kiss him for the first time, and the instant their lips touched, everything around her made a dizzying shift . . .

I'm choking on smoke, eyes tearing as I fumble a door open and lurch inside the van, drawn by the cries of a small child. My heart's racing, hammering. Not this time. I'm not losing this one.

Where is she? Where is she? Can't see a damn thing.

"It's okay, it's okay, I'm coming. Talk to me, kid, talk to me."

The inside of the van is hot, too hot. Just give me time. A little more time . . . and then something warm and soft brushes my fingertips. A bare leg.

I close my fingers around that soft, pudgy leg, trying to be gentle even as the need to hurry clenches in my gut. I use the leg to guide me to a car seat. Strapped in, the seat and the kid. Glimpse of pink flowers on a white T-shirt. A little girl. Oh, Jesus, a little girl. Small and helpless and counting on me.

This child's *not dying, damn it.*

"Just hang on. I won't let you down."

I can't see, can't find the mechanism that releases the straps. And I smell hot metal, burning plastic and rubber, hear a weird, ominous crackle. Flames? Oh, Jesus, oh, Jesus.

Still no straps, hands frantic as they move over the screaming, squirming child, searching, searching. Finally, there it is. The latch. Jesus, the metal's hot.

Everything is so hot, making the sweat pour into my eyes, stinging along with the smoke. Two more seconds, and the latch is free, the girl all but sliding out of the seat into my arms.

A laugh escapes me, a touch hysterical, as I crawl backward, out of the death trap, out into humid, smoke-choked air. My lungs ache, burn, my throat raw.

But I've got the girl, this sweet, warm, wriggly child, in my arms, and nothing else matters. This time, *I saved the—*

An explosion shook the world.

Enter the rich world of historical romance with Berkley Books.

Lynn Kurland

Patricia Potter

Betina Krahn

Jodi Thomas

Anne Gracie

Love is timeless.

penguin.com